PENGUIN BOOKS

COLUMBINE

Raymond Kennedy, a native New Englander, is the author of two earlier novels, *My Father's Orchard* and *Good Night, Jupiter*. He lives in Brooklyn, New York, with his wife, Gloria, and their young daughter, Branwynne.

Columbine

by Raymond Kennedy

PENGUIN BOOKS

Penguin Books Ltd, Harmondsworth,
Middlesex, England
Penguin Books, 625 Madison Avenue,
New York, New York 10022, U.S.A.
Penguin Books Australia Ltd, Ringwood,
Victoria, Australia
Penguin Books Canada Limited, 2801 John Street,
Markham, Ontario, Canada L3R 1B4
Penguin Books (N.Z.) Ltd, 182–190 Wairau Road,
Auckland 10, New Zealand

First published in the United States of America by
Farrar, Straus and Giroux 1980
First published in Canada by
McGraw-Hill Ryerson Limited 1980
Published in Penguin Books 1981

LIBRARY OF CONGRESS CATALOGING IN PUBLICATION DATA
Kennedy, Raymond A
Columbine.
I. Title.
[PS3561.E427C6 1981] 813'.54 80-29380
ISBN 0 14 00.5882 6

Printed in the United States of America by
George Banta Co., Inc., Harrisonburg, Virginia
Set in Video Compano

To my mother,
Orise Marie Belanger Kennedy

Columbine

I

His mother was a saint. Everyone said as much. She attended Mass daily, made regular novenas, and had, it was said, burned enough candles in the little chapel on North Main Street to light the way to Heaven for a million failed souls. The father was another kettle of fish. Cynical toward his neighbors, and distrustful of friends and relatives, he possessed a sarcastic wit and a tongue to go along with it. This union produced—in Henry Starbuck Flynn—neither fish nor fowl. Where the mother was devout, the boy was at best vaguely reverent; where the father was cutting and cantankerous, the son was complacent, easy to get along with, even sometimes the willing butt of other people's jokes and friendly bantering.

Early photos of Henry reflect the emergence of these benign attributes. In infancy, he had a headful of blond curls and a quick, toothy smile of the type that drives mothers wild. An early protrait shows a sandy-haired little boy in Sunday sailor clothes sitting bare-legged on a plush seat with a toy bear on his lap, his tongue lolling embarrassedly. There are two pictures taken of Henry in altar-boy vestments, and another shot of him standing in the sun with a group of boy choristers, his eyes shut tightly in the sunlight. His hair looks white in the sun. In a grade-school class photo, he appears to be buried between two bigger boys. His teeth are bucked slightly, a feature that shows in all these adolescent pictures. There is, finally, a photograph, taken in 1940, when Henry was eighteen, showing a tallish, loose-limbed youth of no particular distinction. It is a picture of a pleasant-faced, amenable young man, dressed casually in dark trousers and a white dress shirt open at the throat, with his shirtsleeves rolled up to reveal a new wristwatch. The face of the youth in this photograph is the upshot of all of the faces in the sequence of his boyhood pictures. The expression is bemused, the attitude both sheepish and innocent. The picture contains no prophecy whatever upon life's future, nothing at all; just a boy standing under a tree, looking at a camera.

This last picture was snapped on a Sunday morning by Helen Kokoriss, the girl next door. Helen was sixteen. Her shadow shows in the picture. A disinterested observer, however, knowing nothing about the history of photography or of Western dress customs, might easily believe this picture dated back ages and ages. It looks antiquated, yellow, and curled; and there is something shadowy and antiquated, too, about the young man depicted in it: Henry Starbuck Flynn.

The Flynns and the Kokorisses lived on a street called Cottage Avenue, which was not a street at all but a row of five frame houses that faced a flagstone path with a common alleyway running behind the back fences. A steep bluff stood directly in front of the houses, just beyond the flagstone walk, and obstructed any view whatever from the front windows and porches. The row of houses lay perpendicular to the broad street that climbed the hill—what Henry's father called "a proper street"—and up which a trolley car came toiling every fifteen minutes or so. On summer evenings, the families that dwelt in this row of houses sat on their front porches sipping cold drinks, gossiping, and listening to the radio while gazing across the stone walkway at the little cliff that rose up before them, with its patches of salmon-colored shale and the scraggly trees and bushes that clung to its side. No one, so far as Henry knew, had ever questioned the wisdom or philosophy of the original builder, the man who had planned and engineered these houses, and was therefore responsible for their facing the wrong way.

Each of the houses was surrounded by a wealth of foliage, particularly about the front porches, as though the tenants wished to obscure themselves from their neighbors going past on the walk, while, at the back of the houses, wooden fences served to assure privacy at the ground level. These wooden barriers, like the footpath traversing the front of the houses, conferred on Cottage Avenue a feeling reminiscent of Old Europe, particularly of the Eastern states of Europe, from which, by chance, a majority of these homeowners had emigrated. The Kokorisses were Lithuanians; the Blyes were Lithuanians; the Trumbowskis were Poles. The parents of these families spoke almost exclusively their native tongues, while the children all spoke English. The strange mixture of languages on the avenue had been a part of Henry Flynn's growing-up years as far back as he could remember, even back to babyhood.

The Flynns lived in the first house, at the head of the avenue, and were thus unique in possessing from their side windows a view of the street that climbed the hill past the paper mill. Henry's room at the top of the house had a small window in the gable at each end, one window looking down the hill toward the mill and the river beyond, the other facing the Kokoriss house next door. Henry was born in this house. His parents were both born in Ireland Parish, the city across the river, and naturally looked upon themselves as native Americans, a view that the father, however, did not extend wholeheartedly to his neighbors. While he was cordial to the Kokorisses, Blyes, and Trumbowskis in public, he was secretly contemptuous of them in the privacy of his house. Or when he sat outdoors on the porch, watching

11

them coming and going on the flagstone walk, he could not suppress the look of disappointment that twisted his lips. Old Mrs. Blye wore a babushka. Nicholas, her only child, was in jail for grand larceny. The Trumbowskis, a childless, middle-aged couple, spoke atrocious English, and were albinos besides. And so on. But it was for Mr. Kokoriss that the older Flynn really reserved his spleen. He felt for the man an animus not easily explained, since the man next door was a silent, moody individual who rarely troubled anyone.

Mr. Kokoriss worked in the coalyard at the paper mill, and when he came home from work in the late afternoon, he was a sight to behold. He came up the steps and into the avenue, covered from head to foot with shiny black coal dust. Trudging solemnly past the Flynn house, his eyes shining like two sapphires in the dusky rectangle of his face, he looked scarcely human. Just seeing him go by on the footpath brought from Henry's father a sudden outburst of malicious delight. "Lock your doors, Mrs. Flynn," he would call back to the kitchen, "I think I just saw the bogeyman!"

It was a fact, however unfortunate, that the poor man did look at such times like something dug up from a pit in the ground. It took Mr. Kokoriss the better part of a quarter hour of brushing, scrubbing, and changing in his back shed before he would reappear in his vegetable garden outside the shed door, his face as white as a parsnip, and looking for all the world like a dead man come from his tomb at the Judgment Hour.

His name was Benedict Kokoriss, and he had come to Massachusetts in 1920 from a farming village in Lithuania. He was a very big man, tall and square-boned, with a pale, chiseled face, narrow eyes, and ears pinned back to his head. He was not a sociable man. Whether he was made sullen by his broken tongue or by the circumstances of life, or whether he

12

was just reticent by nature, no one on the avenue sought to guess, although the quiet tyranny with which he ruled his wife and daughters argued against his being a man of a retiring or sensitive nature. It was known, for example, that on one occasion he had rebuked Mrs. Kokoriss over some petty mischief perpetrated by Sophie, the next to oldest of his four daughters, by striking the girl's mother an impulsive blow on the eye. It was no wonder the girls never spoke of their father in anything but respectful language, or, also, sadly, that they were all faintly disdainful of their mother.

The episode of the black eye had, of course, an unhappier effect on public opinion as it related to Mr. Kokoriss than it might have had upon his daughters. For once, Henry's father was even joined in his criticism of his neighbor by most of the other tenants of the avenue. Everyone, particularly the women, agreed that the use of brutality as a means of encouraging the wifely virtues was a custom that had been better left behind in the old country, where wife kicking and the whipping of children were, so far as anyone knew, still going forward with undiminished vigor. No one thought to say as much, for at that time such awfully worse things were happening in Europe, as in Poland, where the Germans had recently installed themselves by force of arms, and in Lithuania, where uninvited Russian troops were known to be terrorizing the population. It was probably the smell of unreasonable violence concerning Mr. Kokoriss's vicious assault on his wife, coupled with the newspaper headlines publicizing the daily evils going on in Eastern Europe, that raised the hackles of Mr. Kokoriss's neighbors. No one, in any event, interfered. No type of verbal protest was raised. The incident came and went like a spring rainstorm; and all that spring, as in the springs before, Benedict Kokoriss appeared in the evenings in his garden, spading up the earth, shaking sod, and pruning and fertilizing his flowering fruit trees.

That was in April 1940, the same month in which Henry's father was promoted to his post as desk sergeant at the Hadley Falls Police Department. Mrs. Flynn sewed new gold chevrons onto her husband's blue tunic, and Henry, when he heard the news of his father's promotion, greeted the announcement with a peal of laughter that unsettled his father's nerves. Henry's father, being a policeman, had been secretly poked fun at by Henry's friends all during his childhood years, so that the promotion to sergeant seemed to make his father, and therefore himself, once more liable to mockery. Henry was a conservative individual. He did not like change. He had a gentle, womanly side to his nature that haunted him his whole life through. He laughed at his father that morning from embarrassment. Sergeant Flynn came, however, to where Henry was sitting at the breakfast table, and stood over him, with his tunic open and his new gold chevrons glimmering, and glowered at him.

"Why, he's just wet behind the ears," his father spat out. "He doesn't know where his bread and butter come from!" Sergeant Flynn got red in the face as he scolded and badgered his son, even alluding nastily to the token position held by Henry the previous autumn on the high-school football team. "Well, he's just a little waterboy, isn't he?"

Henry was used to being twitted and made fun of by the older Flynn, but the scent of impending violence in the air that morning left him feeling unusually upset. He was only saved from having to punish himself with guilt feelings by a second incident later that same morning. He had gone to do a chore for Mrs. Blye, the old woman who lived by herself in the next to last house in the blind avenue. Mrs. Blye was impoverished. Her husband was dead, and her son, Nicholas, was serving a seven-year term in the Massachusetts penitentiary at Walpole. Thus, Henry's mother sometimes made him available to the widow for chores. On this day, Henry had volunteered to clean Mrs. Blye's cellar. While working downstairs, he dwelt for a while moodily on the strange fact of his father's apparent distaste for him. As an only child, Henry might reasonably have expected his father to love him very much, even to dote on him. As that was not the case, Henry could only conclude, as he often had, that there was something deficient about him as a human being. When thoughts of this type are not challenged by outside realities, they often grow fat upon themselves, like a malignant weed; but on this occasion, Henry was spared the worst of it, for coming upstairs from Mrs. Blye's cellar, he found his mother visiting with the widow in her kitchen—and there, sitting by the window, visiting with them, was Helen Kokoriss.

The young girl's presence was astonishing to Henry, since the Kokoriss girls were forbidden ever to leave their house or grounds, except, of course, for school and errands. Henry had seen Helen a thousand times before, but this time she looked different. She looked like a young woman. That surprised him. He took notice of her long chestnut hair, her high cheekbones, and her dark indigo eyes. She had always been a stranger to him, but now, in quite a different way, she had grown stranger still. She looked lovely. He felt ardent stirrings.

To Henry, the Kokoriss house, standing not fifty feet from his own, had always seemed as remote as a medieval cloister. It was a gray clapboard structure, hidden behind trellises and foliage. At night, its windows were so faintly lighted one might have presumed that only one or two forty-watt bulbs were permitted to burn at the same time. Sometimes, as on summer evenings, when windows were thrown wide, traces of exotic food smells could be detected floating across from the house next door, odd, spicy fragrances that only strengthened

Henry's impression of his neighbors as an alien presence. As a small boy, Henry had been particularly puzzled by the strange cooking smells, for he knew, by direct observation, that the vegetables that grew in Mr. Kokoriss's garden—the cabbages and beets and tomatoes and such—were identical, point for point, to those that grew in his father's own garden. Nor had his father's wry comment on the matter of the vegetables shed much light on the boy's confusion. "God only knows what they do to them when they get them indoors," he had said.

Other factors deepened the mystery of the Kokoriss household, such as Mr. Kokoriss's deep voice rolling softly across the twilight air like distant thunder, the foreign words indecipherable, but the intimation always grave and portentous. The wife, a plump little woman who was turning gray, was more silent still as she went about her daily chores with a stolid, fateful footstep, her face set in the pinched, quizzical expression of someone peering in through a screen door. In all his youthful days, Henry had not set foot on Kokoriss soil perhaps more than a half dozen times. Nor could he remember other children going to play with the girls next door. Finally, too, none of the Kokoriss girls attended the local schools; they went, instead, by municipal bus, across the river to Ireland Parish, to the grammar school and high school of the Mater Dolorosa, a Polish parochial school that charged tuition (and which, if Sergeant Flynn's views upon the subject were of any value, had not yet produced a single notable alumnus).

By the time Henry was eighteen, and Helen sixteen, they had scarcely spoken to one another, even though they had been raised from the very crib in these two neighboring houses. On that April morning when Henry came upstairs into Mrs. Blye's kitchen, having just finished sweeping and hosing down the old lady's cellar, there was probably something fitting about the fact that he was covered with grime and coal dust from head to foot, and that Helen, upon seeing him, did not join in the spontaneous shouts of laughter produced by his mother and Mrs. Blye, but instead rose from her chair and went in a businesslike way to start the tapwater running in Mrs. Blye's kitchen sink.

Years later, when Henry Starbuck Flynn was called upon to tell the story of his first love, he was puzzled to discover how thoroughly Helen had gone out of his mind. He could remember her house with remarkable clarity—the dim interior of the downstairs rooms, the cretonne-covered parlor furnishings, a wind-up Victrola, the piano on which Helen plinked out popular tunes like "South of the Border" —or, more impressively, the sight one evening of the four girls sitting around the table in the dining room, with their dark, glistening manes, quietly eating supper. He remembered sitting on the sofa with Helen one evening, listening to a radio broadcast summarizing the early reports coming in from overseas of the sudden German onslaught upon France and the Low Countries, and recalled glancing up the front stairway and seeing through the balustrade the pale, skinny, thrushlike legs of Helen's little sister as she climbed the steps to bed. That was Columbine. She was about eight. There was a picture of her on the piano, a studio portrait in a gold frame. He could remember that, but he could not remember pictures of Helen, nor, in later times, could he conjure up her face. She was, he said, a brunette, with pale complexion, a fine straight nose, and a rather dreamy look that belied her industrious, unimaginative outlook on life.

But during that spring, summer, and fall, Henry showed all the symptoms of a young man suffering his first mad crush. For one thing, his normal sexual appetites abandoned him; it were as if the physical potency that is the pride and mortification of every

17

youth had turned to vapor and risen to his head. He went about in a haze of idealism, filled with gallant thoughts about Helen. He drew mental comparisons between the girl next door and his mother that were not flattering to Mrs. Flynn. He combed his blond hair into a pompadour; he tried writing poetry; he threw away a brand-new pair of corduroy trousers because, he said, they "whistled." On Fridays, he took Helen to the pictures at the Victory Theater, and they sat afterward in a booth at the back of Caesar Equi's ice-cream parlor, and marveled at the strangeness of their having just discovered one another after living next door all their lives. One night in June, after a heavy rainstorm, they went walking at twilight in the sodden grass by the river, and Helen allowed Henry to kiss her on the lips, during which tender enactment he could feel the flesh at the small of her back quivering under his fingertips. Later on, she let him slip his hand underneath her sweater to fondle her breast.

Henry was by then a regular visitor at Helen's house. He was present, for instance, on the night in July when Helen's mother and father celebrated their twentieth wedding anniversary, the house brimming with their Lithuanian relatives and friends. Two of Helen's cousins, Vincas and Leon Botyrius, played the accordion and balalaika, and the house came alive with singing and dancing. Everyone present was talking Lithuanian, including most of the children, but Helen and her sisters kept Henry entertained. Anna, who was only twelve, played the piano for him. Sophie, who was nearly fifteen, made eyes at Henry whenever Helen stepped away. Only Columbine, the youngest of the four girls, ignored him. Columbine was different from her sisters. She was saucy and independent. When Henry teased her, she showed him a disdainful pout and walked away. Henry asked Helen where Columbine had got such a farfetched name. Helen said her mother had taken it from an afternoon soap opera on the radio.

By that time, Henry's father had stopped using the word "Polack," but whenever Helen went past on the walk, he would gaze down at her with a pained, uncomprehending squint. Nothing, he was sure, could ever come from two such pathetic creatures as his son and this strange, saddle-shoed girl who buttoned her sweaters down the back. "She can't even talk," he would say. "What do you imagine they talk about when they're alone?"

"They talk about what we talked about," said Mrs. Flynn.

"I was working," Sergeant Flynn reminded her quickly, with a thin, bitter smile. "I had a job."

"Henry will find work."

"I was working forty-eight hours a week. They're different," he said, and pointed his pipe stem at the outdoors. "With their phonograph records and comic books."

"Henry doesn't read comic books."

"With their movies every week," he continued, "and the radio going all night. Not a soul among them works, you know. There must be fifty boys standing around at the corner store, and not one of them works." He raised a finger. *Not one.* And it's not the Sisters' fault, either, because they'll still give a boy a good caning. Do you remember the recital in the school hall the night Sister Stanislaus lashed Henry on the neck with her pointer?" Popping forward in his chair, Henry's father clapped his hand to his head. "Jesus, Mary, and Joseph, the howl that came out of him!"

About Henry, what the father said was partly true. After finishing high school, he had not begun looking for work but spent days and weeks lolling about with his unemployed friends in the little park by the corner store. They played cards under the trees, games of hi-lo-jack and blackjack and rummy, and hooted at the girls going past. They played a game with a broomstick and tennis ball that they called swift pitch, or went in a mob down to the Beach Grounds to play softball. Two or three of the boys worked for the WPA, out in the wilderness, where a reservoir was being built, and two or three others had gone off to the CCC camps. Marshall Phelan, the dentist's son, played professional baseball for Sherbrooke in the Can-Am League, and Ozzie Solin was a freshman at Brown. The others hung about, pinching cigarettes, playing the punchboards, talking about girls or about the Selective Service Act and the coming draft, but with scarcely a thought to future careers or professions. There was something portentous about their idleness. They seemed to be waiting for something to happen.

Sergeant Flynn had an observation on that score. "It would take a war to wake them up," he said, "and, God knows, they may get it. I don't see how we can stay out, May."

"What a world we live in," said Mrs. Flynn. "Could it be true, Jerome, about what the Japanese are said to be doing in China? Won't they ever leave China?"

"They're monkeys," said the father blithely. "What's the matter with you?"

"I heard on the radio today that Japanese soldiers will tie two little children back-to-back on a bamboo pole and throw them into the water, and let them just spin and thrash helplessly, until, finally, one is drowned, and then they shoot the other. Merciful God, is that possible, Jerome? Are such things possible?"

"Listen," said Henry's father. "When a Jap builds a house, he puts the roof on first. Now, that," he said, tapping a stack of *Reader's Digests* with his thumbnail, "is a documented fact."

"I never heard such stories as I've heard this year.

It's grisly, Jerome. It's inhuman. God protect Henry," she would say. "I pray for him night and day. If the time comes when they start taking the boys the way they did in 1917—by the millions and millions, Jerome—until we're all childless and driven out of our wits with fear—I think I'll just go down to the chapel and stay there forever. I wouldn't have the strength to go on."

"I'll tell you the way it is, Mrs. Flynn, so you won't have to bury yourself on bread and water in that smelly chapel. America," he would say, balling his fist, "is ready for them. That's right. *Secretly,*" he would say, "we have got ourselves ready, you see." Usually when Henry's father sought to quiet his wife's qualms, by citing the secret plans and preparations going on in the American republic, or by describing in vague detail some of the great engines of war that this country would loose upon any adversary foolish enough to attack her, the effect upon Mrs. Flynn was the opposite of that intended, and she would go stealing away, more frightened than ever. "We have stockpiles of poison gas sufficient to destroy in twenty-four hours every mammal, bird, and insect on the face of the globe. We aren't afraid to use it, either. Why, this nation is so big we can't even comprehend our own awesome dimensions. There are more telephones in the United States than there are people in Germany. There are more factories in the United States than there are telephones in China!" As Henry's father dispensed his Sunday-supplement wisdoms, he would work himself into a red-faced fit. "Oh, yes," he would toss out, with a truculent glint in his eye, "if anywhere in the world there is a nation of nincompoops that wants a real war—and I'm not talking about six or seven freshly painted airplanes diving about in the sky over London for the sake of American newsreels—but a real, honest-to-God hard-punching *war,* well, then, by heavens, won't we be just the ones to accommodate them? What do you think they're doing over at the Stevens Arms factory, with the lights burning all night and the machines banging away? What do you think they're producing over there, by the thousands and thousands? You just wait till November, till that man in the White House gets his mandate, and then you won't see any more pussyfooting, believe me. He'll just tell them, in his polite, gentlemanly way, to quit fighting and go to bed—or else. That's all he'll say. *Or else.*"

"Or else they'll come and take Henry," said Mrs. Flynn, "and every boy like him. I think God must be tired of us all."

Young Henry had his own views on the possibility of war. "They can't come over here," he would say, "and we don't want to go over there. Anyhow," he would add, with a gush of laughter and a toothy smile, "I wouldn't mind if we did."

Henry's dalliance with Helen Kokoriss began to falter toward the end of the year. The Kokoriss girl thought Henry to be aimless and indecisive. Sometimes when she came home from school in the afternoon, she could hear him up in his room playing the trombone. Henry didn't sing in the choir any more, or at family gatherings as he had as a boy, but he had a natural musical gift and taught himself to play trombone. For his part, he was tolerant of Helen's sober-mindedness, and even of her constant urgings that he find work; nevertheless, he found the girl next door to be a little "too old" for him. He wished she were lighter-hearted. Of course, he couldn't fault her for being earnest. She also had a very gentle disposition. She was, for example, gentler and softer by nature (and, if he could admit it, also more lovable-seeming) than the Irish girls with whom he had gone to school; but where those girls were clever-tongued, always joking and laughing and making playful cracks, Helen was slow to warm up to any type of kidding around. She was never merry. She was never spontaneous.

After the President was re-elected in November, a winter lull developed in the European war that made the holiday time seem brighter than anyone had expected. One evening, while coming up the hill, trudging home from the corner store—it was about nine o'clock—Henry fell into step with Helen's sister Sophie. Sophie was carrying a bottle of milk in a paper bag, with her arms wrapped around it, and in the shimmer and glare of the streetlight there was no confusing—even for a fellow reputed to be a little slow on the uptake—the revolutionary point of view that Sophie appeared intent on publicizing. She pointed out that this was the first time they two had ever spoken in private. Not, she said, that she had anything very special to say, but she did know *all* about Helen and him, and that, frankly, if anyone were to ask *her* opinion, which, she acknowledged, they were not doing, she couldn't *help,* she said, but take Henry's side. Sophie said that if anyone had given *her* a beautiful camera for *her* seventeenth birthday, which they had not, of course, if only for the very good reason that she wasn't seventeen—"although I am fifteen, only a year younger than Helen was when you started seeing her"—that she, Sophie, wouldn't worry herself to death about the price of film!

"I'm not saying Helen's a dud," she said, "because you may have some feeling for her—that I *don't* know—but I am saying that if my boyfriend went to the trouble to find me something as original as that —and *I* wouldn't care, Herk, if he worked or stole for it—why, I think I'd photograph just about everything in sight!"

Henry was, confessedly, gratified by Sophie Kokoriss's having thrown a little light on the matter of the Brownie 120 box camera which, wrapped beautifully in red and silver foil, he had given Helen

23

on the occasion of her last birthday. So he didn't discourage Sophie in her treachery. All around the world, after all, the ministers of great governments were negotiating behind one another's back, flattering their opponents and vilifying their friends, so that a little underhandedness between sisters seemed trifling enough. The two of them stood in the lamplight at the foot of the short flight of stone steps leading up to the flagstone walk, while Sophie, wetting her lips, looking away, and looking back again, proceeded, step by step, to tear her sister to pieces.

Clutching the bag with the bottle of milk to her breast, she asked Henry, at last, if she, Helen, wasn't really just too boring for words. "I wouldn't call it boring," Henry replied very judiciously, but in a tone suggesting that it would require a philosopher to improve upon that description. The chill of the night gave Sophie's high cheekbones and water-colored eyes a luminosity that Henry associated with undersea life, as with the gleam of a starfish; and while neither one of them openly avoided climbing the steps, so did neither one of them actually take the lead as they continued along past the stairs and on up the hill, turning in instead at the dirt roadway that ran behind the houses. A radio program called "Cavalcade of America" was either going on or going off the air, for its theme music came seeping out the back windows of the Flynn house as Henry and Sophie sauntered along quietly in the shadow of the fence. Minutes later, they were standing behind Mr. Kokoriss's woodshed, when Sophie came softly against him in the darkness and began kissing his mouth in a delicate but eager and passionate way. He could feel the cold, hard bottle of milk lodged between them in the place where Sophie's breast should have been.

"She can't even read," said Sophie. "I've read *Don Quixote.*"

"Have you?" said Henry.

"I'll write to you in the service, too."

"Oh, they won't take me." Henry disparaged that idea. "They go by numbers," he explained.

"I would be willing to say *anything* in a letter," said Sophie. "Helen wouldn't even write. Besides, I'm smarter than she is."

"I heard that you were," Henry croaked.

"I'm helping her with her homework tonight."

"Isn't that fascinating?" Henry was whispering to her at close range, in a frail, piping voice, just as Sophie's tongue came fluttering into the passageway between his own lips.

That was in December 1940. Within a month, Henry was lying on the rifle range at the Great Lakes Training Station, firing an old bolt-action Springfield rifle for record, the only young man from Hadley Falls to have been inducted into the Navy.

II

A time came when Henry, lying in his bunk at night, would remember the dark treetops above the Kokoriss house, or hear again the late-night sounds of his father moving about restlessly in the downstairs rooms of their house on Cottage Avenue, and wonder if the house and avenue still existed, or had that entire portion of his life vanished into the ocean behind him, like a discarded Coke bottle or one of Petty Officer Pue's burning cigar stubs? By that time, Henry was an old salt. He was not discharged when his term of service ended because of the Japanese aerial assault on the American fleet at Pearl Harbor and the onset of war. Early the next year, he found himself aboard a destroyer, a "tin can" called the U.S.S. *Markham* that steamed its way thousands of miles across the Pacific, and whose chief mission and purpose, so far as Henry or his fellow crewmen could discern, seemed to be to avoid at all costs either spotting or being spotted by any vessel of any nationality.

The Pacific Ocean seemed so big to Henry, so indescribably vast, that he could not imagine how any conflict between mere tiny ships could ever be decisive or have any meaningful territorial bearing, since the victorious ships would merely turn about and retire as they had come, in the form of little black specks vanishing over the horizon, and be thereafter neither more nor less possessing of this dull blue infinitude than their sunken adversaries. For several days, the crew worked at scraping paint. That was to prevent the ship from burning in battle.

At night, because it was stifling in the compartments below, the men slept topside. Stories were plentiful on deck. "The Japs like to cut your head off with a sword." "The Japs killed nineteen nuns in New Guinea. They raped them and chopped them up with their swords." "Japs never give up. They fight to the finish." Henry tried to avoid listening to such claptrap, but spent his time between watches in the ship's library, poring over atlases and sea charts, trying to reconcile his understanding of maps, as inculcated in him at the Sisters' school, with the great monotonous waste of water that stretched out forever fore and aft.

There was a popular theory aboard ship, an idea advanced by a mess attendant named Stryker, that the *Markham*, as one of the few surviving warships of a mostly sunken navy, was supposed to do nothing more consequential than steam about on its own, far from harm's way—down around New Zealand, it was supposed—while back home America built herself a *new* navy; then that new navy, with brand-new ships and guns and crews, would come sailing out into the Pacific to fight the Japs, and that they, Henry and his fellow crewmen, would then steer quietly about and sail home. Further scuttlebutt had it, though, that the *Markham* was to join the screen of destroyers for the carriers *Hornet* and *Enterprise*, believed to be operating far to the south. These aircraft carriers, along with the *Lexington* and *Yorktown*, had escaped the debacle at Pearl, and were—according to the gossip that no one believed—steamed up and spoiling for a fight.

In April 1942, the *Markham* crossed the Equator. Henry was transferred from his post on a 40 mm. gun mount to a rescue team that practiced every day at deploying lifelines and rescue nets, an activity that involved a great deal of running about the deck and shouting, and which the other crewmen looked upon as being a little demoralizing, if not actually bizarre. Early one morning, several days below the Equator, Henry was awakened in his bunk by a steady rhythmic vibrating that set his teeth on edge. Hurrying topside, he emerged on deck to find himself, and the entire destroyer, standing in the shadow of an enormous wall of steel that loomed darkly ahead and above. He was looking up amidships at the U.S.S. *Yorktown*. The morning sun was hidden behind the great carrier, but the rays of the morning light poured out horizontally across the flight deck. Another small vessel, a seaplane tender, stood close by, also in the shadows of the *Yorktown,* while farther out, other ships of varying descriptions appeared to be standing to. The water all around was churned up and white, the air filled with the throbbing roar of engines and wind and a medley of whistles, gongs, loudspeaker squawkings, and bullhorns. Henry, who, like his green fellow shipmates, had not until now truly believed in the reality of war, at least not in any personal sense, felt strangely upset and frightened by his first glimpse at the awesomeness of a carrier. That moment remained with Henry thereafter as a time of a parting of ways, as of between peace and war, or between childhood and manhood. An hour later, a score of ships got underway, and then, with a stiff trade wind blowing, the *Yorktown* (now about a half mile distant) made a slow, stately turn into the wind, and began launching her scouting planes. They came up like bees.

Soon the great carrier and its escort resumed their westerly course, while the destroyer *Markham* concluded its solitary journey by turning about and putting in at Tongatabu, the port from which the *Yorktown* had just sortied. It was there, at Tongatabu, while enjoying shore leave and investigating this exotic little port of call, and exchanging pleasantries with some British seamen, that Henry Flynn and his mates heard news for the first time of the latest

American military disaster, the fall of Corregidor and the Philippines.

Henry guessed that he was more sober-minded than his crewmates, since most of them accepted the news quite nonchalantly and were evidently far more interested in the barefooted, barebreasted Polynesian girls (whose pictures they were snapping left and right) than they were in a distant catastrophe. An Englishman who served as an observer aboard the Catalina patrol planes summed up the matter nicely and in a way that seemed to satisfy the crew's philosophical needs as well as its need to laugh now and again, when he said, "Well, your navy has been smashed, and now the other fellows are having *their* turn, you see. In Europe, it's been just the other way about. We," he said, "had our army smashed up first. That's how wars are fought. First, you have the one smashed to pieces," he said, in a cheerful, singsong voice, "and then, not too much later, you have the other smashed up!" To this grim appraisal of war the British sailor, who gave his name as Harold Holcroft-Hughes, added a view about events taking place on the other side of the world that produced gales of laughter among the men of the *Markham*. "Why," he said, "I wouldn't even want to *be* in Europe today. They're behaving like savages!" he cried. "If you so much as set foot there, by God, you take your life in your hands!"

"They're killing people," said one of the crewmen.

"That's just what I'm driving at!" snapped the Britisher. "Listen," he said, and changed his voice, "why don't you show me how to make one of those planter's punches of yours. After all, I might as well learn something useful out here."

Henry wrote home faithfully. His letters to Sergeant and Mrs. Flynn were models of all the letters ever written home by sons stationed in the four corners of the world. These letters conveyed almost no information whatever; they contained vague assurances on the matter of the writer's good health; they hoped that everyone at home was equally healthy; and they usually concluded with a playful quip. That Henry was, at this time, experiencing lurid dreams at night—dreams in which a particular native girl appeared, a girl with badly stained teeth and a luminous mat of waist-length black hair whom he had noticed watching him down by the docks one evening—was just one of a hundred poignant features of Henry's life that could not have been guessed from his insipid letters. Another was the secret dread he carried around with him that one day, suddenly, he would find himself face to face with individual Japanese combatants, three or four helmeted Nipponese armed with knives and guns, each meaning to mutilate and kill him on the spot. It was not unusual for Henry to drop off to sleep with the face of the smiling black-toothed native girl in his mind, only to awaken in the middle of the night, pouring sweat, about to be carved to bits by three or four grinning sons of Japan. He never dreamed of Helen Kokoriss, or, for that matter, of her sister Sophie. He was certainly unaware of the fact that the Kokorisses and their neighbors were in the meanwhile all proud of him. Sophie had acquired from Henry's mother a photograph that Henry sat for in San Diego, a picture showing the young seaman in summer whites, which she displayed atop the upright piano in a handsome gold frame. Mrs. Blye, for her part, never passed the Flynn house without stopping to ask after Henry. Without his knowing it, Henry had become the beloved representative-at-war of the entire little enclave of houses that composed Cottage Avenue.

Even Henry's father could not fail to be proud. When news of the great naval victory at Midway was released to the public, Sergeant Flynn actually wept. That night, he admitted to his wife in bed what no one might have guessed: that until now he had been frightened and worried about his son. The news from Midway seemed to purge him of his secret terror.

On the evening when Admiral Yamamoto broke off the action at Midway, ordering the supporting remnants of his destroyed carrier force to retire upon his main fleet in the west, Henry Flynn was three thousand miles away. He was still at Tongatabu. In fact, at sunset of that very evening, he was being followed on foot in the shadows of a row of pandanus trees by the tall girl with the long mat of black hair. He was making his way back to the *Markham* but had stopped off briefly to visit his English sailor friends in their compound by the seaplane hangar. He came out of the gate just as the sun was setting. From afar came the soft drone of an approaching PBY. Suddenly, sensing her presence, Henry spun about and saw the girl coming along behind him under the trees. She was, as always, barefooted, and, as always, too, she walked erectly, her head high and her bosom alive to the motion of her legs. She came directly toward him. She had been waiting for him. Henry stood rooted to the spot. The emotion that forbade Henry to turn and flee in fright was, no doubt, a little counterfeit version of that great emotion that holds a man in place in battle; that is, his fear of showing cowardice just barely outweighed his true cowardly feelings. Henry knew her well by sight now. She was a Fijian. That explained her tallness. She was coming straight at him, the instep of her foot flashing like phosphorus at every step she took. Henry, in his confusion, was staring directly at her breasts as she stopped in front of him and, smiling brazenly, said, "Two dollar?"

Henry told this story himself more than once in later years, when he was old enough to realize what a child he had been in those days, but what he did not confess was the medley of wild emotions that assailed him for weeks to come. "I gave her the two dollars," he would say, "pulled it out of my dungarees and handed it to her, and then, to her everlasting amazement, turned about-face and marched back to the ship! God, how she must have laughed over that! When I walked away from her, I had the feeling a man must get when he knows a pistol is trained on his back. I didn't tell a soul!" What Henry also did not tell anyone, though, was that all during that summer he suffered a mild kind of emotional derangement, one which had befallen many white men who had come out to these islands; he wanted to creep back out at night, and forget about all the details of everyday life—about ships and toil and ticking clocks—and take the tall bronze Fijian girl into one of those buglike outriggers, and set sail with her (black teeth and all) for one of the coral islands that he had seen from the air in a Catalina. There were dozens of such islands thereabouts, some of them lush, green, and volcanic, others with coral breakwaters and motionless lagoons, into any one of which he could have vanished like a thought.

Henry did not fall in love with the islands; he fell prey to a tropical languor, a malaise that came over him as swiftly as if he had been bitten by a bug. He grew distant. He stopped playing poker with his mates evenings; he missed many of the movies shown on deck; he withdrew from the friendly beer-drinking and skull sessions aboard ship. In the daytime, he went about his duties lethargically, confining his responses to monosyllabic mutterings and shrugs. Henry's strangeness was not lost upon his shipmates, but before any of his friends could have helped him, Henry was transferred to the signals section on shore. One evening, after taking a long, solitary walk on the beach, he stood and watched as the U.S.S. *Markham* glided silently out to sea.

He never saw the *Markham* again, and it was a long

time before he heard news of her fate. It came under the command of an Admiral Callaghan, who one night led a wild suicidal attack of cruisers and destroyers smack through the heart of a Japanese task force sailing down the "Slot" in the Solomons. The *Markham* went down. Hit hard both port and starboard, the destroyer was lost with all hands. Henry never dwelt much, though, upon his having been saved by fortune from sharing the evil lot of the men with whom he had served for months, but now and again he did have to suppress in his mind a picture of flooded steel chambers containing fishes and seaweed and shiny white bones.

In time his natural spirits returned. Henry shook off his equatorial lethargy and then, for reasons he was never able to uncover, began to lead a new life. He remained the same grinning, good-natured butt of other people's jibes and pranks, but at the back of this deceptive persona he developed also a thoughtful inner life. He began to keep a daily journal, which he called his "Pacific Log," and often found himself involved in philosophical discussions with two or three of his British friends, late-night talks about subjects of an exalted and abstruse nature. He also began to drink gin, which made him loquacious, so that sometimes he astounded even himself by holding forth for several minutes running, expressing thoughts that he had not known himself capable of formulating. He could not even remember by what steady progression his views had so utterly altered that he had come to receive the sobriquet, pinned on him by the British, "that Yank atheist."

"You see," he said, "it's a logical necessity that either I'm right and most of the world is wrong, or else I'm wrong and, at best, mind you, half of the world may be right."

"I don't understand that at all," insisted one Englishman, also glowing from his gin and juice.

"You can't be a Buddhist and a headhunter and a

33

Jew and a Christian Baptist and *all* of you be right,"
said Henry, stopping to mix himself a powerful
draught of Bombay gin and orange juice. He was
sitting at a bamboo table beneath a dim hanging
lantern in the British billet. Electrical power had
failed in the port that evening, but Henry and his
friends continued uninterruptedly their debate of
the temporal versus the eternal verities. *"Either"*—
Henry swallowed and wiped his lips with his fist—
"either half of you are wrong, *or* all of you are
wrong. If you are all wrong, I'm right. Or to state it
differently, if I am right, you are all wrong. Whereas
if I'm wrong, then only half of you may be wrong.
May be wrong," he said. "You still may *all* be
wrong."

"I don't understand that," said a Britisher.

"Don't argue with Herky Flynn," said another of
His Majesty's sailors, who lay half naked on his cot.
"Herky is a fund of paradoxes. What *I'd* like to
know," he said, "is where else on earth do God's
bloody cockroaches *fly?"*

Henry mixed more gin into his drink and tried to
steer the conversation back to its previous heights,
notwithstanding the thick swarm of fireflies and
flying cockroaches going round and round in the
lamplight. "You're not being logical," he argued.
"That's the trouble with coming from an old country. You confuse faith with hidebound tradition.
You take comfort in habit. What *is,"* said Henry,
"must be good simply *because* it is—because it *was*
and *is* and, one hopes, *shall be.* But that's not logical,
you see. Now, *Stateside* everything is new . . ."

And so it went, Henry and his British friends
whiling away whole days and evenings, on through
September into autumn, talking, playing cribbage,
writing letters, performing mechanically their dull
assigned duties, and then more gin and talking, on
through Christmas into the New Year. A special
treat came one night in January 1943, in the form of

a dozen bottles of Japanese *sake,* brought in from Guadalcanal aboard a mail plane, prompting an extemporaneous party at which Henry got desperately drunk and sick on a lethal concoction of gin, *sake,* and coconut milk. All he could remember later was Harold Holcroft-Hughes saying, over and over again, in a voice emptied of human meaningfulness, "I say—this delivers a *punch!* . . . I say there, old man, this delivers a punch! . . ."

Taken in all, Henry's memories of the Pacific never assumed a very coherent or systematic picture. His days at Tongatabu merged into one unending tropical afternoon. There was, he remembered, a typhoon. There was also an Australian cruiser that arrived in broad daylight on fire, trailing oil slick for miles behind her and sending up a funnel of black smoke that reached tremendous heights in the cloudless sky; a black hole gaped in her port bow, and the crewmen on deck were all pressing forward to avoid the suffocating smoke. On another occasion, Henry accompanied a Marine captain and five or six of his men in a motor whaleboat to a nearby island in search of three AWOL American sailors, but all they found was a little thatched-hut village standing back of the beach, and there, big as life, sitting in her father's doorway, was the tall girl with the black teeth; she wore a white plaster cast on one leg, and it was obvious she was many months pregnant. When Henry realized that he had all but forgotten her, he knew that he had been in the Pacific Theater a considerable time. The Marines did not find the AWOLs that morning, and Henry never saw the girl again. By that time, he was drinking more than he should have. He was filling his "Log" with lengthy, high-sounding arguments, to which he affixed such ponderous titles as "The Irreconcilability of God and Democracy," and what's more, he had stopped writing to—and even thinking about—the Kokoriss girls, who lived next door on Cottage

Avenue. Just as the war seemed now to be receding into the northwest, Henry's childhood days were similarly dissolving somewhere back of the morning mists. He grew a mustache; he began to speak of himself as a writer; he even affected a faraway look in his eye in the hope of conveying to others something of the dimension of his solitude and expanding intellectual powers. It was, understandably, a shock for Henry when he learned that he was being ordered back to sea.

Part of the remainder of Henry Flynn's Navy days was spent aboard a destroyer escort among seasoned, hard-bitten men, at least forty of whom had lost their previous ship and been fished out of the burning waters of the Bismarck Sea. Hearing them talk about combat left Henry queasy. While Henry's almost four years of service made him one of the old-timers aboard ship—he was, by then, a petty officer second class—he was, nevertheless, the only hand who had not been in battle. One night in early October 1944, World War II—the greatest and most cataclysmic of all wars—reached out to Henry Starbuck Flynn a fiery tentacle.

The occasion of Henry's baptism at war was a sudden surface skirmish that developed about sixty miles south of Mindanao. The action lasted eight minutes. It commenced with no announcement whatever, no distant gunfire, no bells or sirens, no intercoms, not even a human shout; just a sudden thunderous *crack* from overhead, the report of an unexploded eight-inch shell shearing off a section of armor plate on the bridge as it passed through. Henry (he had just shaved off his mustache and at the moment was regarding himself narcissistically in the mirror attached to his locker) lost his footing under the impact and reeled around against the bulkhead. Henry himself could not tell you what happened next. He made an effort to get topside but was washed back at once by a wall of knee-deep water that simply appeared from nowhere and carried him off his feet. Nevertheless, by some conspiracy of desperation and nervous excitement, Henry scrambled his way up on deck, the ship pitching violently. He remembered only the sight of a second vessel, which, strangely, seemed to be riding high in the water and flaming brightly—that, and a sensation that the very ocean itself was upended and wracked with deafening explosions. Cowering, he passed into shock. One explosion blew his shoes off. By then, the ship's five-inchers were banging away in the darkness, even though the ship itself had swung violently about, its bow passing perilously close to the flaming ship near at hand. Henry did not consciously acknowledge any of the several subsequent explosions, two of which came from the after fire room, nor did he ever ascertain who, precisely, was responsible for tying around him the Mae West in which he was found floating—in total shock—in the oily waters at dawn the next morning.

This engagement was summed up by an officer aboard the medical ship to which Henry and three other wounded crewmen were later transferred by breeches buoy as a fluke. "A couple of 'little boys,'" he said, "stumbled onto a crippled Nip cruiser bound for Brunei Bay. No ships down, no men lost."

Ever afterward, Henry simplified his account of his "days in action" by saying that he was hit during the Battle of Leyte Gulf, the historic sea fight that pitched the Seventh and Third Fleets against the entire remaining Japanese Navy, but which actually began more than two weeks later, at the end of October, by which time Henry was being carried ashore at Honolulu.

The last entry in Henry's "Pacific Log" was also its shortest and most cryptic:

> 4/21/45: *144 days at sea, 176 days Honolulu, 803 days Tongatabu. Goodbye, Tongatabu.*

III

Henry's timing was superlative. He arrived home in early June 1945, two months before the Pacific war's end; by then, Americans everywhere sensed victory to be imminent, and day by day were accustoming themselves to the prospect that millions of fighting men would soon be stacking arms and heading home. Henry's arrival offered a living assurance that that day of sweet reunions was creeping close, for the only soldiers and sailors from Hadley Falls to have reached home ahead of Henry had been those who arrived at the depot in flag-draped caskets with a military escort. Henry came home under his own power. The damage he had sustained to both ankles and to his left leg proved advantageous, as this rather minor infirmity required his carrying a cane for the next several weeks, and of course the sight of the young seaman coming and going at his parents' door in his summer whites, limping a trifle and swinging his cane along before him at every step as he took his first solitary walks up and down the hill to the drugstore and back, brought many of his neighbors directly out onto their porches to call down to him a heartfelt "Well done, Herky! . . . Proud of you, boy!"

In the weeks to come, Henry kept himself neat and trim in every respect. Because he was not discharged from active duty and was required by wartime regulations to wear his uniform at all hours, he made sure never to drink too much. He did not want to disgrace himself. Every afternoon, he caught a bus that took him across the river to Ireland Parish, where he visited a bar called Jockamy's. There he drank three gins and three lemon sodas, then boarded the bus again for home. He did not call upon the Kokorisses next door, because the two older girls, Helen and Sophie, did not live at home any more. Helen was in Washington, D.C., where she worked as a stenographer, and, according to Henry's mother, had recently got engaged to be married. Sophie was working in Boston. One evening, as Henry was returning home from a short walk by the river, he saw Anna standing under the porch light at the back of the Kokoriss house and was struck by her resemblance to her older sisters. Anna was now seventeen, which was as old as, or even a year older than, Helen had been in 1940, when she and Henry had begun dating. The sight of her troubled him. He felt like someone come back from the dead. Everything looked the same, but everything was changed. His friends were gone; the bedroom in which he had slept as a youth seemed narrow and cramped; Anna Kokoriss looked older than Sophie, and Sophie, were she to come home, would doubtless look older than Helen. Even Columbine, the youngest of the Kokoriss children, had shot up from a little schoolchild into a skinny adolescent. Henry's chief consolation was that people everywhere lionized him, thumping him on the back, offering him rides in their autos, and, generally, according him the friendliness, respect, and goodwill typically shown to heroes or to generals of the army. One day, a man whom Henry had never seen before paid for his lunch at the counter in Liggett's. Another time a woman introduced herself to him as the wife of Dick McKenna, the bartender at Jockamy's, and drove Henry all the way home in the family car. Mrs. McKenna said it was a shame that Dicky's ulcers had kept him out of the war, that it mortified her every time she thought about it. She loved sailor uniforms, she said, and had hoped to see Dicky in one. "As soon as he heard from the Selective Service people, he developed his ulcers."

Mrs. McKenna sat behind the wheel of the car and turned herself toward Henry in a way that struck him as being a very attractive pose in a woman; he was impressed, too, by the way she moistened her lips from time to time while talking, as though she had just eaten something sweet and wanted to savor and remember it. When on the following day, at the same hour, Mrs. McKenna showed up in her Buick at the bus stop near Jockamy's Bar and drove Henry home again, she did not stop the car at the little flight of stone steps leading up into Cottage Avenue but drove on up the hill to Highland Street and around the bend, and didn't stop until they were out on the River Road past the radio broadcasting station. She said she hoped Henry wouldn't mind her stopping, but she needed someone to talk to, and she didn't mean just anyone, but someone whom she admired and could trust, somebody who was young enough to understand what she, who was twenty seven, was talking about, because she was thinking of leaving Dick, she said, now that he didn't seem able to make her feel like a complete woman, particularly since he had dodged the draft, and she wanted Henry to know, she said, that she—not in spite of her being Dicky's wife, but because of it—was grateful for what Henry had done overseas to those lousy, yellow-bellied Japs, and that there wasn't anything he could ask of her, she said, that she wouldn't do for him or give to him if he wanted or needed it.

"Anything," she said.

Henry sat in the passenger's seat, with his cane propped between his legs and a frozen grin on his face. He was petrified.

Mrs. McKenna said her name was Dolly, that she had gone to college for a year and a half, and that her education also stood as a barrier between her and

41

Dicky, that half the time he didn't even know what she was talking about, and how often, too, she added, she had wished against wish to be living with someone like Henry, who was college-trained and obviously very intellectual, besides being handsome and having one hell of a war record. When Henry told Mrs. McKenna that he had never been to college, a look of amazement came over her. She said she couldn't believe it. She asked him where he had acquired such a nice way of talking, that she noticed he even had an English accent sometimes, as in the way he had referred to the bus he took from Jockamy's every day as a "bloody fright."

When Henry Flynn blushed, Mrs. McKenna reached for and took possession of his two hands resting atop his cane, and said to him, again, only this time in a very soft, resolved tone of voice, that she would truly like to do anything for him, anywhere, anytime. Anything he wanted. Even right now, she said. Right here.

"In the car," she said.

The stunned bewilderment on Henry's face was the same expression exactly that the rescue team discovered on Henry eight months earlier, the morning they pulled him out of the running black ocean and raised him into the launch, his body dripping and smeared with oil, his dungarees in tatters. If his left shin and calf had not begun to send severe shooting pains up the length of his leg, causing him to grimace and rub his knee, he might never have had a reason for urging Mrs. McKenna to take him home. As it was, Dolly McKenna—while explaining to him how rude and forward of her she knew it to be—came forward on the seat and kissed Henry on the mouth. She put her left hand on his right hip and her right hand behind his head, pressing him down to her; he saw her tongue go darting across her lips in the instant before she attached her mouth to his.

———

That was a Tuesday. Henry did not go to Jockamy's Bar the next day, nor did he go on Thursday or Friday. He did, however, encounter Dick McKenna's wife that Friday evening. He met her under unusual circumstances. Early in the evening Anna Kokoriss had paid Henry's mother a visit to return a novel she had borrowed from Mrs. Flynn, and the woman and the girl were sitting in the kitchen while Henry and his father were sitting in the parlor conducting a conversation on the subject of whether the Japanese were human or not. Henry seemed inclined to favor the view that the majority of Japanese were as human as anybody else, while his father cleaved to a contrary point of view. Sergeant Flynn came home from the police stationhouse for supper every evening, and liked to sit back on the sofa and open his tunic and smoke a pipeful after dinner. At such times, he often grew expansive. "Well, then," he said gently, as he sucked thoughtfully on his pipe, while staring at the glowing bowl, "tell me this. If a creature lives like an animal and behaves like an animal, what is to stop him from being an animal?"

"Everybody knows Japs are human," said Henry, in embarrassment. "Everybody, after all, has their inhuman moments. Only a man *can* behave inhumanly. A squirrel, for example, cannot behave inhumanly."

"I didn't say that!" said his father. "I didn't say he could! I didn't say they were squirrels. Any lummox would know they're not squirrels. Squirrels," he elucidated, "do not cut off each other's head, or stab themselves in the belly. Squirrels," he gestured broadly, "do not run completely amok in the forest!"

"There have been other times in history when men ran amok," said Henry, jiggling his cane nervously against his shoes.

"By the millions?" His father's eyes bulged insinuatingly.

"What about the Golden Horde?" said Henry.

"The Golden Horde, you say!" His father raised his voice musically. "You mean those thousands of yellow skins pouring down from Mongolia? Is that what you're talking about? Because that's what *I'm* talking about."

The discussion was interrupted by May Flynn, who asked her son if he would not care to accompany Anna and herself to the movies at the Rialto.

"Take him to the movies," said his father, "by all means. Look at what the devils did to him." He gestured at Henry's legs and cane. "Look, too," he cried, in a quavering falsetto, "what they did to the women and children of Nanking! Would you call the slaughter and *rapine* of a million women and children —one million women and children—the actions of a rational being? Because I would not. No," he caroled roundly, "I would not regard it that way. Two years ago, for the War Bond effort, a Jap midget submarine was put on display in front of the public library. It was not any bigger than this sofa. A two-man submarine, it was called. I tell you, I couldn't believe my eyes. I said to myself, 'What came into their minds that would cause them to *build* such a contraption?' Did they honestly intend with gadgets like that to fight it out against the United States of America?" He waved a hand at Anna Kokoriss, who stood in the doorway behind Henry's mother. "A young girl in her pigtails would know better," he said. "It had no guns, no torpedoes, no radio, no radar, no place for food, no place to sleep, no windows, no toilet, not anything seaworthy or sensible about it at all. But then, maybe *I* am wrong." He looked at his three auditors in turn. "Who am I to pass judgment on Creation? If God in His wisdom sees fit to create a full seventy million of these so-called Japanese humans, as you call them . . ."

The older Flynn continued to expound his ethnological views as he led the way down the hill toward the stationhouse and movie theater, with Henry at his side and the two women coming along behind them. Henry's father always carried a nightstick, which, as a desk sergeant, he had no business carrying in the street, but it had become a part of his person over the years and was rarely out of his hands. He brandished it when speaking; he twirled it sometimes at blinding speed; he emphasized his words with quick, sharp cuts of the stick in the air. "You see"—up came the stick—"I take a moral view of the world. What is a human being is a moral question. Does *that*," he said, "make sense to you? Tell me if I'm wrong. A cat has a digestive system. A rat," he said, "has eyes, ears, a nose, a mouth. An owl has a heart beating in his chest, doesn't he?"

"Yes, he does," said Henry.

"Does an elephant have a brain?"

"Yes, he does."

"Is that brain bigger than man's brain?"

"I believe it may be bigger," said Henry.

Sergeant Flynn's stick made a sudden vicious revolution and stopped abruptly under Henry's nose. "What makes a man human? Answer me that. Isn't it something moral? Something God-given? Doesn't it reveal itself in behavior? Isn't it something unique among the animals?"

"I think civilization makes a big difference," said Henry, as he looked back sheepishly at his mother and Anna coming along in their wake. Anna, he noticed, had begun looking at him in a certain pleasant and intimate way astonishingly reminiscent of expressions he had seen on both Helen's and Sophie's faces back in '49.

Sergeant Flynn was contemplating Henry with a superior smirk. "Why do you suppose," he asked prettily, "God didn't give civilization to the yellows? Isn't it possible," he went on in a pedantic tone, bulging wide his eyes, "that the yellows are an unsuccessful offshoot of the species? I mean to say," he boomed out in a mellow, facetious tone, "isn't that just possible?"

"Well, anything is possible," Henry conceded idly, while wincing inwardly at the thought of Anna Kokoriss's gathering attentions, "although they have a civilization of their own. Maybe," he said, "they see us as the barbarians and would like to clear the earth of us so they can work out their destiny." Henry tossed out these words without a solid thought behind them, because his mind was dwelling on the absurd notion that he might soon start up with Anna. It gave him the feeling again of being bypassed by life—as in the way these girls, for example, were moving past him into womanhood one by one, while he, ageless and forever innocent, stood somehow shunted to one side.

"Is my hearing gone?" said Sergeant Flynn, looking away in befuddlement. "Or did he say they have a civilization? Is that what you said? Did I hear you correctly?"

As he marched along at his father's side, the two of them presenting an attractive military picture, Henry happened to glance into the roadway just as Mrs. McKenna cruised slowly past in her red Buick coupe, her eyes falling on him and on Anna and his mother coming along behind. Dolly McKenna drove on, but pulled up to the curb at the foot of the hill, where she waited. Henry's heart beat in agitation. He had a horror of Dolly McKenna getting out of her car and creating a sudden scene. As the four of them marched past Mrs. McKenna's parked car, he caught a glimpse of her as she spun about and sent a swift, menacing look at Anna. Mrs. McKenna had her compact in her hands and was pretending to make up her face, but kept looking sidewise at Anna Kokoriss with an expression of malevolent intensity. After Sergeant Flynn had gone his own way, tramping down the side street to the police station, and

Henry had shepherded his mother and the girl next door into the Rialto movie house, he felt powerfully unnerved, so much so that he excused himself during the opening shots of the Movietone news (featuring the naval bombardment of Okinawa) and went out to the lobby. Mrs. McKenna was standing in the theater lobby waiting for him.

Mrs. McKenna started right in. She was not one for mincing words. She didn't waste her time, she said, on guys who cheated on the side. She made no effort to conceal her anger or jealousy, but spoke straight out to the embarrassed sailor, raising her voice to accommodate her rising anger. Not fifteen feet away, the crimson-jacketed high-school boy working the popcorn machine stood listening to the two of them in fascination, while from inside the theater resounded the soft strains of background music that accompanied the crackling voice of the newsreel commentator and the still softer, insistent boom and din of the long-range naval cannonade. It wasn't every girl, Mrs. McKenna said, who would just offer herself to someone, or go chasing after him like a lunatic, even if he was supposed to be some sort of local hero. Beneath Mrs. McKenna's gray suit jacket, her matching gray sweater came swelling forth in a way that left Henry feeling both excited and upset. Dicky, she said, was a "dead issue," and knew it. There was nothing to worry about with Dick, and he, Henry, should know that, because she knew he was worried about something not to have taken advantage—not to have "made good" was how she styled it—on what she had wanted to give him.

"Dicky is a jimoke," she said.

Henry could not remember by what stages he had got himself into this embroilment.

"I could tell you stories about him that would curl your hair," she said.

Mrs. McKenna and Henry stood at the heart of the

ornate vaulted lobby, with its red plush carpeting and gilt ceiling, gazing at one another, Henry appearing red-faced but faint.

"He likes a woman to walk all over him," she added.

Lighting a cigarette, Mrs. McKenna blew a long plume of smoke sideways from her mouth, then carefully picked a grain of tobacco from the tip of her tongue.

"So what are we going to do?" she said in a clear, firm voice. "Where are we going to meet? And *when?*"

Henry was finished with Mrs. McKenna. For one thing, he found her a trifle crude. She was presentable in appearance and well-spoken, he would not deny her that, but the slightest obstruction to her will, he noticed, brought forth a coarse, willful strain in her nature that was not ladylike. At such times, her face took on a cynical set, as if she was waiting for the other party to knuckle under and acknowledge her more realistic way of thinking. Henry even found himself pitying Dick McKenna. More than once in these past three weeks Henry and Dick had passed the time of afternoon together in the bar, listening to "Queen for a Day" on the radio, or taking turns at playing the jukebox, while Henry sipped his gin and lemon soda and Dick made pleasant discourse on a variety of subjects. Henry, who loved trombone, enjoyed sitting in the cool dark of the barroom, listening to Tommy Dorsey. Now, he could not go to Jockamy's any more. Mrs. McKenna had spoiled it. He would have to go some place new, since he did not relish the prospect of suddenly being brought to blows by that sturdy little bartender, or having to go home on the five o'clock bus holding a handkerchief to his bloodied nose, with his Navy whites torn and filthied. He would find another barroom, that was all, and try to keep clear of Dick McKenna's wife. That was his program and policy.

He did not go to the movies any more, and he made sure not to be seen on the street with Anna Kokoriss, since Mrs. McKenna had made it obvious that she would not tolerate "another woman." The truth was that Dolly McKenna's boldness in pursuing him into the movie house that evening had appalled Henry. For several days he actually worried that she might come to his front door and create an ugly scene. He could envision her thrusting her way into the front parlor and lifting her voice contemptuously to Mrs. Flynn, demanding to talk to Henry. Henry wished he had never accepted that first ride home from her, and he made it a governing precept for his future dealings with women that he would not be taken advantage of again in that fashion. "I got mixed up with a bad egg," he said.

Henry's avoidance of the bartender's wife naturally curtailed his movements. Sometimes in the evening he would play Parcheesi in the kitchen with his mother and Anna, or stump his way down the hill on his cane to the police stationhouse to pass a pleasant half hour or so with his father. Henry recognized that the feelings of ennui and dislocation that had settled upon him stemmed from his abrupt passage from the military life, where pointlessness was made bearable by being institutionalized, to this formless, sedate existence at home. Not too far in the future, particularly after being mustered out, his spirits and inner balance would restore themselves. By then, this entire lamentable business with Dolly McKenna would be as faded in memory as his remembrances of life at sea. That was not to say that she was not attractive to Henry, because she was. She made a vivid impression on him, and what's more, her grasping, determined attitude toward him was not unflattering. Mrs. McKenna put Henry in mind of a sentiment expressed by one of his British friends in the Pacific, words to the effect that a woman who evinces great sexual magnetism is usually a woman of great character and resources as well. He could not remember in which discussion these words were spoken, but he did feel that Mrs. McKenna was the living epitome of a woman whose sexual powers were but a surface reflection of a very formidable inner nature. ("It all goes back to the primeval swamp," said the Britisher, "a simple matter of who will survive and who won't. But I'll tell you this, Herky, old hat, it's a sticky business when a moral inferior gains ascendancy over you. That happened with me, until, as I was telling you, I went for her with a knife.")

At odd hours, Henry conjured up arguments in support of his decision not to see the woman any more. He imagined Mrs. McKenna coming to him and pleading her case before him, while he, growing ever more adamant, kept her at bay with grave, long-winded disquisitions on the humanistic morality of atheism, or by explaining to her how he could not see any positive human value in cuckolding Dicky, even though, as she had said, Dicky might himself find some obscure thrill in it. "The absence of pain," Henry fancied himself putting a particularly fine point on this conundrum, "does not certify an action in the moral sense. It never has, and it never will."

Anna was graduated from high school on a Sunday in late June, and Henry saw her standing on the flagstone walk in a white dress that looked like a bridal costume. He went outdoors to talk to her. Mr. and Mrs. Kokoriss presently appeared in their stiff, churchgoing suits and felt hats, and then Columbine, the youngest of the Kokorisses, came outdoors with a camera and took a picture of her parents and Anna standing together in front of a big bush of salmon-yellow tea roses. The look of Anna posing in her genteel, unassuming way, clasping a handful of the tea roses to her waist, touched a chord of emotion in Henry, although he did not know why. Maybe it was something not in Anna at all, but in her two stolid parents flanking her, that made Henry feel a sudden compassion that afternoon toward all people everywhere, who, in all ages, suffered so much and went on with such simple courage, trusting in the Creator they believed in to bear them through to an end the nature and character of which they had not but a glimmering of an understanding. Anna looked pretty in her white dress, and when her mother and she signaled for Henry to join her in another snapshot, even the father, Benedict Kokoriss, managed upon his wooden face to make a smile. Henry stood in uniform next to Anna on the walk, both in white, both looking at the camera, and Mrs. Kokoriss snapped their picture.

A picture of Henry still stood on the piano in the Kokoriss parlor, the one which Sophie had displayed next to her parents' wedding picture and a collection of baby pictures of the four girls. Anna and Henry began to spend more time together. In the days to come, Henry became a visitor once more in the house next door. Sometimes Anna played the piano for him. He liked to sit on the sofa in the Kokoriss parlor, the room that had once seemed to him quite alien and forbidding, and watch her sitting with her back to him at the piano, as she played soft classical pieces for him with tolerable skill. In the beginning he could not bring himself to make intimate overtures toward Anna. When they brushed against each other in walking, they excused themselves. The thought of beginning with her, after his long-ago experiences with Helen and Sophie, seemed to Henry to pertain perhaps to the face of the sailor in the picture on the piano, and not to himself at all. It was to Anna that Henry confessed his feelings of estrangement, and to whom he sought to convey the peculiar revulsion he felt upon entering church each

Sunday morning with his mother and father. He did not explain to her that these same feelings arose in him sometimes when *they* were together, nor did he try to tell her that the war had meant nothing to him, or that he did not know what he was going to do with himself now. He took Anna for short walks to the river and back. She played the piano for him.

If Henry had a pleasure in life during this period, it came in the early morning. The hour after dawn was his favorite time. He liked to sit outdoors on the porch and leaf through yesterday's edition of the evening newspaper. He scanned the paper backward and forward, starting with the wire-service photos on the back sporting pages showing highlights of the big-league baseball games. He riffled past the obituaries and classified material to the entertainment pages, to the photos of the women vocalists appearing in local nightclubs. He did not read the front-page accounts of the death struggle underway on Okinawa, or give more than a passing glance to the pictures of the assault beaches fringed with ragged, wind-blown palms that showed the long files of men slogging their way inland. He examined, though, the faces of girls who were being betrothed, and the faces in groups of local organizations, such as the Ancient Order of Hibernians, or the Golden-Agers. He read the comic strips, *Barney Google* and *Terry and the Pirates.* He read "Jottings from the Police Blotter." Then he turned to the back, and started all over again, maybe reading the box scores of the baseball games. This was his favorite hour. He enjoyed the early-morning silence, the fresh dewiness of the air. In later years, Henry guessed that it was then perhaps, while sitting quietly on his father's porch, that he began nurturing the idea of writing for newspapers. One morning, however, after Henry had folded up his paper, and after exchanging waves with Mr. Kokoriss, who went silently past the porch on his way to work, something happened that had a definite future bearing on Henry's existence.

It began with a sudden riotous squalling, or shrieking, of blue jays overhead. An instant later, there came flashing into view a collection of swirling, infuriated birds. Out of their midst, a grackle plummeted to earth. The bird lit with a thump on the damp grass not ten feet from the porch steps. The blackbird was down in the grass, thrashing about in circles, beating one wing furiously, trying futilely to get airborne, while the screaming blue jays dove at him in deadly earnest. Henry hurried down from the porch, clapping his hands to frighten away the enraged blue jays; then, covering his face with his left forearm, he managed to retrieve the grackle. A broken wing hung limply over Henry's thumb, and he could feel the bird's racing heart in the palm of his hand. A sudden ear-splitting screech directly behind Henry's head sent him hurrying for cover; one of the jays had executed a final victorious pass that carried him within twelve inches of Henry's face. From behind the screen door came the mocking laughter of his father, awakened evidently by the raucous clamor of the birds. *"Of all things!"* he cried merrily. "May, come quick! Ho, ho, ho! . . . Look!" he shouted, as Henry fled across the grass under a new, if less menacing, attack from above.

Henry did not fancy himself losing an eye in order to gamble on the salvation of a bird that was probably ruined already, or to provide his father with a moment of cynical levity; he took cover quickly beneath the boughs of the little maple tree that grew by the Kokoriss fence and waited for the caterwauling of the blue jays to abate. He stood with his back to the fence. When the blackbird moved in his hand, Henry noticed a smudge of blood on his palm. The blood had dripped also onto his blouse, staining the front of his white uniform in the shape of a dark, glittering wafer. Something then moved behind Henry. There was a rustling of leaves in an overhanging bush, and when Henry looked back, turning only his head, she was standing there. It was Columbine. She, too, had heard the tumult of the birds and come outdoors to see. Her sudden presence took Henry by surprise.

She was standing on the other side of the fence, about five feet away. Her face, glowing amid the framework of leaves and blue hydrangea blossoms, shone like porcelain, her hair as black as the grackle. She was not looking at the bird, however, or at the crimson bloodstain on his uniform. She was staring at him. Her face, he noticed, was distorted a little, her mouth open, her lips drawn back as though she might produce a hissing sound. She could have been an apparition. If Columbine had not spoken up, Henry might have wondered if his mind had not played a trick on him. Her face was a picture of primitive suspicion. The blue puzzle of her eyes held Henry momentarily enmeshed, as she put him a question in a tone that forestalled any answer. "Where is your cane?" she said.

Columbine did not wait for the sailor to make a reply, but withdrew silently, drawing her pale-green terry-cloth bathrobe about herself, and going on green-slippered feet up one of the dirt aisles between the rows of her father's tomato plants to her back door. Henry watched her mount the rear steps, her head erect, her back as straight as a ruler, and then vanish with an air of composure into the back doorway. The shutting screen door gave back an echo.

If Henry Flynn was not anything else, he was an honest soul, and he did not like being challenged in that way by a child. The obvious implication that he was a fake spoiled Henry's morning. After all, he had never made himself out to be crippled. Time was knitting together some half dozen shattered bones, and he thought everyone could tell readily by the way he walked and swung his cane that it was just an auxiliary tool kept in hand to transfer a marginal degree of pressure from his leg to the stick. He was astonished, too, that his detractor was a child whose existence had not made any sensible impression upon him before. Henry was just enough perturbed by the incident in the garden that, when he turned with the bird in his hands and made his way to the rear of the house, he quite forgot again that he was not employing his cane. (The grackle lived about five minutes only. Henry wound the bird in an oily rag he found in the tool shed, and buried it in a patch of loam by the azaleas near the back footpath.)

He did not want to see Anna that day, nor did he wish to see her the following day. He sat during the hot afternoons upstairs in his room and practiced the trombone. He played decently. Henry could play the trombone with feeling, so long as the melody was simple and there were no other instruments to make demands on his timing. He produced a very mellow tone. Each day he played "Sleepy Lagoon." On the third day, he took the two o'clock bus across the river and went in search of a new bar.

IV

Henry was home a month. Then he was home six weeks. The days were rolling past. It was July, then it was August. Henry went away for a week to the Naval hospital in Rhode Island, and then he came home again. Soon other boys were coming home, too. They congregated every day and evening on the sidewalk in front of the corner fruit store, and exchanged stories. They talked a great deal about their military days, even though none of them, it seemed, had seen any action, except for Billy Knapp, of course, who was killed in Italy, or Herky, they said, who was hit at Leyte. They talked a lot about the airplanes they had flown in, or their long shipboard ocean crossings, but especially about the women, the women of Tunis, or of Sicily, or of Burma, Cherbourg, and China, all of whom were evidently thrilled over their coming ashore. They talked about the atomic bomb, about the quality of enemy armaments, about radar and sonar and rockets, and about villages and cities they had been posted to from Bougainville to Bizerte. By early fall, the boys were appearing in great numbers, massed under the awnings at the corner store, loafing about, downing the little two-ounce nips of whiskey from the liquor store. Some wore uniforms, some wore their uniform trousers with old sweaters and jackets, or dungarees with Ike jackets, and each week they watched to see who would come home next.

Henry's father said that the boys now were not like the boys in the First War, because back then they came home and went looking for jobs. These fellows were different, he said. He remembered these fellows as not having worked *before* the war, and said that it would take soldiers with bayonets to get them to go to work now. He said there were incidents every night in all the barrooms. He said he was sorry to see such a shiftless bunch hanging about together, and then going across the river to the bars at night, especially to some of the so-called fighting bars, like the one they called the Ack Ack Club on Division Street, and raising riotous Cain over there. Henry reminded his father that these fellows *were* the soldiers with the bayonets, but Sergeant Flynn laughed at that crack and made a derisive whiffling noise through his lips. "That bunch?" he cried. "Why, I know them, every last one of them, from Cherry Burke to the Ziemecki boy with the big eyeglasses. You start thinking about work," he said to Henry.

"I've been thinking about work!" Henry defended himself.

"You stay away from that corner store."

That was in September. Henry was discharged from the Navy at the end of the month. He was given several hundred dollars in mustering-out pay, besides back furlough pay, and sent home again. There he took off his uniform for the last time and packed everything away. He folded up his summer whites and winter blues, and stored them carefully in his duffel bag, along with his dungarees, his pea coat, his low-quarter dress shoes, his blue raincoat and caps, and the various paraphernalia that were so familiar to him. He was pleased that the officer who had addressed the men being discharged was a man of senior grade, and not some ensign pup from Officers' Training. "It's my duty," the man said, "but also my pleasure, to be able to thank you men, in the name of the people of the United States, and in the name of the United States Navy, for your having come forward when you were needed and for having done your duty. It was a great cause, and now it's won, and now you can go home." Henry had liked the man's crisp attitude, and could still hear the words of farewell ringing in his head, as he toted his duffel bag upstairs and stored it in the attic. That was one thing about the military, he thought, there was not a lot of useless bluster and verbiage. We're finished with you, you can go home.

Henry also packed away his cane, some letters and photos, and his "Pacific Log." Finished with that chore, he headed across the river by bus to Ireland Parish and paid a visit to Besse-Hills & Company, the most fashionable men's clothier on High Street, where old Mr. Hills himself helped Henry in the selection and fitting of two suits and several pairs of odd trousers and white shirts. Mr. Hills said that Henry was a "tailor's dream," that he had the posture and bearing of a male mannequin, and that he would, if he were wise, focus a good deal of attention always on his attire. "Clothing makes the man," said Mr. Hills, as he rolled Henry's money up inside the sales slip, inserted the slip into a little brass car, then placed it on the running cables overhead that carried the car with Henry's money in it upstairs to the cashier with breathtaking speed.

After that, Henry permitted the old gentleman to outfit him completely, because, as Mr. Hills said, with all of the boys coming home simultaneously, it was the fellow with "something extra on the ball" who would win the choicest job, or, he added with a wink, the choicest girl. Henry bought from Mr. Hills a gray felt hat, a pair of cordovan shoes, a pair of black wing-tip shoes, six pairs of hose, some garters, several handkerchiefs, a half dozen polka-dot silk neckties, a belt with the letter F monogrammed on the buckle, and an elegant white topcoat. He spent, in all, an enormous sum of money. When he walked down the hill with his father and mother to church that Sunday morning, he was scarcely less the cynosure of all eyes than he had been upon his arrival home from the Pacific. He cut a splendid figure. If Henry had learned nothing else in his Navy days, he had learned the lesson of meticulousness. He dressed and groomed himself to perfection. His mother, fawning over him at breakfast, said he looked like Van Johnson, her favorite movie star. Henry did not notice during Mass that many of the women of the congregation did, in fact, turn to him glances of an approving nature. For all his correctness of dress and manners, Henry Flynn was not vain. He could not really imagine that anyone might look upon him with stirrings of physical desire.

The morning in the church was a memorable one for Henry for other reasons. He felt free. He felt new and rejuvenated. He sat back listening to the tiny red-faced pastor, Father McElligot, sermonizing from the pulpit about certain evil tendencies he saw developing in modern-day youth, as in their wild jitterbug dancing, or in the skimpy skirts and painted faces found commonly now among mere high-school girls, or the tuneless, discordant jazz music—"with a tinge of chaos about it," added the pastor shrewdly—a litany of ideas that Henry wished to rebut. He would have liked to reprove the little tomato-faced clergyman, telling him he should not take so earnest a view of these mundane matters, that music ought to be exhilarating, that dancing ought to be liberating, or that, so far as Henry could tell, girls with lipstick looked prettier. Henry smiled as he imagined one of Admiral Yamamoto's fifteen-inch shells piercing the slate roof of the church and blasting everything in sight to smithereens.

He marveled, too, at the look of exquisite piety shining out of his father's rough, lozenge-shaped face, as Sergeant Flynn, with his two big hands clasped benignly at his waist, returned down the aisle to his seat after receiving the sacrament of Holy Communion. Henry wondered if it was true that his father had extracted by physical force the confession from Mrs. Blye's son, Nicholas, that sent the boy to the penitentiary. He saw his father as a bigoted, opinionated man who could as easily have provided the cause as the victorious solution to World War II. This nettlesome realization led Henry's mind on into even higher spheres of reflection, as he wondered what were these invisible forces that led men like Jerome Flynn, or perhaps himself, as well, to become the butchers of men one day and the virtuous instruments of God's justice upon those same butchers on the morrow. The bloody finger of guilt seemed to Henry to be pointed not at the individual heart, after all—or ever, really—but at some vague underlying social principle perhaps, some historical rottenness, a massive frustration or blind contest between two great social wills. Henry gave up thinking upon the matter of good and evil, however, and tried to enjoy the colorful ceremony of the Mass itself, almost as though he were a Bushman, or Hottentot, someone arrived from afar and intent upon taking a detached view of a curious religious rite. Turning in his seat, and uncrossing his legs, Henry glanced idly about him and found himself gazing directly into Columbine's eyes.

She was looking right at him from two rows back, sitting quite primly, by herself, her head up, her skinny neck as fragile as the stem of a glass flower. Then she was not looking at him, because she was looking through him, or probably had not even seen him, as her blue gaze remained steady, almost opaque. A prickly sensation asserted itself in his temples as he turned away, as though she, the Koko-riss girl, were his special accuser. His senses began a little to swim, a sensation that was not ameliorated by the stuffiness of the atmosphere. Something troublesome was stirring in the darkness at the back of his mind. Words resounded: "The choicest girl." Of all things! Henry realized that when the dapper old haberdasher had produced those words, it was Columbine's face that had flashed into his head! The look of her as she stood behind him, in her father's garden, that summer morning, her face motionless among the leaves, saying, *"Where is your cane?"*

At the ending of the Mass, as Henry knelt forward and thrice with his fist tapped his heart rhythmically over the words "Lord have mercy on us," he didn't wish to stop, or to move, or to stand up, but just to remain kneeling for a while, with his eyes shut. He felt dizzy, as on the day when they lifted him out by breeches buoy over the boiling, spinning sea, and swung him across to the hospital ship.

Later that week Henry reported to the offices of the Veterans Administration in the War Memorial Building in Ireland Parish and signed up for what the boys at the corner called the Fifty-two Twenty Club, a veterans' unemployment benefit that provided twenty dollars a week for fifty-two weeks. From there, however, Henry went directly to High Street to the editorial offices of the local newspaper, where he asked for a reporting job. Mr. Neumann, the managing editor, a short, stocky man with very furry eyebrows and great horn-rimmed spectacles, glanced out the door to where the blond-haired job applicant stood waiting in the outside vestibule. Mr. Neumann liked his looks right away, and came out. He looked the young man over from head to foot, from his service-cut hair down to his gleaming black shoes, admiring, too, the cut of the young man's Glenplaid suit, the freshness of his white shirt, even the modest twist Henry had imparted to his white-spotted crimson silk necktie. Henry's grin, facile and a little buck-toothed, was disarmingly ingenuous, at least so far as Mr. Neumann was concerned, and was just the sort of easy, nonchalant mannerism that could inspire in other people what Mr. Neumann spoke of as the "requisite trust."

"You see, Henry," he said, "if *I* can trust you, and I'm not sure I can, well, maybe somebody else will trust you, somebody in trouble, for example, somebody in peril, somebody...somebody ordinarily *dis*-trustful."

"Yes, sir," said Henry, coloring.

"Can you write?"

"Yes, sir!"

Henry was hired on the spot as a cub reporter—a job description that sent his father into peals of laughter when he heard it that evening.

"Cub? . . . May, come here! Hear it from Herk's own lips. Go on," he said, "tell her. Tell her what they made you today! Listen to this, May. *Sh,"* he said, "Herky's got an announcement to make."

It was true. Henry was excited. He had not felt such excitement in a long time. Now, overnight, he became a fountain of nervous energy. He went to work an hour early every morning, and all day long he skipped about on the job, running here, running there, smiling, chattering away, writing, typing, hurrying out on research assignments, the living embodiment of pointed human activity. He didn't eat lunch. He didn't stop for coffee. And when the end of the workday rolled around, after all the daytime editors and reporters had gone home, Henry Flynn was still at his desk, sitting alone in the big, empty editorial room, looking as fresh as the morning itself, and clack-clack-clattering away on his typewriter. He was thrilled to be alive.

At home, he transformed his bedroom into a proper study. He bought a new bookcase and a handsome brass gooseneck table lamp for his desk table. He bought a new Remington portable typewriter, a ten-dollar gold fountain pen, and a stack of six handsome pocket-sized genuine-leather notebooks. He fell to studying. He became conversant with the writings of H. M. Tomlinson. He read Macaulay and Carlyle deep into the night. He bought the complete works of George Bernard Shaw, an enormous Merriam dictionary, *Roget's International Thesaurus,* Bartlett's *Familiar Quotations,* and a dozen odd volumes on subjects ranging from the trees of North America to the humor of Irvin S. Cobb. Everything in those days was grist to Henry's mill. He was simply in great forward motion. He went six weeks without tasting a sip of gin, without once seeing Anna next door, and without giving so much as a thought to Mrs. McKenna, the barman's wife.

The fellows hanging about the corner lost sight of Henry altogether. He did not go to the fruit store in the daytime any more, nor did he show his face in any of the bars at night. He was earning money, he was working hard, he was making a profession for himself. In November, he exhausted the last of his savings buying a white 1940 Ford V-8 convertible, with a brand-new top, ivory-colored leather seats, amber fog lights up front, and a spotlight on the driver's side that could be operated by an inside handle. By that time, Henry was becoming known also in the gentlemen's bar at the Roger Smith Hotel, which Henry had staked out as an appropriate "watering hole" (as he now styled it) for an up-and-coming young writer and reporter on the staff of the *Ireland Parish Telegram,* and into whose dimly lighted, gracious confines many local men of distinction, as of the various professions, legal, medical, and otherwise, repaired now and again for a little refreshment. (Henry Flynn was the trim, well-tailored, ex-Navy man with the blond crewcut and the toothy smile standing about three-fourths of the way down the bar, talking with Dr. Tannenbaum about the famous Ireland Parish High basketball team of 1919, which played in a great post-season tournament up in Glens Falls, New York, and of which "famous five" Harry Tannenbaum had been the star forward.)

Henry did not think of himself as a success. He

was not ever conceited. He was just elated to be at the newspaper, and to be on the payroll there as a reporter, even though most of his day was absorbed with running errands, reading over copy, carrying messages to the composing room, filling in for absentees (sometimes even in the advertising or circulation departments), and now and then being sent out with a regular reporter on assignment. He went with Mrs. Holmes, the editor of the women's page, to a charity fashion show at the Canoe Club. He went with the sportswriters to the Saturday-afternoon football games, or to the Wednesday-night boxing matches at the Valley Arena—always composing afterward his own account of the event and passing it along dutifully to Mr. Neumann. It was not until December that Henry first saw himself in print.

One evening, during the first snowfall of the year, while Henry was driving home in his Ford, he saw an automobile accident develop on the road in front of him. A car skidded out of control, sideswiped a police cruiser that was advancing from the opposite direction, and then plowed into a fire hydrant. The driver of the car, who was tipsy, was carrying no license or registration, and identified himself to the police as Chief Walking Bear, an American Indian. He said he was born in the Grand Canyon, and that he didn't need a license to drive a car because, as far as he was concerned, he didn't even need a car. Henry accompanied the Indian and the police downtown to the Ireland Parish stationhouse, and in the morning, before going to work, Henry went back a second time to interview the man, who had been in the lockup overnight and was to face drunken-driving charges. Henry wrote up the story in ten sentences, a very terse, rather amusing account of the incident, and gave it to Mr. Neumann. Reading it over, Mr. Neumann said that it was a very fine piece of reportage. He said, though, that the conclusion was so good as to be almost too good. He read the concluding sentence aloud: "During the night Chief Walking Bear tried to hang himself in his cell."

"That touch is either macabre, or is making fun of your subject. It's masterful, Herky, *but,* as I said"— Mr. Neumann smiled up at him through his tortoise-shell glasses—"it's too good. Well, forget it," he threw out carelessly, "we'll run it as it is. He *did* try to hang himself?"

"Yes, sir."

Henry's newspaper career thus opened that evening with the appearance of the Chief Walking Bear story on an inner page of the *Ireland Parish Telegram.* Even Henry's father could not conceal his pride when shown the article and convinced of its authorship; he loosened his tie and, pursing his lips and chuckling restrainedly, read it over a half dozen times from top to bottom. Mrs. Flynn brought the paper next door to show the Kokorisses, and then Anna came over to congratulate Henry, and the two of them went back to the Kokoriss house for a cup of eggnog. Mr. Kokoriss put some brandy in the eggnog and, in his own silent way, raised his cup to salute Henry's triumph and future good fortune. Mr. Kokoriss stood by the piano in the living room, as always cold and aloof, but looking older than Henry had remembered him, and seeming, too, to Henry, to strike in his own breast a poignant note, the meaning of which Henry could not easily discern. Henry guessed it was the knowledge that Mr. Kokoriss was, at one and the same time, both the most solitary of persons he had ever known, and yet also the most devoted to others. Mr. Kokoriss lived to work; he lived just for the benefit of other people, for Mrs. Kokoriss, and for their four daughters. He was utterly an individual, and yet had no individuality.

Henry sat on the sofa, with his topcoat thrown open and the genial smile on his lips camouflaging the rather grave character of his thoughts. Behind him, a pine Christmas wreath with red electric bulbs flared in the window that looked out onto the porch. Anna sat beside him on the sofa, asking Henry questions about his job and about his new car. Mrs. Kokoriss took Mrs. Flynn into the kitchen to show her her new Hamilton Beach electric mixer, and Mr. Kokoriss went back downstairs to his woodworking shop in the cellar. Henry asked Anna if she would like to go for a spin in his convertible (he should have asked her weeks ago), and Anna blushed to a peony pink and said, oh, yes, she would, and she went to get her coat and a wool scarf for her head.

While Anna was gone, Columbine came down from the second floor, descending serenely, and stopped at the foot of the stairs. She looked impassively in at Henry, then came slowly across and into the room without looking at him, dipped her fingers into the eggnog bowl as she passed the piano, and, sucking at her fingertips, moved on unruffledly into the dining room without a word. Henry heard her then going down the cellar steps to join her father. From below came the gathering buzz of an electric drill. Henry drew a mental picture of Columbine in the cellar, sitting on a tall stool by her father's workbench, with the light from the green-shaded bulb overhead illuminating her china-like face. He pictured her sitting with her knees together, her longish, slender legs forming a diagonal line against the cross rungs of the stool. She was in his brain now. He knew that. He knew she knew it, too.

When Anna came back to join him, Henry was gazing into space.

Nothing begins spontaneously. It is as true in human matters as it is in physical nature that all things develop from the smallest coalescences, the coming together, by accident or chance, of the tiniest particles, and just as a soil may be sympathetic to a root, or air to a wing, also perhaps a human word or just the momentary flash of an eye may fix itself upon the mind like a physical burr or bit of pollen. It was in Henry's brain now—she was—and it didn't matter why, since he had no natural repugnance toward it, no mechanism or fluid to discharge or wash it away. It had already begun to grow. She could have been a bit of seed dust floating in the heat of a summer afternoon and he one of a thousand weed stalks standing at the roadside.

Henry did not try to divine her thoughts or will, but he did not believe, either, that she was being flirtatious. Columbine struck him as too remote and cool-hearted for that, despite her tender years. She might, he supposed, have been conceited. Or maybe, too, it was even simpler than that. She might just have got used to seeing his picture there on the piano —for no doubt it would have seemed to Columbine, at thirteen, to have been there for a century—the innocent sailor face, smiling and idealistic—and that she had judged him, first as the man in the uniform last summer with the cane, and now as the man in the white topcoat who wore a brightly striped necktie and who mounted two shiny copper pennies in his loafers, to be a possible fraud against that picture. This explanation gratified Henry; it explained the recriminatory mood in the garden and subsequent supercilious looks, as well as the air of aloofness that she employed, as if to show him that she, the judge, could not descend every five minutes in order to reassure him that he was probably all right. Why, he wondered, couldn't she be just an amiable little girl who lived next door? Helen, at Columbine's age, hadn't been so remote or suspicious-seeming. She hadn't been so austere, so judgmental, so high and mighty. Neither had Sophie or Anna. He guessed Columbine had been spoiled.

Twice in the following days Columbine passed Henry by at close range, not looking at him on either

occasion, but not pretending, either, to look at anything else. She just went by him. She went past him
on her bicycle, skimming along behind the back
fences, as he stood (stopped by her approach) at the
driver's side of his Ford convertible, pedaling right
past him, with her head lifted, her back unbelievably
straight, and then, a second time, walking, coming
up the front steps onto the flagstone path at the head
of Cottage Avenue, this time appearing even a little
insolent toward him, if anything, in reacting to his
stepping aside for her by conspicuously averting her
head, showing him just a bare fraction of her imper-
turbable, porcelain-smooth face. (By that time,
though, both knew. That was plain. Both knew
something was between them, even if that something was only a misunderstanding. Henry felt it
both times she went by, that she was "on parade"
for him and knew it, and that she knew he knew it,
and knew that he was not shocked by it, or by their
both knowing it, so long, at least, as no one else
knew it.)

It was during that month of December, in 1945,
along toward Christmas, that Mr. Kokoriss fell ill.
He missed one day of work, his first absence from
the paper company in years, and as time showed, it
was an evil omen. Henry was the first outsider to
guess at the mortal nature of it, something he saw in
Mrs. Kokoriss's eyes one Saturday morning when he
asked after Mr. Kokoriss's health. There was a sudden flashing look of animal bewilderment, the sheer
incapacity of a human being to cope with this ulti-
mate enigma, the doom of the loved one. Mrs. Kokoriss tried at once to conceal it, but in doing so only
made matters worse, because she lost her voice.
They were outdoors; the doctor had not been gone
even an hour.

The fact of Mr. Kokoriss's impending death colored that season for Henry in a way he never forgot.
In later years when he cast back to the winters he

spent on Cottage Avenue, he remembered the perfect stillness of the pale-blue Christmas lights in his mother's parlor window, or the cold snowless earth of the two gardens lying side by side between their two houses, or it might have been the sight of Mr. Griffin, who occupied the last house in the avenue, coming down the frozen alleyway, with three or four of his beagles running ahead of him in a cluster— Mr. Griffin himself like one of the gnomes of the underworld, with a stony, pocked face, and wearing big rubber mittens and rubber duck boots—and, cast over it all, over the cold earth and the shine of the pale-blue bulbs, the knowledge about the man next door.

The older girls, Helen and Sophie, came home that year for Christmas. Helen came first, by train from Washington, but Henry did not see her first. He thought he saw her—on the walk out front, the rattle of someone's heels approaching on the brittle, frosty stones, and then the sight of a well-dressed young woman in a dark fur coat with dark hair sliding briskly up the walk, her hands thrust sportily in her side pockets and a leather bag swinging on a strap over her shoulder—but it wasn't Helen. It was, to Henry's annoyance, Sophie. Henry had more or less prepared himself for the arrival home of a new, older Helen, a different and more mature Helen, and had even been a bit worried that, after all these past five years, she might have become even a formidable figure for him, just the sort of concern that a twenty-three-year-old might feel over the return after several years of an old girlfriend now affianced. He had forgotten all about Sophie, at least in that regard, and was abashed at the way she carried herself. She went up the walk with the self-assurance of one who had just purchased all the houses on the avenue and was coming to collect the rent. Henry was peeking out through the lace curtains at her when he was suddenly struck by the absurdity of his own behavior.

Henry went upstairs, not to his room, but to the attic, and got his cane, and came back down to the parlor. He had not used his cane in about ten weeks, but he had an urge to use it now. His leg was throbbing. Sometimes, too, in the evening, after a long day, his leg tired. But that was not his reason for fetching the cane now. He had not liked being shamed out of being able to use it, and the embarrassment of catching himself peeking through the curtains to catch a quick glimpse of Helen—or of someone he thought was going to be Helen—brought back the other embarrassment. The incident with Columbine in the garden. Henry felt he should stand up on this point, even though it involved the irony of his introducing upon his person a kind of crutch in going next door to greet Helen and Sophie.

That was a night or two before Christmas. Henry's father had taken Mrs. Flynn to the Knights of Columbus annual holiday dinner. Henry was home alone. He was not having a pleasant evening. He knew he was expected next door, but he could not bring himself to get started. He had a premonition, a vision of Mr. Kokoriss lying like an enormous parsnip in a brand-new suit of clothes in his coffin. He envisioned Columbine in a black veil standing by herself in the graveyard. Henry paced back and forth in the darkness, swinging his cane and meditating. He felt as he had on the night in June when he returned from the Pacific and, coming up the hill on foot, had seen against the sky the shadowy roof of his father's house, and had had to stop in the street and lean against the wall before being able to continue—an experience familiar to wanderers and veterans of all ages, the inability to go the last ten steps up to the door. That was how he felt now. He shut off the room lights and stood in the darkened parlor leaning on his cane and looking out across the garden space to the lighted Kokoriss house.

———

Helen said Henry had changed. Sophie agreed he was very distinguished-looking. Sophie said also that he was too old for Anna, but Helen disagreed, saying that Anna, who was eighteen now and working as a teller at the Hadley Falls bank, was only about five years younger than Henry. She said that Johnny, her own husband-to-be, at twenty-eight, was six years older than she. The sisters were sitting at the breakfast table the next morning, giving their impressions of Henry. Anna, obviously flustered, said that everyone was "jumping the gun," that she and Henry were not even "seeing each other." Sophie tried to end the conversation by saying that for her money she would not like to see anyone get mixed up with Henry, even if he was becoming a sort of success at the newspaper, because underneath it all, she said, he was just a "local yokel."

Helen laughed over her sister's words, but Anna didn't like them and rallied to Henry's defense, saying, with insight, that Sophie only felt that way because she had not liked the way Henry had contradicted her on two or three occasions the night before. Sophie conceded that Henry was, indeed, argumentative. Helen then combined with Anna in asserting that Henry had always been very smart, while Anna, flushing with anger, crowned her defense by exclaiming, "Herky has a beautiful mind!"

The girls could not talk at that time about their father, who lay upstairs mortally ill, because Columbine was present. The three older girls knew about their father. Columbine had been told nothing. She sat at the inside seat of the table by the window, drinking Postum and listening in silence to her sisters. After a pause in the conversation, she decided to make a contribution of her own.

"It would seem to me," she said, "that none of the three of you knows much about what she's talking about."

This proclamation, put forward with characteristic temerity and an air of fabulous serenity, brought all three faces turning to her. Columbine finished her hot drink, got up from the table, and took her cup to the sink. She turned then, and went mirthlessly from the room. "You sound like three old hens," she said.

Henry had not spoken to Columbine since she was a little girl of seven or eight, back in the days before the war. He remembered her as a solitary child, playing by herself on the porch or in the garden, or sometimes coming to where he was, and standing in silence, watching what he was doing. On this day, after the newspaper office had closed early in the afternoon for Christmas, Henry found himself inclined to pay a last visit to the stores. He could not hide from himself the desire he had to buy her a Christmas gift, if only because of the news about her father. When he had gone the evening before to the Kokoriss house, and been greeted by Helen and Sophie and Anna, she, Columbine, had already gone up to bed. Mrs. Kokoriss had stayed upstairs most of the evening with her husband, while the three girls had talked very frankly with Henry about their father. Mr. Kokoriss had cancer. The prognosis, they said, was bleak beyond description.

Anna had played the piano during the evening while Henry and Sophie had argued a little about politics. Sophie said that the war was made by a lot of people who stood to profit by it. Henry said that was a popular view that seemed to him very superficial. Helen chimed in, speaking for Sophie's benefit, saying that it was not very wise or kind to suggest to a veteran that his fighting had only served to line people's pockets, to which Sophie replied that the truth was the truth, nonetheless, and that it sometimes had to hurt somebody. Henry sat for nearly an hour on the piano bench next to Anna, but facing the other way, facing the two older girls on the sofa,

72

with his cane propped on the floor between his feet, and felt dismayed at the way Sophie's opinions were always antagonistic to his own. Helen seemed to possess the same warm and loving nature that he remembered her for, but Henry found himself feeling a trifle resentful toward her. He divined something aloof in Helen's attitude, something indulgent about the way she ignored the talk of politics, or even, for that matter, in the way she defended Henry against her sister. He was made to feel that he was like a sibling here, as if Helen, the oldest sister, saw it as her duty to defend Henry, the younger brother, against another older sister. Anna then made matters worse by mentioning a ride she had taken with Henry in his car, and of how Henry had mentioned to her on that occasion that the American way of life was safe now that the war was over. Hearing that, Sophie burst out laughing derisively, and got up from her place on the sofa and strode importantly across the room and went out to the kitchen. Henry was left blushing furiously, for he was sure he had never said anything to Anna as simplistic as that. That left Helen sitting alone on the sofa on the other side of the room and smiling across at Henry and Anna in a way that made Henry and Anna into a couple.

"Wasn't that what you said?" Anna had then asked in confusion.

Helen kept smiling at them, a small, gentle, simpering smile, and Henry blushed repeatedly. Sophie was out in the kitchen, laughing to herself. Henry got so desperate to recover lost ground that he later launched into a long atheistic harangue that shocked even Sophie. At the door, before leaving, he said that if God had been alive six years ago, He certainly wasn't now.

"I can't see," he said, speaking at that point with an elegant, almost British clip to his voice, and flourishing his cane instructively as he prepared to go out

73

the door, "how a God of wisdom and mercy *could* have survived it, frankly—presupposing that He was, of course, there at the start. Can you?" he said, looking at Sophie.

On reflection, Henry was sorry he had not produced this conversational bludgeon earlier in the evening, and he was, he realized, eager to use it again on both Sophie and Helen. In fact, while he was standing at the perfume counter in the department store, he decided he would not himself initiate the atheistic theme but would wait for Sophie to bring it up, as she surely would, and then lambaste her with philosophical propositions from people like Hobbes and Nietzsche that she could not even comprehend, let alone contradict. In the meanwhile, he purchased a bottle of Antelope perfume for Columbine, and asked that it be wrapped in silver foil and tied with a bright-green ribbon. When finished, the little package was a treasure to the eye, so elegantly done that Henry gave the boy at the wrapping counter a fifty-cent tip. (He was willing to bet, he reflected, that Sophie had never even heard of Immanuel Kant.)

Henry could have saved up his emotive energy, however, because he never got a chance to propound to either of the older Kokoriss girls any of his weightier themes. Mr. Kokoriss died in the night. Everyone had expected he would live for eight or ten weeks, or even several months, but it had not been that way. He died about three o'clock Christmas morning. Mrs. Blye, the old Lithuanian, telephoned about eight o'clock in the morning with the news. When Henry looked out the window at the Kokoriss house, he saw that the window shades had been drawn. Henry's mother cried in the kitchen, and his father went outdoors in his shirtsleeves onto the rear porch and just stood there looking up at the shark-colored sky. Henry, who had not been in the stoutest frame of mind these past weeks and months, did what no other neighbor presumed to do. He put on his coat and went outside and up the flagstone walk to the Kokoriss house. He went onto the porch and looked in through the window of the door just at the instant Columbine arrived at the foot of the inside staircase. She stood there icily, in the front hallway, with her head turned to him, her face even more bloodless than usual. Then she came to the door, and as she opened it, Henry said to her the words he had so often heard spoken by his cousins and his uncles and aunts and grandparents in the moment of bereavement. "I'm sorry for your troubles," he said quietly.

"Thank you for coming," said Columbine.

Henry handed her the silver and green parcel, and Columbine took it and closed the door.

Mr. Kokoriss was waked at the Petras Kuznierz Funeral Home near Hampden Park in Ireland Parish, not far from the school and church of the Mater Dolorosa. Henry came early on Christmas night to pay his respects, but appeared among a rapidly swelling gathering of visitors. Mrs. Kokoriss sat in the midst of a collection of stout, big-breasted women whose cheeks were all streaked from weeping, while the four girls, farther back, were interspersed amid a throng of relatives and friends. Everyone was speaking Lithuanian, and the air was redolent of the thick sweet smell of carnations and roses. Even before Henry had paused, with his hat in one hand, neatly folding his white coat over his arm, he saw Columbine coming through the throng at the back of the room, aiming directly at him. She wore a straight black dress and black shoes, and was so slender and even tall-looking as to make her own sisters seem, by contrast, bovine. Henry paused on the margin of the carpet just inside the foyer and waited, his face registering a series of tiny, clocklike tics, as she approached, coming up to him with a deadpan face and a dignity of bearing that could have been the envy of a Hapsburg heir. From the moment of his arrival, Columbine left no doubt as to whose office it was to receive him. She had taken him at once in hand, and asked in a flat, businesslike voice if he had signed the Visitors Ledger, and then led him to it, held out a fountain pen, and watched with idle concentration, with her lips turned back and compressed inside themselves, as he bent forward and carefully entered his name on the lined page. *Henry S. Flynn.*

That done, she recovered the pen from his fingers and restored it to its place in the horizontal groove cut into the surface of the little wooden desk top. Reaching with both hands, she prepared to relieve Henry of his coat and hat. But Henry didn't move. He was looking at her. Presently, sensing this, her eyes came up. Henry felt a slow geyser of feeling welling up inside him, and after a moment repeated the words he had early that day spoken to her. "I'm sorry for your troubles," he whispered, with apparent emotion.

She—stopped—was looking back at him, unblinkingly, out of blue inscrutable eyes, which then sent an imperceptibly quick look past him at the others, this followed by as faint and glacial a smile as might ever have registered on a human countenance. "Yes, you said that!" she snapped, with a mock curtness that told him that they were still communing out of some privately shared intimacy. This time she succeeded in taking his coat. "Would you like to see my father?" she said, very correctly, as her eyes pointed the way to the flower-decked casket and tall candles standing beyond the archway of the foyer.

Henry prayed on his knees, kneeling on the carpet. He didn't have any faith in the efficacy of prayer, but delivered himself of several of the many he knew. He went then and offered his condolences to Mrs. Kokoriss, reaching over someone's shoulder to squeeze her hand, and then, too, to Helen, Sophie, and Anna, the last of whom was actually limp with grief. Anna, they said, was on the verge of collapse. After that, Henry sat by himself for a while on one of the metal folding chairs, surrounded by a host of foreign-tongued men and women who kept up an insistent rumble of speech, until Columbine reappeared from behind him and sat down next to him. She sat forward on the edge of her chair, with her feet together, her hands on her lap, and her back and neck perfectly straight. Then, as though she had first to get into position, she turned her face to him. Henry waited for her to speak. She was looking at him.

"What does the S. stand for?" she said. "Henry S. Flynn."

"It stands for Starbuck."

Columbine again compressed her mouth, turning her lips back out of sight, and appeared to reflect upon the sound of that name. Then, for the first time since the morning in the garden, Henry saw come upon her face that slightly distasteful grimace, the curling back of her lips and dilation of her nostrils, which he now recognized to be merely a personal quirk in her expressiveness, a sign of focused concentration. "Starbuck," she said.

She was looking away from him, turned fractionally, gazing into space. He was watching her. She was pondering something, as though the word—the name Starbuck—coming from her own lips were calling forth some forgotten reverberation. Her lower lip curled back sensuously. Then they looked at one another.

V

Everything happened at once. On the day before the funeral, Mrs. Blye's son, Nicholas, came home from prison. Henry saw him come up the stone steps into the avenue at twilight, a black-haired figure in a leather jacket moving silently past the bushes on the front walk. To Henry, he appeared like an apparition. Henry realized that he had years ago stopped believing in the actual physical existence of Nicholas Blye. When the Blye boy went to prison, Henry was fifteen or sixteen. During all that intervening time, from Henry's days in high school and on to the Navy and the Pacific, and all during the months and years of port duty and sea duty, and of his hospitalization and convalescence—covering all the tumultuous years—the invasions of Poland, France, Russia, the Battle of Britain, the bombing of Pearl Harbor, the fall of Singapore, all of it, the entire ensuing cataract of armed fury blazing all across the globe—during all that time, the Blye boy was locked up in a prison cell at Walpole.

Henry felt uneasy as he wondered why he had not thought more about Nicholas. He wondered, too, if Nicholas, by being locked away during all that perilous, historic time, did not think of himself as a traitor, or as a ghost perhaps, a Lazarus returning from the dead. The story about Nicholas—of night break-ins, pistols, etc.—seemed to contain no longer for Henry the mythic elements of a movie or radio drama, as it once had, but to be, instead, rather lurid. Henry even thought some about the sheer courage it must have required to commit such acts, realizing himself to be deficient in bravery of that kind. At the far end of the avenue, Mr. Griffin's beagles began to bark, first one or two of them, yapping (the older dogs probably, remembering, and sensing now the Blye boy's approach), and then the entire kennel taking it up. That was Nicholas's welcome-home party, a chorus of eight or ten hounds yodeling unrestrainedly in the icy air.

Henry did not go to the Kokoriss wake that second evening, as he had planned to do. He felt too jumpy; his nerves were a little unstrung by the death of his neighbor, and by the girl he did not allow himself to think about, and now, too, the return to Cottage Avenue of Mrs. Blye's son. He went instead to the bar at the Roger Smith Hotel, where he got into a conversation with a former merchant sailor from Rhode Island who talked about ships with such surpassing knowledge, as to their construction, capacity, displacement, engines, tonnage, and such, that when he asked Henry which branch of the service he had been in, Henry (then in his cups) said, "The Army."

Mostly, he was filled with a sense of foreboding. He was uneasy. He drank his gin and tried to shake it off. He thought about his new assignment, working for the City Editor. He thought about Mrs. McKenna, remembering the look of her silk-stockinged knees when she sat facing him in the car, and of her profound bust, and then about Sophie, and then confusing the two of them in his mind. He could not yet admit to the true nature of his apprehension, although her face—Columbine's—swam repeatedly into his mind. When he went out of the Roger Smith Hotel that evening, he waited outdoors nearly a half hour for the late bus to Hadley Falls before remembering that he owned an automobile, and that he had parked in the street next to the

McAuslin-Wakelin department store.

That night he slept fitfully, but arose at dawn, bathed, and dressed with care.

At the funeral that morning, Henry remained well back in the crowd of mourners, anxious not to intrude himself upon the family. Being a neighbor, he was just the sort of person they would be compelled to acknowledge, and he wished to spare them the trouble. A cold, watery light fell from the sky over the cemetery, and the trees along the narrow asphalt roadway were dripping with a morning wetness. He saw Columbine only at a distance, gazing at her over the heads of others. Anna, he noticed, had to be helped out of the limousine by two men, so distraught she could scarcely walk. Helen and Sophie got on either side of Anna and propped her up, and the three of them moved forward at a snail's pace toward the open grave, with Anna wailing, "No—no —no—" many times, and turning her head strangely this way and that, as though expecting her father suddenly to reappear somewhere behind her in the milling crowd. Henry recognized at that moment the poignancy of the manless, fatherless house next door—as if it were up to Mr. Kokoriss himself to get out of his coffin and help Anna. Even at that distance, Anna's face stood out starkly in the gray air, as blank as a bar of soap.

Father Sulcas took his place at the head of the grave, with Mrs. Kokoriss and her three older daughters on his left. Columbine stood on the other side of the priest, on a spot directly overlooking the grave and casket—probably, Henry thought, to dissociate herself as much as possible from Anna. Columbine was too much of a stoic ever to countenance behavior like that. By standing at the priest's right hand, she appeared rather like the chief mourner, motionless and impassive in her slender black coat. Henry guessed that most of the great women of history must once have been girls like Columbine: individuals with an inborn faculty for revealing themselves on a separate plane from others. That was how she looked: small, tragic, dignified. At the end of the rites, after the priest turned away, Columbine stooped and picked up a blossom from one of the many bouquets, and then walked back, ahead of the others, to the first black car: the driver opened the door for her, and she climbed in and seated herself on the far side of the car, looking out the far window.

Upon leaving the graveyard, Henry caught a glimpse of Nicholas Blye, looking pale and benign, standing with his hands in his jacket pockets, a dark muffler wound around his throat. He was very attentive to his mother, leaning to her, nodding, uttering a word or two, then glancing up at the sky and shuffling his feet nervously on the frozen, rutted earth. Henry conceived how difficult this public appearance must have been for him on the first morning of his freedom; and he couldn't help admiring Mrs. Blye, also, whose gratitude over her son's return was apparent upon her face every moment.

In the days to come, Henry saw none of the Kokorisses. The older sisters went away again, Anna went back to work at the bank, and Columbine to school. Henry put Columbine from his thoughts, although a passage he came upon in a book one night set him thinking about her. It concerned the love of Peter Abélard, the medieval theologian, for Héloïse; the story of a priest's love for his pupil, their secret marriage, Abélard's banishment, Héloïse's subsequent nunhood, her exquisite love letters to him, and, to Henry's shock, a reference to Abélard's mutilation. Henry read the passage over again many times with widened eyes. He could not help putting himself in Abélard's shoes, and actually grew nervous as he imagined the revered doctor being hauled off into the woods somewhere and being brutally deprived of his manhood. Henry had heard of the famous couple in high school, but he had not known the grisly details of Abélard's punishment. Forbidden love, he guessed, found a place in many a human heart. Every age had its favorite stories of doomed, star-crossed lovers placing their sweet passion before all else in the world, but usually winding up drowned, or poisoned, or, as in Abélard's case, with consequences too horrible even to think about. He imagined Columbine going away in sorrow to a cloister, while he was being taken out to the woods somewhere to be castrated.

One night, Henry was awakened by scraping sounds coming from the house next door and, looking out the window, saw Columbine clearing snow from the path at the side of her house. It had snowed heavily; the gardens below were blanketed. The air was still blue with night. Henry looked at his clock, discovering the time to be half-past-four. That was original, he thought. She was shoveling the snow before dawn. That was the first time he had seen her since the morning of the funeral, and he lay on his side now, in bed, watching the silent, fluid, clocklike motion of her body moving in silhouette, as she bent, thrust in the shovel, straightened, then sent a silent white shower of snow flashing sidewise in a glittery gust. Except for the soft, metallic, scraping sound, she might only have been a shadow—coiling and uncoiling in a steady, sensual rhythm that mirrored the dreamy machinations of his own mind. Still in the sleep state, Henry thought of soon putting himself somehow in her way. Dropping off, he found her face waiting for him on the borderline of sleep, her lips turned back, her cool glance passing through him like light.

Henry intended to demonstrate, to his own satisfaction, that she was just a thirteen-year-old child after all, and could never avoid revealing it when put to the test, and that her oddly seductive mannerisms were only as thin as a piece of paper. He devoted a little time that day to devising various stratagems that might bring them together, if only to quench his curiosity about her. At noontime, Henry ran into Anna on the street and, for a moment, actually contemplated using Anna—their friendship, that is, her evident admiration for him—as a means of facilitating an encounter with Columbine. Henry was shamefaced at the mere thought of it, though, and thrust it from his mind. Instead, he took Anna to lunch. Anna made use of the opportunity to apologize to Henry for her behavior at the funeral, and for having neglected him. "I was a mess," she said.

"You were supposed to be in grief," said Henry, trying to appear kindly without being *too* concerned, for Anna was gazing across at him fondly all the while, as if waiting for Henry to say something of an intimate nature to her. Anna, he thought, looked somewhat like Sophie, but with a mind more like Helen's—that in a family where the oldest had the looks and the next-to-oldest the brains. Anna kept looking at him steadily over lunch, causing Henry to smile and to hum, as well as to show an inordinate interest in the ingredients of his club sandwich. He later excoriated himself for having contemplated the idea of visiting Anna in her house only as an excuse for catching a glimpse of her younger sister. That, he thought, shaking his head, would never do.

Henry needn't have exercised himself too much over the matter, though, because when he came home from work that day, Columbine was sitting in the parlor, waiting for him. He had parked his car in the street, and entered at the front door. When he came in, he was already in an agitated state over an unpleasant encounter he had just had with Dolly McKenna, the bartender's wife. Mrs. McKenna had seen Henry with Anna that day, and had come to pay him a visit at his desk in the office. He could still see her sitting across the desk from him, with her coat open and her legs crossed, tapping her burning cigarette on the edge of the ashtray she held in one hand, while having the audacity to question him, not about Anna, not about him and Anna at lunch, but about young Nolan, the new man whom Mr. Neumann had just hired as a cub. Henry was indignant. He felt used. Henry's mind rarely ran to explicit language or characterizations, but he couldn't help feeling Dolly McKenna was trying to use him as a kind of sordid, little go-between. "I don't know anything about him!" he said, scandalized. "Well, call him over," said Mrs. McKenna. "We'll both meet him." Henry supposed there had never been a woman so outspoken and forthright. "He looks like a college man," she said. "He *is* a college man!" Henry shot back. "You," Mrs. McKenna teased, mocking him in a musical voice, "I thought you didn't know anything about him. Is he the Water Commissioner's son?" she asked, half-closing one eye, while shifting about in her chair in a way that Henry had noticed before and which always arrested his attention. "Is he Pert Nolan's son?" "No," said Henry, "he's not." "Is he married?" she asked, as if she had known but forgotten. "No!" "Too bad," she said. "How about you, Herk? You'll be getting married one of these days," she said, in a sugary, ironical tone. "Who *was* that girl today? The one with the big brogans on." "She wasn't wearing brogans," said Henry, "those were snow boots." Mrs. McKenna laughed huskily through her cigarette smoke, and fell to coughing. "Listen, Herky," she said, collecting herself, and then reaching across the desk and placing her hand warmly on top of his, "I want you to know you're free to see whoever you want. Our little escapade"—she signified him and her with a wave of her cigarette—"wasn't worth five cents to me." Spinning suddenly in her seat, Mrs. McKenna sent up a luminous and provocatively familiar smile at young Nolan, who happened at that moment to be hastening by, pulling on his overcoat; she turned all the way around to him as he went by, revolving her torso in a manner that showed herself off to advantage. Henry was still stewing over it when he got home. He knew what he *should* have told Dolly McKenna. He should have got up from his chair, like Lionel Barrymore, and told her to *get out!*

Henry's father was sprawled horsily in his favorite spot at the end of the sofa, while Columbine was sitting on Mrs. Flynn's little needlepoint chair in the middle of the room. She sat primly, with her coat folded on her lap. Her head was high, her expression austere. His father and she were in the midst of a conversation. Sergeant Flynn—home for the supper hour—was doing the talking. He was gesturing with his pipe, drawing tiny arabesques in the air. "That, you see," he was saying, in a shrewd, oily tone, while allowing one eyelid to squeeze a trifle shut, "is speculative, though, isn't it?"

Columbine flashed Henry a quick, polite, mechanical smile, then returned her attention to Henry's father.

"However," said his father crisply, taking a quick, thoughtful puff at his pipe, his eye floating up to the ceiling, "let's look at the other side of the picture, shall we?" He did not acknowledge Henry's arrival, except as he refused to be deflected by the girl's acknowledging smile. "Let's look at it from the Hebrew standpoint. Let's ask ourselves"—Sergeant Flynn puffed at his pipe—"let's ask ourselves why your typical Hebrew is a Communist. Why is your typical Hebrew businessman a Communist? At first glance"—he puffed—"a capitalist cannot be a Communist and still be a capitalist. See my point? The Pope is not an atheist. Housecats do not fly. See what I'm driving at? Businessmen are not Communists. And yet"—he showed Columbine the stem of his pipe through a cloud of smoke—"your typical—

and I say typical to mean ninety-nine and ninety-nine one-hundredths percent of all Hebrews—your typical Hebrew is as red as Marshal Stalin. Why do you suppose that is?" He sucked at his pipe while watching the girl cannily from his comfortable position in the lamplight on the sofa.

Judging both the question and ensuing pause to be rhetorical, Columbine made no effort to reply, but did avail herself of the chance to direct a second glance at Henry, who was puzzled to find the youngest of the Kokoriss girls seated in his own house. He was amazed, too, by her aplomb, as she turned her eyes away once more to his father. Columbine wore her black dress and black shoes, and sat with her skinny legs folded together just so. Her alabaster face, wan and uplifted, was a picture of serenity. Henry's dreamy apprehension of the bizarre scene before him, of his father and Columbine sitting and conversing like two long-acquainted neighbors, was reflected in his movements as he slowly unbuttoned his coat. His father had opened his tunic, revealing an expanse of light-blue shirt offset by a dark necktie fastened with a Knights of Columbus stickpin. Sergeant Flynn had always been for Henry the embodiment of law and order, from his high-cropped hair and starched shirt collars down to the glasslike gleam of his black shoes, but was not, by and large, a reassuring figure in Henry's mind. Mostly, he was thrown by Columbine's presence. She had never, to his knowledge, entered this house before, and yet here she was, big as life, sitting on his mother's prettiest chair, in her prettiest manner, making polite discourse with his father, almost as though she were Henry's date, or girlfriend, or fiancée. Henry had a sudden horror that the girl had taken it into her head to translate into public terms some of the provocative, playful understandings they had secretly shared. He stood in the doorway, gaping at them.

"Do you see what I'm driving at?" said his father.

Columbine spoke up then, evidently in continuation of an earlier line of thought. She did not look at Henry, but continued to regard his father evenly. "Of course, we're Balts, you know, and all Balts despise Russians. Of every stripe," she added, with a smartness of tone to match the weightiness of the subject.

"Balts?" Sergeant Flynn didn't know what she was talking about.

"Balts," said Columbine. "Lithuanians are Balts."

With his pipe clamped in his fist, Henry's father gazed at her in wonderment.

"From the Baltic Sea," Columbine explained.

"Oh, I see!" the policeman came back roundly. "The Baltic Sea, why not?"

"My father"—Columbine widened her eyes— "loathed Russians to his last breath!" She tossed up her hands to epitomize the hopelessness of ever being able to capture in words the extent of her father's racial hatred.

"Still"—Henry's father came back at her in a gruff, assertive voice, while stopping momentarily to suck at his pipe three or four times, making little popping noises with his lips as he did so—"your typical Russian is a poor dirt farmer, while your typical Hebrew is more cosmopolitan. That's why Hitler and his crowd put the commissars and Jews into the same basket, as being all cosmopolitan Communist troublemakers out to get them. I read a very interesting article that would probably interest you, by the way," he said, in a manner meant to flatter the girl by revealing to her his awareness of her intelligence and adultish ways, "not anything for children, you understand, but I think you could grasp its meaning readily enough, a piece dealing with the matter of hybridization in the human world as against hybridization in the plant or animal world. Now, according to this man, the author, who happens to be a Catholic priest and a perfect genius, if you ask me, man hybridizes plants and animals in order to meet his own needs, certainly not for the purpose of meeting the needs of the hybrids. *He* claims"—he regarded Columbine shrewdly—"that if your hybrids were left to nature, left behind to survive on their own in the wild over the ages, that every one of them would either dry up and expire or else fall back into a state more feeble than that of either of the two parent stocks. See what I'm driving at? Do you see his point?"

Henry had advanced tentatively into the room. "If you ask me," he said quietly, "it would seem the author was confusing species with racial stocks."

"Did I?" said his father bitterly, not looking up at Henry, but glowering into space. "Did I ask you?" Sergeant Flynn looked at the clock and got to his feet with an impatient sigh, reaching for his hat and nightstick all in one motion, and, while buttoning his coat, informed Henry that he was to drive Miss Kokoriss (his father appeared unable to recall the girl's given name) to her aunt and uncle's house in Ireland Parish. It was important, he said.

"Nothing serious?" said Henry worriedly.

But Columbine, too, was putting on her coat, the slender black coat she wore for dress purposes, and had already started for the door and made no reply. While the sergeant took his overcoat down from the clothes tree in the hall, Columbine held his stick for him. He regarded himself with satisfaction in the looking glass. Then all three went outdoors in the snow.

By the time they reached Henry's car in the street, his father was delivering himself once more of some of his favorite views, but only for Columbine's benefit. It was apparent to Henry that his father had suddenly taken a shine to the girl. It struck Henry as preposterous that a man of his father's age should be putting on such overt masculine airs, swelling out his chest like a bull moose showing himself off to a pretty calf. Nor could Henry believe that his father's cracked ideas and witticisms would find much sympathy even in a slip of a girl like Columbine. And yet, she had not yet uttered a word to Henry. She seated herself between them on the front seat, still holding the nightstick in her gloved hands, and was devoting her attention to his father.

"A crime," Sergeant Flynn was saying, "is a way of testing not the law, mind you, but the specific practices and beliefs that lie behind the law. Follow me?"

Columbine nodded.

"The law supports those beliefs or customs, you see, whatever they may be. There are people in this world who believe that butterflies are divine. If a man murders a butterfly, the law demands that certain unspeakable penalties be visited upon that man. Personally, I, like most Christians, believe in the sacredness of private property. If a man steals my watch"—Sergeant Flynn paused to dig out his pocket watch, and displayed this glittering appliance on the palm of his hand for Columbine to look at— "in order to make it *his* watch, then I want to know how society intends to recover that watch and prevent it being taken again. I don't care about the philosophy of the criminal. I don't care if he's a Chinaman or a lunatic, and I'll tell you why. Because I want my watch back. I want it back," said the sergeant, "and I don't want it stolen again."

As Henry started the automobile rolling down the cobbled hill, the snow came dropping in great wet flakes, splashing onto the windshield amid the movement of the wipers. He was not listening to his father, but stole random glances at Columbine in profile. A sweet fragrance touched the air, and Henry realized she was wearing the perfume he had given her as a gift on that raw, unhappy morning not long ago.

His father snapped shut the case of his watch.

"Criminals are my deadly enemies, you see. I go after them as the blue racer goes after rattlesnakes. I hunt them," he said, "and I catch them."

His father's braggadocio was dismaying to Henry. It was almost a sexual display, the way he continually ogled her, leaning his head down to her, and moving his arms and hands in various ways suggestive of his ability to grasp people.

"That's my business," he told her. "That's my function. Society has commissioned me to uphold the law. That's why I wear this uniform, this cap and coat. That's what my shield is for."

"And your club," said Columbine.

"Exactly. Why," Sergeant Flynn suggested suddenly, "don't you stop in at the stationhouse late one afternoon, Miss Kokoriss, and I'll show you around our facility?"

"That would be very enjoyable." Columbine responded in a tone of voice suitable to the sergeant's proposal. She was not unaware of her emergence here into adult company, for she had never been treated so respectfully by the police sergeant.

"Of course, we're not the FBI, you understand, just a little local constabulary, but do you know"— he raised his voice gently—"we've played a part in breaking up some rather notorious cases?"

"Like the Mole Hill counterfeiters," said Columbine, pleased as punch at being able to make a timely contribution to the discussion.

"That was one." He blushed with pleasure at the girl's mention of his most famous case. "But there were others. Mostly, I pride myself, though, on my ability to smell a criminal. I have a sixth sense, you see."

"Well, I wouldn't like you to arrest me," said Columbine, in a pretty tone that brought a solid laugh from Henry's father.

"I wouldn't worry about that, if I were you!" he said.

It was at that moment, precisely, just as Henry was pulling away from a traffic light, that he happened to glance around and caught sight of something that took his breath away. The policeman had just taken back his nightstick from Columbine, and was clutching it in a way that struck Henry as downright obscene. He was holding the stick against his groin in the ball of his fist, with the long, dark shaft extending upward in a display of phallic potency that was so obvious as to appear intentional. The grin, too, on his father's face, half hidden as it was in the shadow of his peaked cap, combined with the dark twinkling stick to suggest a mythic, devilish sexual power.

"So long as you keep to the straight and narrow," added his father jovially, while waving the stick slowly to and fro, "I wouldn't worry."

"I'd like very much to see the cells," she said. "Would there be people in them?"

"Sometimes," he crooned.

"I'd like to visit the cells when there are people in them It would be fun looking in at them."

His father exploded with laughter. "Ho, ho, ho! Listen to this one, will you! Well," he said, "I shall certainly try to accommodate you. When I hear that you're coming, my girl, I'll round up a half dozen or so of our local shills and pickpockets and stuff them in the pokey for you. I'll have them put on a fine, pathetic show for you, too, throwing themselves against the bars and begging to be let out."

"Oh, by all means," said Columbine. "That would be exciting."

Henry expected that after his father had got out of the car, trudging his way through the snow up the front walk to the stationhouse, Columbine would become suddenly talkative. He thought she would make polite references to his father, or to his father's stories, or even to his harebrained theories, and revive at once the bright personality she had shown him at the wake the night she came straight to him in the crowded room and had him sign the visitors' book. Columbine, though, merely moved over to the far end of the front seat, where she sat forward, staring out through the dark crescent of the windshield cleared by the wiper. Her face went from light to shadow with the passing street lamps. She hadn't even acknowledged his presence. She hadn't even had the courtesy to thank him for the ride he was giving her. Her coldness, he guessed, was her way of masking the fact that it was she who had drawn his attention to her in the first place. Henry was not smitten with the girl (she was only a child, after all), but he did find himself perplexed and made curious by her.

Henry drove through the snow-soaked streets and onto the river bridge, and still not a word passed between them. On the bridge, Columbine turned her head to the window, and looked down at the black boulders capped with snow in the riverbed below, and upstream to the dam with its icy curtain of falling water lighted by spotlights and extending across the river from one dark cluster of factory buildings on one shore to another on the opposite side. The band of glowing white water appeared to be cascading into existence out of a black void and vanishing at once into another. Henry switched on the radio. But Columbine reached round at once and shut it off.

"Is the heater on?" she complained. "I'm freezing."

"Yes," said Henry, puzzled, "it's on."

"Thank you," she said curtly, and continued looking out the side window.

The streets of the downtown factory district were deserted, the pavements covered with a layer of wet snow. The only lights shining were those in the night watchmen's shanties and gatehouses. Not a pedestrian was abroad. A glimmering of snowflakes fell incessantly through the glare of a streetlight and swept on over the rails of a canal bridge. Columbine had not moved a muscle.

"Are you angry about something?" he asked, finally.

Columbine's head swiveled all the way about, the porcelain face alight with an indignant glow. "Well, wouldn't you be?" Her eyes contained a cold blue fire. "Of course, I am!" She fairly spat the words at him.

Henry's foot went limp on the accelerator, causing the car to slow at once. He couldn't believe his ears. He found it hard to imagine that the girl was drawing him into something like a lovers' tiff. She was staring daggers at him.

"But what about?" said Henry.

"I don't want to talk about it," said Columbine. "Could you turn up the heater, please?"

"It's on high," he told her.

"I can't imagine why anyone would want a convertible in the winter," she said, and glanced around the interior of the car with an ironic, bittersweet twist to her mouth. Her eyes did linger, though, along the panel of soft green lights and dials adorning the dashboard.

"Are you angry at me?" said Henry.

"Could we talk about something else?" said Columbine.

"All right," Henry replied, a trifle flustered. "Where are we going?"

"We're going up Lyman Street to Chestnut. Just drive up Lyman," she said impatiently, "I'll tell you when to stop."

Henry was a creature of great tolerance. It was a natural facet of his character. Where somebody else might take a quick instinctive reaction to insult, Henry was disposed by nature to look upon it from its several sides. In the case of Columbine, he actually felt quite concerned for her—this having nothing to do, he imagined, with the secret communion that had existed between them for several weeks and months.

"Why don't you tell me what's troubling you," he said. "I'd like to know if I did something to displease you."

"I *said,*" said Columbine, "I'd rather not talk about it."

"It isn't fair," he reasoned with her, striking this time an indulgent tone that took account of her immaturity, "to hold a grudge against someone without telling them why."

Suddenly Columbine sat back in her seat, made a little wet clicking noise with her tongue, and crossed her legs. "You're impossible," she said.

At that, Henry gave a sharp laugh. She was winding him into a toil, a subtle, insidious toil!

"Aren't you remarkable," he said.

Columbine turned to him then a placid, haughty aspect, reached her arm languidly along the top of the white leather seat, and fell to appraising once more the satisfying configuration of pale-green lights and luminous dials on the dashboard. She had not ridden in many automobiles. She lifted her gaze levelly to the road and falling snow once again.

"*Are* you angry?" he said, at last.

"*Yes!*" she cried. "Now are you satisfied?"

"Well, if you won't tell me why," said Henry, as amused as he was perplexed, "I won't ask you again."

"I heard about your lunch date today," she said, and showed him that same thin, bittersweet smile.

There it was! Henry gave a shout of laughter. "With Anna?" he said.

"Did you have two?" said Columbine, as promptly as that.

"Anna and I met on the street," he explained patiently.

"Well, I knew you didn't meet under a rock," said Columbine.

"You aren't going to tell me," said Henry, "that you're jealous of Anna?"

"Of my own sister? Of Anna?" Columbine had slid forward and was sitting on the edge of the seat again, with her head up, gazing at him in disbelief. "I think you have the wrong idea about me," she said, "if you think that I could be jealous of Anna. By the way," she put in abruptly, "you just went past Lyman Street!"

"Was that Lyman Street?" Henry glanced up at the rearview mirror.

"No," said Columbine, "it was the Appian Way."

He couldn't help laughing. He would never have dreamed her to be so quick. Quick to anger, too, he thought. She was very bright and impudent. A regular saucebox. Henry made the next turn, and started up the hill. The snow appeared to be flying more thickly, the big spinning flakes swimming down through the headlights and splashing like raindrops on the windshield.

"Thank heavens the heater is working now," said Columbine, as she made a show of extending her legs in the direction of the whirring sound coming from beneath the dash.

"Are you warm enough?" he asked in a kindly voice, all but unaware that he was trying to mollify her.

"Where did you go for lunch?" she said.

"Lunch?" he exclaimed. "Oh, today! With Anna. We went to the Maples. Anna had an extra half hour."

"Anna *made* an extra half hour," said Columbine.

"I don't understand," said Henry.

Columbine gave a sigh of disbelief such as women

have been making over men and other women since the start of time. "Anna," she explained, "has a thirty-minute lunch period. She does not get an hour for lunch."

"Oh, I see," said Henry, with a dawning of understanding. "You mean—" he started to say.

"Yes," said Columbine, "that's exactly what I mean."

Henry knew himself to be entangled in Columbine's delicate toils, but a knowledge of snares is not the same as freedom from them, and he was left to extricate himself at his leisure. The ensuing silence gave him time to contemplate the depths and ramifications of his ignorance. Henry broke the silence himself, but only by committing his most serious blunder so far. First, he switched on the radio, and Columbine switched it off. Then he made the blunder. He said:

"How is school?"

This question Columbine found beneath contempt. It forced her to take an altogether new tack with him. It was impossible to hold a proper conversation with him. Her reactions showed in the way she seemed to wipe her face clean of the entire layer of expressions that had been building there. "We're going to Lyman and Chestnut Streets," she said in a new voice, "and you'll have to wait for me while I go inside. Does your clock work? I'd like to be there by seven. I hope we can make it by seven. *If,*" she added, not rudely, but with a painfully courteous smile, "I'm not frozen to death by then. Did I tell you," she went on, without missing a breath, "that Helen left a picture behind for you? It's an old snapshot of you."

"Is it a good one?" Henry asked.

"How should I know?" she tossed back indifferently, but making a face over the question. "You can ask Anna for it. I'm sure she'd be thrilled to give it to you. I do hope we'll make it by seven o'clock. My

Uncle Alexis will be there till seven. He's *very* entertaining." Columbine had become in a twinkling the soul of feminine charm, sitting up straight on the seat, with little smiles flashing through her face, her eyes sparkling. "Don't your tire chains make a racket?" she said. "I don't know how you can stand it. How many miles have you driven this car? I notice your clock isn't working. Does the speedometer? It seems to be."

"The speedometer works," he managed to say.

"But I suppose it would have to, or you wouldn't know whether you were speeding or not." She flashed him a sudden beguiling smile, and returned her eyes to the hill ahead. "It wasn't even supposed to snow tonight. It was supposed to rain. Whenever I shovel the snow, it rains immediately afterward! Almost as if it knew!" Again, Columbine's face ignited in a glamorous smile, more memorable than anything Henry had ever seen. *'Is* it," she inquired, "seven o'clock? Are you wearing a watch? Mine is broken. It's probably just as well I'm not wearing it. When you're as cold as I am, it's not wise to wear metal next to your skin. I know that much." She rattled on without letup, the picture of an appreciative neighbor returning charm for a favor being done her. "I hope you don't mind my switching off the radio. I never listen to it. The idea of somebody I've never even met talking to me out of a box for hours and hours, *usually,"* she stressed, "about something he doesn't know anything about but is reading from a piece of paper, seems about as stupid as anything I could possibly imagine. Anna listens a great deal. I leave the room. I"—she borrowed here a word from Sister Mary Placida, her nun—*"loathe* the radio. I would rather read a book."

"Do you read much?" Henry interposed hurriedly.

Columbine ignored him. She had become a little volcano of idle patter. "Why do you have that amber

97

knob attached to your steering wheel? Is that what they call a spinner? That is amber, isn't it? Amber," she elucidated, "is sometimes called 'Lithuanian gold.' Did you know that? It's mined, you know. It's pine pitch." She widened her eyes and drew in her cheeks, while waiting this time for his polite acknowledgment.

"I didn't know that." Henry was by now greatly charmed by Columbine's virtuoso performance, knowing it to be her dramatized reply, as it were, to his question about her schooling.

"Yes, it was once pine pitch. You can almost tell by the color. As pine trees die, they just sort of *crumble,*" Columbine said, making a sudden crumpling gesture with her two hands, "and melt into the earth. And it builds up for thousands and thousands of years until it's actually very deep in the ground and has to be mined. It ages," she said, and glared at him, as though this point were of special moment. "Of course, you only find amber where there are pine trees. Or where there used to be pine trees. *Lithuania,*" she exclaimed, and cast up her two hands, "has millions and millions of pine trees. Did you know that the Greeks of olden times traveled all the way to Lithuania for amber? It was the longest trade route in the world." She showed him a pretty smile.

Henry, who could not help comparing Anna as he remembered her at lunch to the vision of theatricality sitting before him, wondered if Columbine was her sister at all, or if she were not some evanescent creature made out of starlight. He was charmed.

"The Lithuanian language is also one of the oldest languages there is," Columbine confided. Henry wanted to interrupt her, to ask her to say something to him in her father's tongue, but Columbine rattled on prettily. "The oldest man in the world lives in Lithuania. He's one hundred and forty-four years old. Also, the biggest man in the world lives in Lithuania. He's over eight feet tall. His wife is seven feet six. They live in an enormous house with special doorways and furniture and very high ceilings."

"How do you say sailor in Lithuanian?" said Henry.

"*Jurininkas,*" she fired out, just like that. "The Lithuanians are a seafaring people, you know. They fish. They eat more fish than probably anyone in the world."

"Off amber plates, I suppose," said Henry.

Columbine laughed sharply, an impulsive burst of laughter over Henry's sudden interjection. Not an instant later—Henry had just stopped for the light at the top of the hill—she swung about in her seat, pointing past him excitedly, and, in an altogether changed voice, cried, "Oh, Starbuck! Look!"

Henry swiveled about so quickly, and was so riveted by what he saw, that he hadn't time even to notice that Columbine had called him Starbuck. For there, not thirty feet away, stood the figure of a man in a parti-colored costume, looking out at them through the snow. He was standing in the shadows of a raised stone porch of the City Hall, a vision— a miracle—in green and blue and red and orange, with a green stocking cap and his face painted a pasty white with the lips rouged in, and patches of color everywhere upon him. Henry set his hand to the side of his face and gawked at him. The man was a living spectacle. He was the only human being in sight. He was a harlequin, but without a reason in the world to be there. The snow flew past between them. After a moment, the man raised his right arm slowly, bringing it up from his side, and he shook a tambourine; the bells tinkled softly in the snowfall.

"That man," said Henry, amused, "is an original." As he pulled away through the intersection, Henry managed a final backward glance. The parti-colored man was evidently following them with his eyes, because the white face had moved around fractionally toward them. The colors—the purples and emeralds and yellows—dissolved in the snow. Columbine was next to Henry on the seat. She was right beside him, only inches away, straining to see. When Henry turned to her, to comment on the gay apparition, her face was next to his. Her closeness had been made natural by the sudden excitement.

"Who do you suppose that was?" she said. A moment later, she smiled over Henry's discomfort. He steered around the far end of the park onto Chestnut Street, and drove on slowly under the white trees. Columbine made no move to withdraw. Henry wasn't looking at her; but she was much too close. She was looking at him. "Can you smell my perfume?" she said. Henry nodded. "Turn left here."

"What?" he said.

"Turn left!"

Henry stamped hurriedly onto the brakes, causing the rear end to slew about on the snowy pavement.

"Now, pull over by that door and wait for me."

The girl was importunate, thought Henry. She was nervy. Very pert and egoistic. Henry did not feel that it was all that attractive in a young girl. She had meanwhile slid across the seat.

"Get closer to the curb," she said. "A little closer. Good," she said. "*Stop!*" She threw open the door. "I'll try to hurry. Teeka is a chatterbox. Keep the motor running for the heater." Slamming the door, Columbine ran through the rainy snowfall and vanished into a tenement house.

While Columbine was indoors, Henry sat at the wheel, with the motor running. He shut off the wipers and played the radio. The city was very quiet. He felt almost relieved to be alone for a minute, as she had led him a merry chase, back and forth across the entire spectrum of human emotions, in the space of a bare quarter hour. He counseled himself to be firm; he would insist, for one thing, that she not sit close beside him again like that. He could just imagine Mr. Neumann or Mr. Meehan from the newspaper suddenly going past and discovering him with a very young girl like that cuddled up close to him at the wheel (even if she was the girl next door). Henry guessed he would have to be a little more forceful with her. If it came to that, he would go so far as never to let her into his car again. She was charming when she wanted to be, and he had no doubt she would sometime be a great beauty, but he would have to let her know that he would not be drawn into adolescent spats or be made the target of her groundless jealousies.

Henry had a good long while to lay his plans in this regard, for Columbine kept him waiting forty-five minutes. That, he decided, was an outrage. Henry could be firm when he wanted to be. He had not spent five years in the United States Navy, stationed in a combat zone and exposed to enemy fire, only to be made a rag of by a thirteen-year-old girl. When she came back to the car, he would give her a reprimand.

Unfortunately, Henry was denied the opportunity to give Columbine a proper scolding that evening; not because she failed to return, but because she brought someone with her to the car. She came out the tenement door leading a small boy by the hand. The boy was bundled up in a snowsuit, with the hood up and a scarf around his face. Columbine opened the door, and swung him effortlessly into the car.

"Look, Starbuck," she cried, "isn't he beautiful?" She clambered in and slammed the door behind her. "I'm sorry I'm late. Oh, it's warm as toast in here," she said, and began at once untying the little boy's hood. *"This* is Casimir," she said, but saying it playfully to the little boy. "My *kudikeli,"* she said, "hm?" and tickled him. "Isn't he priceless? I *am* sorry for being late." She carefully let back the boy's hood, uncovering a brilliant head of blond hair. He was blond to the point of whiteness. The child was indeed beautiful; there was no disputing that. Columbine removed his mittens, stuffing them into her own coat pocket. "Teeka talks and *talks,*" she said of her aunt. "It's a wonder Alexis can stand it. *You,*" she said to Henry, in the way of a compliment founded upon her own intimate grasp of Henry's likes and dislikes, "would find her unbearable! Oh, but, Starbuck," she brought out suddenly, with great familiarity, as she stopped what she was doing to regard him affectionately across the interior of the rolling automobile, "what do you suppose? I told Aunt Teeka about the man in the party costume at the City Hall. She knows him! He's the laughing stock of Ward Four, she says. She says he's a *girtuoklis,* a drinker," said Columbine, "a crazyhead. She saw him in a masquerade costume up on the bandstand in Hampden Park one night just before Christmas, leading a make-believe orchestra! Casimir wants to see him, too. Don't you, pickle? Where he comes from"—she loosened the child's coat—"there are not many sights like that. Casimir," she said to Henry, "came out of Lithuania in a suitcase. That's what they tell me, anyhow."

The boy, Henry noticed, despite his platinum hair, as compared to Columbine's black hair, had eyes of the very same hue as hers. He could have passed for her brother, or, had she been old enough, for her child. He noticed, too, the deftness with which she handled him.

Columbine reached as a matter of habit and switched off the radio. "The car is tremendously warm," she said. While loosening her scarf, she took a sudden deep breath and slowly expelled it. "After I see Aunt Teeka, I always get so talkative. You get all wound up, because she talks about so many things at once, and you can't fit a word in edgewise. Oh, are we here already?"

Henry stopped on the hill by the City Hall, and

the three of them strained to see through the falling snow into the shadows at the stair top, to catch a glimpse of the parti-colored man. But by then, of course, he was not there.

VI

Henry did not pretend to be knowledgeable about girls, and yet he didn't think of his ignorance in this regard as being capable of growth or refinement. Anna, after all, was not more puzzling to him than Helen or Sophie had been. Mrs. McKenna, the bartender's wife, was no less comprehensible. She frightened Henry a little, but she didn't mystify him. It wasn't until Henry became better acquainted with Columbine, the youngest of the Kokoriss girls, that his ignorance began to expand.

For one thing, Columbine struck up a friendship with Henry's father. This friendship was encouraged by Mrs. Flynn, who thought it fitting and appropriate that the girl, deprived now of her own father, should find a friend and surrogate father in the person of Sergeant Flynn, a man of authority in the neighborhood. What puzzled Henry was the way the girl often sided with his father in his frequent ribbing and heckling of Henry. His father had never had an ally in the house before. After Columbine started coming by, he began noticeably to strut and crow in her presence; he began to bait Henry, not maliciously really, but in the spirit of good-natured raillery. Sergeant Flynn, for example, took Columbine one evening to a high-school basketball game, and when they came home and were joined in the parlor by Henry, he began to poke fun at him at once. He recalled how Henry, as a boy, had not liked to play basketball but chose instead to referee. Sergeant Flynn then gave an imitation of Henry that sent Columbine into peals of laughter, as he skipped this way and that across the parlor, blowing an imaginary whistle.

In the beginning, Henry thought Columbine was being clever, using his father as a ruse to get her closer to himself. He thought she was being wonderfully inventive. But a crack never appeared on the surface of her features. She ignored Henry; or, if she was not ignoring him, she was looking at him in pained wonderment, or with impatience, or even, sometimes, with an amused, indulgent look that reminded Henry of one of his aunts. Columbine began to visit his father at the stationhouse, stopping by in the afternoon on her way home from school. He also gave her books to read, and they talked about them afterward. They read, for example, *The Egg and I,* which Sergeant Flynn had set down as a masterpiece of good humor. They read James Oliver Curwood's *The Valley of Silent Men,* and *Scaramouche* by Rafael Sabatini. His father saw to it, too, that Columbine became a regular Sunday-afternoon guest at the Flynn dinner table (sitting opposite Henry, in her black or green or scarlet dress, and eating daintily while hanging on his father's words, or turning to smile at Mrs. Flynn, or sometimes speaking a few words in her brisk, precocious manner, usually aimed at no one in particular). Within the space of five or six weeks, she had become like a little concubine in the house.

"Don't put her coat over there," his father would chide Henry. "What's the matter with you? That's no place for a coat. You would think he was raised in the Flats," he would say to Columbine. "Hang it in the hall closet! And put her rain hat on the shelf. Well, now," he would say, turning to Columbine with the unctuous manner of a palace official attending to the Empress Marie Louise herself, "what do you suppose I could get for you? What do you think you might like? Would you like a little blackberry nectar?"

His father's blackberry nectar was a standing joke in the Flynn house for years. Jerome Flynn was a teetotaler, but when guests were in the house he liked sometimes to strike an air of exaggerated suavity. At such times, he would break out the set of pretty Waterford wineglasses that May Flynn had got from her mother years ago, and then repair to the cellar for one of his blackberry jugs. The blackberry concoction was prepared by a man whose son the sergeant had once saved from drowning; each year at holiday time the man brought him another jugful of this thick, sweet, rich beverage, and each year Henry's father served it to his guests with great ceremony. Each guest was allotted half a glass of the dark, twinkling substance, which portions Sergeant Flynn measured out in the kitchen with a little glass beaker and the eye of an alchemist. As soon, however, as Columbine became a regular guest in the Flynn house, Henry's father's blackberry nectar began to flow at a prodigal rate. All Columbine had to say was, "Isn't this a *treasure?*" and his father was footing his way down cellar once or twice a week to fetch up the jug.

Sometimes Columbine and Henry's father sat together in Sergeant Flynn's den, discussing books and articles and imbibing his father's secret elixir. Henry was a little perturbed by the fact that his father sometimes shut the door, and that there always seemed to be more laughter going on in the den when the door was closed than otherwise. His father's laughter at such times seemed, also, to have a certain soft raucous quality that reminded Henry of the jabbering of ducks or crows. It sounded obscene. Henry got so curious that he actually peeped in on them once, going round through the snow at the side of the house in his shirtsleeves. Columbine was sitting primly on the edge of his father's maple reading chair, holding her wineglass aloft with great delicacy. His father was standing over her, reading to her from a book in his hand. Henry couldn't hear the words, but Columbine's tinkle of laughter and the way she threw back her head while lifting her wine-glass in a kind of salute suggested that his father was communicating something of special charm. As Henry trudged back through the snow to the front door, the picture of Columbine smiling prettily and holding her glass high in the air remained etched in his brain.

Columbine came, too, on weekday evenings, when his father was on duty, and played Parcheesi with Mrs. Flynn in the kitchen. Mrs. Flynn loaned Columbine a novel called *Girl of the Limberlost,* but the next Sunday at the dinner table Columbine confessed that the book was not to her taste.

The father looked up swiftly from his plate. "What book was that?" he demanded, his neck reddening with anger at the thought of someone having trespassed on his territory.

"I found it to be a bit slushy," said Columbine, but regretting immediately the invisible wedge she had just driven in between the mother and father.

"That's not your sort of book, at all," said his father. He had just given Columbine a copy of a book entitled *Seven Came Through* by Eddie Rickenbacker.

"I don't think she will like that book about the seven airmen cast away on a raft." May Flynn smiled helplessly in the face of her husband's more spirited intellect, while looking about to see if everyone was eating the baked haddock.

Sergeant Flynn appeared petulant as he resumed eating. Then he looked up again. "You said she wouldn't like *All Night Long,*" the father reminded her, with excessive politeness. "She liked that."

"I didn't say she wouldn't like it," Mrs. Flynn retreated graciously. "I only said, Jerome, that I didn't think Erskine Caldwell appropriate for her."

"And *Captain Blood?*" said the father. "Is *that* not appropriate?"

"Oh, I found that delightful!" Columbine brightened at once.

"There! Did you hear?" said the father. "Did you hear what she said?"

"Some of those books," said Mrs. Flynn, with gentle dismay, "*I* would not recommend."

"The younger generation is different," said Jerome Flynn.

"I guess they must be," the mother confessed, with just a trace of pique.

"You leave it to me," said Sergeant Flynn. "The girl can read just about anything."

"And has been," said Henry.

"How was that?" said his father, his guard up at once.

"It sounds to me as though she's been reading 'just about anything,' " said Henry darkly, feeling shut out from discussing a subject that he saw as meat and drink to himself.

Columbine grew taut. She was wearing what appeared to be a gray business suit with a snow white blouse that had a ruffle at the throat. A peony color came into her cheekbones. She found Henry's remark offensive.

"What did he say?" said his father, pretending deafness.

"You heard me," said Henry.

"These books are good enough for Clifton Fadiman"—Sergeant Flynn sat back in his chair—"but they're not good enough for him!"

"If you ask me," Henry spoke up even more emphatically, "they're all banal and stupid, these books."

"Yes," said the sergeant, with a tremulous glint flying into his eye, "but then, nobody asked you! Did they?" He set down his fork with exquisite care, as though there were only one little place for it in all the world; then he sat back and folded his arms, and looked at his son.

Columbine was breaking a piece of bread, sitting with her elbows on the table, her hands raised before her. She took up a butter knife, while watching the older and younger Flynn with apprehension.

Abruptly Henry's own true frustrations broke through. "I should think," he said, in a show of sarcasm equal to his father's, "that a child like Columbine should be reading something on the order of Louisa May Alcott."

Instantly Columbine put down her knife with a clatter. "I beg your pardon!" she said.

The outrage that came shining out of Columbine's beautiful face manifested itself with such suddenness that Mrs. Flynn, unable to restrain herself, threw back her head and laughed merrily.

His father's face darkened. "If there's one thing I don't permit in this house," he shouted at Henry, "it's insulting a guest!"

After an awkward interval, all four returned their attentions to their plates, but his father's vexation, like many forces in nature, continued to gather for a while before suddenly breaking out in a more virulent form. Everyone was dining in silence, when his father flicked up his eyes.

"You're not such a big shot," he said, "that I might not take a round out of your hide yet!"

This proclamation had a profound effect on the table. Over the years, Henry's father had never once struck him, save for small, peremptory spankings during childhood, so that this sudden physical threat came down like a bombshell. It caused May Flynn to blanch a deadly white. She looked ill.

"Jerome!" she said.

"I think *I* had better leave," said Columbine, as she put down her napkin and prepared to rise from her chair.

"You stay right where you are," the father commanded. "If anyone is leaving, it won't be you."

Mrs. Flynn interceded also, touching Columbine's sleeve with her fingers. "Pay no attention to them," she said worriedly. "The Irish always fight at supper."

While the others at the table adjusted themselves to the unpleasant circumstance, Henry sat bolt upright, gazing into space as though some fabulous creature unknown to zoology had just marched across his field of vision. No one made any effort to lighten the tension, and the Sunday dinner wound down to a conclusion relieved only by brusque instructions going to and fro among them.

"Pass the salt."

"Pass the bread, please."

"Thank you."

"Pass the tomatoes."

"Thank you."

"Thanks."

Columbine continued to cultivate Mrs. Flynn's good offices in her own behalf, while at the same time not discouraging Sergeant Flynn from preening and strutting a bit whenever she was nearby. Mrs. Flynn and Columbine drank tea together in the evening, and Mrs. Flynn always made sure to have candy corn-cakes and maple creams on hand, as both she and the girl next door had a special liking for these particular sweets. Moreover, when Mrs. Flynn secretly loaned Columbine a copy of A. J. Cronin's *Hatter's Castle*, holding a finger up to her lips to suggest the clandestine character of the transaction, Columbine made sure to be enthusiastic about the book when she brought it back. As for Henry, though, he had still not got over his father's vicious attack upon him. It had not occurred to Henry that he might have been putting on airs about his work at the newspaper, what with his talk of assignments and deadlines and feature stories and such, or that such talk might have rankled in his father's breast.

Henry Flynn was not a show-off. He was not belligerent, either. His first impulse, after having been shouted down and threatened that way by his father, was to absent himself as much as possible from his father's presence. Henry was not home for dinner the following Sunday, nor was he present on the evening when his father and mother took Columbine to the movies with them. He didn't see Columbine for two weeks, except at a distance. He saw her going out to school one morning, in her tan windbreaker and red galoshes; and then, another time, she was coming up the hill when he drove past, pretending not to see her, neither waving to her nor pumping his horn. Henry thought she had been disrespectful toward him in his own house, and had fallen back on his pride with her. That was how he felt the afternoon he drove past her on the hill in his Ford. An hour later, though, Columbine was at the front door of his house.

Henry was home alone when she called, and did not know if it was proper to let her into the parlor —not that his wondering about it mattered, for Columbine came right in anyway, brushing past him into the foyer.

"I have a problem to discuss with you," she said. "I hope no one else is here."

"My mother is at the Sodality meeting."

Columbine removed her scarf and kicked off her red rubber overshoes and, with a shaking out of her short-clipped, black hair, proceeded past him into the living room. "You've been a stranger," she called back airily, over her shoulder, as she snatched up a magazine, scrutinized its cover, and tossed it down again. Henry noticed the faint shiny color on Columbine's lips, the first time he had ever seen makeup on her face. He guessed from that that Columbine knew he was alone in the house, because

Mrs. Flynn was not the sort of woman to condone a "painted face" on a girl as young as Columbine.

In the dining room, Columbine positioned herself by the bow window that looked out onto the gardens and the Kokoriss house. She folded her arms, clasping her elbows in both hands, and stood, thus, rigidly, altogether self-assured, regarding Henry as he came into the room. With the gray glow of dusk shining around the windows behind her, her face was revealed to him more as a mask than a face.

"I don't mind apologizing," she spoke up boldly, "when I feel I've been wrong about something. That's why I'm here." She compressed her lips and looked at him evenly.

"You want to apologize to me?" he said.

"Yes, I do."

"That isn't necessary, Columbine." Henry's voice was soft but resonant in the gloom. He stood in the doorway. In the dim, glowing light, his dark suit and white shirt gave him a priestly look. The girl before him had about her an air of unreality—her face turned to him, her temples and cheeks glowing like a shell. "You and I," he said, "have no basis of an understanding that would require anything like that." Immediately Henry liked the way he had worded that thought. Thrusting back the sides of his suit jacket, he sank his hands into his trouser pockets and stepped soundlessly into the room. He said nothing more, but continued to relish the formal character of his reply.

"I didn't come here to argue with you," Columbine countered at once, on a rising, exceptive note. "I came to explain. If you won't let me speak, then I'll leave. Is that," she said, challenging him, "what you want? For me to leave?"

"I didn't say that." Henry had fallen unconsciously into the pattern of harmless but provocative bickering set by Columbine.

"Because if it is," she said, "I'll go. I don't mind apologizing," she allowed, in that same pert manner, "but I'm not going to make an idiot of myself. I'm not going to behave like Anna. I'm not like that."

"I don't see what Anna has to do with it," Henry argued.

"To do with what?"

"With any of it," Henry said helplessly.

"Well, you used to date her, didn't you? And you don't any more."

"Columbine," Henry went on in the face of what seemed to him a want of strict reasoning in his guest's retorts, but affected still by the wan gray light in the room and Columbine's silhouette, "I'm not following too well the train of your thought." He smiled with effort.

"Well, everyone *knows,*" she came back saucily, "that you only have to call her. Anna," she said, "is a wallflower."

"Columbine!"

"I'm not. I never will be."

"I'm sure you won't," he said.

"I'm not like that."

A silence then grew up between them. Henry could not divine the meaning of the girl's visit, and Columbine's appearance, shadowy and motionless in the twilit room, added to the mystery.

"Why are you here?" he said, at last.

"I came to apologize," she said.

Another silence followed. Henry could not see outdoors through the glowing windows behind her, but a wintry wind slapped and rattled a telephone line against the side of the house. When the wind went past, the light changed in the room, then changed again. He wondered in passing whether or not to light a lamp. He wanted to dispel his uneasiness, but didn't wish to break this curious spell. So he did nothing. He stood in the doorway, with his hands in his pockets, staring across the room at the prim, silent figure before him. He would wait for her to explain herself.

Columbine, however, was not eager to conclude matters, and chose instead to pursue the more nerve-rattling side of things.

"Do you want me to stay?" she said.

"I'll leave that answer to you," said Henry.

"If you leave it to me," she replied, "I'll go."

Henry experienced a moment of confusion and indecision.

"Shall I go?" she persisted, more challengingly than before. Her head moved slightly, as though she was conscious of a strain or stiffness in her neck, but then she was staring at him again, perfectly motionless from head to toe.

Being human, Henry tried to frame a reply that would reconcile the demands of pride and pleasure, and said, "Well, I would like to know why you came."

This answer, he realized at once, failed of its purpose, for Columbine left the windows immediately and went briskly past him. She didn't look at him. She went by him in the doorway, and on into the parlor, with her head in the air, and continued out to the front hallway. When Henry overtook her, she had already got her tan windbreaker in hand, and was putting it on. She was ignoring him. Henry appeared a little pained. He wished they were not in his house, for all of his past was immanent and at work here. In a moment of weakness, he even felt that Columbine should better have comprehended his dilemma. Of course, with that realization, he knew he was skidding.

With her jacket on, drawing up her zipper, she cast a sidelong glance at him. Her face bore that flawless, opalescent aspect. Without taking her eyes from him, she pulled a pair of red woolen gloves from her pocket and fitted them one by one onto her hands. "Do you want me to stay?"

There was no light of triumph in the ice-blue eyes. She was simply looking at him. All the moments of their silent communications of these past several months had now collected in a question requiring the simplest of all answers.

"Shall I stay?" she said.

"Yes," he said.

As quickly as that, Columbine peeled off her windbreaker, hanging it up on the hall tree, and launched into a fresh topic, leaving the impression that something unpleasant but necessary had been got over.

"Before I get around to my apology," she said brightly, smiling at Henry with easy familiarity as she strode past him once more into the parlor, "I want to ask you something silly. You must know Andrew Sullivan," she said. "He lives out back, on Old Bridge Street."

"His name is Salty," said Henry, "and everybody knows him." Henry was still in the front hall. "He's a living terror."

"That's him, then," said Columbine. "I didn't know he was called Salty, though."

"He isn't called anything else," Henry answered from the hall.

"He told me," said Columbine, "that his name was Andrew."

Henry came quickly into the room. "You were talking to Salty Sullivan?"

Columbine had seated herself on the arm of a wing chair, and looked up in innocent wonder. "I hope," she said, "that you're not going to tell me who I can talk to." Her eyes shone.

"Were you talking to Salty Sullivan?" Henry insisted. He had forgotten all about Columbine's supposed apology, and about the oddly compelling apparition of her silhouette a moment ago in the twilit dining room. Switching on the lamp, he repeated: *"Were you?"*

Gleams of disbelief chased one another across Columbine's face, as though these questions pertained to some altogether distant matter from what she was talking about.

"Is that a *crime?"* she said.

"It should be," said Henry rapidly. "Were you talking to him?"

"Well, if you must know," she said, making a face, "I was."

"What about?"

"Just a minute," said Columbine, letting her hands drop onto her lap as she straightened her shoulders, while appearing—or appearing to appear—a little confused, as if she had not heard him correctly. "Am I supposed to tell you everything that I say to people, and what they say to me?"

Her face sparkled with disbelief.

"Columbine," Henry scolded her, "that wasn't a wise thing for you to do. Salty Sullivan was once arrested for doing something very ugly to another boy."

"He did?"

"He was," said Henry.

"Was what?" Columbine asked.

"Was arrested!"

"Yes, but what did he do?"

"He did something obscene, something no one was even able to put into words."

"I wish someone would put it into words," Columbine exclaimed.

"He did something vile."

"You just said that."

"You shouldn't talk to people like that."

"Don't *scold,"* said Columbine. "I haven't told you what he said."

Columbine was being very adultish now, not arguing with Henry, or even objecting to his point of view, so much as maintaining a lively discussion between equals. Sitting on the chair arm, she had crossed her legs in a way that revealed a portion of one thigh.

"Don't worry," she exclaimed, "he didn't touch me."

Henry, who had a nervous habit of always trying to keep order about himself, a kind of obsession, had at that moment fallen to arranging things, knocking out one of his father's pipes, then pausing to pluck a yellow leaf from a potted philodendron. "I wasn't worried about that," he muttered.

"You *weren't?*" said Columbine, teasing him. "I'd think you would have been." She followed Henry with her eyes as he bent to pick up a red skein of wool from the carpet. "Now I am surprised," she said.

"It isn't amusing, Columbine!" he fired at her.

"Why, Starbuck," she said, "I believe you're jealous."

"Of course I'm not jealous!" he cried.

"What did Andrew do, by the way?" Columbine asked, as if she had known but forgotten.

"I can't tell you that."

"It won't *shock* me." She made a face. "Was it sodomy?"

"Was it what?" Henry looked at her.

"What Andrew did."

"It wasn't *Andrew.*" Henry spat out the name. "His name is Salty. Believe me," said Henry, with agitation, "his name will never be Andrew!"

"What did he force the other boy to do?"

"I didn't say force."

"Well, you all but said it." Columbine was swinging her leg. She reached and touched her hair. She was enjoying herself.

"I said he did something obscene."

"You said that about eight times," she said.

"He wasn't a child, either. That happened in 1939."

"That was seven years ago!" Columbine cried. *"Was* it that long ago?"

"What did the two of you talk about?" said Henry. "That's what I want to know."

"He asked me to go out with him," said Columbine, offhandedly. "He wants to take me to dinner. Oh, don't worry," she brought out rapidly, as Henry turned to her in amazement, "I'm not going with him. But not," she stressed, "because he's a criminal. I just don't like the way he talks. I don't like the language he uses. He doesn't say 'right,' you know. He says 'reet.' " Columbine mimicked him. " 'Oh, *reet!*' Isn't that disgusting? He calls his clothing his 'threads' and he says that things are *what am.* He's buying a new Packard *what am!*" Columbine laughed gaily, and threw back her head. "Isn't that re*pul*sive? Also," she added, "he has dirty fingernails."

"Salty is about nineteen years old!" Henry reminded her.

"He's twenty," Columbine corrected, looking up at him in a mocking, telltale way, her leg still swinging.

"That's too old for you!" Henry lectured her.

"You should talk," said Columbine, but at that moment turned, as she heard someone approaching from outdoors.

Mrs. Flynn's key rattled in the lock. Columbine shot Henry a look, and ran her tongue nervously over her colored lips. When Henry's mother came into the room, she found the two of them, one standing and one sitting, looking like stone effigies in a tomb. A look of concern passed over Mrs. Flynn's face, but was quickly repressed, as she managed a smile and went on through the parlor and dining room toward the kitchen.

"I should have rung the bell," she said.

———

VII

Until now, Columbine's life was governed by the simple, ancient routines of rising in the morning, dressing in a cold room, muddling through a breakfast of toast and oatmeal, and then bundling up for the drafty bus ride across the river to the Mater Dolorosa school, where a second series of ancient routines was repeated day in and day out: morning prayers, pledgings to the flag, and hours of taking down lessons in ink onto fuzzy yellow exercise paper that blotted and tore under the scratch of the pen. There were enormous wall maps, and blackboards, and three tall windows that looked out onto a row of bleak tenement houses. There was also a nun, a stern disciplinarian, who blew on a flat, black pitch pipe when calling for order, or went whispering about the room in her long, black habit, peeping over shoulders. That was Sister Mary Placida, a tall, angular creature with crooked chalky fingers and a face like dusty parchment. Sister's most fascinating feature was her grave, twinkling eyes. She had a favorite oak ruler that she carried concealed in the folds of her habit on days when she was feeling restless and punitive. Sister preferred little boys to little girls, and made no secret of it. When a girl in class made a blunder of her recitation, saying *eram* for *ero* or *ab virtutem* for *propter virtutem,* or was caught talking, or daydreaming, Sister (if she was feeling merry) would make her stand up; then she would go herself to the head of the class, blow on her pitch pipe, and, with a series of hearty physical gestures, lead all the boys of the class in resounding chorus:

Rachel, Rachel, I've been thinking,
What a fine world this would be,
If the girls were all transported
Far beyond the Northern Sea!

If Sister was feeling other than merry, she would bring her steel-edged foot rule crashing down with explosive force onto the desk top of the feckless child; or seize the girl sharply by the ear, or pull up her hair, or, in the extreme, march the blanching child out of the class to the cloakroom for a taste of corporal punishment.

The only advantage to a child being whacked on the hands by Sister swinging her ruler in the cloakroom, Columbine had noticed, was that when Sister came back to class from the cloakroom she was usually rosy and flushed, as though the thrashing had been a tonic for her spirits. While the offending child sat licking and pampering his or her burning hands at the back of the room, Sister would stand up before the class and discourse to them at length, in a soft, rather lovely voice, on the theme of how wonderful it was to be a child in school, to be young and protected and with all life before them, and how she, Sister Mary Placida, wished against wish that she could recover her own happy days in school, to go back again to those smiling hours when she and her girlfriends and the Sisters of St. Joseph read Vergil and Livy together in Latin, and *The Lives of the Saints*, and how they all adored St. Theresa, etc.

Columbine had also noticed that there were never two thrashings in one day, no matter how unruly a pupil might behave during the blissful aftermath of a beating. Once Sister's thirst for inflicting physical punishment was sated, there was no other such impulse that day. Strangest of all, though, was the fact that, despite Sister's misogyny, it was she, Sister Mary Placida, who became one of Columbine's earliest admirers.

Sister Mary Placida's admiration of Columbine went back to the previous autumn, to the morning of the first day of school, when Sister was going slowly about the class, dealing out workbooks and paper and pausing over each child to fix him or her with a cold, gray, watery eye as a kind of soulful admonition that was meant to soak in. If the child did not respond to Sister's admonitory glare, Sister would stand there and wait patiently until the child did, and wait, too, until the youngster's answering gaze withered and was withdrawn; then Sister would lift up her head and move along slowly to the next child.

Thus she went, from desk to desk. When she came, however, to the desk of the skinny, black-haired girl sitting by the window, she paused and stood over Columbine, with her colorless eyes twinkling and her face filling up with a dusty pink color. She actually smiled at Columbine. Her lips formed a kind of aristocratic moue, as if she had recognized at once in the Kokoriss girl the presence of a spirit consonant with her own. She looked at Columbine's hair, her eyes, her mouth, the delicate lift of her head, and examined, too, her white, long-fingered hands.

Sister Mary Placida lingered over Columbine perhaps not longer than over any other pupil, but her absorption caused her to forget to give Columbine her materials. In time, Sister raised her head, straightened her carriage, and began softly to step along toward the next student, when Columbine spoke up petulantly.

"Sister!" she said. "Am I not *also* going to get a book and paper?"

The nun's breathless, ruffled reaction brought a snort of laughter from Joseph Kussman, the boy sitting behind Columbine, which Sister appeared scarcely to notice, as she came wavering back to Columbine with simpering lips and glittering eyes.

The deep ruby blush on her cheeks was accentuated a hundred times by the immaculate white oval of her starched coif, as she reached with tender care and laid Columbine's materials on her desk. From that morning forward, Sister's favoritism toward Columbine was as constant as school itself.

She never criticized Columbine in the presence of the class. There had been not one instance of her actually scolding the Kokoriss girl. And while Columbine was only an average-to-above-average scholar, she was often treated by Sister Mary Placida as a court of last appeal in resolving a difficult question. At such times, Sister would rail out against the class at large, excoriating them one and all for their sloth and delinquency in study, but, while doing so, would trickle out the correct answer to the problem, and then, a moment or two later, turn to Columbine, saying, "Well, perhaps, then, Miss Kokoriss will save the hour for us once again."

Columbine was young enough to be taken in by Sister's prejudices and by her shrewd techniques, enough so that when her report cards began to reflect a level of excellence in her school work that she had never attained before, she was encouraged to extend her study hours and to consider intellectual pursuits also as gratifying. Of course, Columbine was still more concerned with the graceful sweep of her handwriting on the page, or with the lovely blue-violet hue of the Carter's ink in her fountain pen, than she was with the actual words she was setting down on paper.

Still, life in the schoolroom had become a little more tolerable under Sister Mary Placida's iron-fisted regime than it had been for Columbine in the lower grades, when certain little boys and girls had been singled out by the nuns year after year as models of what an industrious well-behaved schoolchild ought to be. One girl in particular, Marjorie Piska— a pale, intelligent child who had a habit of claiming in class to have a personal vocation toward the religious life, and who had often brought attention and praise upon herself by asking the teacher sycophantic questions about life in the religious orders—had been coddled and extolled by the nuns for as long as Columbine could remember. However, in Sister Mary Placida's universe, Marjorie could not make headway at all. Sister was not interested in Marjorie Piska's vocation, except, it seemed, as Marjorie might have had a vocation to live in terror. Sister had singled out Marjorie early for severe treatment. In the month of September alone, she had taken three trips to the cloakroom and been given sound whackings (a rather sinister novelty that Columbine looked upon as being somehow redeeming of Sister's harshness). In time, Columbine even kept a written tally on Marjorie, a scorecard jotted in violet ink on the inside back cover of her Latin grammar, showing that Miss Piska, who had never in her life been struck by a nun, had sustained nine lickings in the space of twenty-two weeks under the capricious tutelage of Mary Placida.

"You *will* knuckle down," said Sister to Marjorie, leaning her two bony fists on Marjorie's desk, "you *will* keep up with the others in the class, won't you? After all, we are not armadillos. We know what an armadillo is?"

The soft reply: "Yes, Sister."

"What is an armadillo, Miss Piska?" Sister's eyes became two white, clouded orbs shimmering lustrously behind the lenses of her eyeglasses.

"I believe it is an animal with a shell." Marjorie looked away nervously from Sister, then looked back, then away again. "I believe it . . . lives in the ground." The tremulous pupil sat waiting for the sudden boom of Sister's ruler descending from nowhere like a thunderclap onto her desk.

"Go on," Sister encouraged, in a thin, breathless tone of voice, her eyes glittering depthlessly.

"I believe it lives in Texas."

"Texas?" Sister sang back, and here a little dry whisper in the folds of her dark habit intimated action to come from that quarter.

"I . . . I think so."

"You *do?"*

"Yes, Sister."

As Marjorie here typically lost her voice, Sister Mary Placida here typically lost her patience and, leaning swiftly over the flinching child, laid the tip of a long, chalky finger upon the numerals at the foot of the page of Marjorie's book.

"An armadillo," she shouted resoundingly, "is a girl on page eighty-seven when everyone else is on page eighty-eight!"

Marjorie, who had always looked upon Columbine as a sharp-tongued troublemaker, swallowed her pride nevertheless, and asked the favored Columbine why she thought Sister hated her so.

But Columbine was not helpful. "Because you're repulsive!" she said.

Columbine was named to committees. She headed the committee that oversaw the patrol leaders of the lower grades, and was also a member of the committee that helped Father Bora arrange the indoor and outdoor track meets for winter and spring. While she performed these duties grudgingly, she continued to be exemplary in Sister's eyes. When Columbine returned to school after the winter holidays, following the death of her father, Sister Mary Placida took the entire class to chapel to offer special prayers for Mr. Kokoriss's departed spirit. At recess, when the children of all grades mingled noisily in the schoolyard, Columbine sometimes stood in the doorway with the nun. Sister, strangely enough, was more talkative on days when she was ill-humored than at those times when she managed to purge herself of her anger by taking physical measures against a pupil. In fact, when Sister was feeling rather happy and buoyant, she would stride out big as life into the schoolyard, and go walking about in the wind and sun with a light, swinging tread and the ends of her black gown leaping behind her, calling cheerful greetings to former students, or shouting happily to the little tots on the swings or monkey bars to be careful. Columbine was also aware that when Sister *was* feeling jolly, she often appeared distracted. Her gaze darted and floated, and she was either unable or disinclined to talk at length on one subject only. One day, she saw Sister actually run a few steps on the playground, with her arms upraised and her skirts blowing, to catch a soaring volleyball, and return it with a smooth, roundhouse, underhand blow of her fist that sent the ball hurtling sky-high. Sister was an enigma. However, when she was her more usual self, thin-lipped and somber, she liked to keep Columbine by her side at recess time, standing either by the door inside the vestibule or outdoors on the big granite step. By late winter, Sister Mary Placida's affection for the black-haired Kokoriss girl was growing more pronounced.

There was, for example, the matter of Columbine's shoes. Shortly after her father's death, Columbine began wearing to school a pair of black patent-leather shoes with raised heels. The shoes violated the dress code at school, and when she was stopped in the corridor one afternoon by Sister Superior, who condemned the shoes and forbade her to wear them again, Columbine collected her nerve and appealed after school to Mary Placida.

"You would have to show a reasonable excuse for wearing them," Sister replied automatically. "As, for example, if the shoes were in some way corrective, Miss Kokoriss."

"They are," Columbine lied smoothly, responding at once to Sister's cue.

Sister had been writing something at her desk, and

immediately slapped down her pen and stood up. "In that case, we shall see about it." She left the room to call on Sister Superior. She was back in a twinkling. "You wear whatever shoes you want," she said.

Columbine was naturally pleased. She saw herself as superior to her classmates, and had seized upon the shoes as a sort of symbol of her superiority. She was already much taller than the other girls, and the raised heels simply put her out of sight. Of course, Sister's favoritism further puffed up Columbine's vanity. She was still flattered by it, particularly as Sister was so reviled and feared by everyone.

Sister had begun, by then, to steer their private conversations onto a personal plane. One morning, while they were talking together in the vestibule, she told Columbine that the Creator must have been very pleased with her to have made her so beautiful —a line of thought which, as it posited an existence for Columbine that antedated her attributes, as well as pointing to certain divine judgments about her that antedated her creation, made no more sense to Columbine than it would have to anyone else, but she was impressed nonetheless with the enchanting idea that her beauty was a deliberate reward from God, that He had thus set her above other people, since it was doubtful, after all, that God ever lavished gifts on the undeserving. Columbine even came in time to look upon Sister Mary Placida, with all her dark moods and paradoxes, as a fitting kind of extension of God, and of the mystery of God, of His unfathomable workings, for she, the nun, seemed to personify an almost inhuman combination of cunning terror with sudden unexpected flashes of good humor. The destruction of Sodom and Gomorrah, the web of tricks played upon Job, or even upon Abraham, or the sudden voice in the Garden when God caught Adam and Eve—such skills and deceptions were as natural as breathing to Mary Placida.

Not that Columbine looked up to Sister as being superhuman, but the nun did seem to resolve in her person certain mysteries of Catholic teaching that puzzled Columbine, while also embodying, quite wonderfully, really, the dark, airless, and both hallowed and menacing atmosphere of Church life altogether, of cold morning chapels, of candlelit interiors, of lisped prayers and confession box whisperings. Sister was powerful, she was immaculate, she was wise and devious; she was violent and vindictive, but, at the same time, possessed also a blithe, sentimental side to her. True, she was not very forgiving—insofar, that is, as a proscribed soul like Marjorie Piska could try every form of wheedling blandishment that was ever invented and not get a step closer to Sister's "good side"—but that seemed less important to Columbine than Sister's loyalty to her word, and her inflexible will. Columbine had been taught in her catechism that the two routes open to God, one through Fear and the other through Love, were not favored by God one over the other. Who was to say, then, that Sister might not also have been accessible through love, but that in the beginning, or at least in her dealings with students, had discovered raw terror to be much more easily awakened in the human breast than feelings of love, or selflessness?

Sister Mary Placida became, in short, Columbine's favorite teacher of all time. Columbine sometimes came back to Sister in after-school hours, as if to ask Sister's advice about something, but really just to initiate another of their warm conversations. Academic subjects were rarely touched on. The nun encouraged Columbine to talk about herself; about her past, her family and family life, her aspirations, personal tastes, and the like. In fact, it was Sister Mary

Placida who turned Columbine into a voracious reader that year.

Nothing cemented their friendship so much, however, as the service that Sister performed the day that Columbine had an "accident" in class. As cool-hearted as Columbine usually was, she found herself on this day sitting petrified at her desk. She had noticed a strangeness the day before when she had gone into Starbuck's house and was standing in the glowing light by the bow windows. A sudden dizziness had come over her, then passed. It happened again later that night, in her room. She was play-acting in front of the mirror, trying on lipsticks, when the room began to swim. Now it happened again.

Columbine was terrified. She could feel warm liquid under her legs. Her brain was going round and round, and the pauses between the audible clicks of the minute hand on the wall clock grew impossibly longer between each one and the next, until, finally, she was so dizzy she put her head down on her arms and closed her eyes. Sister was lecturing at the time, talking about the Gadsden Purchase, waving her pointer up at the big colorful wall map, when she turned and saw the Kokoriss girl waver sickishly and then collapse onto her desk. Columbine had visions of the red ooze dripping from her seat, and of being mortified by it in everyone's eyes, and was tending along toward an unconscious state. The cool wood smell of her desk rose to her nostrils. She heard the drone of Sister's voice and then the usual hubbub of closing books and desk tops and foot shufflings that accompanied the end of classes. Except that class was not over. Sister was marching everyone downstairs to the audio-visual room. Then she was standing alone over Columbine. Sister had guessed right.

"I'm bleeding," said Columbine.

Sister took her to the faculty washroom and ministered to her needs with cold, nurselike detachment, while giving a quick biological description of what was happening. She explained to Columbine how the fright and drama of this bodily revolution was God's way of illuminating the responsibility that womanhood carried, and of how regularly these signs would manifest themselves. The nun did not trouble to ask Columbine what she knew, but chose to tell her everything, the meaning of it and the care she should regularly show herself.

"It's more sacred than scarifying," she said sternly, while wrapping Columbine's soiled under-clothes in a paper towel, then washing her hands under the faucet.

Columbine sat with her black pleated uniform skirt hiked high above her waist. Her long bare legs had goose bumps all over. Sister had her stand up, and came to her and swabbed with a wet towel under her buttocks, washing her front and back. Columbine was helpless. She was gripping the sink for balance. The nun washed and dried the inside of her thighs, while Columbine gazed abjectly at herself in the mirror. She was helpless as an infant.

"Apart from all that," the nun was saying, "it means absolutely nothing at all."

Sister Mary Placida paid Columbine a social call at home on a Saturday afternoon in February. Columbine had never had a formal guest before. The little boy Casimir was staying at the Kokoriss house that week, and it was a sight, everyone agreed, to see the stern, retributive, gray-eyed nun sitting in the living room with the chubby, white-haired boy propped on her lap. Sister said that was quite a story about Casimir coming out of Lithuania in a suitcase. While Sister drank tea and consumed one or two of the little honeycakes that Mrs. Kokoriss had prepared for the occasion, Columbine modeled some of her clothes for her. As the youngest of four daughters, Columbine had fallen heir to a considerable collection of hand-me-downs, and had already shown herself to be very original in working up complex costumes out of her sisters' leftovers. Sister sat in the red cretonne wing chair, bouncing Casimir on her knee, while going into little raptures over each of Columbine's costumes.

The girl showed her a black and mauve mohair sweater that Helen had knitted for her for Christmas, and then there was a pair of twill jodhpurs that had once belonged to Sophie, and after that a green satin dress given to her by her Aunt Teeka. As Sister Mary Placida's enthusiasm gathered, Columbine grew more and more theatrical, striking playfully fashionable poses or striding briskly across the room with her arms swinging like a marionette.

It was a sunshiny afternoon, with a white disc of a sun over the roof of the Kokoriss house, as Columbine led Sister outdoors and showed her about the grounds. She identified the two pear trees that grew on a slant by the cellar door. She pointed out the dry stubble of peonies and hydrangea and other perennials by the back gate. Columbine even showed her the shed where she kept her Schwinn bicycle and where, for years, her father had customarily washed himself of coal grime when arriving home from work each afternoon. Sister nodded and clucked at every step, as though each mundane detail were inspiring a recollection of something personal and precious, as though she might have lived here once herself in past times, or maybe just in a setting not remarkably different.

"Of course," said Columbine, in her usual prim, urbane fashion, deprecating everything in sight, "it's all wonderfully ordinary."

"Not at all," Sister objected.

"*And* very boring," said Columbine.

"Not boring at all! Lead the way, my child. I'm enjoying myself."

130

"Aren't you kind," Columbine snapped briskly, as she shut the shed door.

"Yes, it's been quite an afternoon. Quite a treat for me. Very refreshing, Miss Kokoriss. Very refreshing. So this," she said, "is where you were born." Sister put her hands on her hips and surveyed the house and avenue. "What a *very* lovely place to come from." Sister lifted her hems to avoid trailing her habit in the mud and speckled patches of old snow, as she and Columbine made their way back to the front walk.

Before the afternoon was over, Columbine introduced Sister Mary Placida to Henry's father, Sergeant Flynn, who was at home for the day and had stepped outdoors expressly to be introduced. Henry drove up in his car while the three of them were talking. As he came forward to meet them, he heard his father concluding one of his anecdotes. Columbine and her teacher were already laughing as his father brought his story to a close.

"So I turned around and I said to him, 'If you want to be a Gypsy, oil yourself up and be one, Mudgy, but for the love of Mike, don't try coming into a Catholic church with whatever that is you're carrying. What *is* that?' I said to him. '*A goldfish bowl?*' Whoops!" his father cried. "You should have seen his face drop! He wished he was seven miles under the ground!" Sergeant Flynn stamped his foot on the ground, and popped forward in a kink of laughter. Henry was meanwhile left standing at the edge of things, as his father excused himself and went indoors.

"This is his son," said Columbine.

Sister looked around at Henry with her big lustrous, unfriendly gray eyes, and said nothing, but turned back to Columbine. "Show me up the walk, now, to the other houses, like a good girl."

Henry was left standing, as the two of them pivoted about and betook themselves away, strolling languidly, both of them, up the flagstone path. Henry had never been dismissed like that in his life. *"This is his son."* It was a deliberate humiliation. It was intended, no doubt, to impress Sister. To show Sister how summarily she could discharge people. Henry even imagined he had heard the nun chortle under her breath as they were leaving. He had known nuns like that one before—from his own schooldays—with her big gooseberry eyes sparkling voluptuously. Henry watched the two of them going up the walk past the Trumbowski house, walking in the shadow of the high leafless bushes. Columbine was wearing the black dress shoes with raised heels that made her appear very tall, even when walking next to the tall nun.

Now and then, she would raise her hand toward some point of interest, something pertaining to the houses or grounds along the avenue, while the nun, floating along at her side, would pause in her walking, bob her head slowly once or twice, and then languidly they would resume their stroll. Sister, seen that way through the naked gray bushes, with her black woolen cloak tossing at her sides, resembled a great condor hovering over the earth, flapping and fluttering in the wind, rising and settling.

A white streamer of smoke rose from the Kokoriss chimney. Mrs. Kokoriss was down in the cellar putting coal in the furnace. One of Mr. Griffin's dogs was barking sorrowfully.

Henry had a dismal week of it. On Monday, a tooth, erupting in pain, suddenly abscessed, and that same afternoon his superior at the newspaper, Mr. Meehan, reprimanded him for certain inaccuracies in a research assignment. A tall, stout bachelor, Mr. Meehan was a man of sudden moods. One moment he was hearty and affable, thumping Henry on the back, ribbing the secretaries, or rushing out of the room to play a prank on the boys in the circulation department; but not a quarter hour later, he was scowling and raising his voice. In the beginning Henry had avoided Mr. Meehan; he had learned long ago to be wary of Irishmen of this sort, men who would nurture your trust in them only long enough to catch you flat-footed with a vicious remark. Henry's own father was like that. So was his Uncle Matt. But Mr. Meehan was worse. In his black moods his face actually appeared to grow sooty. When he leaned over Henry and glared at him from behind his big rimless eyeglasses, the man revealed a brutish look that gave his onslaught a diabolical dimension; his jowls were heavy, his meaty cheeks dotted with tiny black pockmarks, and his breath came down in pungent gusts.

"I didn't ask you for scientific formulae," he thundered at Henry. "My reader is not an atomic physicist! He doesn't want Einsteinian theory. And because he doesn't, *I* don't! I wanted three dates for the Manhattan Project, and, God save me," he bellowed, "*you* mixed them up!"

Henry was thrown into a sweat by the man's deafening rebuke, especially as he detected the keen interest being secretly shown by everyone else in the room, including Nolan, the other new cub. Speechless, Henry gazed down at the sheet of paper on which he had typed the dates and details; the paper lay crumpled under Mr. Meehan's stout hand. The tirade continued, with a dark rose hue coloring Mr. Meehan's temples, when suddenly the big man dealt Henry an even more embarrassing affront. "The sad truth is," said he in a loud, controlled tone, as he straightened to full height, "I took you off the Denver Pratt story and gave it to Nolan because I thought your treatment was mush. Just plain *mush.* This is a business of facts! My reader," he went on, again appropriating to himself the combined readership of the newspaper, "wants the facts, Herky! He wants them correct, he wants them in good order, and he wants them now! *Today!*"

On Tuesday, Henry's dentist, Bob Lewis, pulled the tooth. That evening at supper, Henry's father compounded matters when he claimed to have noticed an incipient bald spot developing on the top of Henry's head, and made merciless fun of Henry for an hour. Henry's mother kindly objected to the father making sport of Henry that way, especially as Henry had a sore mouth. Mrs. Flynn then examined Henry's head herself and announced that his father must be dreaming. Later, however, upstairs, Henry employed two mirrors and a bright light in a contortionistic effort to confirm his mother's findings, only to discover that his father's raillery enjoyed some basis in fact; for there, in dim outline, was a circular patch of scalp peering out through the thinning hair on the crown of his head.

Henry lay awake that night with the bloody cavity in his mouth throbbing, and visions coming and going in his head of the man he must someday become. He saw a stoutish, graying figure in glasses with the whole top of his head shining baldly, the face of a failed businessman or merchant, of an accountant or priest who had not made a success of his life; and in it, Henry recognized himself. He felt painfully mortal.

His deepest shock, though, came on Wednesday, at about quitting time, when he saw Columbine go past the newspaper offices on High Street in a big black-and-cream-colored Packard. She was sitting up stiffly in the front seat with her face turned to the driver, whom Henry recognized instantly. Salty Sullivan was a caricature of his time. He wore "glad rags"—collarless gabardine sport jackets in pastel hues, pegged trousers, and pointy spectator shoes. He combed his carroty hair into a shiny pompadour that gave his face the crazed, attenuated aspect of a woodpecker. Known to his companions as a skilled gambler and womanizer, Salty was a near-mythical figure in Hadley Falls. As a boy he was believed to have parachuted from the top of a sixty-foot water tower with an umbrella; he was supposed also to have drunk his own father under the table. He was a boy whom no one wished to demythify. He was a "cult boy." Older men thought him colorful and original, while his juniors manufactured rafts of stories about him of the wildest improbability. Fires of suspicious origin were attributed to his incendiary hand as a matter of course. He was said to own an arsenal of handguns, even though he was rarely, if ever, seen to brandish one. He was fabled to be very quick with his fists; but, again, even in that regard, his reputation seemed to stem as much from his own fine talk as from his exploits. What was known was that he had been arrested at age twelve following a sexual assault on another boy, that he sometimes got roaring drunk, and that he was fearless to the point of being reckless in pursuing other men's wives. To Henry, who was his senior by three or four years, Salty Sullivan was nothing more than a nuisance, a bad apple, a lazy shanty-Irish boy on his way to becoming a barfly and lush.

Just seeing Columbine go by in Salty's Packard threw Henry's mind into a whirl. Strangely enough, until now Henry had never thought of Columbine as physically a girl. He had always seen her under the total aspect of the "girl next door," of the pert black-haired adolescent bundled up in sweaters and mufflers, in long stockings, in woolen caps and gloves, or even sitting at the Flynn dinner table in a black sheath of a dress with a silver pin over her breast, or in the red-and-blue-fringed tartan skirt that she fastened at the hip with a decorative safety pin. That, after all, was who she was. A precocious girl with stylish ways. A porcelain face of undeniable beauty. Now he had another way to think about her. Henry had a discomfiting vision of her: a picture in his mind of her reclining at her ease, a picture of her as, of course, she really was, of her ivory torso and ivory limbs, and, at the heart of it, the soft pubic shadow.

VIII

Columbine's star brightened. There was in Ireland Parish in those days a woman who called herself Madame Muntrum and claimed to have been in her prime a distinguished ballerina. This lady lived in poverty on the top floor of a tenement house in the Polish neighborhood not far from the church and school of the Mater Dolorosa. To her neighbors she was an eccentric. She kept to herself mostly, going outdoors only on her weekly shopping excursions. When she did take to the street, however, she cut a noticeable figure, dashing along briskly through the park on tiny high-heeled shoes amid a flurry of feathers and veils; a look of ruling-class impatience seemed to spur her every step. Her thriftiness among the fruit and vegetable stalls of the Growers' Outlet, where she squeezed every orange, grapefruit, and plum in sight before making her selection, was a tradition in itself. Madame was a fixture in Ward Four. She gave piano lessons to children of the neighborhood in a tiny ground-floor room at the back of her tenement house. This room, which was not much more than a spacious broom closet, accommodating an upright piano, a chair for Madame, and just space enough for Madame to pace back and forth while speaking and gesturing in exaggerated syncopation with the music lesson, was Madame Muntrum's "studio." Every afternoon the upstairs tenants could hear the repetitive chords and lessons being thrummed out on the piano below, interspersed by outbursts of Madame's tempestuous temper. ("No, no, no, no, no, *no!*" she would cry.) For these services Madame charged her pupils a dollar or two; and so far as was known, the woman satisfied the material requirements of her life in this way.

Columbine was taken up by Madame Muntrum. On Ash Wednesday morning, as Columbine was going from the church to the school at the start of classes, the great woman put herself in Columbine's way. Where, Madame wished to know, had so rare a creature been keeping herself? She held Columbine out at arm's length and extolled her "pure animal graces." She made Columbine take off her coat. She twirled her about with one hand, as though the girl were a rare vase being examined at auction. "Aren't you breathtaking!" she exclaimed. While Columbine's classmates trooped past, their foreheads bearing the sign of the burnt ashes, Columbine stood trancelike, greatly affected by this stylish woman with the overbearing European ways. Under the smart, diagonal slash of her hat brim, the woman's face appeared to Columbine as a pale triangle with black, pellucid eyes. It was impossible not to look at her. With a flourish of her bejeweled hand, Madame extracted from a tiny beaded purse her card, and abandoned it, as it were, to Columbine. "You visit me at three o'clock this afternoon"—Madame narrowed one fabulous eye—"and we shall talk."

No tenant in Madame Muntrum's building could ever recall her having received a bona fide guest in her quarters. Not one person, to anyone's knowledge, had ever stepped across that top-floor threshold; and yet here, abruptly, was an adolescent girl now coming and going on the stairs with great regularity. Madame Muntrum's old-fashioned Victrola was now blasting away overhead, with cymbals and drums reverberating, with a soaring of violins and cellos, and Madame shouting to be heard above the din. Neighbors got accustomed to an accompanying staccato of footsteps, to the throb and beat of Columbine's feet as she went through her paces. She was rehearsing her exercises in Madame's parlor, drilling away tirelessly at her basic ballet steps. If Madame had not long ago impressed and intimidated her neighbors with her overpowering upper-class hauteur—a living reflection to some of them of that very tyranny of privilege from under which, in the old country, they had barely managed to crawl out—they might even have complained to the landlord.

"Glissade derrière! Devant! . . . Dessus! Good! *Bon!* Now! *En avant! . . . En arrière!* No, no, no! Not like a fish. *En arrière!* Again. *En arrière!"*

Madame Muntrum smoked black-papered cigarettes that she rolled herself on a little tin machine with a crank on the side and a rubber belt. Her Turkish tobacco came in red and blue tins that she kept in the lacquered chest by the windows; it was very aromatic. After each dance session, Columbine helped Madame put the furniture back in place, the two of them toiling side by side to push out the upholstered Morris chair, the girl then lighting the green bulb in the bridge lamp and the white bulb in the china lamp, while Madame flew about on stiletto heels, closing the faded draperies and setting about the vital business of drawing tea from the silver samovar on the sideboard. They sipped from a delicate white and gold tea service that Madame said was manufactured in Tiflis a long time ago and was a gift of a Georgian nobleman. While Columbine sat sweating in her tights with a blanket around her—propped stiffly on a chair hand-carved to simulate the coiled limbs of an Oriental dragon—Madame held forth on subjects of a personal and romantic nature.

Columbine came to visit twice weekly. Each time she stayed two hours: fifteen minutes of limbering up, forty-five minutes of dance practice, and then one hour of tea and exalted discourse. Madame sat under the green light, appearing very remote and

arcane, while drawing pictures from memory of a
life that had receded from view—a world of horse-
pulled carriages, sable lap blankets, gaslit theaters
and drawing rooms. Columbine sat absorbing it all,
endeavoring never to appear gauche, of course, but
always properly innocent and curious. In time she
began matching some of Madame's telltale gestures
(a flourish of the hand to signify the insignificant, a
slow closing of the eyes to represent some otherwise
inexpressible passion), and grew apt at leading Madame back from digressions through calculated
questions.

"So," Madame would blurt with a bitter chuckle,
waving a braceleted arm to take in the circumference
of the strange green-lighted parlor with its mélange
of curious possessions, "this is where I am to be
found. It was for this that I aspired—gave it all up
—to dance, to achieve renown, you see. All of that"
—she gestured—"for this. That is what life is, my
dear Miss Columbine. Here it is, staring you in the
face. Never be poor, my dear. I should have been
shot to death like one of Nicholas's aged racehorses.
Instead, I live among the lowest element of the Poles.
I instruct their children." Madame's philosophy,
more wistful than bleak, was evident in the languorous sweep of her arm. "I read my books, brew my
tea, enjoy a little tobacco. I suppose I shouldn't com-
plain, should I?"

"I suppose not." Columbine evinced a mixture of
admiration and precocious sagacity.

"This is, after all, where I want to be. Hidden
away! Locked up like an old ball gown. I could
scarcely tell you the name of this city! I've lived here
twenty-five years. I was married at forty to a man of
sixty who brought me here from Istanbul in 1920.
He wanted a place to hide!"

Columbine laughed prettily over Madame's spirited irony. "It seems a wonderful place to hide."

"He found an even better place." Madame raised

her teacup to her lips. "He died that first summer."
She gave out a tinkle of laughter. "He was a very
elegant gentleman. Very distinguished. Civilized in
a way that is forgotten now everywhere." Rummaging
then hurriedly through a trunk of papers and
keepsakes near at hand, Madame Muntrum produced
for Columbine a bridal photo set in a gray
cardboard frame with gold letters of the studio name
stenciled on it in a strange alphabet. The picture
showed Madame appearing diminutive next to her
husband, a tall, lanky man with a blond mustache
and thinning hair. He held a gray cylinder hat atop
his left arm. Madame was dressed all in white, and
looked characteristically herself, very composed and
candid, but a good deal younger.

"That was the end," said Madame, "to everything
that went before it, and this, of course, these rooms,
et cetera, is the end to that." She sent the photo
skimming into the chest.

"Yes," said the girl, unaffected by the woman's
morbid turn of mind, but steering her back once
more to the golden past and Madame's lustrous
place in it, "but you were saying about the Naval
cadets in the Hermitage that summer, the year your
sister became pregnant."

"I'm telling you about it," Madame came chiming
back with renewed ebullience. "I was almost as
young as you, my dear. I was beautiful, too, just as
you are. I was a child of sixteen. There was always
something memorable about the sky over St. Petersburg,
about its clarity, the perfect blueness of it.
Maybe the North gets that way in summer. An arctic
purity. That's what I remember. White uniforms,
young men with swords coming down the steps, and
a sky like cornflowers. One of them, you see, one of
the cadets, was the father, the father-to-be, and *my*
father, *our* father, my sister Raissa's and mine, had
come up by train from the provinces, from Panevezys,
from Lithuania—my father was Lithuanian—"

"I didn't know that!" Columbine struck in.

"—while my mother, a Great Russian in every sense of the word, lived in Lithuania with my father and Raissa and me with about as much satisfaction as you would expect of a polar bear living in Montevideo."

Thrilled to discover this racial affinity with Madame, Columbine pursued her own lights. "I'm a Balt!" she cried.

"Keep quiet," said the woman. "I'm talking. Hand me a cigarette. Get us another tea. Oh, this is a lovely story!" Madame Muntrum selected a wooden match from a box of Ohio blue tips, scratched it, and brought the sparkling flame up to her cigarette in the green lamplight, talking all the while. "Father had a peculiar habit of stammering in Russian, but only in St. Petersburg. In the border towns he sounded like the Czar's own ambassador, but drop him into the great city itself and his tongue grew as thick as that table. Anyhow, we met Father at the Finland Station, and of course, my sister was *holding in her breath* . . ."

Columbine owned at that time a little canvas rehearsal bag that she slung over her shoulder, which contained her tights and the dancing slippers Madame had given her, as well as her writing tools and school books, and the presence of which lent her that casual if studied air of a prima donna on her way to a workout—a certain dressed-down, devil-may-care theatricality of which Columbine was herself by no means unconscious, particularly as that was precisely the way she saw herself these days. It was no wonder that Sister Mary Placida, when visiting Columbine at her home, had found the girl to be rather cool and curt; Sister was unaware that her favorite pupil had entered through her imagination into a land inhabited by beautiful ballerinas and handsome cadets, for Columbine was entirely sold on the idea planted in her head by the old ballerina that she, the girl, was as out of place here, or in that preposterous little schoolhouse on Lyman Street, as Pavlova or Isadora Duncan might have been, or, indeed, as Madame Muntrum in fact *was* out of place here.

What's more, if Andrew Sullivan wanted to go out of his way to pick her up at school and drive her to Madame's in the afternoon, or even to drive her home, in his black and cream Packard (which left even the high-school girls breathless with envy), or if he wanted to wait downstairs in the street outside Madame's house for her, while she, Columbine, kept him waiting a good long time by prolonging her tea hour with Madame—listening perhaps to the story about the beautiful cadet from Tula who impregnated Madame's sister while pleasure-cruising on Lake Ladoga in 1896—was that so outrageous? Andrew Sullivan might have been desirable in the eyes of the girls in a local parochial school, but he was not, by any stretch of the imagination, a St. Petersburg cadet. Much as he might have *thought* himself to be one. As for Starbuck, who was Andrew's superior in just about every way, although not in every *single* way, there was the question of what *he* would think about that. He would probably not be so vain about his white convertible Ford with the amber fog lights and white leather seats, or about ever asking to take anybody for a ride someplace! She could see him in her mind's eye, standing in the dining room in the gray light shining on him from the bow windows at the moment when she felt the first dizziness, when womanhood first began to come on inside her; her priestly swain.

The rigorous exercises Columbine performed at home every evening, a program of "changements" laid down for her by her mentor, had given her a wonderful sense of her body and of the unsuspected strengths hidden in her legs. Columbine never walked now but paraded, aware of every facet of her body working in smooth coordination with every other vital part of her. It was really a pity that other people walked as they did, shambling along with their heads down and their eyes on the ground before them, as though being taken off somewhere to be shot, when they could at least *try,* she thought, to straighten their spines and keep their eyes and heads up. Of course, none of them would ever walk as *she* walked, because she was a ballerina, after all, or soon would be, and it was natural that they *should* admire her deportment, as so many of them in passing seemed regularly to do.

Walking through the park, Columbine veered around the far side of the bandstand, making a slight detour of it on her way to visit Madame, just so that the three postmen and the elderly couple sitting on the bench beyond them would all have an opportunity to see her go by. They would not know who she was, of course, certainly not by name, but they would know by the way she walked and by the casual way she carried her rehearsal bag that she was somebody important beyond her years and beyond, too, the scope of this town and this little park. This more circuitous route would also carry her past the gaping front doors of the firehouse on Maple Street, where the "braves" inside would show their usual appreciation in the form of some whoops and whistles. If Starbuck had just half an idea of the excitement she was generating these days, he would probably come to his senses. If he didn't telephone her soon, or offer to take her for a drive, she would teach him a lesson he would not forget. People like Starbuck, who could talk rings around you, had to be put in their place.

Columbine went gliding past the fire station to the predictable shouts and whistles of the men inside with no more than a perceptible little pushing out of her pelvis and an averting of her head in the direction of the street. That, she had discovered, was one of the funny characteristics of men; that the more you cut them dead, the more excited and demonstrative they became. Walking along the street, Columbine studied herself momentarily in the mirror of her compact, inspecting the makeup she had put on immediately after school. Snapping the lid shut, she swung down her canvas bag, letting it hang casually at her side, where it fell into easy syncopation with her stride. She unzipped her tan windbreaker to reveal, if only for her own satisfaction, the tasteful matching of her mauve and black mohair sweater with her charcoal pleated uniform skirt. In school today, for the third or fourth time this year, Marjorie Piska had buttered up Columbine, but in this case had actually debased herself a little by suddenly blurting out in a voice breathless with admiration, "It's no wonder you're Sister's favorite this year!" But Columbine was by now beyond acknowledging tribute from the likes of pasty-faced little grinds who brown-nosed anyone who would let them, and who really *ought* to be locked up in one of the convents they were always talking about.

Such were the thoughts coursing through Columbine's head as she made her way over Maple Street from the ice-cream parlor where she made up her face to Madame's house. What a lucky stroke Madame had been. For all her adolescent egoism and airs, Columbine was enthralled with the old dancer and with every detail of her fabulous apartment atop the old tenement house, from the old-fashioned beaded lamp shades and the walls of the parlor decked with framed photographs and pretty watercolor paintings to the assortment of glass-encased bric-a-brac, tiny bronze dogs, handpainted candy dishes, exotic vases, and of course her black cigarettes and her green tea and her record albums; and there was Igor Stravinsky's personal signature on the theater program next to Madame's own printed name, and a signed note written to her in that strange Cyrillic script by Vaslav Nijinsky. And, of course, Madame herself at the very core of it, smelling of her musky perfumes, and with her exquisite unpainted nails, and the double and triple layers of necklaces of white beads and black beads and crystal, not to mention Madame's physical poise, the way she got up from a chair, or lowered herself to sit, or turned on her heel while widening her eyes and elevating her arms to express the wonder of the dance—all of which caused Columbine to increase her pace as she approached Madame's downstairs door.

As the door shut behind her, and as she began with composure to mount the steps, wondering at the same time how precisely a ballerina should best carry herself up a staircase, if indeed there *was* a better or best way, Columbine caught sight of someone standing at the turning above, waiting for her. It was a girl whom Columbine recognized at once. Her name was Susannah Kelleher. She had dark red hair and was best known as the girl whom Andrew Sullivan had recently jilted. She was not supposed to be in this building. Columbine stopped instinctively, pausing on the second step of the staircase, as the Kelleher girl came forward in the shadows. She was looking at Columbine. Until the last instant, Columbine felt certain their meeting was accidental; then, for a split second, she thought perhaps the girl with the red hair was going to beseech her to leave Andrew alone. That would have surprised Columbine, as the Kelleher girl was much older than Columbine. Suddenly, though, the girl's expression changed. Reaching, she gave Columbine a vicious, open-handed blow on the face. It knocked her down the steps.

"You little slut," said the girl. She seized Columbine by the hair and began to shake and pummel her. Columbine was shrieking. Her scalp was on fire. She saw the floor go past one way, then stop, and go past the other way, as the Kelleher girl yanked her head from side to side. "Cheap fucking Polack slut," she was saying. Then the blows began to fall in earnest. Columbine was punched hard in the face. She was being killed!

Columbine screamed in terror, but the girl clamped her hand over her mouth and began to beat Columbine's head against the plaster wall. She continued to look the redhead in the face, though her head was slamming back and forth, her ears ringing. She couldn't begin to struggle. She would not have thought a girl—even a much older girl of sixteen or seventeen—could have been so strong. Her eyes were riveted in alarm to the twinkling hazel eyes of the redhead. The look of pure hatred pouring from the girl's eyes demoralized her. With a lunge Columbine got her mouth free, and without knowing what she was saying, cried, "Starbuck! Help me!" The Kelleher girl then finished with three or four sharp punches flush into Columbine's face, followed by a hearty shove that sent her sprawling full-length on the dark linoleum; her canvas bag flew open, scattering her books and dancing slippers in every direction.

After the outside door had closed, Columbine continued to lie face down, with her hands over her head, her clothing in disarray. She dared not move, and could scarcely catch breath sufficient to support her crying.

The Kokoriss house was in ferment that evening. Columbine had locked herself in her room and would not come out, despite the pleas and demonstrations of Anna and her mother. In due course Henry's father was summoned. That was about seven o'clock. Sergeant Flynn arrived with another policeman in a radio car, coming up the hill with the siren wailing and the amber light spinning. Still,

Columbine would not open her door. Henry's father threatened to knock it in, but Columbine was adamant. The house was meanwhile filling up with alarmed neighbors. Mrs. Blye arrived with her son, Nicholas. While Mrs. Flynn was cautioning her husband to show restraint, Nicholas put forward the suggestion that he could himself go around to the back of the house and force his way into her room. When Nicholas said that, Sergeant Flynn looked around at him in a funny sort of way, because the last time Nicholas let himself in through an upstairs window, he was tried and sent to prison for it.

By the time Henry appeared on the scene, everyone was standing in a cluster at the top of the stairs outside Columbine's door. Mrs. Flynn was the only one who noticed Henry's reaction to the news of what had happened to Columbine; Henry's face went to pieces. Everyone else was looking at Nicholas and the police.

"I could go in there easy as anything," said Nicholas, with the modest forthrightness of a true professional.

"Oh, I'm sure you could!" Sergeant Flynn's face lit up. The second policeman laughed nastily and looked away.

"There's a roof," Nicholas began to explain.

"And the locked window," the sergeant piped up in a voice dripping with sarcasm, "would be a piece of cake, I suppose."

"I wouldn't have any trouble with the window," Nicholas went on innocently, puzzled by their amusement. "Any sort of jimmy. Mrs. Kokoriss, you wouldn't have a metal ruler I could borrow? Or a dinner knife?"

The sergeant was gazing at Nicholas with big, glassy eyes. "Next thing you'll be telling me we should call the police."

"The police?" Nicholas was confused.

"If anyone is going to break into her room," the

sergeant said, touching the tip of his finger to his dark necktie, "it will be me."

Here, however, Anna spoke up, siding with Nicholas, saying his idea was not a bad one, for breaking her door in could traumatize Columbine, she said.

"Herky, get me my ladder," Sergeant Flynn called down the stairs.

"Nicholas was just trying to help," said Anna, with a sudden note of fondness in her voice that was more transparent than intended. Mrs. Blye glanced swiftly at Anna, then at Nicholas, and then at Mrs. Flynn, because Mrs. Flynn had shown a corresponding alertness. Nicholas looked appreciatively at Anna. Then he looked at her again, because Anna was looking at him in a way she never had before. Henry, meanwhile, had not moved. He had not even heard his father's command. The news of Columbine's distress had unnerved him; he couldn't bear the thought of her being hurt. He was aware, too, of the irony that he, of all people, was powerless to act; by trammeling and hiding his affection for her, he had trammeled everything else. It was appropriate that she had given him another name—Starbuck—because there was that other person inside him, the one with the secret feelings for her.

Henry needn't have gone for the ladder, anyhow, because soon, while everyone was talking and milling about, the bedroom door opened and Columbine appeared in the doorway. She stood there impassively, with one hand on the knob, holding in her feelings. Her face was a sight.

"I have a headache," she announced. "I want to go to bed. Everyone go home, please."

"Don't close the door," Henry brought out hurriedly from the foot of the stairs, but Columbine closed the door and locked it.

The next day Columbine told her story. She telephoned Henry's father at the police station and asked if he would pay her a formal call that evening. Her manner on the telephone was that of a person of fame and influence trying to pretend that she was just another citizen. Henry's father, she knew, was champing at the bit to get his two big hands around someone's throat, so she was not disappointed to discover that he, too, was making a facetious pretense of being calm and methodical and bureaucratic about it all. They were speaking a private language.

"Very good, Miss Kokoriss," he droned in a gentle, unctuous voice laden with venom, while evidently writing himself a note. "Would seven o'clock be satisfactory?"

"Seven o'clock would be marvelous," she said.

"Perhaps," said the sergeant in that same oily voice that contained a wrathful forecast for some wrongdoer, "we might even take a little drive together across the river to visit some of my—ah—you know, some of my colleagues over at police headquarters in Ireland Parish?"

"That sounds sensible," said Columbine, holding the mouthpiece high, almost up to her nose, and pivoting at the same time on one heel while she stared blankly into the parlor to where Anna and her mother sat side by side on the sofa, listening absorbedly. She could picture the little half-formed smile tugging at Sergeant Flynn's mouth as he savored the fun of giving someone a murderous pounding with a rubber truncheon.

"You're certain, Miss Kokoriss, that this won't cause you too much of a strain?"

"Not a bit," said she.

"We could postpone for a day."

"No, no," said Columbine, pivoting on the other heel, "not at all."

"Just as well," he returned oilily. "Might as well put this—ah—unpleasantness to rest once and for all. I'll have Officer Fleming drive me up to your place at seven sharp, and," he said, "we'll see if we

150

can't bring this matter to a speedy close. I'm sure," he crooned, "you'll have satisfaction."

"Thank you, Sergeant."

"Quite all right, Miss Kokoriss."

"I hope," Columbine added, in an obvious reference to Henry, "that you won't bring anyone else. I don't want anyone from the—from the press," she said.

"Strictly a police matter between ourselves," he assured her. "Everything in the strictest confidence."

It was very useful to have friends in important posts, Columbine later reflected while sitting with her dark glasses on in front of the vanity mirror. Of course, she would have to show the police her face. Her looks were ruined. Also, it would be necessary to gloss over the part about Andrew "Salty" Sullivan. She knew what the police thought of him. A little notoriety was all right, but only a very little.

IX

Henry's father gave an amusing account at the supper table the following night of the way he had humiliated the Sullivan youth in the eyes of a half dozen Ireland Parish policemen. "Him in his fancy duds, with his hair combed up like a rooster, and wearing a big yellow tie and a yellow hat. 'You can't bully me,' he said." Sergeant Flynn laughed between mouthfuls. *"So,"* he said, "I just reached over—nice and easy like—like this"—Henry's father reached and slid his finger down the back of Henry's own collar—"and gave him a nice, friendly squeeze, you see."

At once Henry set down his fork and squirmed to free himself of his father's grip. His face flushed a quick crimson.

"Oh, don't worry," his father crowed, "the boys over there know a trick or two about managing the likes of a punk like that. Not one man in the room batted an eye," he boasted.

Henry extricated himself at last from his father's grasp, but continued to blush in anger.

"What amazes me," Mrs. Flynn put in, with disappointment, "is that Columbine would get herself mixed up in such a sordid affair. The very idea of her accepting a ride in that boy's automobile in the first place!"

"He's not such a boy," said Sergeant Flynn, as he began to salt a glistening ear of corn.

"That's what I mean," said Mrs. Flynn.

"He's nineteen years old," said the sergeant, as he held up the ear of corn and scrutinized it a moment with dreamy eyes before attacking it.

"Wouldn't it be a sad thing," Henry's mother went on, "after all these years, after all her father's and mother's hard work, struggling as they have in a foreign country, and now with the father's death and all, if they lost their youngest daughter to—well, I don't know *what* you would call it. Sometimes," Mrs. Flynn confessed, "*I* find Columbine trying. I worry, too, now that the war is over, what's going to happen next. I really do. After the First War, people changed so. They began to mock everything, all of the old ways, the Church, the family, all of it. This time will probably be worse."

"It won't," Henry muttered.

"It won't if I have anything to say about it," said his father.

"God's world isn't recognizable any more," Mrs. Flynn complained. Her temples grew pink with indignation. "When I think of the families in the Dillon block, when I was a girl, with all the windows thrown open in the summertime and the sound of the singing and the pianos playing, and of how helpful and neighborly everyone was."

"Yes," his father teased her, "and old Michael coming home plastered in the middle of the night and trying to dismantle the banister of the stairway from the first floor to the fifth."

Mrs. Flynn laughed merrily over the memory of her father. "First floor to the fifth," she deprecated.

"And then," Henry spoke up facetiously, as he reached for the teapot, "there were the little bronchial children with their faces as white as milk, dying like flies. That was in the Dillon block."

"Don't speak about things you don't understand!" his mother flared up. Lately, she had grown peculiarly moody, her temperament changing rapidly from dark to light.

"Also," Henry corrected his mother, "the Kokorisses don't live in a foreign country."

"If you ask my opinion," said Sergeant Flynn, working his lips and tongue back and forth over his teeth, "our little neighbor will leave all the rest of you in the dust."

"To listen to the two of you"—Henry's mother colored anew—"you would think she was God's own gift to the human race!"

Henry offered one of his rare spoken opinions about Columbine: "She's different from her sisters."

"You can say that again," said his father.

"The sisters are all lovely," Mrs. Flynn insisted. "Earnest girls, well-mannered and devout."

"They're certainly earnest," said Henry.

"Anna is very sensitive and sweet-tempered," his mother went on. "And she plays the piano beautifully. Sometime," she added, "I would like to hear Henry sing and Anna play. Do you remember, Jerome, when you had the Studebaker, our driving home at night from the movies, how we would all three sing? Henry was only about five or six then." She looked across lovingly at her son, who sought to conceal his embarrassment.

"Herky had himself quite a voice there," his father acknowledged grudgingly, without raising his eyes. "Yes, he did."

"I remember him standing in the parlor on the day he was confirmed, in his navy-blue suit with a white satin necktie and satin armband, and singing for all the family—my sister Ruth and her girls were there, and the Smiths, and your mother was there, Jerome, wearing a big hat with pink flowers, and looking like the mother of an angel."

"She was the mother of an angel," said Henry, with a snort of laughter.

"Never a hair on her head out of place," Mrs. Flynn rhapsodized, "and the figure of a schoolgirl till the day she died."

"I remember it well enough." Sergeant Flynn's eyes strayed outdoors to the garden.

"Henry sang the 'Ave Maria.' You could have heard a pin drop, it was that quiet." After a moment, Mrs. Flynn glanced up at her son. "I think you could do worse," she said mystifyingly.

Henry looked up in perplexity. "Worse than what?"

"Worse than Anna," said she.

A silence fell over the table. Henry had a sudden intimation that his mother had somehow discovered —had divined through her maternal instincts—the nature of his secret feelings toward the girl next door. He felt caught out. A wave of dread flooded his brain. He had never done or said anything to betray his secret ardor, but he felt his mother's knowledge pass through him like light going silently through glass. Before he could respond, however, his mother explained. "I think something is developing between Anna and Nicholas Blye."

"Oh," said Henry, in a show of relief, "is that what you were thinking?"

"I saw them going out," said his mother.

"I'm surprised to hear that," said Henry.

"More power to them," said Henry's father, with a broad sigh, as he reached for his newspaper.

"Nicholas is going to work for the Gas and Electric Company. He's going to learn to climb the poles," said Mrs. Flynn.

"Nicholas can already climb the poles," said Sergeant Flynn. "If you ask me, Mr. Nicholas Blye might teach the people at the gas company a trick or two about climbing the poles."

"Nicholas is a human fly," said Henry.

"You might as well teach a grasshopper to hop." Sergeant Flynn shook out his newspaper and buried himself behind it, with just the tips of his fingers showing.

"There was a time, not so long ago," said Mrs. Flynn lightly, "when I thought that Henry and Anna were taking a shine to one another."

"You did?" Henry affected astonishment.

"I did," said his mother.

"Maybe he's waiting for the little one," said his father. "He's tried out all the others." He laughed thickly behind his newspaper. "If it were me," he added, "*I* would wait. Not that it would do our Herky here any good. That girl will be finding herself a millionaire someday, you mark my words. She's cut from a different part of the hog. Young Herky would never keep up with the likes of that one. You should have seen her in the stationhouse, sitting there with her hands on her lap and the big dark sunglasses on, just as calm and snooty as could be, mind you."

"I say it's a disgrace!" Instantly Henry's mother lost her poise. "I'm tired of hearing about her! I'm tired of the dirty little stories. Six months ago no one knew she was alive. For years, I thought the cat had her tongue. She never spoke, never smiled much, never had girlfriends over to play with. Now suddenly it's Columbine this and Columbine that, and everyone laughing at everyone else, at her mother, at her sisters, at me. I don't understand it!"

During Mrs. Flynn's unexpected tirade, Henry's father lowered his newspaper and gazed across the table in wonderment at his wife. Henry sat stone-like, looking at his plate.

"If you fancy her so much," Mrs. Flynn shot out at her husband in fiery tones, "why don't you kidnap her and take her off someplace out of my sight, to some Shangri-la on the other side of the mountains where fifty-five-year-old policemen make themselves a carnal paradise out of living with little thirteen-year-old strumpets!"

The father and the son were speechless in the face of Mrs. Flynn's fury.

"I don't like the way she walks, and I don't like the way she talks! With her highfalutin airs! There are people in this world who would shave her head for her. If you ask me, she's the sorry example of what women do to one another! And it's all the fault of dirty-minded old men preying on young girls and putting high-and-mighty ideas into their heads, of treating them like little princesses of the palace, when what they really need is the belt. It's disgraceful. Sitting in the *police station,* at her age, with her face puffed up out of recognition, and acting as if she were a star on loan from a Hollywood studio!" Mrs. Flynn got up from the table, tossing plates and silverware into a pile before her, and then suddenly left the room, but continued, from the dining room, to remonstrate. Henry had never known his mother to fly off the handle so abruptly, nor had he ever seen his father look so thunderstruck or worried.

"She treats *me,"* cried Mrs. Flynn, from the adjoining room, "as though I were something the cat dragged in!"

Henry's father rose from his place and went on tiptoe to fetch his raincoat.

"I have feelings, too," Mrs. Flynn added. "I have a heart, also."

Henry's own heart sank at these words, but he could only watch in helplessness as his father, with his coat folded over his arm, went through the doorway into the dining room. A moment later he heard his father talking in undertones.

"I know that," his mother said more softly. "But I have feelings."

Then his father spoke again, his voice soft and mollifying.

"Yes," said his mother, even more subduedly. "I know that, Jerome."

After that, the two voices grew softer and softer. Henry took himself quietly from the room, stepping out through the back shed onto the rear porch. The wind at twilight had plastered his car with wet leaves.

In the days to come, Columbine remained incognito, and appeared outdoors only rarely. When going to school in the morning, or riding off hurriedly on her bicycle in the afternoon, she was always hidden behind the dark glasses. She avoided Henry and never came to the door of the Flynn house.

Henry, too, evinced some mysterious symptoms. For one thing, he paid a second memorable visit to the Besse-Hills clothier, where he spent a small fortune on outfitting himself—not an extravagant act in itself, except as Henry insisted on being shown everything in stock that was white. He bought a white linen suit. He bought white duck trousers and white dress shirts. Even the neckties he selected were specimens featuring spots and stripes against a white ground. Friends of his childhood days—veterans of the war like Cherry Burke and Zekie Ziemecki— watched him go whizzing past the corner fruit store in his open white convertible dressed all in white. (It was to Cherry Burke that the comment was attributed about Henry having "a pin loose in his transmission.")

At the newspaper Henry's predilection for white vesture also aroused some concern, but since Henry was working so devotedly on his assignments, neither Mr. Neumann nor Mr. Meehan chose to express their puzzlement. Mr. Meehan continued to rib Henry good-naturedly one day, while subjecting him to storms of abuse the next. The sad truth was that Mr. Meehan had got Henry securely under his thumb, and Mr. Neumann was not doing a thing to mitigate Mr. Meehan's tyranny. Mr. Meehan said that Henry would work solely upon the researching of articles for the other newsmen—even for young Nolan—until he had learned to respect his facts! Mr. Meehan swore he would keep Henry working as a researcher until hell itself froze over, if that was necessary. Henry did not like, either, the way Mr. Meehan often took him to one side and lectured and berated him, while standing over him and breathing on his face, and making some very strange allusions, too, about men and women, or about the institution of marriage, or about boys and girls dating, or dancing, or of how only a man could be trusted to tell another man the honest-to-God truth about himself. More than once Mr. Meehan was overtly insulting to Henry. "Being a fancy Dan would never cut any ice with me," he once said. "With me, you have to prove yourself on your merits. You have to show me what you can do! You have to knuckle down and produce! . . . You have to make me happy, Herky!"

During this passing of winter into spring, Henry spent most of his free time alone. He spent hours on end in his room, reading the evenings away. He was determined to improve himself, to educate himself, but it seemed, the more he read, the less he seemed to know. He felt sometimes awash in his studies. He was like a sailor traveling all over the world without charts or compass, having been everywhere and nowhere at one and the same time, but sailing on again to yet another unmarked, unfamiliar port. He even thought of the public library as a metaphor for madness, with the information pouring into it faster than anyone could master it, the new books arriving by the dozens every day. He saw himself sitting all alone in an empty room at a long walnut table reading his way furiously through book after book, turning the pages like mad, reading the words as rapidly as he could, turning the leaf, scanning another page, and then another, faster and faster, while behind him the new books were arriving ten and twenty at a clip. He imagined hearing the shouts of the library boys rushing to and fro, pushing their rubber-wheeled trucks over the marble floor, the trucks brimming with stacks of newly arrived books.

In one evening Henry skipped from Havelock Ellis to Herodotus, and from Samuel Purchas to *The Book of Kings.* He read a section of a book about higher mathematics, and a mishmash of theosophy and Egyptology by a man named Ouspensky, and a half dozen Petrarchan sonnets, before becoming absorbed in the opening chapters of a sea adventure by Herman Melville. All the while, he kept notes on everything. Henry even recalled with nostalgia and despair how in his Navy days he used to hold forth brilliantly on the most abstruse subjects in the world without ever having read anything.

Sometimes he fell asleep at his desk table. Or sometimes he doused the light and gazed out through the darkness to the lighted house next door. Sometimes he could see the silhouette of Columbine dancing in the window light of her room. Henry knew nothing of the girl's ballet exercises, other than what he saw in the nighttime from his bedroom window. One day in late March, Henry paid a call at the Alling Rubber sporting-goods store in Ireland Parish and purchased a pair of high-powered field glasses. He hid the glasses in his closet. Then, oftentimes, at night, when the girl's light flashed on in her room across the way, Henry would darken his own room and fetch his binoculars from the closet.

He watched her dance. He watched her performing her elaborate calisthenics and was impressed with the limberness and aplomb of her movements: standing beautifully balanced on the tip of one toe and raising her other leg, stiff as could be, and then sweeping that leg about in a slow, graceful, beautifully modulated arc. Her body yielded itself to the most remarkable contortions. She wore gray leotards that covered her body from her neck and her wrists down to her dancing slippers, and which showed her to possess almost no breasts at all. Henry was reminded by her silent dreamlike gyrations of a storybook sylph, an apparition, an imaginary narcissistic spirit enamored of herself and dancing away in solipsistic ecstasy for her own pleasure. Often Columbine danced in front of her vanity mirror, and when she did that, he could train his glasses directly upon her reflected image. He could see her face in the glass, and in front of that the back of her head and neck, her straining back and outstretched arms.

In time Henry came to recognize that Columbine was conscious of her audience. She knew he was watching. Henry was certain of that because one evening after she had switched on her room light, and after he, Henry, had then extinguished the light in his own room, Columbine had in turn put out her own light and waited in the dark. When Henry at last lighted up his own room again and prepared to resume reading, Columbine quickly switched on her light, showing him that she had caught him out. She did not come to the window, however, or make any overt sign of having discovered him, but simply lapsed into her usual preliminary warming-up exercises. The spectacle became thereafter an almost nightly affair. At nine o'clock, or a few minutes past, Columbine would enter her room and put on the light, and Henry, a minute or two later, would kill the reading lamp and dig out his binoculars.

The dance had become like a rite of spring. Henry was not ignorant of the fact that his alliance with Columbine had, in this way, transposed itself almost out of reality. The garden space between their two houses had become like the little chink in the wall through which the mythical Pyramus and Thisbe once communed in secret; it was the conduit of their secret bond, the channel across which she transmitted to him, in silence, certain obscure but memorable significations of his meaningfulness to her, just as, also, however, it signified a new gulf that had opened between them. He began to lose sight of the fact that Columbine and he had once been familiar together, had spoken together, had ridden together in the darkness in his automobile. She had worn perfume that influenced the air he breathed. She had called him Starbuck. He went back in memory to the look of her face that summer morning in the garden, the slow curling back of her lips, the dilation of her nostrils, or the look of her head in profile against the glowing bow windows the night his mother surprised them together. That was in the past. Now there were these two lighted rooms, like boxes suspended in space, the lights flashing on and off in sequence, and her image coming up to full size upon the lenses of his glasses.

In the beginning her performance was mechanical; she would clutch the back of the white bridge chair with one hand, for balance, and pass through a seemingly endless series of exercises. It was only after a week or so that she began to perform, to improvise, as if her own instincts toward creating variety were attuned exactly to the limits of Henry's capacity to be enthralled by sheer raw mechanics. Henry admired her control. He couldn't believe that she would not succumb finally to histrionics; and yet she never did. She never tried to portray an explicit message, though her performance varied in feeling from night to night. She had evolved a strict format: she began always by warming up, re-enacting the same set of exercises, point for point, night after night, for about fifteen minutes; then, with that out of the way, she danced freely, sometimes (usually) for her own benefit, facing the looking glass, but occasionally, on perhaps one night in three, aiming herself and the total effect of her movements upon the windows, as if the gardens below were her theater and he a favored patron looking on from his box with his opera glasses. Sometimes she appeared happy; sometimes the feeling was one of delight, of self-love; but once or twice, when facing away from him, he could feel, by virtue of her repeating over and over again one specific sequence of movements, that the distance between them was growing deeper and deeper. Her movements were like the syllables of a line reiterated over and over. One night, while

Henry was watching her, he switched his glasses around toward a movement he detected at the front of the house, and saw, in magnification, Anna and Nicholas standing on the front porch, kissing in the shadows.

The older girls, Helen and Sophie, came home for the Easter weekend that year. Henry had not spent an Easter at home in six years, not since the spring of 1940, and had forgotten what a gay, frivolous day it had always been until he saw the Kokoriss girls appear in their back yard that morning, all four of them trooping out into the sunshine in a rainbow of colors. It was the last time Henry Flynn ever saw the four of them together quite like that. The girls wore big hats, and at a distance Henry had difficulty identifying the older ones. Momentarily he mistook Helen for Anna because of the billowy blue dress Helen wore and the big hat with straw-colored blossoms; he was used to seeing Anna in blue. Anna, a frail baby, had been consecrated at birth to the Virgin Mother, and during much of her childhood wore clothing of the traditional blue. Henry reflected what a power of trouble the girls must have gone through that morning to get themselves up so prettily. Sophie, surprisingly, was the most flamboyant of all, bedecked in a shimmering yellow satin dress with a white crocheted shawl that blew in the wind. She wore white shoes and long gloves and a white picture hat, and had a band of white flowers upon her hat. Anna was in pink and red, and Columbine wore a purple dress and a purple straw hat. Henry was enthralled with the picture of the four sisters as they moved over the dry grass amid a spectrum of blowing colors. He thought he had never seen a sight to match it. Their shoes were blue and white and pink and purple; the girls were forever reaching a hand up to steady their hats in place, or smoothing down their jumping skirts. Through the open window came the medley of their voices. But it was the sheer gratuitous gaiety of it all that impressed Henry most, as though the slow tedious preparations inside the house had set off, at last, this overflow of exuberance and sent them pouring outdoors into open space, as magical as the sudden blowing open of wildflowers in a corner of a woodlot or field.

He would not see them like that again. This was the moment of the inflorescence of all their childhoods in their father's house, and Henry, though no such thought touched his conscious mind, somehow knew it. The generation was complete. The last of them, Columbine, came trailing a step or two behind the others. When the girls reached the fence bordering the back of the property, they paused, milled about momentarily, laughing and talking among themselves, alive to the beauty of the morning, a little self-conscious over their own unaccustomed splendor, and started then slowly to saunter back along the edge of the fallow garden plot. Mr. Griffin, stamping past in the alleyway with three or four of his dogs, shouted a hello, and all the girls turned and waved to Mr. Griffin.

Henry didn't talk to Columbine that day, nor did he meet even once with any of the sisters over that entire weekend. Neither Helen nor Sophie sought him out. He saw Anna and Nicholas walking together down the hill in the evening, Anna hatless and wearing a dark coat over her Easter dress, and Nicholas going along at her side, very modest-seeming and attentive and solicitous. The Flynns had company. Aunt Ruth, his mother's sister, came to dinner with Uncle Stephen, and after dinner the aunt and uncle had a bitter family fight. Aunt Ruth's face grew pink with anger whenever Stephen answered her back. She said he was "a disobedient son, an irresponsible husband, and a bad father!" Years ago, she said, he had heard the story of how his namesake, St. Stephen, the first Christian martyr, had been stoned to death, and he, Uncle Stephen, had been getting stoned to death ever since. Uncle Stephen cited that remark as only the latest instance of his wife's vicious tongue. Aunt Ruth then accused Uncle Stephen of drinking away every penny he had ever earned, while she, struggling week in and week out to make ends meet, had been shamed in the eyes of every solitary human being who had ever knocked upon their door. Henry's father, although a teetotaler, kept a bottle of whiskey in the kitchen pantry for moments like this, and he brought Uncle Stephen a drink in the front room while May Flynn consoled her weeping sister at the dinner table. Henry was shocked by his Aunt Ruth's behavior and was inclined to see this pathetic episode as bringing to a close that generation of lively, boisterous, tale-telling relatives on both sides of the family tree who had foregathered here, in this house, year after year at holiday time.

He could hear them, the aunt and uncle, in counterpoint:

"We are the only Irish still living in Ward Four," Aunt Ruth complained in a quavering, bitter tone.

"She's the only woman I know," said Uncle Stephen, "who went through the changes at age thirty. Ask her," he cried hoarsely, "if you don't believe me. She had two babies and dried up like a fig."

Aunt Ruth was quick in her rejoinder. "Between the dingle and the dam there are a dozen gin mills that couldn't open their doors tomorrow morning if it weren't for himself!"

Uncle Stephen raised his own voice in a bandying shout: "Yes, and plenty of good reason for keeping them open, too!"

After the departure of the aunt and uncle, the two of them going out of the house morosely and driving off in Uncle Stephen's 1938 Buick Special, a feather of black smoke arising from Uncle Stephen's exhaust pipe, Henry went upstairs to his typewriter. He wanted to compose something for Columbine, something to her, or for her, or about her. He wished he could write something of an imaginative nature that would correspond to the strange aesthetic of the ritual of her dancing for him in the window light. He pecked away all evening at his typewriter, throwing away page after page, effort after effort. It was only after he had shut off his light and gone to bed, after he had quit trying and lay back in tranquillity, that he felt capable of composing a lucid thought or two. Rising, he tried again; but again, unfortunately, the words would not come. Henry even considered cribbing something from one of his books, maybe some sentiment or other of Jonathan Swift's, as in his letters to Stella or Vanessa, or something even a trifle more lurid. Henry leafed through a volume of the works of Charles Baudelaire. He fell back then on Catullus. He possessed rather a facile grasp of Latin, after all. Nothing, though, seemed suitable, inasmuch as Henry had no precise conviction about what he wished to say. He wanted to express something, but it eluded him.

He paced to and fro in the long, low-ceiled attic bedroom, going back and forth meditatively, gazing out one gable window, then pacing back and gazing down from the window opposite. He was standing in the window that looked out onto the street—the "proper street"—the street on the hill where years ago the trolley used to go past and from which, even now, he could look out beyond the dark hulk of the paper mill to the distant river itself. Lights twinkled on the black surface of the river; a dull-red pulsating glow on the far horizon, in the vicinity of the Army airbase, gave the night a soft ephemeral beat. Henry gazed skyward, thinking long thoughts about Swift and Keats and Gaius Catullus, when a car came slowly up the hill and drew up silently at the curb just beyond the stone staircase that led into the avenue. The car was a black Packard sedan with cream-colored fenders. The side door of the Packard opened and Columbine got out. The time was nearly midnight. The car belonged to Salty Sullivan. Columbine strode quickly along the walk, vanished for a second behind the overhanging shrubs, and then emerged into view coming up the steps. The purple of her straw hat produced a sudden bluish metallic gleam as she passed under the lamplight, then she was out of view.

The driver of the car shifted gears and backed around in the street. Henry saw him. The light touched his face and hands. From the driver's window a flipped cigarette described an insolent crimson arc. Salty shifted into low; then the car was rolling over the cobbles and started down the hill once more.

From the opposite window he saw Columbine striding quickly through the darkness along the side of the house to her back door. Henry didn't hear the door open, nor did a light come on in the Kokoriss house. Henry was so upset that his mind would not function properly but dwelt instead, obstinately, upon little extraneous details, such as the gleam in the light of her purple hat, the purple menacing glint of it, reminding him of the tin-pot helmets of British and Japanese soldiers. Henry couldn't think straight. His mind was in a whirl. His evening's work at the typewriter struck him as the product of a simple-hearted fool, and he recalled Mr. Meehan leaning over him at his desk and breathing sourly upon his face and vilifying his work on the Denver Pratt story as "mush."

That night Columbine invaded Henry's mind with a vengeance. She had become a gleaming blue wood sprite, naked but helmeted, an invention in blue metal, with gun-blued arms and thighs, moving with rigid, machine-like grace through a forest of prurience. At about four o'clock in the morning

Henry rose and went through the upper hallway to the lavatory, and there ministered to his own needs, in calculated frenzy.

"Are you speaking about Andrew?" said Columbine. "Is this," she added, "an inquisition?"

She was sitting in the front seat of Henry's car. He had drawn up at the stoplight by the Post Office, three or four blocks from the Mater Dolorosa school, where he had gone to get her.

"Because if it is," she said, "someone else could give me a lift to where I'm going."

"Where are you going?" said Henry.

"Just continue overstreet," she instructed regally, "and I'll tell you when to stop."

She was wearing her purple straw hat and sunglasses, but while speaking removed her glasses, put them into her handbag, and took out the bottle of Antelope perfume that Henry had given her Christmas morning. Of the bruise around her eye only a tiny blue crescent now remained. Columbine inverted the bottle deftly two or three times, touched her fingertip to her throat, then stoppered the bottle and dropped it into her bag. Henry was too perturbed, though, to be amused by Columbine's adultish mannerisms. She closed her bag, then straightened the brim of her hat carefully with both hands.

"The light is green. You can drive," she said. Her haughtiness was glacial.

Henry continued scolding her. "I should think you'd know better," he said. "You could create a scandal!"

"Couldn't anyone? . . . Why aren't you working today?"

"I'm working at the library this afternoon."

Columbine smoothed her skirt with the flat of her hand while slowly crossing her legs and examining the toe of her patent-leather shoe. "I never see your name in the paper any more," she let fall in a bored tone.

"They don't like my work," he said moodily.

"There's a fib," said Columbine absently. She was reviewing the dashboard panel and then lifting her eyes calmly to the road ahead.

"No," said Henry, "it isn't. I think they've hired somebody in my place."

"Nobody writes articles as well as you do." Her want of concern was empyrean.

"They say I write mush!"

"Nobody *writes* the way you do, *and,*" she stressed, "nobody *studies* the way you do." Columbine was alluding covertly here to the nighttime correspondence that they were keeping between their two windows. "You study all night," she said with a mocking light in her eyes as she turned deadpan to look at him. "I would think you'd get a headache."

Henry nodded ironically. "I get a headache."

Not anxious to arrive at any destination, Henry was driving slowly under the trees hugging the curb. He was not himself. Mr. Meehan had not talked to him at all today. Last week he had given Henry three intimate talkings to, cornering him each time in the vestibule outside the washroom and lecturing him to the point of exhaustion, until Henry's brain was overflowing like a sodden sponge. Also, Mr. Meehan had salted each of his critiques with little off-color asides about the young men and women in the office. He said that Tillie Flood, the telephone girl, had a rump you could hide a sheep inside, and that the girls downstairs called her Tillie the Toiler, not because she worked hard, but because of the way she climbed the stairs. Mr. Meehan then launched into one of his impersonations. Clutching an imaginary baluster with one hand and rolling his beam from one side to the other, he waddled slowly across the vestibule in the manner of Miss Flood toiling her way upstairs. Mr. Meehan coughed and gagged on his own laughter. And while he was speaking of sheep, he said, did Henry know that a sheep's vagina was closer to that of woman than any other in nature? Mr. Meehan was taking on, for Henry, the sordid aspect of a devil in street clothes. There was also, too, of course, Henry's even deeper perturbation over his having seen Columbine disembark from Salty's Packard late the night before, not to mention his own nocturnal excess.

"Somebody," Henry grumbled with a touch of paranoia, "would like to see me sacked."

"Don't talk rubbish," said Columbine. She had taken two lipstick tubes from her straw bag. "Which shade do you like? This one is called cinnamon. Look," she said, and displayed them one at a time. She gave the first tube a clockwise twist and showed him the cinnamon tip. "That one?" she recited. *"Or,"* she screwed up the tip of the second lipstick tube, "the coral?"

"They're both very nice," Henry muttered dully.

"Oh, you're a big help." Reaching up, Columbine twisted Henry's rearview mirror to face her, first peering into it as though to ascertain the fact of her existence, then compressing her lips and looking down at the two colors. "The coral is new," she said. "I think I'll try the coral."

Henry was still nodding and scowling a little. "You should have been born a hundred years from now. Somewhere in the very distant future."

"I'm glad I wasn't born a hundred years ago!" she replied, and began importantly to apply a layer of coral gloss along her upper lip. "I'd rather live now than any other time."

"Why do you say that?" Henry was genuinely curious, being one of those persons who hold the past in high esteem.

"Because I don't see myself making butter in a churn."

"Well, I hadn't thought of that."

"Women used to have twenty babies. They made meals and clothing for twenty babies while their husbands made a big tub of whiskey and rode out to shoot buffalo. That doesn't sound like fun." Columbine spread the coral lipstick, then pressed her lips together. "My mother grew up on sunflower seeds. My Grandfather Balderis had an acre of sunflowers. That's all they had. That"—Columbine eyed herself critically in the rearview mirror—"does not sound like fun."

"Maybe it was better," said Henry, "and then it got worse."

But Columbine was finished with that topic. "I'm going for photos today," she said.

"Photos?" said Henry, casting a quick, puzzled look forward through the windshield as though expecting to see a photographer materialize out of the sunlit asphalt.

Turning, Columbine showed him her mouth; she made a perfect blank of her face. "Do you like the coral?"

"It's all right," Henry said.

"I think so, too." She snapped shut her handbag.

"Where are you going?" Henry inquired in an injured tone.

"By the way," Columbine turned on him archly, "aren't you *embarrassed* at having me in your car?"

"You were in it before."

"Yes," said Columbine, "that night months ago when I went to get Casimir. But that time," she said, "you had an excuse. Today you don't."

"I don't need an excuse," Henry responded feebly.

"Well, some people don't." She looked away with a smirk. She appeared irritated. "Have you ever heard of Laurence Pratt?"

"I met Denver Pratt. I wrote a story about her for the newspaper. They never printed it."

"Laurence Pratt is her son."

171

"I know," said Henry. "He's a little strange. Not strange, actually, but a sort of wealthy idler with some peculiar notions. He wanted to build a museum here to exhibit paper products, not just products from the mills, but all sorts of things that have been made from paper throughout history—stamps, money, books, newspapers, ancient documents. He was going to foot part of the bill himself." It was a relief for Henry to be able to speak to Columbine about someone other than herself.

"Isn't that fascinating," she brought out with a keenness of interest she rarely showed toward anything. Shadows from the passing trees moved softly over her face.

"Denver Pratt didn't think so," Henry continued, happy to be adopting a more comfortably authoritative tone with Columbine, "and neither did sixty thousand other people in town, including the mayor and the board of aldermen. Another time he wanted to inaugurate an international volleyball tournament here. An annual festival. Volleyball was invented here."

"Isn't that interesting? How do you know so much, Starbuck?" Columbine dropped his name effortlessly.

"Because I study all night." He looked at her significantly.

"I guess you must. I admire men with brains. I hope you won't be angry," she continued intimately, while turning to him with the look of concern of a newlywed breaking fresh ground. "I'm going to Mr. Pratt's house this afternoon." Seeing the astonishment leap into Henry's face, Columbine added, "For pictures."

"What kind of pictures?" Henry took his foot from the accelerator.

"I *knew* you'd be furious." Columbine made an anxious face and gazed at the road ahead.

"I don't know what you're talking about," he said.

"Laurence Pratt, in case you didn't know it," Columbine retorted peevishly and made Henry a simpering, superior expression, "is a world-famous amateur photographer. Oh, don't worry," she cried in the hasty maddening tone of someone encountering unreasonable jealousy, "I won't be posing in the nude! *If,*" she added icily, "that's what's worrying you."

Henry Flynn could not keep abreast of these new developments. He had not made sense yet of the Salty Sullivan episode and was already being assailed from a new quarter.

"It's nothing special," she exacerbated matters by minimizing them. "Laurence likes to shoot girls. My dance coach suggested me to him. I study dance, you know." She regarded Henry with a bland expression, as though testing his capacity to maintain a pretense of ignorance. "Did you know I dance?"

"I didn't know!" he said angrily.

In a rare outburst of merriment Columbine threw back her head and laughed freely.

"And Mr. Pratt"—Henry's mind was aswim—"is going to photograph you?"

"Turn on Essex Street." Columbine pointed a long arm. "Turn left."

"You're going to his house?"

"I went to his house last Friday," said Columbine, "and *Mr.* Pratt, as you call him, said we could begin shooting today. Why, Starbuck," she said, "are you jealous?"

The question struck Henry like a blow on the face.

"I would never believe that," she went on, "from someone who's so *busy* all the time, buying new clothes and Simonizing his car, or going off for rides in the evening by himself or with girls from Ireland Parish."

"I don't go out with girls," he exclaimed.

Puzzled, Columbine appeared to lean closer to him by a fraction of an inch. Her smooth conchlike face shone with a puzzling light. "You *don't?*" she asked softly.

"No," he said.

This admission left Columbine authentically perplexed; she looked up at herself in the mirror for an instant, then at the road, then at Henry again. "Then why haven't you called me?" she inquired.

Henry turned on her. "I can't do that!" he cried. "What's the matter with you?"

"Other people do," she replied more firmly.

"Well, they shouldn't," said Henry. That was his point.

The peony color was rising in Columbine's face, invading in particular the tips of her cheekbones. "Well, those who want to will," she said with a sharpening edge to her tongue, "and those who don't won't."

"I won't," said Henry.

"Well, others will."

"I'm sorry I picked you up today."

"I didn't ask you to!"

"I won't again," said Henry.

"Then *don't!*" she cried, infuriated.

Henry drew to a stop in front of the gate of the old Pratt house. Laurence Pratt, Denver's son, lived alone here in what was originally his great-grandfather's house; it was the house in which Denver was born, a tall, narrow Victorian edifice with a slate roof and brown-yellow stucco sides. A stuccoed wall crowned with iron pickets enclosed a grassless yard. The yard was empty save for three tall, scraggy American pines, two of which peeped over the roof while the third stood by itself as in peevish isolation next to the surrounding wall. All of the lower branches of the trees had been severed years ago. Situated in the old downtown district of Ireland Parish, the house was fittingly decrepit, but in styling and size imposing all the same.

Without a word of goodbye, Columbine took her

leave of Henry. This time she was angry. She was not play-acting. He watched her thrust open the iron gate, enter the grounds, close the gate behind her, and pace forth with her longish stride and usual dignity up the sunlit brick walk to the front door. A woman in a starched uniform dress answered the door. Columbine went in and the door closed.

The balance of the afternoon passed, for Henry, in a haze. He could not later remember the sequence of his actions but knew he had returned to the library, completed his work there for the newspaper, and then isolated himself for a while upstairs. He sat at a wooden table behind the book stacks, leafing through the pages of an ancient yellow tome entitled *Skeat's Etymological English Dictionary.* The big book had been in the library for decades, and yet some of the pages, he discovered, had never been cut. Showing a pardonable sentimentality, Henry reached with his fountain pen inside the fold of an uncut page of the big book and wrote, awkwardly, in a pale-blue hand, the names Starbuck and Columbine across the face of the inner yellowed page. The pure bathos of it all caused his temples to heat up, as, continuing, he scratched out, as best he could, a series of Roman numerals commemorating the month, day, and year of this inditement:

IV XVIII MCMXLVI

A book that had never been read, or perhaps opened, appealed to Henry as a suitable repository for the recording of this contemporary but futureless passion. He withdrew his fist slowly from the paper fold, being as careful as could be not to split or tear the page, then closed the volume and restored it in its otherwise virginal condition to its berth on a high shelf. The upstairs flooring was formed of old-fashioned glass tiles, big translucent blocks that absorbed noise and returned to the eye only a dim reflection of the overhead light or of the light shining up from below, and in the glassen face of which Henry descried a blurry image of himself, a shapeless white blotch.

That evening, following a struggle with his conscience, Henry telephoned Columbine. Alone in the house, he stood in the center of the darkened parlor listening to the mechanical trill in the receiver as the phone rang next door. He could see across the darkened gardens into the illuminated window at the side of her house as the girl herself, arriving in view, took up the telephone. He heard then the sound of her voice in his ear. Henry was speechless, however. Across the way the figure in the window light turned to face him. She could not see him, but knew—was certain—it was he. *"Starbuck?"* she said, at last, in a whisper.

"Yes," said Henry, but lost his voice as soon as he had found it. There was a windlike humming on the line, a sound denotative to Henry of immeasurable distances. Henry turned away from the window and was gazing into the darkness in the corner of the room.

"I know what you want," she said in a suppressed tone.

"Do you?" said he.

"Yes," said Columbine.

Again, however, Henry lost his voice. Turning to the window, he discovered her facing him in silhouette, standing in the vertical oblong of light like a caryatid, her head supporting effortlessly an entablature as big as the night itself. If Columbine, who proved herself sometimes to be the soul of diplomacy, had not spoken, Henry might have stood there in silence forever. His mind was empty. There was no spontaneity. Soon, however, Columbine spoke up softly, rather under her breath.

"When would you like to see me?" she said.

X

On Wednesdays and Fridays Columbine went to Madame Muntrum's house to dance, and on Thursdays to Mr. Pratt for photographs. Madame said the photographer would help Columbine. Madame said it was probably good for the ballerina's form; she was not sure, but it was certainly good for the ballerina's ego. Madame did not discourage vanity. Not once so far had the older woman really rebuked her protégée for showing self-esteem or a sudden flash of the prima-donna temperament. On the contrary, Madame encouraged Columbine's natural disposition in that regard, so much so that it was not unusual for the coach and her pupil to engage in toe-to-toe quarrels that blossomed into fiery shouting matches.

"Because," Madame would upbraid her, "I *tell* you to!"

"I will not!"

"Believe me, my little tiger cat, you will, or I'll punish you. You will begin again from the start!"

"Well, I won't," Columbine would shout, throwing down a towel or tearing angrily at the bow of her slipper. "I won't begin again! There isn't room for it here, anyhow, and I'm finished for today!"

At that point Madame would fix Columbine with a cold, black, jelly-like eye and stare at her relentlessly, as if determined to keep her rooted there to the floor for all time if necessary, only, at last, to throw up her arms in a sudden physical discharge of emotion, crying, "She's a vixen! I'm powerless to teach her! Powerless. Very well, then. We *are* finished for today. I'm too exhausted to fight with you. My head is swimming. That stubbornness! Such temperament! What *is* the use? What *is* the sense? She's worse than I was. I just want to sit down. I want my tea! Go on," she would shout, "draw my tea, you spitfire. God will punish you, not I. God and the public, I suppose. I'm *exhausted* over you. What *is* the use?"

Columbine was noticeably more patient in her dealings with Mr. Laurence Pratt than she was with Madame. That was because of Madame Muntrum's affection for Columbine, and partly because Madame kept up a breezy kind of European persona that enabled her to display a variety of emotions without ever being insulting or hurtful. But Mr. Pratt was a more shadowy personality. He came from a family of old-line Americans of Calvinist stock that was moody and shrewd in one generation and half crazy in the next. Laurence Pratt was one of those persons who was more complex than he needed to be. He drove a 1933 Chevrolet, a tinny model with rusted fenders and squealing mechanical brakes, and boasted that every stitch of clothing on his back derived from the same wardrobe he had brought with him to Dartmouth College in the fall of 1926. Strangely enough, however, to this frugal side of his nature he added the unlikely characteristic of despising the workaday world. Ten years earlier, complaining of migraine headaches, he had withdrawn from the family papermaking business. Since then, he had pursued an assortment of interests, such as collecting early New England glass and gaining a modest reputation for himself as an amateur photographer.

The furnishings of the Pratt house were both venerable and shabby, but the rooms were kept in reasonably good order by Mrs. Straight, the housekeeper. To forestall any gossip about herself and the well-to-do bachelor, Mrs. Straight wore a white uniform dress to work. Geraldine Straight had been involved in a scandal as a young woman. Mr. Pratt told Columbine the story. Columbine was surprised at the forthrightness with which he expressed himself on the matter, not because of her own tender age, but because the woman was working in a nearby room.

"It used to be believed," said Mr. Pratt, while sitting at a big oak table, riffling through a batch of negatives, "that if a fellow could show that his pregnant sweetheart had been involved amorously with six other men, a total of seven in all, he could be absolved by law from any responsibility toward the offspring. Too many possible sires." Mr. Pratt smiled thinly. "That was the idea, you see. In fact, that *was* the scandal. Leon Straight tried to put together the necessary seven fellows, and of course, it raised quite a stink around town. It was all very humorous, as you can imagine," he continued dryly. "People were coming forward, you see. Men were coming forward from every direction, in fact." He looked up at Columbine. "Mrs. Straight was a good-looking woman."

"She still is," said Columbine.

Down came Mr. Pratt's head. "Indeed, she still is. You're right as rain there. Trouble was, though"—his voice went up an octave—"some of the local fellows were too anxious, too convincing—oh, men whom she'd probably thrown over, I suppose, and so, in the end, Leon upped one day and married her."

"He was jealous," said Columbine.

Mr. Pratt winked. "You've put your finger on it."

"Are they happy now?"

"He's happy," said Mr. Pratt, "she's not."

"Isn't that amusing," said Columbine, affecting the light blasé tone she thought appropriate in making small talk with a person of inherited wealth. She appreciated Mr. Pratt taking her into his confidence. She liked his manners, too, which were quietly def-

erential and fitted nicely with the comfortable rumpled look of his clothing and his air of absentmind-
edness. Mr. Pratt was a Yankee.

The second time Columbine visited Mr. Pratt, on
the day Henry drove her to the gate, Mr. Pratt
photographed her outdoors. Behind the house was a
derelict garden where great masses of leafless vines
and shrubberies ran riot over rotting trellises, almost
choking from view a stunted apple tree and spilling
across the stone surface of a small dry fish pond. The
old stone walkway was all but hidden. In the midst
of this wild tangle stood a cast-iron bench. Mr. Pratt
posed Columbine in her school clothes and straw
hat, sitting on the iron bench with her school books
on her lap, a picture of freshness amid the wintry
rose vines. He posed her also by the stuccoed wall,
in a dallying attitude, peering wistfully over the
spikes toward the passing roadway. He compli-
mented her incessantly. Madame was right as rain in
calling Columbine one of a kind, he said. Mr. Pratt
was wonderful at making her feel at ease. He was
particularly interested in her life and background, as
in the way he questioned her about the early death
of her father, all the while he moved silently about
in his white canvas shoes, working the light meter
and camera. Mr. Pratt said in jest that if he had a
daughter as lovely as Columbine he would make
sure not to die for a very long time.

After the picture taking he treated Columbine to
a lunch of soda crackers and cheese and lemonade.
Columbine's heart filled up when she talked about
her father, for she realized, only now, months after
his passing, that she would never see him again.
Somehow she had not understood that before. She
remembered the tall, big-shouldered size of him, as
when he passed through a doorway, or the way he
stood over his woodwork in the cellar with a chisel
poised delicately in his fingers, humming softly to
himself one of the sweet alien melodies from his

boyhood. She recalled the sound of his footstep on the porch. She would like to have gone home that afternoon and heard the sound of him moving about among his things in the cellar below. She would run to the door and say, "Papa!"

On her third visit Mr. Pratt photographed Columbine indoors in her dancing gear. She wore white tights and slippers and a new white tutu. Columbine did not own a tutu, and Madame said, what was more, that she'd be a long time earning the right to wear one—but then had surprised Columbine two days ago by bringing out a little white frilled garment and helping Columbine to fix it about her waist. In her excitement Columbine kissed the old woman on the cheek, causing Madame's face to crumple into a smile that was very wide and pathetic. At Laurence Pratt's, Columbine felt proud, not because of the tutu itself, for she knew that even little girls wore them in dance training, but because Madame had invested it with special importance. Columbine couldn't help it, but when Mr. Pratt showed her upstairs to the big empty music room on the third floor, following her up the staircase, droning on behind her about lenses and shutter speeds and the quality of the daylight and such, she felt very superior. She went up the stairs silently, setting her slippered feet down just so upon each step, neither hurrying nor dallying, but stepping along beautifully, with her head high and her arms at her sides. She couldn't help it, but she felt superior to Mr. Pratt. She knew he was looking at her bottom in the tutu and that he was not thinking about what he was saying but about what he was looking at, and she even had a momentary impulse to say something very short to him, a sudden reproof, the way a Balanchine ballerina might be expected to silence a talkative camera bug. Columbine liked Mr. Laurence Pratt, but there was something about him, she felt, that was inviting her to turn on him.

The music room at the top of the house was built as a ballroom. Mr. Pratt explained how the ballroom floor had been laid to allow for two or three inches of sway, built as it was to accommodate an orchestra and a roomful of dancing couples. Of course the room had never been used, he said. Such rooms never were. While Mr. Pratt went on long-windedly about the builder of the house and about the ballroom, using fancy words like "fenestration" and "cull boards" and "housewrights," Columbine warmed up her muscles by grasping the knob of the closed door and executing a series of exercises. At her host's request she identified each exercise by name as she executed it, rather in the manner of Madame Muntrum calling out the commands to her in French. Mr. Pratt snapped a picture or two, consulted his light meter, then peered through the viewer at her while talking quietly to himself. The girl knew he was aiming the camera straight at her pelvis, so she straightened, gave him a sudden reproachful look, reversed her position altogether, and took hold of the doorknob with her other hand, putting him thus behind her.

"Tendu à la seconde!" she was saying. *"En troisième! . . . Plié en troisième!"*

"Isn't that charming," Mr. Pratt commented. Columbine could hear the repeated clicks of the camera going off behind her and knew he was photographing her bottom. "Just imagine you're alone in the room, Miss Kokoriss," he suggested.

"I will," she said snootily, "don't worry."

"Can you stand on your toes?" he called to her from behind.

"On my *points?"* Columbine corrected him.

"If that's what you call 'em," said Mr. Pratt pleasantly.

"I'm not supposed to do point work this year," she said importantly, but as though giving the matter consideration, "although Madame says I rise on my

points easily and naturally. Most students don't."
An instant later Columbine rose effortlessly onto the
woolen-padded toes of her slippers, going up into a
very pretty elongation of her body that drew a soft
whistle of disbelief from Mr. Pratt.

"That is enchanting!" he cried.

"I'm not supposed to do that," she explained
primly, and lowered herself.

"I wish I had caught it on film," he complained.

"You *didn't?*" Columbine showed quick disap-
proval over her shoulder. She couldn't help feeling
that Mr. Pratt was asking her to be fresh.

"All I can say," Mr. Pratt sighed with a shrug of
embarrassment, "is *darn it all.*"

With a sigh of impatience Columbine resumed her
exercises, her back to the camera once more. After
several minutes of warm-up, she began to execute
more elaborate movements, set pieces, little arabesques and pirouettes, while working her way to
the center of the room. She imagined she was a delicate white swan floating silently upon water and
Laurence Pratt was a little mammal peeping out of
the bushes at her. He had taken many shots by this
time and was working now with a second camera.
The straps of the two cameras crisscrossed on his
chest like bandoliers.

"When I'm shooting," he said, "I feel invisible. A
most peculiar sensation."

"That is peculiar," Columbine let fall.

"I feel very far away. You can probably feel it
yourself."

"Feel what?" snapped Columbine.

"My being sort of . . . detached." He was speaking
from behind her. At regular intervals came the click
of the camera. "Distance is the *sine qua non* of the
artistic temperament."

From the tail of her eye Columbine could make
out Mr. Pratt squatted behind her on his haunches
with his face hidden by the camera—first turning the

183

camera laterally and peering into it that way, then vertically and peering again, all the while prating away about art and beauty. Half the time Columbine didn't know what he was talking about, but she was perspicacious enough to know that Mr. Pratt was probably making sense. He was not like an Andrew Sullivan, who used words incorrectly and who swore and used slang to make up for it. Andrew used big words for their comical effect, as in his saying "Indubitably!" or "Copacetic!" He used foul, unpleasant words, too, like "pecker" and "honyocker" and "crud." But he could also be gallant and entertaining in his way, such as the time he bullied his friend Petie Zidek into spreading his coat over a puddle for Columbine to walk on.

She was practicing a port de bras, opening her arms delicately, when Laurence came noiselessly by in his canvas shoes. He stopped, studied her with a half-closed eye, gauged the light coming in at the windows, then squatted on his haunches before her. Whenever Columbine's eyes happened to fall on the camera in his hands, she looked straight through it, through the lens, and through Mr. Pratt as well. She was thinking back on an incident with Andrew Sullivan in the penny arcade when Andrew was standing behind her while she was peeping into a coin-operated movie machine; he had pretended he was helping her with the machine, when she felt him pushing softly against her, something warm and cylindrical pressing in against the cleft of her buttocks. Even the recollection of it left her senses in disarray.

Mr. Pratt was speaking from behind the camera "Can you feel my detachment?"

"Yes, I can!" she threw out brazenly.

She shifted position. She could not see her slippered feet beneath the stiffened net of her tutu, but with her feet splayed at a one-hundred-and-eighty-degree angle she could feel the strained perfection of her posture through the pull of the muscles of her ankles and calves.

"I've never photographed a young girl before," said Mr. Pratt, "let alone a ballerina, but I suppose you can tell that!"

"Yes, I can," she said pertly. She didn't know why he was goading her to be insolent.

"You are certainly a nonpareil," said he. "The old woman was right about that."

In the next instant Columbine, seized from within by a sudden impulse of freshness, was showing Mr. Pratt her tongue. It was what Joseph Kussman, a boy at school, called in Lithuanian the *liezuzis*. She parted her lips, set the tip of her tongue against her bottom teeth, and rolled the top of her tongue up into view. She made a face then and blew a quick snort of air at him through her nostrils. This spontaneous display of impudence, of effrontery and contempt for Mr. Pratt, brought a yelp of laughter from behind the camera, and Mr. Pratt began to snap pictures with great rapidity. He wanted to capture her inner essence at a time, he said, when she was feeling so irreverent and rebellious. Columbine then treated Mr. Pratt to his heart's desire by favoring him with a series of truly disdainful looks, gestures, and mannerisms that threw him into an orgy of picture taking. "Isn't it marvelous how I brought you out?" he congratulated himself.

Mr. Pratt then took the girl downstairs and posed her lying full-length on her side atop a dining table fully set with china and silver and glassware. She lay lengthwise along the table, propping up her head with one hand and gazing into space, with an expression of exquisite weariness turning her lips. Mr. Pratt was beside himself with accolades. She was a miracle, a vision, a delicacy. Pretty as a butterfly. A bibelot, he called her, and photographed her reclining sensually among the dinnerware and wineglasses from a dozen angles; the white frill of her tutu jutted up like a dazzling centerpiece amid the sparkling crystal and tall candles. Columbine's face and hands appeared as translucent as the glassware. He sat her then atop an eight-foot armoire, directly above the doors, with her legs casually crossed and, after that, on the floor again, rising on the tips of her slippered feet while opening with both arms the big double doors of the armoire onto the blackness within. Mr. Pratt said that she was the most beautiful Pandora he had ever seen. He was working with speed. He loaded and reloaded his cameras, stalking about on silent canvas soles, while Columbine gave expression to every passing emotion. She was growing almost exhilarated. At Mr. Pratt's behest she leaned her head forward gracefully and set her lips with an expression of thoughtful ardor against the back of her own hand, kissing herself tenderly. She swung one leg straight up above her head and planted the sole of her slippered foot flush against the wall, while holding in her hands a small leather-bound book of poems that she pretended to be perusing with an inviolate romantic detachment. He seated her in an empty room on a severe oak chair, holding an old brass Army bugle in her hands and gazing off sideways into a darkened doorway as though despairing at last of the approach or return of someone long awaited.

Catching her in moments of joy, petulance, arrogance, and ennui, Laurence Pratt attempted countless facial shots; he took profiles of her neck and head, isolated shots of her hands and fingers, and even a close-up shot of the ribbon bows at the back of Columbine's ankles. When he had finally exhausted his supply of film, Mr. Pratt flung himself backward into an old armchair and appeared to be utterly sapped. His arms drooped like broken wings over the sides of the chair.

"I'll never photograph another tree," he declared,

cutting the air with his hand, "or another automobile or chimney as long as I live."

For all her usual sangfroid, Columbine, too, was charmed and exhilarated by what had happened. Her appearance was quite cool, however. She was very composed and dry-skinned. Columbine rarely perspired.

"Are you feeling well?" she asked in a superior tone.

"I am bushed," said Mr. Pratt. "I am beat."

"You certainly look it."

"I feel absolutely weightless." He was sprawled in the chair, his legs out, his arms hanging down. "Don't go away, Miss Kokoriss," he interposed as she turned to leave, "we'll have some supper. I want you to be here when I start developing."

Columbine paused in the doorway. "I'm afraid that won't be possible," she chirped, and showed him a sweet smile. "I have a date for supper." She regarded him significantly, then strode into the next room and peered out to the street. Rain was falling. Henry Starbuck Flynn's white convertible stood glistening by the gate.

"Well, golly, I'm sorry you won't be able to stay," said Mr. Pratt, as Columbine went past him on her way to change clothes. Her face bore an expression of sublime indifference.

"Maybe another time," she said.

Outdoors, Columbine opened her umbrella, cast a resigned upward glance at the sky, then came briskly down the walk to where Henry sat waiting for her in his Ford. He gaped as she came hurrying down the brick walkway in high-heeled shoes.

Shaking out her umbrella, Columbine clambered into the car. "Sorry I'm late," she piped busily, "but I've changed clothes three times today."

"Where is your school dress?" said Henry, as he detected a flash of green satin peeping out from beneath her raincoat. She had decorated her eyes with a pale-green tincture and wore a set of silver earrings. Her shoes he recognized as having belonged once to one of her sisters; they were spike-heeled with ankle straps.

"Well, I'm not *that* dumb! How do I look?" She thrust her face close to Henry and showed him a blank, sultry look. "Not that you would ever answer." She tossed her umbrella into the back seat, as Henry, looking befuddled, shifted gears and pulled the car away from the curb. Columbine's attitude contained a mixture of intimacy and haughtiness that suggested to Henry's mind that she saw herself now as his girlfriend. "Oh, look," she exclaimed. "Laurence is watching from the window."

Henry turned just in time to catch sight of a figure spying from behind the curtains in a front window of the old house.

"That was him," said Columbine. "I'll bet he's wondering who you are!" She shook out her hair. "He certainly knows how to pose a person."

"Does he?" said Henry in a darkening tone.

"Oh, yes. He brings you out something marvelous. Of course," she said, "I like to show off, anyhow. You're not like that, Starbuck. You're modest. The M.P.—that's Sister—calls that hiding your light under a bushel." Columbine settled herself comfortably in her seat, situated about halfway between Henry and the door on her side, and crossed her legs. "Of course, I like you to be modest. I think it's very becoming." She looked at Henry to see if he was appreciative of the smartness of her locutions. "I think it's better that only one of us be a show-off. Besides," she said, "you like me to show off. In *private,* of course." She favored Henry with a spectacular smile. "Where are we going to dinner?"

"To Arizona," said Henry.

Columbine laughed gaily. "Did you attend Sisters' school, Starbuck? . . . Aren't they the horrors? Helen

188

took me to school on my first day. There were two nuns standing in the doorway. The minute I saw them I let out a blood-curdling scream. I thought they were going to eat me! I've hated them all. All except the M.P. You met Sister." Columbine smiled secretively at Henry.

"You introduced us."

Columbine laughed aloud and changed her position on the seat. Henry was blushing faintly.

"She seemed very admiring of you," he added.

"That's why I like her," said Columbine. "The others hated me. That's because I wouldn't brown-nose them."

"That's not a nice word," said Henry.

"It's true. The brown-nosers spoil it for everybody. Mary Placida doesn't like brown-nosers. Cuddling up to her, that's what she calls it. She beats them! Today she gave Marjorie Piska a vicious beating." Columbine's face lighted radiantly.

"It's not nice to take pleasure in other people's misfortune, either."

"Do you know what Sister said to Marjorie? *I'm going to give you the father and the mother of a thrashing!* And she did, too. Marjorie couldn't even pick up her pencil when it came time to vote for class officers. We voted for officers today. Which was very dull. I voted for myself for president. I got two votes. One from Joseph Kussman, the drip who sits behind me, and one from myself. The funny part is that Joseph was elected president. He got thirteen votes and didn't even vote for himself. It was the first time he ever won an election."

"It probably won't be the last."

"Do you know how he spent the afternoon? Carving out the insides of a horse chestnut with his jack-knife, and then making a little make-believe pipe out of it by sticking a pencil in the side. That was *after* he was elected president."

Henry laughed despite himself. He scarcely knew

where he was driving. He was going down South Street toward the old French Quarter. A green and gray freight car stood shining in the rain atop a concrete trestle in the railroad yards.

"I'll bet you were president, Starbuck. Or class poet."

"I won the Bishop's Prize for Latin."

"Were you ever beaten?"

"No, I wasn't."

"Never?" Columbine stared at him incredulously. "Not *once?"*

Henry shook his head. His reaction to Columbine's appearance, her makeup and earrings and high-heeled shoes, was abating now, so that by the time they drove out across the river bridge he was becoming more focused on what they were talking about. He always found Columbine interesting.

"You must have been the biggest brown-noser in America. You went through Sisters' school *all the way,"* she exclaimed, "and never received one beating? Were you all A's, Starbuck?"

"Mostly," Henry confessed.

"I'll bet you had all the correct answers stacked up," she cried, "one behind the other in your head, like little soldiers. I'll bet all the girls who were brown-nosers were mad about you. Girls like that always like the same kind of boys. Marjorie Piska likes Edward Dabrowsky. Edward has a little round head like a golf ball and a round face with a flat nose on it and he wears round eyeglasses with iron rims. He looks hypnotized most of the time, and he," Columbine stressed, "has never got one licking."

Examining her in profile, Henry felt that he would scarcely have recognized Columbine under different circumstances. The earrings provided the crowning touch. In all, she looked very glamorous, although in a precocious, theatrical way. Henry had a sudden premonition of his being led into a police station somewhere in handcuffs.

"I just threw myself together," she was saying, as she opened her coat, set her canvas bag to one side, and fluffed up her hair with her hand. "Can't you just imagine Marjorie and Edward on a date? They went out together Easter Sunday, to walk in the drag, and then Edward went with Marjorie and her parents to see *Lassie, Come Home!*" Columbine gave out a roll of venomous laughter. Henry would have laughed also but for the chilling realization that Marjorie Piska and Edward Dabrowsky were Columbine's peers. "That," Columbine pointed out emphatically, "is not my idea of a date!" She was reviewing the gleaming appointments in the interior of Henry's V-8. "How long were you in the Navy?" she asked, bringing the topic around smoothly now to Henry's credentials. "Anna said you never talk about your days in the Navy, but *I* thought that was probably because she never asked you. Anna can be stupid, you know." Columbine put forth this observation in the spirit of one whose devotion to truth was stronger than family ties. "Even Sophie said so. When Sophie heard that Anna was seeing Nicholas, she said the two of them together will have enough brains now for either one of them."

Henry switched on his headlights. They were driving east. Night was falling, but through a rift in the swirling black rain clouds lay a band of pale-blue sky, like a blue sword.

"Of course, Sophie is ugly," Columbine added.

"She didn't use to be," said Henry.

"When was that?" said Columbine. "In the year one? Sophie has an ugly disposition, Starbuck. She talks about people in a nasty way. She lives with a girl in Boston and you should hear the way she talks to her on the telephone. She bosses her around and *yells* at her on the phone. I heard her yelling at her on the telephone the night before Easter. She said, *'If you wear a stitch of my clothing while I'm gone, I'll slap you silly!'*"

"Sophie said that?" Henry grimaced. "That is ugly."

"Helen wanted Sophie to be her bridesmaid, but Sophie said no."

"I didn't even know that Helen had fixed the date," said Henry.

"Sophie said a person would have to be off her skin to get married. She says marriage is a trick men use to turn girls into pumpkins. Sophie said she would rather have a good woman friend any day, because a woman has a gentle heart. She says the Church forces women to treat men like big shots."

"If you ask me," Henry spoke with pique, "Sophie has a lot to say."

"She called you a fathead," Columbine added.

This last revelation sent the color rising to Henry's forehead, for he was still amazed by Sophie's rancor toward him.

"She sounds like a lesbian!"

"If that means what I think it means," said Columbine, in an apparent access of maidenly virtue, "you shouldn't say it to me."

"Someone should say it." Henry was steaming.

"Well, that's true," said Columbine, edging nearer to him on the seat and preparing a blank elegant face against the moment when he should turn to look at her. She reached for and picked a thread from his shoulder. They were driving north now, following the river road, driving in the shadow of the mountain. A plane with pontoons passed overhead twice in the dusk. It came from the east each time. It was silver and glittered against the tops of the leafless trees on the riverbank. Henry pulled to the side of the road, and he and Columbine watched as the pilot circled once more for a landing on the river. The pilot appeared unsure of himself in the gathering darkness.

Columbine was sitting behind Henry, looking over his shoulder toward the river. The plane banked in the distance and started across through the darkness with a feathery drone. On the third approach it lit on the surface of the river with a sudden white eruption of water. Henry was kissing Columbine, but couldn't even remember having turned his head. Her lips were sticky. She was perfectly motionless, her eyes shut. The flesh at the back of her neck was warm under his fingertips. He felt a sudden warm swooning sensation. Then the car lurched a little and he stamped on the brake pedal.

"I must tell you," Columbine later complained, "it's not going to be fun breaking this to Anna."

"What was that?" said Henry.

The two of them were sitting opposite one another in an atmospheric little roadhouse west of Amherst. Henry was introducing Columbine to pizza. She had never heard of it. Pizza was new to America. Henry had ordered a martini for himself and a Canada Dry for Columbine.

"About you and me," she said. "I think she's carrying a torch for you."

"What about you and me?" he said.

"Well, what do you *think?*" she said. "We're not going to be able to keep this a secret."

"We'd better," he cried. "I could be tarred and feathered for this!"

"That would be amusing."

"I could lose my job!"

"Don't scold," said Columbine. "Don't think just because you kissed me that you can boss me around. You have lipstick on your collar," she added.

"Eat your pizza."

"I don't like it," she said.

"Columbine"—Henry's patience was dwindling —"you haven't tasted it!"

"Don't," she said, with a menacing flash of her eyes, "scold me."

"It's getting cold."

"Besides, I don't know how to pick it up. You take my portion. I don't like the looks of it. It looks like the chef suddenly got sick. If," she added, "they have a chef. Why is the ginger ale warm?" she asked. She looked around the room with a critical air, at the wall murals showing Italian peasants and fisherfolk cheerfully plying their trades, at the little red-shaded lamps on brass sconces, and at the jukebox with its bubbling lights. The wooden tables in the middle of the room were gouged and pitted with the names and class years of local college men. She and Henry were sitting in a high-backed wooden booth.

"I don't think it would be wise," said Henry, at last, "for either of us to talk to anyone about tonight."

"I'm not *going* to," she emphasized. "Will you please stop harping on it, darling?" Columbine paused long enough for the word "darling" to sink in. "No one is going to tar and feather you." The tip of her shoe grazed his leg under the table. She took a sip from his martini and made a face.

"They'll put us out," said Henry.

"If they do, you can take me to Wiggins' Tavern. How far *is* Wiggins' Tavern?"

"Half the time I don't know what you're talking about."

"That's because you don't listen. You," she said, "are just thinking about getting me outside in your car."

This remark provided Henry with his first solid laugh of the evening.

"It's not *true?*" said Columbine archly, as she put on her most glamorous expression. "All I said was I'd like to go to Wiggins' Tavern, and you," she said, "hit the ceiling!"

"I thought you liked it here." Henry was not incapable of being dismayed by Columbine's disappointment; he glanced helplessly about at their congenial surroundings.

"Did I say I liked it?"

"You seemed happy. When we came in," said Henry, "you seemed pleased. I wanted you to eat something." He spoke to her in a pained, fatherly tone.

"Shall I look at the menu again?" She rolled her eyes.

"No, no, no," said Henry.

"Pizza," she said, "ravioli, manicotti. Ravioli, manicotti, pizza. Manicotti, spaghetti, spumoni, ravioli, pizza."

"What do you like?" Henry implored. He was staring at her worriedly. "Do you like steak?"

"I do," said Columbine smoothly, "yes."

"You do?" He wanted to be certain.

"I like steak very much." She looked away from the table, compressing her lips.

"Shall we," he said, "go someplace else?"

"I don't want you to spend a fortune," she replied reasonably, forcing down her voice.

"I'll get a check," said Henry.

"I know you're not made of money."

"We"ll go someplace else."

Columbine didn't budge. "Where?" she said.

At Wiggins' Tavern Columbine devoured a filet mignon, drank half of Henry's martini, and kept up gay, sociable chatter all through dinner. Over Henry's gentle remonstrations she had insisted on a table at the heart of the big candlelit dining room. By now, though, Henry was feeling more relaxed. The mature atmosphere somehow increased their plausibility. No one in the crowded room was paying them any mind. Why should they? Henry sat back comfortably with his drink, his foot crossed over his knee, and entertained Columbine with a story or two about Mr. Meehan. Anyone in the tavern would think the two of them to be teacher and pupil, he reflected; or uncle and niece. Henry began to wonder what he had been so jumpy about in the first place. After all, he had taken out all three of her sisters. She was the girl next door. He was a respected journalist. Goodness knows, he wasn't trying to seduce the girl! Any donkey could tell that at a glance. Henry ordered another martini.

"You look very beautiful tonight," he said.

"Thank you, darling." Columbine was cutting vigorously into a baked potato. She looked radiant in the soft ambience of the candles. Her earrings and eyes flashed. She was dining busily, reaching about for the bread, the butter, the salt, her water, and smiling, too, at the waiter and various patrons going past.

"I enjoy watching you eat," Henry observed.

"You should have saved your appetite." Columbine flashed Henry a brilliant, glamorous smile. She was tipping vinegar from the crystal cruet onto her salad, while chewing, smiling, talking. The green satin of her dress shimmered like foil in the soft, wavering light. "Are you finished eating? May I?" She reached with knife and fork and retrieved half a steak from Henry's plate. "I haven't eaten since breakfast. At school today they had melted cheese with green peas stirred in. Perfect swill. I wouldn't eat it. Remind me to give you a picture from the batch Laurence took today. *Some* of them," she affected being shocked, "seemed quite exciting."

"That's what I was afraid of," Henry jested. He was feeling better by the minute. He was enjoying himself for a change.

She made him a pretty smile. "I'll sign it."

"And I," said Henry, "will hide it."

"You'll probably have to."

"That's what I mean."

The waiter, a man whom Henry set down as a certain urbane, untrustworthy Mediterranean type, came to the table repeatedly to refill Columbine's water glass. In fact, each time she took a drink he came back and refilled her glass.

"Isn't he sweet?" she said.

"In nature," said Henry, "that's called the bee and the flower. Except he doesn't take anything away with him when he leaves, thank God."

Columbine laughed merrily over that one. "Oh, Starbuck," she said suddenly, putting down her fork, "this is the most fun I've ever had."

An hour later, in the parking lot, Columbine put her arms around Henry's neck, and the two of them engaged in a kiss of mythical dimensions. Her lips drew back in the unintended but sensual sneer that he had grown used to seeing as she pressed against him, fragrant and weightless. A perfume rose from her hair. There was a little wet hissing intake of air passing in through her teeth as she gave him her mouth. She tasted the gin on his lips and tongue. To compensate for her meager breasts, Columbine rose instinctively on her toes, swayed forward, and sank her pelvis forcefully against his. A blue diamond glint of light flashed in the slits of her eyes.

The rain had blown away, leaving a luminous spring night with the Milky Way forming a glittering arch in a moonless sky.

XI

Cherry Burke offered him some advice. Henry had come down with the grippe, as his mother called it, and was laid up in bed when Cherry came to call late one afternoon. Henry heard him enter the downstairs hallway from outdoors and call a playful greeting to Henry's mother. Cherry had not set foot in the Flynn house in more than six years, but he thrust open the front door, just as always, without knocking, and barged right in. Henry got out of bed and went on slippered feet to the stairhead just in time to see Cherry—in his voluminous chocolate-brown gabardine suit, maroon necktie, and size-13 wing-tip cordovan shoes—flirting with Mrs. Flynn. The hair neatly combed and oiled atop Cherry's head was of the same hue as his suit.

"Oh, Charles," Henry's mother rhapsodized, "what a pleasant surprise!"

From above, Cherry's shoulders were massive-seeming. He was squeezing Mrs. Flynn with one arm, then leaning and kissing her cheek. "I'd've come sooner," he whispered heavily in a playfully amorous voice, "but I heard you were living with another man."

"Not one letter from you," she said, flushing pinkly, "all during the war. Where were you, Charles? Frannie told me you were stationed in the Azores. Where are the Azores?" she inquired suddenly, as though calling to mind a point of recurring wonderment.

"Ask my father," Cherry replied boisterously. 'He read somewhere during the war about a plane bound from Rio to the Azores, a flight of five thousand miles. So when anyone asked him where are these islands, he'd say"—Cherry puckered his face into the likeness of a mobile, toothless mass—"I don't knows *essactly,* but—but—but—but dey's five towsand miles from Rio!"

Henry's mother chimed in with Cherry in his laughter, but biting her lip and shaking her head dolefully over the sinfulness of his mocking his father like that.

Henry remembered the Burke household in the days of the Depression, when Cherry's father, unable to find work from week to week and month to month, sat in his rocker by the kitchen stove—the pitted, hawklike profile—sucking on his cold pipe, eaten up with bitterness and despair. The old father never spoke a civil word to anyone. Cherry had once been deeply humiliated himself when he was discovered at school to be wearing a length of clothesline rope for a belt on his trousers. At the moment, however, Henry found himself shocked at the familiar way in which Cherry appeared to be embracing his mother, with his big arm looped affectionately about her, and squeezing her to him each time he laughed. Henry was standing on the stair top, with his pale hair fluffed up from sleep, the waistcord of his pajamas dangling to his knees. His head was hot and stuffy; he had suffered the dry heaves all morning.

"Henry," Mrs. Flynn called cheerfully up the stairs, "look who's here. It's Charles."

Henry was frowning. "Yes, I see him," he replied without enthusiasm.

Cherry visited Henry in his room upstairs, sprawling himself horsily in Henry's desk chair by the window. He was so big that his torso and legs all but concealed the chair from view. Cherry marveled over the dimensions of Henry's room, the walls and ceilings of which seemed to have shrunk into a miniaturized replica of his old friend's boyhood bedroom. Henry, though, was morose. He felt feverish. He sat back against the metal pipes of the white bedstead and responded to Cherry's friendly jibes with suspicious grunts. Henry's suspicions were confirmed in the minutes to follow.

From outdoors came the grinding mechanical complaint of a rusted wheel, and a moment later Mr. Griffin appeared at the back of the Kokoriss house. He was pushing a wheelbarrow. The barrow was piled high with a powdery, colorless substance. Mr. Griffin wore a red and black woolen cap with a peak and a long denim jacket with coppery buttons that glittered. His gnarled stature and the insistent, forward tilt of his body gave Mr. Griffin a grim, plutonian aspect; he had shaggy eyebrows, too, and a truculent glint to his gaze. Behind him, coming in at the gate, was Columbine. She strode along with dignity behind the knotty little man pushing the wheelbarrow.

Mr. Griffin kept a compost heap in the derelict orchard behind his house, and every spring had given Columbine's father a barrowful to fertilize his grass and garden. It was considerate of Mr. Griffin, Henry thought, to be re-enacting that springtime ritual in spite of the father's death. Of course, Henry realized, Columbine might have taken matters into her own hands and gone up the avenue to collect from Mr. Griffin her father's free share of Mr. Griffin's valuable refuse. She was like that, he thought, strange in her mixture of conservatism and license. Henry was sitting up in bed. Cherry was watching him cannily.

"That's a well-looking little bitch," Cherry observed, at last.

Before Henry could reply, however, an altercation broke out next door. Mr. Griffin, it was obvious, was determined to spread the fertilizer, but Columbine was opposing him in her usual overbearing manner.

They were contending for the shovel. Columbine managed finally to wrest the shovel from Mr. Griffin's hands, but the old man began to scold her in rising tones. He took off his cap and wiped his forehead with his sleeve. Columbine paused to listen to him, but it was apparent from her superior air, with one fist planted on her hip, that she was showing him the forebearance of an aristocratic lady toward a loyal peasant. She was wearing green shorts and a blue sweatshirt, which emphasized the slenderness of her neck and legs. Next to Mr. Griffin she looked tall and skinny as a bird. Then she was speaking. She was speaking crisply to Mr. Griffin. It was apparent to Henry and his friend that Columbine was dismissing Mr. Griffin.

Suddenly the old man lost his temper. *"You cahn't do that!"* He shouted in a thick brogue: "You'll break your damned fool back, girl!" An instant later Mr. Griffin and Columbine were wrestling for the shovel. Cherry let out a whoop of laughter.

"Look at the old geezer!" he cried. "Look at him, Herk! Look at him!" Without taking his eyes from the spectacle in the garden, Cherry drew a whiskey bottle from his suit-coat pocket and unscrewed the top.

For the first time Columbine's voice came ringing up through the vibrant spring air. "I demand you give me that shovel!"

Mr. Griffin had the shovel in one hand and was struggling to subdue Columbine with the other, his big, rasping, hornlike voice sounding almost inhuman. He finally got his free arm around her waist, although Columbine continued thrashing about to free herself. *"You're a very bahd girl!"* he was bellowing.

The dispute ended with Mr. Griffin helping Columbine to turn over the earth in the garden. When Henry realized what was happening, he couldn't help feeling proud of the girl. It reflected in her makeup the presence of an ingredient that nature had denied her sisters. None of the three older girls possessed the breadth of character that sent Columbine outdoors on this sunny spring afternoon to prepare her father's garden. But there they were, she and Mr. Griffin, down in the garden, taking turns with the shovel.

Henry accepted the whiskey bottle proffered him by his friend, took a sip, and gave it back. Cherry began to explain then the purpose of his visit. It seemed that Henry had become the subject of certain scandalous stories in circulation.

"Mind you," said Cherry, "it doesn't mean a blessed thing to me."

"Go on," said Henry in a deathly voice.

"We were never any great shakes with the ladies, you and I. Am I telling you the truth?"

A ruby band of color had appeared on Henry's sallow forehead. "Go on," he said.

"Somebody told Zekie that you were seeing that girl." Cherry pointed with the bottle. "*That* girl."

Henry sat up in bed with a slapped expression. "That's the most preposterous thing I've ever heard!" he said.

"I *know* that. Don't you think I know that? Of course, I know it."

"Zekie has a rotten dirty mind," said Henry.

"You're just learning that?" Cherry laughed thickly and gazed out the window. "Zekie calls her the girl with the flashy twat."

Henry closed his eyes and brought his hand up to his head. He had not realized the extent of human vice until now.

"Zekie says you could balance a grapefruit on it."

"Is that what Zekie says?" was Henry's bitter retort.

"You should hear the story he tells about Fitter and his sister."

"I don't want to hear about it."

Cherry chuckled thickly. "Fitter's sister bought a saddle horse—"

"I don't want to hear about it!"

"Zekie's mind is in the gutter, anyhow."

"You're just learning that?" Henry cried.

"Zekie has an aunt who's a sword swallower, and he says she ate her husband from head to toe." Cherry gave a bark of laughter. "They were only married two days. The uncle said if she could swallow a sword she could sure as hell swallow him, and Zekie says she did, too, right on the spot, clothes and all."

"Zekie has a filthy, corrupt mind." Henry was indignant.

"I offered to buy him a milk shake at the Spa last night, and he said, 'No, thanks, I'm dating Mimi Silver now.'" Cherry gestured to signify surfeit, then fell into such a fit of merriment that he lost control of his breathing and began to emit wet whickering noises while tossing himself from side to side on his chair.

"And I suppose you're a party to this conspiracy?" The flesh of Henry's face had taken on a lemony hue against the whiteness of the bedstead and wall. Pinpoints of paranoia shone in his eyes. "People with minds like that," he said bitterly, "are spreading stories about me. I've known her since she was a baby!"

"Nobody is blaming you," said Cherry. "After all, a poke is a poke. She's a well-looking bitch."

"I gave her a ride home from town one night. I had the top down."

"Yes, I know," Cherry confirmed swiftly, "but, for God's sake, Herk, if she's wearing jewelry and a party dress and high-heeled shoes and is sitting in the middle of the front seat looking like Hedy Lamarr, people will talk. You must have been scorched."

"I was drinking a little," Henry allowed, his mind racing now as he recognized the scope of the rumors.

Cherry made a face, uncapped his bottle, drank, and set his fist to his mouth. "I wouldn't worry about it." He laughed softly. "Nobody believes it. You can always tell whether or not someone believes the story he's telling you because if he believes the story himself he laughs before he tells it, but if he doesn't believe it he laughs at the end."

Henry pondered this homely wisdom while reaching to accept Cherry's bottle. "But you," he said, at length, "laughed at the beginning."

"I was talking about Zekie and the others." Cherry smiled.

Henry drank and grimaced. "Then only you believe it."

"I didn't say that."

"But it follows by logic."

"You and I were best friends. We served at the Mass together, Herk. I know you have a crazy streak in you. Listen," he said, "I've seen you eat grasshoppers. I've seen you chew them up in your mouth." Cherry lapsed into suppressed mirth.

Henry, however, did not laugh. "You always mention that," he said peevishly. "I was about ten years old."

"You ate a praying mantis in high school." Cherry came right back in a melodious rebuttal. "Am I lying," he said, "or telling the truth?"

"That's a lie."

"Father Nicholson said there was a five-dollar fine in Massachusetts for anyone caught destroying a praying mantis, and Oakey brought one to Mechanical Drawing and you ate it, Herky." A whistling snicker escaped Cherry, and he began to sway his head to and fro in amusement.

"I don't see any bearing in that," Henry replied with the same note of chagrin and petulance that always set his friend to twitting him all the more. Henry had been the butt of Cherry's sardonic humor for as long as he could remember, but Cherry's witty onslaught this afternoon, on the occasion of their first face-to-face meeting in six years, was unwelcome. For one thing, Henry saw himself as a sober-minded, hard-working journalist now, a man of the world, even perhaps an intellectual. He hadn't time any more to frequent the corner fruit store, or the taste for joining the regular Saturday-night forays into the Ireland Parish bars, especially the fighting bars, and the long nights of hard drinking and fistfights; he had seen them, in bloodied, torn white shirts, hanging over the marble counter at the corner store on Sunday mornings, with swollen faces and loosened teeth, ordering "eggth and toatht" in snarling, incoherent voices. Cherry's skinned knuckles attested to his own want of innocence in that regard. Henry was not like that.

"You can't just drive down High Street with a little bitch like that and not start people talking. Take her off in the toolies," Cherry said. "After all, you did take out all her sisters. You ought to get first shot. How's the leg?" he asked suddenly.

Henry nodded morosely. His mind was going in circles.

"Thank God for that," said Cherry. "You remember Bonus Bob, don't you? The old-timer who got gassed in France? *He* had that leg, you know. It never went away." Cherry drank. "The limp, I mean. That was why they called him Bonus. From the check in the mail every month. Why," said Cherry deprecatingly, "that man wouldn't have gone to work if they stripped him naked and beat him with sticks."

"He's all right," said Henry, recalling the man in question as a guiltless, pathetic figure whose only crime, to Henry's thinking, was the misfortune of being caught in the midst of a killing mayhem in a foreign country.

"He's more than all right," sang Cherry, "he's got a wife that works fifty-two weeks a year, keeps his house, and gives him breakfast and supper every day. And judging by the look of her, probably gives him some nice warm nookie on a regular basis, too. I'd call that all right."

Henry turned away and looked at the wall.

Cherry puffed from his cigarette. "The old woman's got a leg on her. I've seen her on the Mount Holyoke bus. You know her, Herk."

"She's about fifty," said Henry. He was not looking at Cherry. He was looking at the wall. He wished Cherry would leave. Henry lay with his back to the windows. Outdoors, Mr. Griffin was showing Columbine how to prepare the soil for planting. They stood together in the sunlight. Henry was thinking about her. He wished she were in the room. He was having love feelings. He was bored with his old friend.

"How old is she?" asked Cherry, as if reading Henry's thoughts, as he raised his cigarette to his lips with a studied motion. "About thirteen?" He squinted at Henry through the web of smoke ascending from his lips. "Take her out by the car tracks, by the old German club. It's beautiful out there. Tell her you have something important to talk about. Take her in the woods."

"Thanks, Cher."

"Do it by the numbers. The important thing is to keep her in the dark. Tell her you want to look after her. Her father died, didn't he? Put your arm around her. Begin to rub her a little with your hands."

"Oh, for Chrissake." Henry rolled onto his back and looked at the ceiling.

From time to time Cherry paused to send a swift, stealthy glance toward the door and stairway. "But once you start, Herk, don't stop," he whispered. "You'll never get a second chance. Do you know why? Because she won't know what she was afraid of, and she'll hate you for it. Once you get down to it," he stressed, "really lay it to her."

"And that's your advice," said Henry in a thin, querulous voice.

Nodding, Cherry ticked off the essential points on his fingers. "Do it by the numbers. Do it far away. And don't quit!"

In the garden below, Mr. Griffin had resumed turning over the soil while Columbine raked. She handled the rake awkwardly while the knotted man beside her moved with a steady, purposeful, rhythmic motion. Behind them, the windows of Columbine's house glittered like mirrors.

"After the first time, she'll be like putty in your hands." Cherry laughed lustfully. "You'll be Mr. Wonderful."

Cherry finished his whiskey and dropped his cigarette sizzling into the bottle. Henry was sitting listlessly against the pillows, his arms at his sides, inert as a mannequin. The look on Cherry Burke's face dismayed him.

"Once you're inside her, Herk, you won't believe it. Ask Fitter. If there's anybody who knows, it's Fitter. Am I telling you the truth?"

Henry, however, was finished talking.

"At that age, they're tight as a gorilla," said Cherry.

XII

Nearly every afternoon that week Columbine worked in her father's garden, while Henry, lying ill in bed, watched her. She was regular as clockwork. Promptly at four o'clock, after arriving home from school, she would appear outdoors, coming down the porch steps in her green shorts and blue sweatshirt. Each day she worked steadily until twilight, about two hours later. Sometimes Mr. Griffin looked in on her. Columbine would put up her tools very methodically and wait for Mr. Griffin to come to her. She would stand before him, striking the same rigid, comfortable pose that made people standing near her appear a little shapeless or out of focus, a flawless bearing that carried with it a sense of her centricity. If Mr. Griffin bent down to root out a dandelion with his jackknife, or thrust the blade of his hand into the soft loam at the edge of the garden while expanding on some point of horticultural interest, an impartial observer, Henry felt, would not be watching Mr. Griffin so much as he would be watching Columbine watching Mr. Griffin—to see whether she approved of what he was doing or saying, or whether, perhaps, she might not dismiss the effort (as she sometimes did) by turning away from him and starting a new subject altogether, thus leaving Mr. Griffin to collect himself, get to his feet, dust off his hands, and then have to come all the way around her once more, to get in front of her, to get back into the picture, back into focus.

Henry was also given reason that week to suspect that Columbine was probably not an animal lover, for on one occasion when Mr. Griffin stopped by, accompanied by three of his hounds, she was quick to show her displeasure with them. One of the beagles got underfoot just as she was turning on her heel to watch Mr. Griffin going past her, opening out a carpenter's six-foot rule, and she actually stamped her foot. Henry sat up in bed in delight. He had never seen a person so vexed as to stamp a foot. Mr. Griffin was measuring out and marking imaginary rows in Columbine's garden and failed to notice her sudden fury. She didn't move a muscle but stared icily at the offending dog. Until then, the three dogs had been moiling about on the grass, impatient to be gone, but now all three, one after the other, withdrew and flopped down sulkily, dropping their heads onto their forepaws, while Columbine continued to glare at them, as though daring them to behave like dogs in her presence.

On Friday afternoon Columbine called on Henry. She came to the back door of the house at dusk and rapped on the doorjamb and called in through the screen to Mrs. Flynn. She'd heard, she said, that Henry was down with the grippe and wondered if she might not help in some way. Unknown to Henry, Columbine had been waiting for him to communicate with her. As she had not seen him since their "evening out," Henry's silence had begun taking on peculiar dimensions. Concerned, Columbine took matters in hand and went to his house. When Henry's mother came to the door, however, with just the dim oval of her face showing through the screen in the twilight, Columbine felt a chill. The encounter was an unfortunate one for Columbine. Henry's mother had lately begun to exhibit symptoms of change in her psychological outlook; she was growing secretive and suspicious. She kept to herself more than usual and she cried easily. She complained that the deliverymen and local merchants were cheating her, and spent a lot of time going through her drawers and closets in search of misplaced articles—valueless things, as a rule, which she said "could not have walked away." When others were about, Mrs. Flynn was able to force back these strange, sinister feelings, even though it was precisely this type of self-control that might wind up in a sudden crying jag. She was more freely herself when alone. When Columbine came to the back door that afternoon, Mrs. Flynn was in the living room, kneeling on the carpet, going through hundreds of photographs. The empty cedar chest nearby attested to the scope of her search. The floor about her was awash with photo albums and loose pictures. She was missing a picture. Somehow Mrs. Flynn knew it would be missing even before she started hunting for it.

"I thought," said Columbine, speaking through the screen, "that I might go to the library for him, if he'd like, or even run an errand to the newspaper. Tomorrow is Saturday," she continued, when Mrs. Flynn merely gazed back blankly at her, "and I'll be free."

Mrs. Flynn's face hung spectrally in the gloom just inside the kitchen door. Perplexed by her neighbor's eerie reticence, Columbine stood stock-still in the twilight, waiting for a reply to materialize. Mrs. Flynn would neither speak nor open the door. Columbine waited. Mrs. Flynn was staring at her.

"Is something wrong?" said the girl.

In the past week she had developed her first possessive feelings toward Henry. She found herself during school hours scrawling his name and hers— Starbuck and Columbine—in flourishes of green ink, or violet, in her textbooks. She rehearsed the smart subjects she would broach the next time they were together. Of course, she saw herself and Henry as being very much above the multitude. She was so uppity in class these days, in fact, so disdainful and overbearing toward the pupils around her, even sassing Mary Placida once or twice, that she came within an eyelash of receiving her first licking of the year. ("I didn't answer you," she snapped at Sister, with fire in her eyes, "because I didn't *want* to answer!" This reply stunned Sister and cast a stony hush over the class. Sister blushed furiously and sought to conceal her wounded feelings behind a frozen, crooked smile. To avoid having to thrash her favorite pupil, the poor nun hastily produced a stratagem, explaining that the class was going to be given a proof of the reality of miracles this afternoon by actually *seeing one*—for it was only by the agency of a miracle, said Sister, that *someone* in the room was not being "severely rebuked for her impudence.")

Henry's mother, however, was another matter altogether. Columbine had lately detected a vein of malice in Mrs. Flynn's attitude toward her. She guessed that Mrs. Flynn's ill feelings arose from jealousy. She had sensed this on a deep, instinctive level and had made up her mind to deal with it by being outwardly even more respectful than usual to the older woman. After all, Columbine felt, a day would come when Mrs. Flynn would learn about her and her son, and it was always good to prepare in advance for events of such moment. Columbine was wise enough in her adolescent heart to suspect that when that day arrived, Mrs. Flynn would *not* be thrilled over the news. There was, in Mrs. Flynn, a hidden, deep-down current of superiority feelings— feelings of her own superiority, and of the superiority of her family over Columbine's, which the older woman tried to hide but which Columbine sensed and which she knew she must someday eradicate. But for now she would present herself as the bright, comely, hard-working, respectful girl next door. Ultimately there would be a showdown, which she, Columbine, would easily win, after which Mrs. Flynn would retire to lick her wounds, taking her place modestly behind the scenes, probably even as a wellwisher, for the older woman was not at heart a bitter type. Columbine had worked it out. In fact, when she went to the door to ask about Henry's health and to offer her services, it was also to open a new era between herself and Mrs. Flynn. For one thing, she was going to ask Mrs. Flynn if they mightn't start playing Parcheesi again, just the two of them. Columbine loathed the game, but saw it as a vehicle for advancing her purposes. What she could never have guessed, though, was that Mrs. Flynn was crazy that evening.

"What are you planting?" said Mrs. Flynn, at last, through the screen, in a sinister, recriminatory whisper. *"Forget-me-nots?"*

Columbine could not remember a time when she had not been coming onto this porch to knock upon this door, as when sent by her mother during the food-rationing war years to borrow a cup of sugar or a little flour or coffee, or to deliver a plate of freshly baked biscuits covered in waxed paper, or for any of a hundred innocent childish reasons; but never once had she been greeted with such unconcealed distaste. Columbine was speechless. She felt a chill. She gaped at her.

"I know your tricks," said Mrs. Flynn, with a glimmer in her eye. "I know what you're up to every minute of the day." She brought her face close to the screen. "Whose picture have you planted in your garden this year?" she asked eerily. "Mine?"

After Mrs. Flynn had closed the inner door, shutting it tightly, and gone back to the parlor and knelt down in the lamplight on the carpet to resume her search among the sea of family pictures spread about her on the floor, Columbine wandered home in a daze. She guessed, naturally enough, that Mrs. Flynn had got wind of what was going on between her son and herself, and was horrified. Columbine was haunted all that evening by the memory of the spectral face in the doorway. Shortly after supper, Anna went out to the movies with Nicholas Blye, leaving Columbine and her mother alone in the house. Mrs. Kokoriss sat in the front room, pretending as always to be reading the evening paper, even though she was effectively illiterate and struggled just to make sense of the captions under the pictures, while Columbine withdrew to her room upstairs. She had the willies all evening. To make matters worse, there was a rumor going around that a madman had escaped from the state hospital for the insane and was at large in a nearby town. The man was alleged to have destroyed more than a dozen of his father's milk cows by slicing off their udders with a knife, the mere thought of which turned her insides to jelly.

She wished someone else were in the house. She wished Starbuck were here. Someone to take her father's place tonight. Her father should have been sleeping in his bed across the hall. She visualized him, lying on his back, his rocklike face, his chest filling up with air, his breathing stirring the gray-black hairs in his nostrils. He was like granite. Later, in bed, after Anna had come home, Columbine forgot about Mrs. Flynn and about the madman with the butcher knife, and curled up out of sight and fondled herself with her fingers. She drifted in a warm, sleeplike state. She was both dreaming and waking. She was standing over a coin-in-the-slot movie viewer at the amusement park, with someone pressing warmly against her from behind, but it was not Andrew, it was Starbuck, and he was wearing his Navy whites. He was leaning over her with one arm fitted snugly around her waist and his hand tucked comfortably under her pelvis, as he reassured her about his mother. He was talking under his breath while she peered into the viewer. He was saying things to her in Latin, soft, alien intonations, while caressing her with his fingers. She knew what he was saying but could not understand any of the words.

It sounded holy and loving. She fell asleep with her knees drawn up, her arm about the pillow, and one longish, slender foot jutting out of the bedcovers in the moonlight.

Several days went by before Columbine next caught sight of Henry. Unknown to her, he had gone to Boston with Mr. Meehan to attend a convention of New England publishers. Henry had never before been in Boston and would have enjoyed himself thoroughly if Mr. Meehan hadn't had six or eight drinks in the hotel bar each afternoon and then inflicted himself on Henry for hours on end, burning his ears with stories that bored and exasperated him. Henry did not want to hear Mr. Meehan's ghoulish description of the hundreds of charred bodies he had seen extricated after the Coconut Grove fire, or of how in 1940 a female descendant of Cotton Mather was arrested as a whore in Scollay Square. Henry was offended, too, by the older man's constant recurring in his speech and anecdotes to sexual phenomena of a male nature, as to catamites and pederasts and eunuchs. Nor was Henry amused to be told that the vocal talents which he, Henry, had possessed as a choirboy might never have lapsed at all, but for the want of a little surgical incision before puberty. Mr. Meehan had known for months about Henry's reputation as a boy tenor and was forever ragging him about it. He made references from morning to night to Henry's "silver throat," to his "lilies," his "tonsils," his "pipes." Mr. Meehan went so far as to say that a tenor in the Navy must be the most popular man aboard ship.

Henry had been teased and needled all his life, but Mr. Meehan's innuendoes seemed to strike at his manhood. Late one afternoon in Boston, Mr. Meehan took Henry for a ride in one of the swan boats in the Public Gardens and dismayed the younger man by constantly thumping him on the back and slapping his leg. Every time, too, that Henry opened his mouth to say anything, as to make perhaps an evasive reply to one of Mr. Meehan's off-color witticisms, Mr. Meehan's meat-colored face and pale, azoic eyes would light up and he would throw himself about in a paroxysm of laughter, as if Henry had said something incredibly comical. The older man had a habit, too, of thrusting his fist into his crotch every time he popped forward with laughter. By the time Henry got home from Boston, about midnight Thursday evening, he was exhausted. He went straight from the newspaper to Jockamy's Bar. He had forgotten all about his resolution never to patronize again the establishment that employed Dolly McKenna's husband. Henry was, however, shaken that evening. When Mr. McKenna brought Henry his gin, and expressed his pleasure at seeing him again, Henry was unable to respond with reciprocal good humor. He was pale. He sat at the bar, in his gray Glen-plaid suit, with his royal-blue necktie showing to effect against his snowy shirt, and tried to quell the trembling of his fingers. He looked ghastly.

During the three-hour drive home from Boston, at a dark stretch of the road somewhere in the Brookfields, Mr. Meehan had asked Henry to stop the car. Mr. Meehan got out of the Ford to relieve himself. He was drinking all the while and had the bottle with him when he got out. He called Henry out of the car, supposedly in order not to interrupt the flow of his conversation. Mr. Meehan then offered Henry the bottle. He was standing on the opposite side of the car, with his head turned partially toward Henry. Mr. Meehan was drinking from the bottle and urinating at the same time. His eyeglasses had fogged over. Whether this was caused by the heat coming from Mr. Meehan's face or by the change in the atmosphere outdoors, Henry could not be sure; but Mr. Meehan's silvered eyeglasses gave his face the look of an immense bug. Well, what about it, Mr. Meehan was asking from the side of his mouth, *did* Henry, or did he not, want a drink? Henry declined politely but felt the hair rising on the back of his neck. He stood in the roadway wishing an automobile would appear. Mr. Meehan then said that if someone offered him a drink, he would take it gladly. He asked Henry then, in a drunken tone, if he, Henry, was offering him, Jack Meehan, a drink. Henry said that he didn't have a drink to offer. Well, said Mr. Meehan angrily, *he* did. Mr. Meehan said he could offer Henry a pint, a quart, or half a goddamned *gallon,* if he wanted it. Mr. Meehan's abusive tone sent a chill up Henry's spine.

"You want a pint, sailor boy?" said Mr. Meehan, glaring at Henry through opaque glasses while clutching himself. "You want one potent pint?"

As before, Henry demurred. He averted his eyes and pretended to be watching the moths swarming about in the headlights.

"Twice," said Mr. Meehan, in a drunken snarl, "I have offered him a crown, and *twice* he has put it by! There are some people," he fired out, "who'd shove it down your throat for you." To this, Henry replied that he could not trust himself to drive with alcohol in his system. Mr. Meehan said, "Oh, I'll fetch you up something more stimulating than alcohol, don't worry your pretty little head about that. Won't I ever!" he said. "I'll give you something to fire your tonsils." Mr. Meehan rid himself of his whiskey bottle with a sweep of his arm, while continuing to grasp himself with his right hand.

After that, Henry got back into his car, his head reeling, but Mr. Meehan remained outdoors. He continued to taunt Henry over his shoulder, snarling at him. He called Henry "sailor boy." He called him "Virginia" and "Miss Bucktooth" and other names that Henry later strove to forget. He challenged Henry to come out of the car and "get even." His language was foul, and left Henry sitting behind the wheel in a petrified daze, gazing into space.

"If she thought it was her last chance," Mr. Meehan altered Henry's gender, while peering into the car through the moist, silvery lenses of his glasses, "she'd be out here begging me for it!"

Not an automobile passed in the space of five minutes, during which time Mr. Meehan remained in place and, so far as Henry could surmise, gave gratification to his troubled spirit.

When, at midnight, Dick McKenna, the barman, brought Henry his gin, and when, not a minute later, Mrs. McKenna came forward from a booth at the back of the bar and sat down beside Henry, he was ready to be consoled. The barman was noticeably solicitous toward Henry, recalling how he had not seen Henry since his days in uniform. He said it was as much a pleasure today as it was then to wait on someone who had done for his country what Herky Flynn had done for his. Other people were too quick to forget about the war and the sacrifice and the heroism, but Dick McKenna attested that he was not like that. Leaning forward with his two hands planted on the nickel bar, he addressed himself impartially to Henry and to his own wife. Mrs. McKenna was, meanwhile, looking Henry over in a speculative way, as Henry nodded and smiled agreeably over the barman's words. Henry finished his glass of gin in short order.

"I remember the day Herky walked in that door," said Mr. McKenna, "with his spiffy white uniform and white cap. He even looked like a hero. I spotted him straight off as the fellow in the newspaper story. He was carrying a cane. Do you remember that?" he said to Henry. "There are some things you don't forget, and," he added intimately, "there are some people you don't forget."

"Isn't it the truth," Dolly McKenna let fall in a bored, vacant tone, while pointing to a bottle behind the bar. The man reached for the bottle and poured his wife a drink. Henry felt compassion for Mr. McKenna. He noticed the fondness in the way he looked at Dolly, and wondered if she was not merely a flirt, for he could feel a rapport going back and forth between the man and the woman. Mrs. McKenna called her husband "Dicky-bird," and after Mr. McKenna appeared to have exhausted himself of eulogies upon Henry and his war record, she suggested to her husband that he betake himself round to the jukebox and play something. "Put a jit in the Wurlitzer" was how she styled it.

"Shall I?" Mr. McKenna polled Henry.

"Play Elmo Tanner," she said. "Play 'Heartaches.'"

"You like 'Heartaches'?" Mr. McKenna asked Henry.

"*I* like 'Heartaches,'" said Mrs. McKenna forcefully.

"'Heartaches' is fine," said Henry, smiling embarrassedly.

"Isn't he dense?" she said, as Mr. McKenna withdrew to the rear of the bar. The bubbling lights of the jukebox illuminated the side of Mr. McKenna's head and shone upward onto the ceiling in a slow-moving fountain of colors.

Henry felt compassion for him. "He's very decent," said Henry. He looked around again at Mr. McKenna.

"I said dense." Mrs. McKenna raised her voice. "You can be decent and dense," she said, and gestured hopelessly, as though Henry ought to know that better than most. When Mrs. McKenna turned sideways, she revealed a parrotlike profile. Henry had not noticed that before. It affected him oddly. She was talking about her husband and his father. Mr. McKenna's father was fire marshal of a nearby town.

"Yes," Henry interrupted her, "I heard that story."

"His house burned down," said Mrs. McKenna.

"Yes, I know."

"He has two brothers in the fire department, and his father is chief, and their house burned down." Mrs. McKenna was gazing at Henry over the rim of her glass.

"Well," said Henry, suppressing a smile, "anyone's house can burn down."

"The hydrant was dry," she said.

"Yes," Henry said, "I know."

"That runs in the family," she said.

Henry was trying not to smile.

"How could the fire hydrant be dry in front of the fire marshal's burning house if the fire marshal is all there? They all live in a tenement now over the hardware store." Mrs. McKenna reached and straightened Henry's necktie. "Dumbness is like tar. When it sets, you can drive a truck over it."

Henry loosed a sudden peal of laughter, and Mrs. McKenna chimed right in. She had a quick, salacious laugh.

"You always look like a thousand dollars," she said. She was fondling Henry's royal-blue shantung necktie, passing it to and fro between her fingers. She admired, too, his shoes gleaming like black glass on the rung of the bar stool. "Why don't you and I ankle out of here?" she said.

"We can't do that," Henry protested, dropping his voice at once into a hoarse whisper barely perceptible beneath the soaring liquid tones of Elmo Tanner's whistling. He was scarcely conscious that in a matter of seconds he had re-entered utterly the conspiratorial world that he had forsworn forever last summer.

"Dicky-bird," Dolly McKenna called to her husband, as she excused herself to Henry and started for the ladies' room, "Herky's driving me home."

"That's very nice of him," said the barman with perfect ingenuousness. He moved along behind the bar to where Henry was sitting.

"We'll wait for you." Henry colored with embarrassment.

"Don't wait for me!" the barman piped up, glancing at Henry, then thrusting both arms into a sinkful of soapy water. "You two just go along."

By this time Henry had begun to detect a certain peculiar vein in the barman's attitude, almost as if Mr. McKenna were encouraging Henry to leave with his wife. Mr. McKenna certainly did nothing to alter this impression when he smiled up at Henry and tilted his head toward the restrooms, saying, in a cryptic tone, "That's some kind of woman, wouldn't you say?"

"Yes, I would," said Henry, after which he sat stock-still at the bar. Mr. McKenna was swabbing glasses with a wire-handled brush, rinsing them, setting them aside to dry. There was a muffled sound of glasses rolling about in the water on the bottom of the sink. The jukebox had fallen silent. Outside the door the shadows of leaves wavered on the sidewalk. Henry was looking at the crown of Mr. McKenna's head, at the gray points of his brush-cut hair, and at his muscular, stubby arms covered with soap bubbles. The next moment he was able to imagine the sight of Columbine lying asleep in her bed, her short black hair disheveled against the pillow. That was when he realized that his more relaxed manner toward Mrs. McKenna tonight was, oddly, merely a facet of his feelings for Columbine, as if he had been married to Columbine and could therefore let down his guard with others. This realization struck Henry with some force. He was falling in love with Columbine.

Whatever the case, when Mrs. McKenna rejoined Henry at the bar, pulling on her suede coat and saying goodbye to her husband, Henry made no further effort to thwart her. After four days of torture with Mr. Meehan, it was a pleasure to be consorting with human beings again. Henry dismounted from his stool, bade Dick McKenna a pleasant good evening, and escorted Mr. McKenna's wife to the door. The barman sauntered along behind them, seeing the two of them out to the street, as it were, and even spoke up to say how pleased he was that Dolly had somebody like Henry to drive her home. Mr. McKenna was acting like a father seeing his daughter off on a date, and Henry could not help noticing how the man's polite and cheerful manner was studiously maintained, rather as if he were following the words and directions of a scenario he had rehearsed. He sounded too sincere to be human, while Mrs. McKenna, for her part, never so much as looked at her husband (although she had made sure to give them both a good eyeful when she was putting on her coat). Henry didn't care. Mr. McKenna was harmless next to what Henry had been up against with Mr. Meehan. Compared to Mr. Meehan, Dicky-bird was a saint. He was like near-beer next to Mr. Meehan.

While walking in the street under the elms, Mrs. McKenna took hold of Henry's arm, and Henry didn't care about that, either. She was talking animatedly. She had a lively sense of humor. Two or three times she brushed against him with her hip. When he opened the car door for her, he glanced back at the bar. Mr. McKenna was standing in his white apron in the doorway, watching them.

"Why don't you put the top down?" said Mrs. McKenna when Henry got in behind the wheel.

"Just to drive up the hill?"

"Is that where we're going?" said Mrs. McKenna.

Henry looked at her as he put the key into the ignition. "That's where you live, isn't it?"

"It's all right with me," Mrs. McKenna came back

at him. "I didn't think you'd want to. Drive on," she said. "By all means. Take me home."

At first, Henry was intending to discharge Mrs. McKenna from his car with the detached air of a taxicab driver, but by the time they got up the hill, he was in the midst of telling his companion all about the hair-raising episode with Mr. Meehan. Henry was a man of many virtues, but he was not a close-mouthed individual. Once he had begun to talk about it, and could feel Mrs. McKenna's angry sympathy building up for him, he couldn't stop. Mrs. McKenna observed with disgust that Henry should have beaten the daylights out of him. Henry replied that he was not a prizefighter, and was thankful just to have escaped the man's clutches. "You could have used a tire iron," she said. "A fairy who will pull a trick like that should be locked up in a dungeon. A fairy like that is a menace. Some fairies are not like that. *Most* fairies," she corrected herself, "are not like that."

"You would say, then," Henry put forward in a very judicial tone, "that he definitely is a fairy, though?"

Mrs. McKenna put her hand flat to her head in disbelief. "Jesus Christ," she said.

"What I mean to say," Henry stammered out hurriedly, lest Mrs. McKenna think him an idiot, "he acts very masculine. He treats *me* like a fairy."

"A fairy," said Dolly McKenna knowledgeably, "will treat you like a fairy if he wants you to be a fairy. To a fairy, everybody's a fairy. A fairy I know claims that Jesus was a fairy. He says that Shakespeare was a fairy and that F.D.R. was a fairy. Everybody who's ever been famous is a fairy. He says President Truman's not a fairy but is a bum President."

"I see your point." Henry had parked with the motor running underneath the street lamp in front of the McKenna house on Nonotuck Street; he had

222

to admit he was enjoying his talk with Mrs. McKenna. He thought about Mr. McKenna standing in the doorway in his white apron. He thought about Columbine lying asleep in her bed.

"I know one thing," said Henry, touching upon Mr. Meehan's hygiene, "he's a ripe one."

"They call him One-eyed Jack," said Mrs. McKenna.

Henry was feeling better. "He is one ripe owl!"

"To a big, ugly fairy like that," said Mrs. McKenna, "you look like Peter Pan. When he wakes up tomorrow morning and remembers what happened tonight, he's going to break out in a cold sweat."

"I thought about that," said Henry truthfully.

"You won't have to worry about him any more."

"Yes," Henry acknowledged, "I was thinking about that."

"He won't eat breakfast for a week. By noontime tomorrow, he'll be on the wagon."

"You are right about that," said Henry. He truly had thought about it, and she was right. He was feeling better. He was enjoying his talk with Mrs. McKenna. He didn't know what was wrong with Mr. McKenna, but he didn't care a great deal, either. He guessed that the bartender liked to be titillated by his wife. If that was the case, thought Henry, he had married the right woman. Mrs. McKenna was in a rather benign, talkative mood herself tonight, and when she lifted Henry's hand and placed it gently over her breast, and when he felt the heat of her breast inside his hand, and the way her breast seemed to have been molded by nature to occupy itself there, filling the compass of his whole hand, he continued talking with scarcely a skipped breath. He and Mrs. McKenna were becoming old friends. She, apparently, was not in any rush, either, for when Henry later changed the subject, and recounted to Dolly something about his mother's crying fits and recent paranoia, expressing to her his true worry about his mother, she, Mrs. McKenna, took her time to allay Henry's fears by explaining to him that his mother's mid-life strangeness would pass. Mrs. McKenna cited several examples of women in her own family who had evinced symptoms remarkably similar to those shown by Mrs. Flynn. Henry was visibly relieved. Mrs. McKenna's balanced views on the subject, and her sincere, patient portrayal of those views, went a long way toward appeasing Henry's anxiety. He was grateful to her for that.

"I haven't talked to my father about it," he explained, "because my father is not very apt to talk about such things with me."

"Your father is a bonehead," said Mrs. McKenna. "He's one of those big-mouthed lummoxes who know it all. He'd probably like to lock her up in a cage. She'll be fit as a fiddle in six months."

Mrs. McKenna took Henry by the arm and led him into her house. Henry was not being seduced. At least, he did not feel he was being seduced. He was merely accompanying her up the front walk, and then following her into the side door and up the darkened staircase. If he had felt a little fright in his heart, a stab of guilt, or even an honest anticipation that something new and unusual was about to happen, he might then have felt he was being seduced. His head, though, was clear. He knew where he was, and that it was one o'clock now, closing time at Jockamy's, and yet none of it seemed to matter. In the darkness at the top of the stairs, Mrs. McKenna paused. There was a soft jangling of keys and then a rattle and the report of a lock snapping open. Henry judged he had better say something pretty soon, but for the moment nothing came to mind. A breath of air passed over him as the apartment door swung inward, with the sudden pale channel of the doorway revealing pinpoints of light within, the glimmering of vases, glass doors, a mirror on the wall. He could not recall later what he was thinking about, but at every step he became surer that the man who lived in this house would never appear, not so long, at least, as the white Ford sat parked in front of the house, like a white stallion tethered to the lamp post to warn the homecoming tenant that a certain awesome seignorial prerogative was being exercised upstairs.

The only light that came on was the soft yellow glow of the radio dial when Mrs. McKenna tuned up some music. Henry would like to have talked some more. He had no feelings of affection for Dolly McKenna, no pulse of romance, but the intimacy that grew up so swiftly between them at Jockamy's had blossomed stage by stage, and he wished to prolong it. His self-possession of the moment was like a sleepwalker's, in that he felt entirely free to act and yet somehow constrained to coast along inertially with the flow of events. Again, Mrs. McKenna was likewise in no special rush and might willingly, too, have pursued any of their various topics, but in the absence of Henry's initiating any, she was in the meanwhile getting undressed. She was not hurrying. In fact, she even paused to remove a locket and chain that encircled her neck, an unself-conscious gesture that was not meant to attract attention but which Henry found compelling nevertheless. As he accustomed his eyes to the weak light, he examined the details of a tastefully furnished living room. Filmy white curtains and half-shuttered venetian blinds formed pale rectangles against the light of the street below. The radio station faded momentarily, then gathered power anew, only to fade once more: a late-night sound, the distant voice of an announcer rising and receding against a soft crosscurrent of the beepings of a Morse signal. Mrs. McKenna was standing in the light of the window, removing her slip. Henry was pleased at the calmness persisting in him. When she came to him and put her arms

around his neck, he knew still that nothing was ir-
revocable. He could still turn back. The cool neutral-
ity of his heart was remarkable. He could stay, or go.

"I didn't expect you to come up here," she said.

"I didn't expect to be here," said Henry.

Mrs. McKenna took Henry onto the sofa. "Tell me
about Boston," she said, as though preferring to mix
in further conversation. "I've never been there.
Dicky-bird doesn't like big cities. He doesn't like
crowds and he doesn't like corruption. Did you
climb the Bunker Hill monument?"

"No, I didn't," said Henry. He was affected by a
sort of avidity in Mrs. McKenna's nose and mouth.
He was sitting back with the woman moving on top
of him. She was looking at him expressionlessly at
point-blank range. He could still get up and leave.
Nothing was ruled out. His fingertips moved beneath Mrs. McKenna's underclothes.

"Men make sure that women wear simple clothing," Mrs. McKenna observed, "to make us easy to
get at, but then wear complicated clothing themselves." She touched his lips with her tongue. "That
probably encourages a man to have second
thoughts."

"That's an interesting theory," Henry replied.

"You don't seem worried," she said.

"I was wondering about that," said Henry in earnest. Gazing over her shoulder to the eminence of
her buttocks inside the pink silk panties where his
hand was, and beyond that to the sight of her foot
jutting up in the air, with the heel of her shoe aimed
at the ceiling and slowly wavering to and fro, Henry
felt urged to agree with the bartender's earlier pro-
nouncement on his wife: Mrs. McKenna was some
kind of woman.

"Did you see Old Ironsides?" she said. She put the
question in a soft, absentminded manner.

"No," said Henry, "I didn't."

"The Red Sox?" Her breasts were upon Henry's chest and she was moving.

"No," he replied, "but I wished I had."

Mrs. McKenna nodded understandingly. "I love baseball. I love to watch baseball," she whispered. "Dicky-bird likes fishing. Bartenders love to fish."

"I didn't know that," said Henry, always alert to new knowledge.

"He's probably out looking for night crawlers right now," she said. "He keeps a shovel and a pail of dirt in the trunk of his car."

Mrs. McKenna's lips, Henry noticed, were gummy. He guessed his own were, too. "Where does he fish?" he said. "In the river?"

Mrs. McKenna was smiling now because she had hold of Henry with her hand; she had loosened his trousers and got hold of him. "I never go," she said, "so I wouldn't know."

"He probably goes to the river."

"This time of year he uses night crawlers. In the summer he uses flies. I tied some flies for him once. He said they were the most beautiful flies he had ever seen. They were very pretty," she allowed. "Will you take me to see the Red Sox?"

"I don't see why not," said Henry.

"I think I'd like to live in Boston. I'd like to live in Boston and come home weekends. Someday soon," she said, "you and I will go to Boston. Would you like to see my body?"

"Yes, I would," Henry replied.

Mrs. McKenna got to her feet, unfastened her brassiere, and dropped it onto the carpet. Then she stepped out of her panties, balancing very nicely on one leg, then the other. "By the way," she said, "don't worry about Dicky-bird." She stood over Henry, showing him her body. "I'm not overweight," she pointed out, "I'm supposed to look like this."

"You look beautiful," said Henry. He was a little dismayed, however, at the sight of himself, of his own rumpled trousers, and particularly of his erection standing forth where Mrs. McKenna had momentarily abandoned it. He thought then about Columbine, but with a little dismay this time, as he knew he would be staying awhile.

"Dicky-bird thinks you're the living end," said Mrs. McKenna. She slid a sofa cushion onto the floor and sat on it. "Why do you suppose that is?"

"I don't know. It probably says more about him than about me."

"You said a mouthful there," she said.

Henry posed an interesting question. "Is Dicky-bird a fairy?" he asked.

Mrs. McKenna reflected. "I don't think so," she said skeptically.

Henry agreed. "I guess if he were a fairy, he would never have married you. Dicky is crazy about you."

"He likes my body."

"I could tell," said Henry.

"He'd probably like to see us together," said Mrs. McKenna. "You and me."

Henry still possessed that calm, lucid outlook as he joined Mrs. McKenna on the floor. He was glad she was talking. He was glad she had dispelled for him the ugly business with Mr. Meehan that he had experienced on the road coming home from Boston. He felt very calm and virile. He was not worried about anything. His job was safe. His mother would be all right. He felt relaxed.

"You could take me out anytime," said Mrs. McKenna. "I'll bet if you and *I* were married, Herk, you wouldn't be so free and easy with me as Dicky-bird is."

"No, I wouldn't!" Henry averred.

"That's good," she said. "I'm glad you said that." Mrs. McKenna was kissing Henry and he was kissing her back. She was underneath him, making him

228

feel the fullness of her breasts against him, and moving her legs rhythmically. "I wouldn't like you to be free with me, Herk. Not like that." A moment later she was taking hold of him again, using both her hands. "You could do it to me right in front of Dicky-bird, I wouldn't even mind."

"I wouldn't either!" Henry was losing his presence of mind now. He was losing control of his judgment.

"I don't think anyone would mind," she said. "Not even him."

"I don't think he would either."

"He would know," said Mrs. McKenna, "that you were better, and that I wanted you."

"He would understand!" said Henry.

"You're a good size." Mrs. McKenna was whispering now. She was moving everywhere. "I'm glad you said that," she whispered breathlessly, "about not being free and easy with me."

The look of avidity in Mrs. McKenna's face set Henry vibrating. "I wouldn't let anyone near you!" he said.

"I'm glad you said that."

"I'd shoot them!" Henry was atop her, clutching her for dear life, while allowing her to steer him in with her hands.

Also, Mrs. McKenna's voice was becoming more like a raving. "You're going to have me anytime!" she said. "You can take me anywhere you want, any place, any time. Tomorrow, if you want! Tomorrow night."

Henry winced in pain, then gave an instinctive lunge. A cry escaped him. In the instant of entering her, Henry felt like a light bulb flashing on, heating up everywhere at once.

She kept talking. "You could come with us on vacation this summer," she was saying. "With Dicky-bird and me. The three of us! We go to Winnipesaukee."

By this time, though, Henry was not able to follow rationally the thread of their bizarre conversation.

"And Dicky-bird wouldn't be able to touch me while the three of us were together," she added.

"I wouldn't want him to," Henry said. "I really wouldn't want him to."

"If you didn't want him to, he wouldn't!" she said. "That would be final."

"But *I* would," said Henry.

"You would have me as much as you wanted," she said, panting. "Any time you wanted. You would do anything you wanted—any time. I wouldn't even let him look at me, or talk to me, not without your say-so."

"We wouldn't even need him to be there," said Henry, in a flash of sagacity.

"He would only be there to watch," said Mrs. McKenna, while helping Henry establish a physical beat, undulating beneath him.

"To watch and learn," said Henry. His brain was on its own now, like a balloon cut free and climbing. He was heaving rhythmically and clutching Mrs. McKenna, as she crossed her legs behind his back. She, too, was breathless, and was moving her hands with a restless, feverish possessiveness all about his waist and back. Henry was still wearing his Glen-plaid suit and his shirt and necktie. He could feel the floor under his knees.

"He would listen to you," said Mrs. McKenna. "He admires you. He'd do whatever you said."

Henry gave another cry, a sudden outburst of anguish mixed with primitive joy.

"He would have to stay out of the way!" Henry cried. "He could be there, but he would have to keep out of the way!"

"Whenever you got a hard-on, he would have to go outside," she said.

"He could go fishing! . . . Winnipesaukee is a lake, isn't it?"

"He could go any place he wanted, so long as he got out of our way. He could look through a key-hole, if he wanted!"

Mrs. McKenna's many references to her husband watching her and Henry making love gave Henry to wonder if they were not perhaps being watched right now. Henry remembered the glass doors behind them.

"He thinks the world of you," she said.

"He thinks the world of you, too," said Henry.

"He's going to be seeing plenty of us from now on," Mrs. McKenna proclaimed in that voice of iron determination that had once scared Henry. "He can like it or lump it."

Henry's own capacity for speech was running out, replaced by heavy breathing and rhythmic gasps and by the clumsy efforts he was making with his mouth to taste again Mrs. McKenna's tongue.

"I don't care *who* sees us together. I should care," she said, "with a man like you! We make sense! This is the real stuff! Oh, baby," she was saying, "I don't give a shit about anybody. Not now, I don't. Where did *that* come from?" she cried. "Do that," she said. "Do it."

Twice Henry felt certain he had heard noises from behind the glass doors in back of him, but he was too busy undoing his virginity to stop and look back now.

"*Do* that," she said.

"I'm doing it," he said.

"Keep doing it," she said. "Keep *doing* it, baby!"

"I am," he said.

Mrs. McKenna then uttered an obscenity that Henry had never heard before, and buried her tongue in his mouth.

XIII

About equidistant from the Flynn and Kokoriss houses, situated on the far side of the flagstone path, stood an ancient pine tree. It stood by the low cliff that fronted all the houses of Cottage Avenue and was partly obscured by a screen of slender young birches and aspens. Probably because of the thin, sandy soil in which it grew and an underlying stratum of rock, the tree was not tall as pines go, nor was it handsome to look at. Its needles were more black than green. Its shape was lopsided. Over the years several boughs had come down in the wind, while others had fallen to the depredations of boys armed with handsaws or hatchets, so that now, in its old age, having withstood many storms and hard winters, the old American pine had taken on a bitter aspect. It leaned out toward the sidewalk, flinging its haggard boughs forward as in a black imprecation upon anyone going into or out of the avenue.

This tree was venerable, though, in the annals of the two or three generations of boys and girls who had grown up here. For several decades it had served as the focus and meeting place of neighborhood boys coming out of their houses on summer days. So far as human memory went, the pine was always full-grown. It was a mature tree on the morning when the surveyor came to mark out the original building lots, and it was a mature tree that received into its branches the first eager climbers, boys ascending into its upper reaches for the sheer fun of climbing. No one now living on the avenue could remember the tree house someone had built in it many years ago, even though a close scrutiny of the trunk at a spot about twenty feet up would have revealed, still embedded there, the remains of three or four rusted spikes. Small children had often played on the needle bed in its shade, too, digging in the dark loam with shovels and tin pails, or sticks or teaspoons, excavating tunnels underneath the worn roots, passageways through which tiny cast-iron carriages passed wonderfully to and fro. Little trenches and redoubts were built there to accommodate the squad of lead soldiers that was brought to the scene in a wooden cheese box fitted with a sliding cover and tied all round with a double strand of grocer's twine. The Williamsons, a family of five boys that lived originally in the house belonging now to Mrs. Blye, used the old pine tree as the support for a prodigious swing consisting of a stout rope and an automobile tire. The boys threw themselves with heart-stopping abandon off the cliff top, straddling the tire and swinging far out in the air above the front walk, while giving throat, of course, to appropriate daredevil cries.

The old tree had known its share of the life of the avenue; but like all institutions, it lost favor. Even before Henry's time, when there was a dearth of boys growing up on the avenue, the great tree fell into neglect. Its popularity went with its usefulness. Grass crept into the margins, and bushes grew up before it along the stone walk. Mankind had, as it were, moved along, and, in going, left no signs really to attest to that lively, crowded past. Had the old tree been a sentient thing, armed with a memory and feelings, it might well have looked back with a certain nostalgia on the thousand somnolent summer days of its middle years, when it had provided the shelter and support and focus of a life blown joyously full in the lungs and limbs of its children. The orange beads of pitch that shone like amber tears frozen in the crevices of its bark might have had a meaning that surpassed the meaning of trees.

Columbine was lying in her bed early that May morning when she heard from outdoors a moaning sound, a groan like that of a wounded animal, a noise that persisted while rising in tone. It was a bright, blowy morning, but the wind was light, tossing up bits of newspaper, or coming suddenly around the corner of the house to rattle a window or curl back a loose tar shingle on the roof. Columbine heard then a sharp cracking sound, and a tremor ran through the house. The windows jiggled and the reflected images in the vanity mirror trembled. There was a shadow and then a rush of air at the window, as the pine tree let go and fell whistling to earth, falling into the space between the two houses, and smashing everything in its path. The thunderous impact shattered two cellar windows and sent chinaware rolling off shelves. The boughs exploded like firecrackers going off in series, creating a sudden hail of splinters. The old pine came down across the two gardens. A low pipe fence at the edge of the Flynns' front lawn was smashed into the concrete, while the fence dividing the two gardens was destroyed from one end to the other, as though it had been built expressly to provide the perfect axis for the tree's fall. The little maple tree that had stood for fifteen years on the Flynn side of the fence was obliterated as a tree. One moment the two gardens were quiet sunlit oblongs, and the next, the great black-needled monster lay trembling upon them.

When Henry came home from work that Friday afternoon and saw the great fallen hulk of the pine tree lying across the flagstone path and gardens, he was amazed to realize that such a great individual tree had been residing nearby all this while. He thought he had never seen it before. The sweet smell of pine was everywhere on the air. Broken boughs and needle clumps lay scattered in all directions. The stone walk was blocked by the tree trunk for days thereafter. Not being superstitious, Henry attached no special value to the time or occasion of the tree's fall, but went on indoors to supper. He certainly didn't equate any of it with his own moral condition. He didn't even give a thought to its perhaps having done some damage to somebody, as to Columbine, for example, in the sudden wanton destruction of her garden.

Henry felt like a new man. He saw himself in a new light now. He had become something of a rake. Even his footstep was jauntier. He strolled about the editorial rooms of the newspaper with his hands in his pockets and an eye out for the ladies. He liked, for instance, the way Mrs. Sanderson, the paste-up lady, emphasized the smallness of her waist and the amplitude of her bosom and hips through the device of that aquamarine sash she wore with her black dress. That was Mrs. Sanderson's way, Henry conjectured, of advertising the persisting usefulness of her body. That and her ready smile. Henry guessed that all girls and women had a strong hankering to be carried up to the hayloft.

He was happy, too, with the way Jack Meehan had driven himself into a corner. It tickled Henry to watch the big, malodorous fellow trying repeatedly to make light of the ugly business that took place that night in the Brookfields by attributing his behavior to the effects of alcohol. "Was I shellacked," said Mr. Meehan. *"Was* I shellacked! Wasn't I?"

"Yes, you were," Henry said.

"We both were!" cried Mr. Meehan. "I tell you," he said, "we were fried! Herky and I," he explained to others standing nearby, and including Henry in his narrative in such a way as to cultivate anew Henry's trust, "started at three o'clock in the afternoon and were going like two diesels at midnight! I couldn't even think straight! This fellow can hold his tonic! Or"—Mr. Meehan made an amusing face— "should I say *'tawnic'?"* Everyone laughed heartily over Mr. Meehan's mimicry of the speech of Bostonians, especially as the big man stamped about among the desks, whooping with laughter. With Henry, he confined his remarks to man-to-man observations about women. He commended to Henry's attention the Chief's new secretary, "the one with the schoolmarm eyeglasses and the legs that go on forever," he said.

Henry was not fooled by Mr. Meehan's new angle of attack, but his own invigorated spirits were such that the big man's ravings and bizarre outlook produced in him only the shadow of an effect. Henry went twice that week to the bar of the Roger Smith Hotel, where he enjoyed letting fall certain insinuations concerning his romantic life. Henry was not loath to imply that he was dabbling on the side with a married woman. He also bought himself a new cord suit for the coming summer, and paid a visit to the Ford showroom to examine the first postwar automobiles. The fact that the new cars were almost indistinguishable in design from the 1941 models did not dim his enthusiasm. The cars were handsome and luxurious-looking under the glare of the showroom lights. Henry was only discouraged from closing a deal on a new convertible by the constant talk he heard at work of an impending economic depression. "There's never been a war that wasn't followed by a crash" was the constant refrain. Henry was working at that time for Bill Steadman, the editor of the sports page. His finest piece of the season was an interview with Willie Hoppe, the billiards master, which Mr. Steadman characterized as "a crackerjack article."

Unfortunately, Henry's happiness these days was a little spoiled by Mrs. McKenna herself. She telephoned him at the newspaper every day. She called him Sugar and Baby, and sometimes even favored him with an intimate obscenity or two. It was one of the ironics of life that Dolly McKenna, who was the proximate cause of Henry's revolutionary view of himself as a Don Juan, should now have become the fly in the amber; for he was of two minds about her. What troubled him most was Mrs. McKenna's unwillingness to brook any impediment to her will. At first, Henry put her off politely. He made excuses. He invoked his mother's illness. He trotted out his work schedule, his appointments, his assignments. After a few days, however, Mrs. McKenna's patience evaporated.

"Listen, sugar, I'm not Joan of Arc. I'm not a Carmelite nun," she said. "I'm not trying to set an endurance record. I don't spend a week like this."

Cupping his hand over the telephone lest his fellow employees eavesdrop on him, Henry suggested an assignation in the state park on the mountain. "In two or three days," he added.

"We'll use the bed," said Mrs. McKenna.

"I don't think your house is wise," Henry whispered.

"It's all right," she said. "Dicky-bird knows."

"He *knows?*"

"So we don't have to go trooping off into the forest. We'll use my bed—like two grownups."

"Dicky-bird knows?" Henry was gazing walleyed into space. "Jesus Christ," he said.

"He knows all about it. He's right here," she added. "He can hear every word. Shall I put him on?"

"Don't," said Henry.

"I want to see you tonight."

"I'll call you back," Henry whispered.

"Dicky-bird is resigned to the fact. It was inevitable, he says. He's only happy it was you. Those are his own words."

Henry's ordinary pallor was replaced by a new one, like new snow fallen on old.

"I'm at the bar," she said. "We're listening to the radio. I'm bored."

"I'll call you back," said Henry.

"You'd better," she said.

"I will."

"You do that!"

Not a few minutes passed before Henry's telephone was buzzing again. This time, however, the caller said nothing. He could hear someone breathing on the line and saw himself becoming enmeshed now in a strange, satanic triangle. He was about to hang up the receiver when he suddenly divined the identity of the caller. He could feel her presence on the line, almost as surely as if his senses had manufactured the smell of her Antelope perfume. "Columbine?" he said.

"How did you know?" said she, speaking softly. A silence ensued. He could hear her breathing. "Are you busy?"

"Not really." Henry closed his eyes, as he found himself in thrall to forces he could not have anticipated. "No," he said, "I'm not busy at all."

"I wanted to ask if you were angry with me," she said. Columbine's nervousness was palpable.

"Of course, I'm not angry. I never get angry."

"I do," she said.

"Yes, I know." Columbine's voice returned to him completely the intimacy of their last encounter. Her telephone voice was remarkably characteristic of herself, of her precocious intelligence, her diplomacy, and of those deeper, more mysterious attributes that give life to a personality. He was touched most of all, though, by the sweetness of her voice.

"I was in Boston," he explained, "and before that, I was ill for a week."

Columbine waited, listening, while Henry explained his absence from her. "I've been home with the grippe," she said.

"That was what I had."

"You must have given it to me!" she added brightly. "I've been home all week. I've been watching the city men sawing up the tree. Did you know," she inquired softly, "that a tree fell between our houses?"

"Of course," said Henry. "I saw it last Friday."

"They have it nearly chopped up now. It's stacked in piles like firewood. The men," she said, "are quite a colorful crew. I've been watching them from my bed. One of the men wears long underwear and baggy pants with blue suspenders. His name is Dinty," she said. "He blows his nose with his thumb!" Columbine made a honking sound that set Henry laughing.

Henry's affection was apparent in his voice. "You sound as if you're having fun."

"Wait," she said, "I haven't finished. Every morning at dawn, Mr. Griffin comes sneaking down the alley and steals a wheelbarrowful of the wood. I've been awake, and I see him. He comes while it's still dark out, just before sunup, and loads up his wheelbarrow. This morning he was late and showed up in his bathrobe and pajamas. Pink pajamas!" She gave a peal of laughter. "You should have seen him, Starbuck, working like the devil. In his pajamas!"

"He *is* a devil!" said Henry with delight.

"The old thief!" Columbine cried. "I'll bet he's hiding it in his cellar. Not only that," she went on. "He's so clever. He doesn't take the wood all from one place but selects pieces from all the different piles, so no one will notice. He goes around on tiptoe, with the hair on his head standing up like a bush, and looking all about him very shiftily. I've been having a lot of fun in my room this week. I just finished reading *The Magnificent Ambersons*," she said. "Sophie left it behind at Easter. That was a wonderful book. I'm going to read it again. My mother is outside, raking the yard. That's how I was able to call. Are you happy I called?"

"Yes, I am," said Henry. He was alone now in the corner of the editorial room. Minutes earlier, Mr. Steadman had departed the office for the day. All the desks nearby were unoccupied.

"Did you know," Columbine went on, "that Helen is due home? She's going to be married a week from Saturday."

"I didn't know," said Henry.

"Yes," said Columbine, "and Anna and Nicholas are planning to post the banns."

"I didn't know that, either."

"Everyone is getting married," she said. "Helen is coming home at suppertime today. Maybe," Columbine suggested a little warily, "you could come over tonight . . . as if to see Helen." She coughed nervously over her words.

"I will," he said.

"I wish you would." Columbine dropped her voice playfully. "I promise to be *very* clever."

Henry had forgotten that he was speaking to so young a girl. He wished to say something endearing, but nothing came to mind. He had all but put Mrs. McKenna from his mind.

"I hope you don't mind my calling," said Columbine. "I won't do it again. I don't think girls should call their boyfriends at work." The sudden reference to him as her boyfriend did not produce a disagreeable effect on Henry. He was simultaneously touched by her almost childish candor and moved in his heart to admit it was true.

"It was very nice talking with you," he confessed.

"Well," she piped up, mimicking him, "it was very nice talking to you!" With that, Columbine hung up.

Henry went to the Kokoriss house that evening, as invited, but before going he telephoned Mrs. McKenna. He was late calling her, and she was naturally very short-tempered with him. Henry did not mind her fiery character, so long as she kept her temper in check and did not compromise him in some outward way. Henry didn't want to be embarrassed in the eyes of others. He was honest enough to admit that the bartender's wife was an extraordinary woman. She was attractive in many ways, and he was not insensible to those attractions. In his secret heart Henry enjoyed being pursued by her. He knew it. He could not recall anyone ever having pursued him before, and showed a forgivable degree of human weakness in being flattered by the woman's obvious desire for him. If his responses to the older woman were a little like those of a virginal maiden, that, too, was understandable, as he had been, after all, a virgin until Mrs. McKenna came along, and now he was not, and he couldn't help feeling a certain degree of allegiance toward her. So when Mrs. McKenna instructed him on the telephone about a certain "ache" that she was suffering, and which she expected Henry forthwith to alleviate ("And not in some cow pasture, either," she said), Henry was not indifferent to her demands. There was even a touch of coyness about the constant excuses he gave whenever she called, a quality that Mrs. McKenna until now regarded as harmless, an appealing bashfulness, a boyish superfluence that was exciting to overcome. She was getting impatient, though.

"I'm not going to hang around this gin mill night after night, playing pinochle with every rummy that comes through the door. I mean it, cupcake. I have a good lech on."

"I know you have."

"You don't know the half of it," she said.

"I'll see you Saturday evening," said Henry.

"You'll see me tomorrow evening," Mrs. McKenna corrected him.

"Is Dicky-bird there?" asked Henry suddenly, appalled at his own temerity in asking such a question.

"Of course, he's here. He knows about us. That's how it is sometimes," said Mrs. McKenna, instructing Henry in one of the more recondite facets of illicit love. "Sometimes they know."

"I find that amazing," said Henry.

"You're in the driver's seat now," she said. "When is our date?"

"Saturday evening," Henry replied.

"I'll see you Saturday afternoon and Saturday evening both. That's our date." Mrs. McKenna's voice came down like a stamp on a document.

"Assuming especially," he said, "that my mother is feeling better."

"You'll see me Saturday afternoon and Saturday night," she said, "if your mother is croaking on the goddamned floor!"

Mrs. McKenna, Henry had to confess, had a definite way with words.

Before going outdoors, to pay his call at the Kokorisses, Henry stopped in the kitchen to look in on his mother. She was sitting at the kitchen table with three decks of playing cards before her. She had counted the cards in each deck, and one of the decks was missing one card. Now she had divided the cards of the incomplete deck face up on the oilcloth in packets of four to identify the missing card. The deuce of hearts was missing. "Someone stole the two of hearts," she said.

"Maybe it was misplaced," said Henry.

"Who would misplace a two of hearts?" His mother looked up at him with blue, suspicious eyes. The chalkiness of Mrs. Flynn's flesh and her graying hair attested to the relentless passage of time, filling Henry with a sudden sense of life's poignancy.

"Do you remember when you used to stand by the piano, and I played and you sang?" Mrs. Flynn's eyes retained a pale swirling light. "You sang 'Beautiful Dreamer.'" She turned back to her playing cards. "That was my favorite." She began quietly to sing and hum.

Henry made his way outdoors and walked across the gardens in the dusk. The fence that stood for years between the houses had vanished. The two yards lay covered with a thick film of sawdust. The earth was chewed up in places, the forsythia and snowball bushes twisted out of shape. The front walkway was swept clean. Before climbing the porch steps, Henry turned and glanced back at his own house. Across the ravaged space, it looked different and yet the same.

Henry wished Helen Kokoriss great happiness in her marriage, as Helen seated Henry at the dining-room table and showed him a photo of her fiancé. Henry smiled and nodded over the picture and paid Helen a shy compliment or two on her having landed a figure who struck Henry as being rather a dull, upstanding type of fellow with an easy smile, but doubtless an appropriate match. Mrs. Kokoriss joined them at the table, the three of them smiling and nodding over the picture, while overhead could be heard the occasional footsteps of Columbine striding back and forth in her room. Sometimes when the footsteps stopped, Henry would glance about into the living room, expecting Columbine to appear; then, a moment later, the footsteps resounded again on the floor above. Henry had not seen her face in two weeks.

"And Anna and Nicholas are talking," said Mrs. Kokoriss, implying further marital plans. "I'm losing all my daughters."

"It must be a good year for it," said Henry.

"Everyone is getting married this year." Helen colored a little, shot Henry a nervous smile, and exhaled visibly.

"Well, the boys are home," said Mrs. Kokoriss, in her remote, soft-spoken manner, "and they want families. I," she said, "almost married a boy in the year after the last war. In the old country," she added.

Henry found it hard to believe that the quiet, pudgy-faced mother of the four girls had herself once been a young girl with thoughts of marriage.

"Well, you'll have this one at home for a while," said Helen, with a flick of the eyes. Henry looked about and discovered Columbine standing behind him in the arched doorway.

"Are you talking about me?" said Columbine with haughtiness, as she advanced into the room. "Has Helen shown you her heartthrob?" Columbine proceeded coolly past the table into the kitchen. Henry was surprised that she was wearing her gardening costume, her shorts and sweatshirt, with the heeled shoes that she now wore to school. Helen had noticed also.

"Columbine," she was quick to call after her, "I don't think that's much of an outfit you're wearing." Listening for a reply, Helen squinted into space. There was no answer from the kitchen, however, save the report of the refrigerator door closing and then the sound of Columbine's heels on the linoleum flooring. "Your legs are long enough," Helen scolded with that same pinched, abstract expression in her eyes, "without wearing shorts with shoes like those!"

Columbine reappeared in the kitchen doorway, but only fractionally, standing, that is, where only Henry could see her. She posed for him, closing her eyes in a theatrical approximation of a lady of great vogue, then spun about on the toe of one shoe while knifing the other leg sharply through the air, as she stepped out of sight once more.

"It's like talking to a stone," Helen said.

"She doesn't listen," Mrs. Kokoriss confirmed in the way of a confession tinged with motherly pride.

"It began with that dancing teacher," said Helen. "She's been putting ideas into her head. Sometimes,

Mama, you have to slap her down. If I were home," she said, "I would do it."

"But you *won't* be home," Columbine called back tartly. "Will you?"

"She's so fresh." Helen was still smoldering over Columbine's disparaging attitude and remark about the man in the picture. Helen continued to berate her sister, but an opened water faucet in the kitchen drowned out her words. Columbine came back, eating an apple. She seated herself elegantly at the table.

"Would you like one?" she said to Henry in a pert, superior tone, signifying the apple.

"No, thank you," said Henry.

"What would you do with a sister like that?" said Helen.

"What *would* you do?" Columbine showed Henry a set of sea-blue eyes above the apple in her hand, then bit into the apple noisily.

"*I* give up," said Helen. Mrs. Kokoriss laughed relievedly.

"Why don't you show him your gown?" said Columbine. "Helen bought it at Garfinckel's in Washington. Johnny helped her pick it out. It's not fashionable," she said to Henry, "but it's not bad."

"It *is* fashionable," countered Helen.

"It is *not.*" Columbine turned on her hotly.

"Columbine!" said Mrs. Kokoriss.

The younger girl was staring fixedly at her sister. "It's frumpy," she said. "It's not bad, but it's frumpy."

"Why don't you show it to Herky?" Mrs. Kokoriss put in wisely.

Helen blushed painfully. Finding himself in the midst of a typical set-to between the sisters, Henry decided to sit back and enjoy himself. He had forgotten, too, how beautiful Columbine was. It was a pleasure to be here. He could feel the secret electricity coming to him from inside. Henry was smiling pleasantly, drumming his fingertips on the table.

"Would you like to see it?" Helen asked, in an effort to dispel her anger, bashfulness, and worry all at one stroke.

"Yes, I would, very much," said Henry.

"He would very much," Columbine repeated, and sat back smugly and crossed her legs on Henry's side of the table.

Helen paused an instant in her place, setting the fingertips of her two hands on the edge of the table, as if pondering the idea a second, or marshaling herself physically before getting up.

"Go on," said Columbine, prompting her with a supercilious look.

After Helen had thrust herself up from her chair and started out of the room, Columbine turned to Mrs. Kokoriss. "May I have some Postum, Mama?" she said.

"You know where it is!" Helen cried at her from the doorway.

"I didn't ask you!" Columbine blazed back.

"Mother isn't supposed to wait on you hand and foot," said Helen.

Mrs. Kokoriss offered Henry a cup of tea, however, and arose and went to the kitchen to prepare it, leaving Henry and Columbine at the table. Columbine stared after her, then, slowly, brought her attention round again, first turning her head, then her eyes, and contemplating Henry in a solemn way. She was sitting ruler-straight in her chair, looking at him. Now and then, her gaze slid past him, and he remembered there was a mirror on the wall behind him. She was looking in the mirror at herself, and then returning the expression to him, as if refining the look, trying to get it just right. It was a look that Columbine was sure her sisters were incapable of generating. "You can smoke if you'd like," she said.

Before Henry could reply to this startling announcement, Columbine was on her feet. She swept around behind him and around the table, making sure that the gracefulness of her stride was exaggerated enough to spark notice. She introduced a new topic while pulling open the china-closet door. "Nicholas is going to have a stag party in July at Malek's Inn." She rolled her eyes. "With blue movie . Can you imagine Nicholas," she cried, "watching something like that?" She took a green velvet headband from a bowl in the china closet and, raising both hands, proceeded to affix it to her head, while pivoting and coming back to the table. Her mannerisms placed her safely above her subject matter. "Anna is opposed to it, of course. As if it *mattered,*" she drew out the word. "As if it would make Nicholas any better or worse." She was tying the velvet band at the back of her neck. "Can you imagine fighting over something like that? Isn't it pathetic?"

"I think everybody's entitled to his own tastes," Henry replied unconcernedly.

"Well, I don't," said Columbine.

The two of them had fallen easily into their usual conversational pattern.

"Everyone should be forced to show good taste! Why shouldn't they? Would you," she inquired, challenging him, "have a stag party?"

"If I were getting married?" Henry realized that Columbine was comparing him and her as a couple to the others.

"Naturally, if you were getting married!" She sat and crossed her legs. She was tying the headband. He was looking at her hair.

"I don't believe I would," said Henry.

"I'm glad to hear you say *that.* Could you imagine the Prince of Wales having a stag party in Ward Four, with his friends hollering and stamping their feet over a dirty movie?"

"Is there a Prince of Wales?" said Henry.

247

"Could you imagine the Duke of Windsor?"

"The royal houses are all dead," said Henry.

"They wouldn't be," said Columbine, "if I had anything to say about it."

"You'd probably bring back the wheel and the guillotine."

"I wouldn't kill people, if that's what you mean." She showed Henry a look. "But I don't see anything wrong with locking people up."

"What I would like," said Henry, "is to see the blue movies without the stag party."

"Oh, you'll see plenty of blue movies," she came right back at him provocatively. "If," she added, "that's what tickles you."

Helen reappeared then in the doorway carrying a voluminous wedding gown on a hanger, her expression one of apologetic modesty mixed with the natural apprehension of a bride-to-be. Upon seeing her, Henry was quick to show an enthusiastic response, while Columbine looked away.

"I'm not very flashy," said Helen.

"It's beautiful," said Henry, suddenly touched by the older girl's remark, and moved, too, by the affection he had always felt toward Helen, the remembrance of her having been always, truly, the girl next door, his first girlfriend, and showing him now her wedding gown. He knew, too, that Helen, more than the others, had always been a little mystified by him, as a sister might be mystified by her older brother's skill at Latin, or by his talk of baseball and automobiles, or just by the size and look of him. It was a way of looking that she possessed that Sophie and Anna and Columbine could never quite comprehend. "You're going to be a very beautiful bride," he said.

Mrs. Kokoriss was just returning to the dining room and was about to speak, when Helen came forward spontaneously, on an impulse that was as complex as the sum of her own lifelong responses to Henry, and, leaning swiftly, kissed him on the face.

"I won't worry about it any more," she said.

"You're supposed to be worried," Henry exclaimed.

"That's what *I* told her," said Mrs. Kokoriss.

"That's the fun of it," Henry said. "You're supposed to be scared stiff! I would be." He threw his hands testifyingly to his chest.

"Would you?" said Helen, appearing more relieved, as though the advent of the approving man in a fatherless house had righted everything.

"Holy mackerel," Henry cried, "I'd be petrified!" He showed them what he meant by petrified as he bulged out his eyes and struck a comical pose with his two hands frozen in space. "They would have to bring me in on a board. They would!" Henry elicited a general round of laughter, even from Columbine, as he repeated his comical depiction of terror.

"Don't worry," Helen said, "when that day comes, we'll all pick you up and carry you off to the church!"

Columbine was stirring her Postum, her hand going round and round, while she eyed the three of them with forbearance, waiting patiently for the silliness to subside. That she might have been a little unhappy over Henry's reluctance or incapacity to make better use of their proximity after a long separation was not apparent. It was certainly not apparent to Henry, although he had not for a moment confused his feelings of nostalgia over Helen with the more powerful impact made on him by the black-haired girl sitting close by, feelings which had assailed him since the moment she came into the room. The business of Helen's wedding, and of her producing her wedding gown for him, was reminiscent to Henry of feelings he had experienced on the night he graduated high school, or the day a year ago when he came out of the Naval hospital in Rhode Island and walked out to the bus stop, knowing on each occasion that something quite vague but enormous had come to an everlasting stop. Already his childhood had become a fixed historical period, like an era in the history books, something that could be altered only in the interpretation, but which in itself was forever impervious to change. The war had provided Henry with a convenient historical conclusion to the old innocence, a kind of sudden Vesuvian eruption whose liquid ash had covered and destroyed the very thing that it preserved in effigy.

In the course of the next several minutes Columbine's impatience became visible. She sighed aloud, fidgeted, and crossed and recrossed her legs. She was swinging her foot back and forth, tapping the toe of her shoe each time against the floor, like a metronome marking off her aggravation into regular intervals. Henry was explaining to Helen and Mrs. Kokoriss something about his mother's recent "troubles," her flashes of irrationality, her sudden prejudices and paranoia, and of how he and his father, along with Dr. Gold, hoped and expected her to recover her balance any day. Helen and Mrs. Kokoriss made no reply but listened in sympathy and embarrassed silence, for Mrs. Flynn's condition had become by then a trifle notorious in the neighborhood. Abruptly Columbine got up from the table and, taking her cup with her, stalked out of the room. She had not been listening, or at least had not comprehended what she heard. Her departure was made dramatic by the sudden scrape of her chair, the injured, arrogant look she affected in rising, and the noisy clack of her heels going out.

"Do you see what I mean, Mama?" Helen interrupted at once, to call attention to her sister's insolence. "Did you see what she just did? She's gotten too big for her britches. She should be taken down a peg. You should punish her, Mother. She's becoming unbearable. I don't like the way she dresses, or walks, or looks at people."

Her mother averted her eyes helplessly. Columbine could be heard mounting the stairs, then marching across the floor overhead. A radio came on.

"She's so rude." Helen sat back, with her hands limp in her lap.

"That's since her father," said Mrs. Kokoriss, muttering.

"She was always rude, but not like this," said Helen. "She's worse, Mama, than Sophie *ever* was. She's in a class by herself. She's so stuck-up!"

Although baffled himself by Columbine's rude leave-taking, Henry chose to pursue a peacemaking path. "I didn't notice anything," he said. "What happened?"

"I have half a mind to go upstairs," said Helen threateningly.

"Don't," said her mother.

All three gazed up at the ceiling, at the sound of Columbine's footsteps coming back the other way. The radio was silenced, and a moment later she could be heard descending the front stairs once more. Everyone was looking up at the doorway expectantly when she came whisking back into the room. She was wearing a green cotton skirt and carrying her cup of Postum regally. She did not look at anyone directly, but returned to her place at the table, sat, crossed her legs, smoothed her skirt with one hand, and looked up then at Helen. "I'm rude," she said, "but I'm not dumb."

"I give up," said Helen.

Columbine's return to the table had a mollifying effect on everyone, but in the minutes to come, no one, it might have been observed, elected to speak without being certain to include her as a listener of equal importance. Columbine had left the table in an attack of pique, but had thought better of it upstairs, and had made use of the cotton skirt to effect her return. At one point, Helen teased Columbine.

"Have you noticed, Mother," she said, "that she's changed clothes six times since Herky came in? You would think," she said in a saccharine tongue, "she had a crush on him."

"Would that be so bad?" Columbine snapped with a speed that left Henry marveling at her composure.

"That's why she was talking about him at supper!" Helen turned smilingly to Henry. "She was talking about you all through supper."

"Not all through supper," Columbine replied, with a caustic smile. "You were talking about suppositories."

"Columbine!" said Helen.

"You were!"

"Please," said Mrs. Kokoriss. She got up from the table.

"She was," said Columbine. "Weren't you?" she asked Helen. *"Wasn't* she?" she asked her mother. Instantly she turned to Henry. *"Do* you like my skirt?"

"We all give up," said Henry.

"We do—all give up." Smiling, Helen rose and took up her bridal gown. She excused herself. "I'll be back." Moments later, when her mother left Henry and Columbine sitting together at the table, Columbine turned to him swiftly.

She did not speak aloud, but mouthed the words almost soundlessly with her lips. *"Don't* treat me like a juvenile," she said, and showed him her icy blue eyes.

"Do you mean to say," Henry replied calmly in his natural voice, "that it was I who did something?"

"Don't," she repeated, with that same soundless venom, moving her lips exaggeratedly, "treat me like a juvenile." She then spoke up naturally. "That's a very nice-looking suit." She looked him over from head to foot with wifely approval. "It's very becoming. I like cord. Is it new?"

Henry laughed and sat back in his seat. Columbine brought her cup crashing down onto the table.

"That's *just* what I'm talking about!" she said.

"I did it again," said Henry.

"If you do it once more"—she showed him her now-familiar bittersweet smile—"I'll leave and I won't come back."

Unbeknownst to both Henry and Columbine, Mrs. Kokoriss was standing in the kitchen doorway, watching them and listening to their whisperings and posturings, and showing great puzzlement over their air of secrecy and familiarity.

"I think," Henry was saying, "that you see slights where there aren't any."

"I know when I'm being insulted."

Her mother stood frozen in the doorway, unable to go forward or back, while Columbine was trying to make the most of what she imagined to be their brief moment of privacy, and had forgotten about being clever.

"Did you miss me?" she said.

"Yes," said Henry truthfully, although he was put in mind at once of the barman's wife, of that vigorous, attractive, resentful woman and of their love-making together, and he even wondered, tangentially, if that might not represent a threat to something precious, after all, as if morality had a way of imposing its own rewards and penalties without requiring the offices of other people. Henry, more than the girl, should have noticed Mrs. Kokoriss in the doorway, since he was half facing her. She was behind Columbine. Henry was feeling some remorse. He was preoccupied.

"I'm glad," said Columbine. "I did, also."

Columbine, being a girl-woman, was probably the

ideal figure upon whom Henry's remorse could attach itself; she was such an excellent combination of innocence and earthly beauty. The somber hue returned to her gaze. She sat unmoving, her face shining under the glow of the chandelier. Her foot had stopped swinging. Everything came to a stop. Columbine's lip curled back sensually. As the moment between them deepened, they remained unaware of Mrs. Kokoriss's presence all the while in the room. Her face was ashen.

When Henry later bade Helen good night, and went out by the front door, his head was swimming. From the corner of the house he could see his own footprints in the white sawdust on the surface of the gardens. He had taken only a step or two into the gardens when he saw her coming hurriedly toward him in the dark. She was half running in the shadow of the wall of the house. Her pale skirt flared in the window light. Henry's senses were in disorder. Her face materialized in the dark, and her final few steps came in a rush, as though she were throwing herself forward into pure space. She came solidly against him in the dark. "I love you, Starbuck," she said. Henry was embracing her, surprised by the strength of her arms around his neck and the solid pressure of her body.

The silence of the gardens was lunar. If, in the minutes to come, they found themselves on the opposite side of the house, in the shallow space between the house and the flowering lilacs next door, it was not because Columbine had led them there. They were just there. "I have one minute," she was saying. "Just one minute. I wanted to tell you something. I had a dream last night. That was what I wanted to tell you. It was a dream of an old man with a white beard. I think it was you," she said. "I dreamed I washed his feet. You had a beard, Starbuck. You looked like Mr. Shaw, the playwright. That's how you will become."

"Not I," said Henry.

"Yes," she said, "because I would make you that way. That's my promise to you. And when you're old and gray, I'll bathe your feet. That's my promise."

Columbine turned then and moved away rapidly along the side of the house, her skirt flaring in the darkness.

XIV

Henry's undoing was prompt and complete. Nature provided a spectacular setting for it, too, a day of great beauty. The trees in Hampden Park were in full leaf, the leaves astir, and the benches lining the sun-lit walks filled to overflowing with occupants anxious to taste the summer sun. It was the first hot, summery day of the year, the start of June. It was probably fitting, too, that Henry's companion, the dark-haired woman with the pretty features and the self-confident demeanor, should have been, as Henry was, wearing white that day. Mrs. McKenna had put on a new tailored suit of spring-weight worsted, and was wearing black and white shoes and a black and white hat. She had turned herself out for the occasion, so that she and Henry cut a brilliant figure, strolling on the walkway among the trees and iris beds. Probably fitting, too, was the fact that Mrs. McKenna, for all her exaggerated qualities, was, after all, a considerable woman. She knew it, too. She knew it better than Henry did. She knew many things that Henry did not know. If an investigator had delved into the records of the public schools in Ireland Parish, riffling back over the past ten to twenty years, he would have discovered that Mrs. McKenna had been a brilliant student, a girl possessed of outstanding native intelligence.

When she took hold of Henry's arm in the park, the gesture was decisive, but not because she had decided to show everyone she was rebellious, or that she had captivated Henry, or that she wished to make a goat of her spouse. She was not like that.

Others might have been, but she was not. For one thing, walking with Henry at noon hour on a lovely June day got her looked at. That, partly, was what she was like. She enjoyed being noticed. Her companion, of course, helped. If Henry had been Mayor Pfeiffer, or Senator Saltonstall himself, that would have been better. Mrs. McKenna simply did not care what others thought about that, so long as the man was a good man, and so long as he could be cultivated into a fine craze for her now and then. Henry was an accessory. She was attracted to him, but she could never see him in any way outside of his being an extension of herself, an embellishment, a trophy. It would be next to impossible to describe Mrs. McKenna's attitude toward someone like Henry if it were not for the prevalence of a very ancient and revered human custom, namely the complex institution of husband and wife, the chief departure being that Dolly McKenna did not look upon herself as the wife. She liked to use a man a little. She liked to decorate herself with him; to have him suffer a little uxorial anxiety in the face of her exploits. Not that she was heartless or mercenary, for she wasn't, not any more, at any rate, than the typical husband. She wasn't a man hater, either. She was really quite fond of men. She was certainly fond of Henry. It didn't trouble Dolly, either, that she was married to a man whose views of men and women were unique under the sun. She was fond of Dicky, too, and would like to keep him around.

"Of course, that would depend on you," she was saying to Henry, as they arrived at the center of the park, "but it would depend on a lot of other things, too."

"It would certainly depend on Dicky," Henry replied. Henry was preparing himself to unravel the bond he shared with Mrs. McKenna, but he was, so far, slow to begin. That was partly because he felt comfortable in her presence.

The bright sunlight accentuated the pinkness of Mrs. McKenna's complexion, while the whiteness of her costume gave her a plump look, partly optical in origin, that struck Henry as harmonizing nicely with the fullness of her face and her fine, birdlike profile. It was the aspect of a well-fed, self-satisfied pouter pigeon.

"You let me worry about Dicky." Mrs. McKenna ignored the flowers and flowering shrubs along the way, as she was not affected by nature in that respect, but was steering Henry by the elbow, parading him before the multitude, as it were. Everyone on the benches watched them go past, especially the elders, their faces upturned, some grinning. Henry wore a white flannel suit and a striped necktie of silver and cobalt blue. Together they formed a picture of life's promise. Mrs. McKenna was swaggering a little. Her hand was warm inside his arm. She sometimes looked at him, he thought, in a strange way, a sudden prospective glitter in her eyes, as if he were an exotic dish that she had coveted for ages and to which she would now, momentarily, address herself. It amused Henry to think of her as a merry but baleful creature who had some nefarious plan in mind for him, something probably not dissimilar to Dicky-bird's fate. "For all I know," she said, "the dummy's probably skulking about in the bushes somewhere right now." She showed Henry the aquiline, lascivious look that unnerved him. Her eyes danced.

"Watching us?" he said.

"Would you mind?" She steered Henry around the graceful sculpted figure of Victory standing in the heart of the park. "We'll take my car," she said. "You drive."

Another thing about Dolly McKenna that was not unpleasant to Henry was the fact that he didn't have to formulate many decisions. He didn't have to be resourceful or inventive.

"Keep my sunglasses in your pocket," she said. "I lost the case. On second thought, give them back to me." She stopped walking. "I'll put them on. I can't stand looking at some of these faces. Did you see the woman with the lump back there?" She gestured over her shoulder with the glasses, then put them on. She looked at him. "Pretty, aren't they?"

"You look good in sunglasses. I look like an idiot in them," he said.

"Shall we kiss soulfully right here," she said in jest, "or shall we continue walking?" She studied him through her tinted lenses.

"I think we should walk," said Henry, amused, but troubled, too, by his inability to disabuse Mrs. McKenna of some of her views about him. Anyhow, he had the right intentions. There was time. He had no doubt that he could unburden himself of her. She was a strong-minded woman, but she was a realistic woman. It was something else. He found something very congenial in her, something congenial to parts of his character that he did not fully understand. He was thinking then, too, about fidelity, and of how the smallest pernicious act could poison everything. A drop of solution may turn litmus blue, or red, or a drop of venom, he thought, stop a heartbeat. One infidelity was every infidelity. That was the maxim of Pandora.

Mrs. McKenna jostled against his hip. "If you don't put your arm around me," she said, with nonsensical logic, "people will think we're in love."

"If I don't?" said Henry, missing the point of her quip.

"Do," said Mrs. McKenna. Henry, compliant, easy to get along with, slipped his arm around her. Dolly took Henry's wrist gently in her gloved fingers, and moved his hand down flat onto her abdomen. "For Dicky-bird's sake," she said.

Together, resplendent in white, they had the look of a bridal couple promenading in the tropics. Mrs.

McKenna's black and white cloche-style hat, sweeping back impressively from her smooth brow, resembled a gorgeous plumage, curving and streamlined. Henry smiled in bemusement at the thought of the barman peeping out of the bushes at them, his eyes glued in fascination to that hand riding warmly upon Mrs. McKenna's smooth, undulating belly.

This time there were no footprints, as in the glowing lunar sawdust, to record their coming together, but when Henry and his companion came strolling down the walk past the crowded benches and on between the masses of blue irises, she was already there. She was in the park. She was sitting on the bandstand steps.

Always an early riser, Columbine had spent a restive night; by the time dawn colored the air blue outside the kitchen window, she had already finished breakfast. She remained at the table for two hours, reading *The Magnificent Ambersons,* before she heard the others stirring overhead and made her way outdoors to the bus stop. She took her umbrella; the early-morning air was fogged and drizzly. A light rain was falling. The little trees by the low cliff were dripping incessantly, making a music in the leaves. The big pine behind them was missing, the tree that she had noticed only in its absence, much as she had come to comprehend her father through the vacancy he left behind. She descended the stone steps to the street. She could wait thirty minutes for a bus, or walk down the hill in ten and catch the incoming bus from Granby, but chose to remain here, at the bus stop opposite Cottage Avenue, with her black umbrella up, and her back as straight as the lamp post behind her and practice for a half hour being the lady of high degree that she was to become. She did not, for instance, look at the faces of the passing motorists, nor did she turn even to steal a glance at the second-floor window in the Flynn house across the way. She was waiting for the bus, and even a simple, inconsequential act like that could be given a touch of the sublime, a certain dignity or elevation, as Madame Muntrum had drummed into her head a thousand times. The great ones, said Madame, lighted up small things. Waiting for the bus could become a study in human excellence. Thus, when Columbine turned to look up the street in the direction of the anticipated bus, she pivoted on the heel of one foot and the toe of the other, moving her body and head and the umbrella in her hands all smoothly about as one integral piece. She held the umbrella just so, too, with both hands, holding it perfectly upright, like a candle or sword or holy standard. When Columbine boarded the bus, she did not try fishing the token from her wicker bag while the vehicle was in motion, either, but seated herself first, shook out her umbrella, folded it and put it aside, and *then* went looking in her bag for her bus token. Bus drivers who started their buses with a rough jolt even before a boarding passenger could sit down were looked upon by Columbine with disfavor. In fact, she did not say good morning to them a second time.

"We're out bright and early," the driver had greeted her pleasantly, after Columbine had dropped her token into the box and seated herself on the worn leather seat behind him. She didn't answer, of course, or even raise her eyes, but just opened her book and, despite the jouncing and the vibration from the tires on the traprock road, affected to read. She was not thinking about the book, though, but about making it up with Helen, who, after all, really didn't know any better, having probably never even opened an issue of *Vogue* magazine or ever heard of Mainbocher, or Schiaparelli, or anyone like them. It was not nice to tease or make fun of people like Helen. She promised herself she would not ridicule Helen again about her enormous wedding gown, particularly since it was not hard for Columbine to visualize herself on some future day in an elegant ivory sheath of a bridal dress, with a long train to it, and somebody attending to her train (maybe her little cousin Casimir dressed like a page boy in a velvet jacket and velvet knickers with ribbons at the knees, his little shoes shining like anthracite). She had time to think about that. She did know, however, that Starbuck would very much like her to treat Helen kindly, as they two had been childhood sweethearts, and she guessed, too, that he, Starbuck, had a sort of soft spot for Helen, particularly as he could see now how sluggish and dull she was turning out to be. He was sentimental like that—which, she was quick to concede, was a nice trait in a man.

Last night, Columbine had lain in her bed naked, face down on the sheets, with her eyes shut. She was not thinking about Helen then, or Anna, or her father, or even at first about Starbuck, but about herself, about her breasts, which were too small, and her feet, which were too long. Most of the girls at school had very small feet, and that was why she was sensitive about hers. Valentina Rubulis wore size-four shoes, which would have been very nice for Valentina if her mother let her wear narrow, pretty shoes that came to a point; instead, her mother bought her square-toed gillies that made Valentina's feet look like little hoofs, like a Shetland pony's. Her mind drifted. She lay on her belly, enjoying the cool firmness of the sheets under her thighs, until, as at other times, she felt herself growing warm and moist between her legs. Something inside her pelvis, or pressing upward against her pelvis, hardened. She guessed that was how Andrew Sullivan felt when he stood behind her that time at the movie machine, or even how Joseph Kussman felt in school when he stood before the class once with his hands in his pockets and you could actually *see* why the other boys were laughing and why he was so uncomfortable, blushing and stammering, and looking up at the ceiling and hoping everyone else would look up, too. Columbine had her toes locked over the edges on both sides of the mattress. She was moving slowly on her belly with her eyes shut, and that sweet, maddening hardness was there like a mound under the mattress, and she was kissing Starbuck with her tongue, knowing that it was somehow his hand that was creating the hardness and the good feelings that radiated like heat across her abdomen and gave her legs that odd muscular tightness. As for the size of her breasts, that didn't matter if it was cool outdoors and she could wear her sweaters and jackets to cover herself up on top, or the big loose navy-blue sweatshirt, and make them look at her legs instead, or the beauty of her walking. She was chewing on the corner of the pillow, tasting the dry cotton on her tongue, like the taste of wetting a handkerchief to remove a speck from your eye, and her buttocks were moving out and back like the head of a petted cat. She was spread-eagled. Starbuck's face was there. It had that look of desire mingled with faintness, as when she had left him in the darkness a night ago and should have gone back to him, as she knew he wanted her to do so that he could put his hand here and say that he loved her like mad and how Helen was very sweet and old-fashioned and they would not hurt her feelings while he was squeezing her like this and they were lying in Mama's bed in the empty house and she could see the golden hair around his penis or cock like golden scrolls and he had that pale, fainting look of being overcome by what was going to happen between them, and of who she was, and of how Helen and Anna could blow up for all he cared. For she had won him now by his wanting her so bad he could probably not even sleep. It would be a delicious secret, too, until they were caught, of course, and by then he would not care because he would realize that *everyone* wanted her and that it was quite a feather in his cap, after all, even if her breasts were this small or her feet too long, or because of her age, or his age, or so on, or so forth.

That was all she remembered of it, but she felt unaccountably proud this morning over having built it up that way by herself and gone through it all so pleasurably in her bed, thinking about Starbuck and about his hand and even the secrecy of the words "penis" and "cock" and such—while in the meantime the Hadley Falls bus on which she was riding had become the Elmwood West Dwight Street bus (the driver reaching up and cranking the new sign into place) and she could see from the bridge where the foaming river was receding so much now that the trees growing in the riverbed below the dam were completely visible again, standing on islands. She decided to get up from her seat before the bus actually stopped at the City Hall, so that the driver could see her from the back as she waited by the door to disembark, with her canvas bag over her shoulder and her umbrella and book under her arm, and realize that she was not just a schoolgirl to be flirted with by bus drivers.

With her umbrella up and her book tucked safely out of sight now beneath her ballet slippers and tights in her canvas bag, Columbine started over the street in the rain toward Mater Dolorosa. It was eight o'clock, but as it was Saturday morning, the automobile and foot traffic was light in the streets. The park was empty, its wooden benches glimmering wetly among the trees. A dog lying asleep under the bandstand stirred as she went clicking past on the walk. She had decided to call first on Sister Mary Placida. She had begun lately to think of the M.P., not as her favorite figure in the Church so much as her chief admirer in the Church, and therefore an appropriate *religieuse* to be utilized on a genteel basis.

She could imagine herself kneeling on the stone floor in a shadowy cove of the apse, with a pale pencil of daylight illuminating softly her forehead, while Sister Mary stood over her, all but hidden from sight by the blackness of her garments, reciting a brand-new prayer she had composed in Latin for this occasion, calling on the saints and Church fathers to lend their special protection hereafter "to this young woman whom I commend to you now and forevermore"— or something like that. Sister would probably be flattered to have such a part, too, because she was a natural when it came to strutting about and playing the role of a giant among pygmies, and could easily see herself as a dark, mysterious intercessor.

Sister was not the only figure in Columbine's select circle, either. There was also Laurence Pratt, her well-to-do photographer; Madame Muntrum, her dance coach and social adviser; Andrew Sullivan, her fun-loving, happy-go-lucky courtier; and various other admirers and guardians each of whom sought to please and flatter her in his own special way. There was Valentina at school, who always rushed ahead to open the door for her, and then smiled at Columbine with a pinkish blush if Columbine said "Thank you." But as Columbine, the cynosure of this group, had now fallen in love, she felt it appropriate this morning to make the rounds, particularly among the major members of her circle, such as Sister herself, and, if there was time, to stop in the church also for a brief visit at the altar. She could not reveal to anyone the exact nature of her great happiness, of course, but she could pay them each the courtesy of a visit. (Mrs. Wallis Simpson had probably had a coterie of such followers, kowtowing friends who fell all over themselves in their desire to please her whenever she came to call.) Columbine even thought she might call on the outlandish, ill-kempt Mr. Griffin this afternoon. She could just imagine the old gnome bluffing as best he could to hide the thrill of actually seeing her come to his door!

Sister invited Columbine upstairs into her room, delighted by Columbine's unannounced visit. When Columbine entered the foyer of the Sisters' residence house, Sister Mary Placida had collared one of the younger nuns, Sister Catherine, who was not much more than a novice, and was in the midst of giving her a good talking-to. Columbine did not catch Sister's actual words but saw on the M.P.'s face and in the cold gray reptilian eye the familiar heart-chilling look that invariably appeared when she was questioning someone like Marjorie Piska in the moments leading up to a thrashing—Sister's eyes bugging and her lips and jaws working quietly round and round as if she were sucking on something tasteful in her mouth, like the pit of a half-eaten cherry, or perhaps a raisin taken from the little silver tin that she kept under lock and key in her desk, while posing the same unanswerable questions over and over again: "Why *are* you ill-prepared?" Or, with mocking sweetness: "What *shall* I do then . . . with the likes of you?"

But Columbine's appearance in the foyer dispelled Sister's black mood in a fraction of a second, leaving the hurriedly dismissed young nun only to smile gratefully at Sister's unexpected guest, as she went brushing past Columbine on whispering feet, her face as white as the porcelain knobs on the foyer doors. Sister treated Columbine at once like a peer, saying indulgently of Sister Catherine, "Youngsters will be youngsters *even,* apparently, when they have chosen to render solemn vows." Once upstairs, Sister was thrilled when Columbine showed her her dancing shoes and tutu, and she exhorted Columbine to tie on the slippers, a request that Columbine was not about to satisfy. Their visit was cut short almost at once, anyhow, when Sister was called away on some matter pertaining to the parents' association, but she walked Columbine to the downstairs door and saw her out with the formality of a papal dignitary taking leave of a royal guest. Columbine's spirits were continuing to climb. Pacing down the rubber-carpeted aisle of the nave of the Mater Dolorosa minutes later, she felt invincible.

All by herself in the heart of the big, windy church, kneeling upright, she prayed with an air of importance. She prayed for herself, then she prayed for herself and Starbuck. Then she prayed for her father and for her family and friends and for Sister Mary Placida. Then she prayed for Starbuck once more. She prayed that Starbuck should never be unhappy, but that if he were to be unhappy he should be unhappy in the way that she wanted him to be unhappy.

Columbine spent the better part of an hour in Madame Muntrum's tenement that morning, listening to music mostly and not dancing, for Madame became suddenly engrossed in a story of hers about the Golden Horn, an account of how she and her husband had hidden themselves from Bolshevik agents for two days and two nights in a waterfront warehouse that reeked of olives. Madame later took Columbine with her on a shopping errand to the Growers' Outlet, a big fragrant emporium filled with dozens of fruit and vegetable stalls, wherein Columbine emulated Madame's behavior perfectly, point for point, her way of walking, and of looking brazenly at people, or of picking up oranges or lemons or lettuce heads and squeezing them with her fingers while examining them with a jeweler's eye. The outing was spoiled for Columbine only by the appearance of a familiar face, that of her schoolmate Joseph Kussman, who suddenly called out to her. He was wearing a white apron and went bolting up the next aisle carrying in his arms a peck of potatoes that bowed him over backward. "Hi!" he shouted at her.

Columbine stopped dead and fixed him with a look.

Madame turned her head. "Who was that boy?" she inquired.

"Just an idiot from my school," she said.

"I've seen that boy," Madame declared. "A bright little fellow! Hard-working!"

Columbine turned in time to see Joseph vanishing in another direction, carrying this time an enormous armful of celery, and emitting piercing whistles through his teeth to warn shoppers out of the way. Madame was concluding her shopping, and Columbine was carrying Madame's judicious purchases in three or four small bags. Before they got out the front door, however, Joseph came darting into view once more. "Hi, Mrs. Muntrum," he said. "Hi, Cole!"

"Also," said Madame, coloring a little, a trifle flattered, "he remembers names."

"Only not the right ones," said Columbine.

Here Madame showed her protégée a gloved finger of admonition. "A successful person remembers names!"

Columbine went into the park at noon to sit in the sun and read and be admired a little. She was sitting on the steps of the bandstand, sunning her feet and legs. She had written Henry a letter the day before. She had a supply of apple-green stationery at home which her father had brought her from the paper mill for her birthday last June. The only reason Columbine wrote letters, as to Helen and Sophie, was that the paper was so pretty, with its rough deckle edge and handsome apple-green envelopes to match. The violet ink formed a surprisingly tasteful impression, she thought. And, of course, too, there was the recent innovation she had introduced upon her signature, for she did not sign her name any longer in the way she had been taught to do. The name Columbine now appeared under her hand with an enormous capital letter *C,* as large always as space would allow, grand and sweeping, with the rest of her name below it in a small, round, controlled hand, and with the dot of the *i* a mere speck floating high up inside the elegant curve of the capital. The creation of this signature corresponded in Columbine to something relating to Starbuck, a meaning she could not begin to make conscious (nor even dreamed to try), although the great capital letter might have resembled a gossamer lariat thrown out into space to catch and enclose something. She was not, that is, so alive to the possible interpretations of a delicate ovoid structure that enclosed within itself a little floating fishlike speck as Starbuck might have been self-attuned on the day he invaded with his fist the envelope of the unbroken page in Mr. Skeat's ancient dictionary. She was rereading the letter now, while keeping an eye on the passing human parade. Hundreds of blue irises were in full bloom in flower beds parallel to the walks. Three boys with baseball gloves were playing catch nearby. One of the boys looked over at her many times. Columbine ignored him. Then she saw Henry approach. He was dressed in white; so was the woman with him. Columbine's heart jumped wildly. She froze in place.

She had never seen Henry looking so superb, so refined, so splendid. Maybe it was the beauty of the day, but he looked very handsome and lean and gallant. Maybe there is one day, one precise moment, in every lifetime when one passes through the zenith of youth, of physical harmony. This was that moment. He was luminous; he was beautiful. She was staring at him. The woman at his side moved with a mature, sensual rhythm. Her gait was dreamy and undulant. She moved as naturally as sunlight opening out in a field. She was like one of the gods' own mares. Columbine recognized the woman. She had driven him home once long ago when he was still in uniform. She was the woman with the big bosom and the very sexual way of looking at him that had frightened her a little. As they approached on the walk, the urge to get up and run mounted steadily in Columbine's breast, but she couldn't detach her eyes from them. Her face distorted in horror. She managed, at last, to turn away fractionally, and gazed with fixed, animal-like eyes at the trunk of a nearby tree. Henry and Mrs. McKenna stopped walking on the path.

The woman was putting on her sunglasses. She was saying something intimate and suggestive to him; then they were walking again. He was putting his arm around her waist. They had not seen Columbine. They passed within ten feet of the bandstand steps, but failed to see her. Columbine did not follow them with her eyes, but retained a vivid impression of the black and white feathers in the woman's hat, and of the black toes of her shoes, and of his hand riding low upon her belly. She was petrified. In fact, she was so engrossed in herself that when she finally got to her feet and bolted, spilling her book, letter, and umbrella onto the grass, she was heedless of everything going on about her. Her heart was racing. She started off on a beeline in the opposite direction from Henry and didn't notice the boys with the baseball, or hear the sudden shout. An instant later, the thrown hardball struck her temple. Her skull resounded with a crack. Without stopping, she ran headlong from the park. The storefronts and gawking pedestrians were but dimly perceived as forming the corridor of her escape. She was running in the street, holding her canvas bag before her by the two straps like a satchel of explosives to be flung into the river. She was out of control.

Anyone familiar with Columbine and with the facts of the coincidental encounter between herself and the two figures in the park would have been puzzled by her responses. For one thing, she was cool-hearted. Her self-composure was not a mask. As far as that goes, her superciliousness was not a contrivance, either. She was not a modest girl. As for her relationship to the blond-haired young man in the white suit, hers was not supposed to be the vulnerable role. Young as she was, even she, Columbine, knew that. Hers was the steelier soul. If anyone was supposed to become flustered or discombobulated, it was not she, Columbine; it was he, Starbuck. Nor was this just the egoism of an adolescent. Starbuck was her suitor. In a sense he always had been. She had grown up with his photograph on the piano in the parlor. The smiling, distant face of the sailor next door was the companion of her soul on a hundred rainy afternoons. She had talked to him in the picture. She had grown up waiting for him to come home. Helen and Sophie and Anna had talked about him many times, but the watchful eyes of the distant sailor face were watchful of her. She was too young to think of the sailor on the piano as coming home someday to his family. He was coming home to her. It had always been like that. His face was registered in the first archives of her memory. It was imprinted on her soul. He belonged to her. He had *always* been coming home to her.

She couldn't recall later whether she had got back to Cottage Avenue on foot or by bus, but found herself down in the cellar of her house sitting on the high wooden stool in front of her father's workbench. She had become like two people. While sitting there, in shock, she seemed also to be standing apart, as it were, watching herself. In this way her normal feelings returned. Outdoors, it was high afternoon. The sunshine fell almost vertically. The cellar stood noiseless about her in its noonday gloom, bringing back resonances of her father. She remembered when they kept potatoes in the bin by the stairway. She recalled her father repairing the hatch-

271

way doors one summer. He didn't talk much. He didn't smile much, either. He was very big and very powerful. She had a fanciful impression of having seen him naked once, but she was not certain whether she had seen him or dreamed she had, for she could not recall anything of his genitals or of his having moved or spoken. She guessed she had dreamed it.

His tools still lay on the workbench in the very attitude in which he had left them one autumn night just last year. A grayish curlicue wood shaving encircled the blade of a silvery chisel. A block of graying wood was locked in the vise. There had been a bowl of eggnog on the piano upstairs that night. That was the night Starbuck realized who she was. As if that evening he had been able to look back inside her and had found himself there, inside her, back in the very first ages of her existence. Time was like a geography, a series of tablelands and descents rolling away smoothly behind you, backward, rolling downward and on and out of sight, and on backward still into the gardens of creation. Leaning, Columbine placed her two hands on the edge of the workbench and vomited onto the floor. She gagged and then vomited again. In the pool on the floor she could see the undigested raisins from the muffins she had eaten at Madame's.

Columbine went upstairs and put on her purple dress. That was her Easter dress. She regarded herself in the vanity glass. The room was very warm with the sun directly on the roof above, and through the open window came the steady, insistent drone of insects in the grass below and among the bushes along the fence. Columbine dressed methodically. She pulled up her dress and put on a pair of Anna's stockings and the white garter belt she kept hidden in her bureau. Then she sat on the white chair in front of the vanity and made up her face. She followed the directions she had learned from a magazine, keeping the color delicate and graduating it here and there, until her cheekbones came forward and her eye sockets deepened. She had never seen herself look so pretty. She colored her eyelids and darkened her eyelashes and eyebrows, then put on her coral lipstick. Crossing her leg, she admired her stockinged foot in the glass. In the glass her feet looked shorter. She colored her nails and blew on them. The color was pale pink, like the inside of a seashell. She was not thinking about Starbuck or her father or about anyone really, but was feeling very neutral. She spent ten minutes brushing her hair, brushing it in every direction and then combing it vigorously, till at last it lay flat and smooth as a crow's wing above her ear. Then she put on her shoes. They were Anna's graduation shoes. They were originally white. Anna had dyed them for her for Easter. There was nothing wrong with dyeing shoes, not according to the magazines. The shoes looked dark and pretty in her hands. Columbine put them on, and then, getting up and moving the chair to one side, observed herself in the full-length mirror. She looked like somebody else. She looked beautiful.

A blue darning needle flew in at the window, circled the room once in reconnaissance, then flew out the other window. It vanished among the pear leaves. Mr. Griffin was coming up the alleyway. He was carrying a stick and striking languidly before him at the heads of goldenrod drooping in the sultry air. He glanced inquiringly toward the Kokoriss house. He was looking to see if she was there. Mr. Griffin liked her. He was a grass widower whose wife ran off years ago with another man. Columbine had an impulse to go to the window and lift up her dress for Mr. Griffin. She felt sort of spooky. A shaft of sunlight had tilted in over the windowsill and drew a fine, shimmering stripe across the linoleum. It was two o'clock in the afternoon.

Minutes later she was walking up the hill, passing under the shadow of the great water tank. She was walking on the roadside, her heels making wells in the sand. There was a faint smell of sewage in the air, as she turned her steps in at the corner of Old Bridge Street. The derelict condition of the houses in there brought a smirk to her lips. The sidewalk was cracked and overgrown; bits of broken glass lay burning in the sand. She was feeling cool and unemotional. She never perspired, anyhow. Some of the houses, she noticed, didn't even have walks. The neighborhood was scrubby and disreputable. The big flowering lilac tree at the side of the Sullivan house provided the entire street with its only grace.

XV

Columbine was having impure thoughts. She was riding in the Packard with her arm out the window and the breeze from the vents setting her crepe dress rustling and shaking, and she was experiencing unpleasant thoughts and feelings. She felt violated and cheapened. A pout came and went on her lips. Her feelings would run away in one direction, until it seemed she might cry, but then, because she never did cry—ever—those feelings would stop, leaving her bereft momentarily of all feeling. Then something different would start up inside her and go the other way, taking her off into a kind of surliness. She felt surly and unpleasant. She felt vindictive, and a little dirty. Then she would pout again. Then it would start all over again.

Every time her companion tried to draw a response from her, Columbine would put him off with a rude comment or an air of sulky self-absorption and a silence flavored to discourage further entreaties.

"Do you know," Salty would say, piping up in a voice contrived to express still another level of wonderment, "you must be some kind of human miracle!"

"I *said,*" Columbine would reply, "I'm not feeling talkative."

"And I," he would say, "am supposed to drive her around." Salty would thump the steering wheel with his fist or strike his temple a looping blow. "She's a miracle."

"Just take me riding," she said.

She sat against the passenger door, watching the wall of trees rolling past. They were driving west on the Apremont Highway, the road named for the village in France where an Ireland Parish infantry regiment had fought in the First War. Mr. Griffin had been there. He told her about it one afternoon in the garden. She asked him if he had ever killed anyone. He said he had wounded a horse with a machine gun. He said it was an American horse. Columbine asked him what was the difference between an American horse and a German horse, and Mr. Griffin said that the German horses spoke German. Columbine smiled. Everyone had their lies. Even Starbuck, she thought, had lied to her. She pouted.

She was not looking at Salty, but when he turned the radio on a second time, she switched it off. "Don't," she said, "put it on again."

"Somebody is going to be walking home," said Salty.

"I'd rather walk than listen to that," said Columbine. "I don't listen to the radio." She was being terrifically fresh and high-handed now, not raising her voice, but giving him an icy, daggerlike look. Her eyes twinkled with menace.

"*Is* the radio playing?" he said, at last.

Columbine said nothing, but redirected her attention to the road before them, looking out to the valley far ahead, which was dark and somber and seemed to swallow up the sun. She was in a surly, unpleasant mood.

"*Is,*" he said again, "the radio playing? Somebody," he said, "has a bee in her bonnet. Somebody," he said, "has a bee in her ass."

"Andrew," Columbine spoke this time with the gentler tone of a nurse or doctor addressing a terminal patient about some failure in his earthly life that it was perhaps too late to correct, "I don't like vulgar words, especially about me." She was lecturing him now, but that funny ugly feeling was coming on inside her. "I don't have a bee in my ass," she said, "and I don't like talking about my ass, and I don't like you talking about it." She was looking at him insolently. She looked at his hand resting on the shift. His hand looked white and pulpy, like a mushroom, but with tiny freckles on it and little red hairs. It gave her a funny feeling. "I know you have a vulgar tongue," she said, prolonging the subject, "and I really don't mind. But if you use vulgar words about me, I'll make you take me home." It was fun treating him like dirt.

"All I said was, you had a bee in your ass."

"And what if I do?" she snapped. She turned on him. She was looking him over dispraisingly from head to foot. He was wearing a primrose jacket and chartreuse gabardine pants, which, combined with his lemon-colored shirt, big flowery necktie, and two-toned spectator shoes, gave him an altogether verdant look. His head jutted a trifle. He had glossy red hair and red eyebrows and lashes, and green eyes that glittered like a toad's. His features, though, were comely. He was, Columbine realized, a good-looking man, but the lineaments of his face saw a constant parade of expressions passing outward through them, expressions of ignorance and wonder and low shrewdness which served to destroy his handsomeness. The spirit corrupted the form. Of course, Columbine was a snob. To her, Andrew Sullivan was low-class. He could be amusing, and there was something thrilling in the electrical air of danger and violence surrounding him, but she had a suspicion that if she were to reach surreptitiously and raise his pant leg an inch or two, she would discover underneath, not a human leg, but rather the pastern and tufted fetlock of a horse or a goat.

Columbine began then to toy with Salty, playing upon his vanity in a sullen, provocative way. "Just," she said, "because you're nice-looking and have a beautiful automobile doesn't give you the right to use such speech with me."

Scarcely able to credit his ears, Salty showed Columbine a bright, inquisitive gaze. He couldn't imagine she had paid him a compliment. Columbine was regarding him steadily. Sitting languidly against the door, with her pale legs stretched out straight before her and her purple dress fluttering and whispering, she looked like an elegant flower, like a purple larkspur laid out carefully upon the seat, its petals quivering.

"Just," she said, "because you have money in your pocket, or because you may own a pistol, for all I know, or because you buy expensive suits of clothes, doesn't give you that right." Her face was a blank tablet. A moment later, she straightened up and, with a sultry crossness in her lips and eyes, moved closer to him on the seat. She stretched her arm along the seat behind him. She was watching him sullenly. She could detect the telltale signs of Andrew growing restive and upset with himself. He didn't know how to talk to her. He felt outclassed and intimidated. Columbine could just imagine somebody's shock at seeing her sitting so close to Andrew Sullivan like this, and looking at him in a pouting, provocative way. She could imagine Starbuck watching her. She wished she had not seen Starbuck at all that day, but could just have gone on trusting him in innocence.

Beyond the farthest treetops could be seen the silver, winking surfaces of Hampton Ponds, shining like coins in the black valley, with the sky and clouds reflected in them. In a juniper-dotted pasture at the foot of the hill, twenty or more Jersey cows stood motionless in the sun, as they shot past. Minutes later, Salty steered from the highway onto a gravel road that divided the pasture in two and vanished in the woods ahead. Then they were under the trees, with spangles of sunlight dancing on the hood and the polished fenders sideswiping branches. A greenish light came and went in the interior of the sedan.

"Where are you taking me?" said Columbine, with patent disrelish.

"Buck Pond." He was tongue-tied, she imagined.

"Is that where you summer?" she asked tartly, and was amazed herself at the sophisticated edge of her own sarcastic retort.

"A friend of mine has a camp here."

"I can imagine what it looks like." Columbine had taken a cigarette and lighted it, and sighed now in such a way that the smoke came streaming from her mouth in a long gray and blue jet. Grinning elfishly, Salty turned from the gravel road into a drive that revealed itself among the trees as little more than a stripe of bright-green grass with dead leaves on either side of it, curving like a tunnel into the woods.

"Even when you're sassy, Blackbird, I still like you." Salty appeared to marvel no end here over the dimensions of the tolerance engendered in him by his companion.

The name Blackbird brought Columbine's head around instantly, but she said nothing. She guessed that men like Andrew Sullivan gave their girls such names. She didn't want to discourage him too much. She wanted to behave as though she were his girl. She wished she had been walking in Hampden Park with him this morning and had met Starbuck coming the other way, with Andrew beside her in his yellow and green verdant costume looking like a big cauliflower with a magnified red-haired bug peeping out of it. The thought of Starbuck lying somewhere in love with that woman made Columbine's knees shake as she got out of the car at the water's edge.

At first, it was windy. The summer camps along the shore were boarded up still from the winter. The wind made a dry whistling sound in the open space underneath the camps, most of which were built up from the ground on cement staddles; the wind rippled the sunlit water. Salty walked beside her. His eyes were the same emerald hue as the bottle of beer in his hand. His hand around the bottle was oversized and pulpy. It was not a boy's hand. She could imagine him reaching down behind her and clasping her softly back there. That gave her a chill. She was repelled by his bushy red eyebrows and the agate glint of his eyes, but being repelled only added to the funniness of her feelings. She would like to have been seen looking very pretty and sexual and enjoying herself with someone who looked like a devil. It was fun having gone and got him like that, getting all dressed up and not even knowing why until she found herself walking on the broken sidewalk near his house and having that first funny feeling of wanting him to touch her with his hand. Salty was smiling to himself. They were walking by the shore. Columbine picked her way carefully in her purple high-heeled shoes.

The sun made yellow splash marks on the brown surface of the pond; it lighted the white diving rafts, and twinkled in windows of camps on the far shore. A motorboat moved through the shadows of the trees across the pond, its engine echoing softly in the branches directly overhead. Columbine had an impulse to say something flattering to Andrew; to look at him in an intimate, scornful way, but in a way that was scornful not of him but of everything, because that was how girls who belonged to men like Andrew were supposed to look, and then to say something outrageous. He incited in her the kind of fascination one might feel in a museum toward spiders or snakes. It would be fun to treat him with a kind of respect, as if he were her peer, or as if she were really quite degraded, after all, and was therefore *his* peer. It was fun imagining they were equals and in getting her face to show it, to show that she not only respected herself but could respect him, too, even if low-class manners required a cynical way of putting it.

"Next to you," she said, "most people don't know which end is up." Turning, she showed Salty a smug, vain look which, by contraries, was meant to reflect tartly upon Salty's vaunted worldliness. "That's why people talk about you."

Columbine introduced a certain surliness into her gait. It was the first time she had ever spoken to Andrew in a civil and apparently sincere way like that, and she was not surprised by the glow of pleasure that burnished his cheeks.

"You ain't just whistling," he said, and smiled past her in the direction of the water.

Columbine was looking at him as she walked, her aerial-blue eyes humorless, her lips shut. She was (to borrow Sophie's word for it) slumming.

She was in front of him then, picking her way through the grass with great care, making sure to demonstrate to her companion the difficulty of traversing uneven ground in high-heeled shoes, but not being so flagrant about it as to sacrifice her natural ladylike poise. The trick was to walk on the balls of the feet, she thought, using the heel just for extra balance, maintaining all the while a smooth, thoughtful stride. She could envision her companion coming along behind her, sauntering casually, with his hands in his pockets. He had rid himself of the emptied beer bottle. She heard it go whistling away in the air, revolving. Unlike Starbuck, Andrew right now would be leering at her every movement; she could feel his green, suspicious eyes on her legs as she walked. If it was Starbuck behind her, she would have gone under the pines, in where the walking was smoother and where, in the gloom, he would not have had any excuse for not kissing her; but with

Andrew she kept to the water's edge, lest he think she was encouraging him. You had to deal differently with different people. She was learning that. With Andrew, she would stay by the shore, where they would be visible but not conspicuous. Columbine smiled at the thought of Starbuck going past in a boat and seeing her now, walking at the edge of the woods in her Easter dress, with Salty Sullivan shambling along behind her in his flashy shoes and pegged pants, and Starbuck knowing full well what was in *his* mind, Andrew's mind, especially as she was so prettily made up today, and seemed to be enjoying herself, and making a point, too, of being friendly toward Andrew, of treating him almost politely, paying him compliments and treating him like her equal, like a proper date—even, she thought, like Starbuck himself. The best part in that regard would come when he, Andrew, would actually touch her with his hand. His hand gave her the heebie-jeebies. It was like toadstools. It frightened her. She wanted him, though, to put his hand on her, to touch her flesh with his hand, just once, as if to leave a spot. That was how she felt. She also had an impulse to cry, but that was more a rolling feeling in her chest than a conscious unhappiness. Turning, Columbine spoke over her shoulder, showing him just the profile of her face. He was, she could see from the corner of her eye, trailing along behind her just as she had guessed, a few paces back, with his hands in his pockets, and, also, of course, looking her up and down like mad. He had a dandelion in his mouth.

"People *do* talk about you, don't they?" she said. She glanced at him with approving sulkiness, then glanced away over the water to where the distant motorboat was throbbing along quietly in the shadows of trees, its stern very low in the water. The boat was red and white.

Salty took the dandelion from his mouth and looked at the bitter-tasting stem, while contributing a timely litotes. "You're no donkey yourself," he said.

Columbine allowed the shadow of a sneer to distort her lips and nose, an expression she imagined as being distinctly low-class. "Your girlfriend," she said derisively, "should see you now."

"I don't have a girlfriend," he said.

"You did," she retaliated icily.

"I did," he conceded philosophically, "but I don't any more."

Columbine looked over her shoulder at him expressionlessly.

"I got rid of her," he said. "She was a tomato. Next to you"—Salty made a slow, lateral cut of his hand —"that girl was a tomato."

"Next to me?" Columbine challenged him with a backward glance, while not missing a step, however, in her slow, languorous, ladylike stride, and not failing, either, to mix a certain bantering note into her amazement.

"Well, why not?"

"Why not *whut?*" she said saucily. "She was your girlfriend."

"Do you know," Salty replied in an incredulous, musical tone, while scrunching up his face, "she never really was."

"Oh, there's a fib!" Columbine threw out, but regretted at once the use of such a childish word.

"She *thought* she was," he drawled, "but she never really was." Salty expressed this sentiment with that air of rare impersonal wonderment usually reserved for subjects of a very remote or ancient character, such as questions pertaining to interstellar space or the vanished dinosaurs. Salty put Miss Kelleher in the past tense. "She had no style, Blackbird, and," he added significantly, "she was thick to boot. Skirts like that give me a pain. Hey," he said, "she was a donkey, why kid ourselves."

Columbine regarded him placidly, as he drew

abreast of her. "I don't like being compared to tomatoes," she said, relishing the use of the slang word and scanning him sullenly from head to foot.

"You're different, Blackbird," he went on.

"I should hope so."

"You," he said, "come from a good family."

"Well, you," she replied with that same air of intimate insolence toward the rest of the world, "were too good for a tomato like that."

"She was a bum," said Salty. He blew the dandelion from his mouth. They were walking side by side. "She was a tramp and a bum. Her sister is a tramp and her brother is a tramp. The only one who's not a tramp is her brother Eddie, and he's a priest in Milwaukee." Here Salty spread his hands before him to signify an enormous stomach. "Eddie's got a beer belly like this, and they sent him to Milwaukee. I could never understand that."

Columbine was learning that low-class individuals like Andrew saw themselves as self-respecting, but to do that they looked down on one another. They looked down on one another because there was no one else to look down on. To Andrew, she, Columbine, was as unattainable as a fashion plate in Palm Beach society, she thought. That was why the Kelleher girl had attacked her, too, because to her Columbine was a figure of the hated upper class. Columbine knew that there were not three classes, as Mary Placida had taught at school. There was not an upper class and a middle class and a lower class. There were two classes. There was an upper class and a lower class. That was why Andrew was afraid to put his hand on her. To him, she was like a creature made out of precious materials, a creation whose perfumed flesh he was forbidden by birth ever to touch. That was why, too, his hands were repellent to her. But it was also why she wanted him to touch her. When Sophie once said she had gone slumming, it must have been to get this deliciously

284

horrible feeling of being next to something unnatural, something coarse and fleshy and unclean. That was why rich people went slumming. She had seen the tiny spears of orange hairs showing in Andrew's nostrils which resembled something furry and six-legged hiding in there. Columbine shivered, and folded her arms. From behind, she could hear the approaching putt-putt-putt of the motorboat coming along slowly in the shadows of the trees close to shore.

Columbine's thoughts grew more childish still, as she contemplated turning her head to him and showing him a quick, fleeting glimpse inside herself, a sudden frankness of the eye that would excite him. She would pretend that he was not different from Starbuck. That was how she would repay Starbuck for what he had done. In reprisal, she would give her eyes momentarily to Andrew. She would let him actually see inside her, see who she was, and how delicate and precious she really was, and how fine. Then she would look away, and he, Andrew, would never afterward see her like that again.

She was setting her feet down carefully in the grass, walking with grace, not stepping on the dandelions underfoot, and avoiding the gray coils of last summer's dog droppings. Andrew was beside her. The motorboat came past about twenty feet offshore, its engine thrumming noisily. The boat was reassuring. She could smell Salty's talcum. She was aware of the dandelions going down under his feet. The time had come. Turning, she brought her head slowly around to him, turning her face to him in a smooth dramatic manner that was a testimonial it-self to her bearing and posture. She looked at him deeply, his eyes shining back at her with a depthless, feline puzzlement. He was looking right inside her, or trying to. He was trying to fathom her. When he smiled, she observed a green pencil-line stain on the upper edges of his teeth; the fingers of his left hand closed then around Columbine's upper arm. He had reached around behind her back, and was clasping her left biceps in his hand. She was still looking at him in that deep candid way, keeping her eyes all the while wide and sincere, and still walking smoothly, too, not missing a pace, not stepping on the yellow, upright flowers or on the dried dung or on the fallen twigs strewn in the grass. It was frightening, but she kept walking. She was walking and looking at him.

His hand encircling her whole arm, gripping it in the place where her vaccination mark was, was the crowning part of it. Starbuck should have seen her now. He should have seen her, in her purple crêpe dress with the crêpe ruffles, walking along the shore of the pond in the embrace of someone who was known to be notorious, and looking at this person very soulfully at the same time, while walking.

They marched on together past three boarded-up camps, and on past a rotted jetty and the sunken remains of a gray dory that was filled with mud and water and leaves. A dragonfly hovered in the sun directly over the submerged boat, its wings shimmering iridescently. The sun was still high but was behind the trees, and was running behind clouds; it cast sudden milky, colorless spangles of light, like coins, across the earth before them, only to vanish again instantly. Columbine had withdrawn her eyes from her companion and was gazing steadily before her. He would never see that look again. That was his fate in being low-class, just as it would be Starbuck's fate to beg forgiveness of her on his knees. Andrew was still gripping her arm warmly in his hand. She could feel his arm about her back. The only apparent movement was that of their feet at the periphery of her vision, the recurrence to view of the purple pointed toe of her shoe, and of the brown and white perforated wing tip of his—his crushing down everything it met, hers avoiding every impediment.

She was savoring the clutch of his hand on her arm and the feel of his arm behind her, and the constant cluster of sensations upon her, the faint fetid odor of the pond, the talcum smell, the smell of humus and of the leaf mold under the oaks by the boarded-up boathouse. They walked onto a tiny bathing beach and past a shut summer cottage with a white flagpole standing in front of it, and then onto the grass once more, and on again under the trees. She was treating him like an equal now; that was the best part of it, putting herself into that frame of mind. She looked at him sidelong once more with just the sort of smug insolence that a Kelleher-type girl would use in looking at her boyfriend. Their walk was becoming a promenade, something deliciously ritualistic and arcane. She could not explain the rolling sensation in her chest, or the proclivity toward tears that brought a pout to her lips, but it was all part of the one gratification. She felt both damaged and inoculated against harm by what was happening. Following the contour of the shore, she caught sight, far behind them, of the black and cream automobile parked underneath the ash tree by the water. Salty was speaking to her as they walked. If anyone ever harmed Columbine again, said Salty, making a past assumption of his protectiveness toward her now, "I'd blow a hole in them you could see through."

Columbine wished to turn back, but was skeptical of introducing any novelty of movement that might be interpreted as an invitation for intimacies. Her horror of his actually stopping and taking hold of her with his hands and arms was as real as the surprising emptiness of all the summer camps they had passed, or as the late-afternoon silence that seemed to Columbine as physical as the coolness of the air.

"That," she replied calmly, "is because you're violent."

"I ain't violent," said Salty, grinning at her from

the corner of his eyes. At such times Columbine thought him more comical than wicked. The orange pompadour atop his head gave him a crazed, rooster-like look; his big purple and lavender necktie was like the tongue of a lizard.

"Shall we go back to the car?" she said, and at the same time led him obliquely toward the water. Pausing, she turned then, in the pale, milky sunlight, and started slowly to stride back toward the car. Surprisingly, her companion acceded without a word, although he continued to hold her arm, and she could now and then feel the entire length of his body brushing and touching against her. They walked under the trees and out past the summer cottage with the white flagpole, and were walking on leaves and acorns, with the colorless sunbeams flitting down upon them and retracting and dimming, when Salty released her arm and dropped his hand casually around her waist. He moved his hand softly forward till it rested flat on her belly. Columbine continued pacing, but her brain had slowed down. Her head felt cold. His hand was open on her belly, the fingers spread out across her whole abdomen from one side to the other. Salty was a little behind her now, with his hip against her right buttock, his left leg moving in smooth conjunction with her right. They were strolling in unison, like one, when Columbine stole a downward glance at his hand. It lay flush upon her belly, white and isolated, resting on the purple crêpe of her dress. The skin was so pale as to be luminous. The fingernails were long and uneven. The thumbnail was cracked. Each finger was coated with a mat of glossy red hair.

Stranger still, Columbine discovered that she had been talking all the while. She began talking when they paused at the water, and was talking when he placed his hand on her belly, and was still talking now. A part of her had even been listening to herself talking. Half her brain was cold, and the other part was talking. She was talking about Helen and her wedding this month, but as soon as she realized she was talking, she forgot what she had been talking about. She was looking straight ahead, walking like a somnambulist. His hand on her belly was the perfection of defilement. She knew that. He could not have improved on that. It was pulpy with freckles on it. It was like a starfish sleeping on her dress.

"Sometimes I chatter away," she said.

"You make sense," said Salty.

"That's because you understand what I'm talking about." Columbine continued to flatter him. She didn't know why she was doing that. She promised herself she would never again go to such a remote, desolate place with an individual like Andrew. His hand and his hip felt warm against her, almost hot. She guessed he was very excited. He was pretending not to be. When she stole a glance at him, his eyes brightened to a shine. A piquant, cunning glow arose in his features, and he bit his lip and looked away. It was so quiet by the pond that she could hear the grainy whisper of her silk-sheathed legs. At every step the toe of her purple shoe peeped up from below the ruffled hem of her dress. The tumult in her breast was subsiding.

From time to time, too, she discovered him stealing glances at her, his eyes a sudden green witchfire. He was biting his lip. "To me," he said, smiling, "you're special."

This endearment struck Columbine as somehow a matchless vulgarism, as though he had been a devil with a tail and knew that she had seen his tail, and was now pretending that he had not noticed her noticing. Still, she showed him an insolent, brightening glance, and looked away. She was egging him on. She had done that with others. She had done it with Joseph at school. She had done it with strangers. She had done it with Starbuck. It was not meant to injure anyone. She had ridden past Starbuck on her bicycle last year, back in the days when he used to sit on his front porch in his sailor whites, and she knew he was looking at her; she could feel it in her whole body as she pedaled past. Or when she got off her bicycle at the end of the flagstone path, in order to let her bike down the steps, while making a show of her legs, and she could actually feel him wanting to get up from his seat on the porch and come out to help her. He was waiting for her to look up and acknowledge his presence, but she never did. That was her way of effecting the improbable. He, the sailor in the photo, was paying attention to her because she was *not* paying attention to him. She was supposed to look at him. She was supposed to smile and greet him. She had been waiting forever for him to come home. But by not looking at him, she had surprised him into looking at her. That was what she wanted. That was how it was supposed to be. That was her way of showing him that she actually was looking at him.

"You know, Blackbird," Salty was saying, while eyeing her sidewise, "I would like to take you someplace special. You're not the sort of girl I'd take to a movie, or for a boat ride. You take a tomato to a movie. You," he said, "I'd take to Tosca's."

Columbine looked at him. Tosca's was a fast downtown nightclub with a young, brash, hard-drinking clientele, a bar and restaurant crowded on weekend evenings with droves of pleasure-seeking airmen from the nearby base and their girlfriends, and with local high-school youths who came looking for fights. "You would?" she said, not averse to notoriety. Columbine could imagine herself entering Tosca's smoky rooms, with Andrew Sullivan's hand reposing on her belly. She would pause at the door with an expression of quiet disdain on her face. Someone would see her like that, and they would tell Starbuck. She would feel safe, too. She would feel safer then than now.

The quiet of the afternoon was surprising. From afar came the muffled stutter of the outboard. It was leaving the pond. The sound was coming from inside the concrete viaduct under the distant highway, the pipe through which the waters of Buck Pond communicated with the other ponds. That was far away. Quite abruptly, the echo of the red and white motorboat faded altogether. Her sense of well-being dwindled again as the solitude of the sunlit pond gathered meaning. No one was anywhere about. Columbine realized how important it was not to show fear, because people, like animals, smelled fear and took advantage of it. If, for instance, she was too emphatic about not wanting Andrew to embrace her, to keep his arm circled about her, he would become suspicious. He might even get angry. It was better to be clever. In an effort to show him that his closeness did not frighten her, but even more importantly, to induce him to think now about leaving Buck Pond, which was awfully bare and desolate, Columbine asked if they might not go to Tosca's together tonight.

The redhead's eyes changed color, like a vacuum tube heating up. "I don't see why not," he said, moistening his lips.

Columbine asked then if it would be necessary for her to dress up to go there, and Salty replied that she already was dressed up.

"I wear this dress in the daytime," said Columbine, but with a certain pathos evident in her want of haughtiness now.

"You could wear it at night," said Salty unconcernedly, at the same time, though, creating a little pressure with his hand on her stomach.

"In the evening," she added softly, "I would wear something different. This dress is nice for church or for walking in the Easter drag, which I do *not* do," she amended quickly. While speaking, she was steering their steps surefootedly toward the car. "I'm sorry," she went on casually, in an effort to obscure her fear, "that I didn't bring a bathing suit with me today." She gazed about then with deliberate thoughtfulness at the picture of the silent cottages on the far shore. "There isn't much to do here if you don't swim."

"Oh, I don't know," said Salty suggestively, while stealing a look at the girl in the curl of his arm. Anyhow, he explained, the water was too cold for her. "I wouldn't let you go in, Kitten," he said, and tightened his arm about her protectively. "You're too delicate."

When Andrew said that, Columbine got that strange, spooky feeling again. The idea of someone like Andrew Sullivan calling her delicate, someone who didn't even know the meaning of the word, and of the way his eyes shone with a voluptuous puzzle when he made a point of being paternal toward her! She was getting used to the feeling, though, of his arm wound around her; it was like a python sleeping all the way around her, heavy but weightless. His arm inside the pastel sleeve of his jacket coiled all about her like that was very defiling. That was what Sister meant by the word, as when something clean and pure was insulted or made dirty, such as defiling a church with impure thoughts. He, Andrew, would not understand that; but she could feel it.

They had stopped walking now, and Andrew was standing behind her with his hand still resting flat on her stomach. They stood on the shore where the ruins of the dory lay submerged in the brown shallows, half hidden in mud and fallen leaves, its gray outline perceptible from bow to stern. Tiny brown clouds appeared and disappeared in the shallows, with the comings and goings of little fishes. No one was anywhere about. The water stood in shadow. The patches of daylight and gloom around the edges of the pond accentuated the stillness of the day. It hadn't even mattered, she now realized, whether the automobile was near or far. That had been an illusion of security. It hadn't mattered at all. The pond was deserted. Columbine's eyes closed with a sudden fatigue, a faintness from fear, as she felt his other hand come around her waist and pause atop her belly. He had both arms around her and was standing behind her, and exerting light pressure on her stomach with his hands. She could feel him pressing softly against her, against her buttocks. She was thinking about the boats, about the red and white motorboat and about the gray dory lying forgotten under the water with the fishes making brown puffs of mud smoke inside it. Men had little fishes inside them. They had special organs that produced little fishes which swam inside you looking for an egg to swim into and hatch. One girl, Annaliese Baran, whose real name was Baranauskas, said at school one day that the man squirted his fishes into you with a force like a syringe. Everyone had laughed that day at school when she, Columbine, had replied that it must be true if Annaliese said it, since Annaliese had a face like a fish.

Columbine could see the toes of her purple shoes in the grass at the water's edge. She could see, too, in the water above the sunken boat, the reflection of Andrew's head on the dark surface. Bits of chaff and brown maple wings floated over the image of his face, and then she could see, dimly, that it was not his face at all but the oval of her own face inset within the shadowy framework of his reflected head and hair and ears.

"Please take me to the car," she said quietly.

"Know what's the matter with you?" said Salty in a low, rather hoarse, billing kind of voice. "You're too young, Kitten, even to know what's good for you." Salty began then to massage Columbine's stomach with both his hands. Then, leaning to her, tilting his head, he kissed the back of her neck gently. Columbine's eyes shut; a shiver passed over her at the moist touch of his mouth on her flesh.

"Only kids," he muttered softly, "walk in the Easter parade."

"I don't," she murmured.

"The hell you don't. I saw you." Salty laughed softly. He was caressing her belly.

Columbine stared glassily ahead. "Not this year," she said. She wanted to move. She wanted to continue to the car, but couldn't start. He was revolving one hand slowly round and round on her pelvis, while setting his lips to her neck once more.

"You were with your father," he said.

"My father never walked in the Easter parade." She could hear the wind licking underneath one of the empty cottages; it jiggled a metal fixture on the flagpole and then corrugated the pond.

"You're a liar," said Salty.

The fingertips of his left hand were underneath her breasts now; she was frightened. She couldn't move.

"My father is dead."

"Well, I know that," he said unctuously. "Don't you think I know that? I knew your father."

"I want to go home," said Columbine, with weakness.

While continuously massaging her, Salty rested his chin on her shoulder. "That father of yours was some kind of gentleman. I met him," he exclaimed. "I met him in Augustine's barbershop. Hey," Salty cried, "I'll bet you didn't even know that."

Columbine was poised at the edge of the water, her two feet together, her hands clasped at her waist. His fingertips were moving to and fro on the underside of her breasts. She could feel the tears coming, but fought them back. It was not wise to exhibit fear. She stood rooted to the earth.

"You have a beautiful neck," he said.

Columbine said nothing.

"It's like an Indian pipe," he said. "You know what an Indian pipe is?"

Columbine shook her head. "No," she managed to reply, in a small voice, for he was fondling her nipples now. In a swoon of fear she was trying desperately to think of something to say that would compel him to stop what he was doing. His voice was frightening.

"Do you want to see an Indian pipe?" he said.

"No," said the girl. "I would like to go home, please."

He was kissing her neck. "I could show you one," he added.

She shook her head. He was talking about something frightening, she was sure of that, but she didn't know what it was. His voice was peculiar.

"You don't even know what's good for you," he whispered ardently in her ear. His eyes, fixed microscopically on a distant point somewhere across the pond, sparkled. "I'll show you around," he confided. He was whispering to her and massaging and fondling her. "Girls like you are exciting. You need to go places. I'll take you to clubs. I'll take you dancing. Hey, I'll take you to cockfights. I'll take you any place you want, Blackbird. You name it."

"I want you to take me home."

"I'll take you jitterbugging. You just leave it to old Saltyballs." His right hand was pressing in underneath her now, pushing in her dress, probing inward. She was unstrung.

A moment later, however, sensing her fear, Salty released her, and resumed walking with her. This time he clutched her close to him in both arms, almost as though she were a mannequin he was carrying. He was vaporing away about a crap game of the night before in which he had "cleaned house." He showed Columbine a fat cylinder of bills.

"You should have heard them," he cried, and launched into a lively impersonation of his opponents at dice. *" 'Give me a five, one time. Little Phoebe. Phoebe in the fuckhouse, one time. One time! Eighter from Decatur. Little Joe. Tennessee Toddy, all ass 'n no body! One time! One time! Big Joe! Little Joe!' "* Lurching forward, Salty loosed a screech of laughter. "Old *Army* men," he said, rolling his eyes. "Hell, I got those *bones* one time! Five naturals," he said. "I just laid them out, pretty as your two little feet. Slam, *bam,*" said Salty, "the alaca*zam* man!" He bit his lip and squinted his eyes to convey an infallible, hypnotic state, then blew into his fist and cast an imaginary "natural." Snapping his fingers, he gave a sudden englishing kick of the leg. *"Wham,"* he said, "you are looking at it!"

Vulgar displays of this sort usually drew a haughty response from Columbine, but on this occasion she continued in a straight line toward the car. Salty overtook her and put his arm comfortably about her. He called her his kitten now. "I'm going to buy something really nice for my kitten," he said. He asked Columbine if she would like a nickel-plated .25-caliber pistol. "A little one-shot French job," he said. Or maybe she would like some alligator shoes. "I'm crazy about women's high-heeled shoes."

Columbine was breathing more easily. "They can be very pretty," she said, trying to get her agitated heart back in compass.

"How do you walk in them, Blackbird?" Salty was a picture of admiration.

"You just walk in them." Columbine showed him a quick flash of her azure eyes, as she tried to take a sounding of his intentions. Her spirits revived a little bit. "Why don't you buy a pair and put them on?" she said.

With a whoop of laughter, Salty popped forward in glee.

"I could teach you," she added. Her strength was coming back. Columbine felt she had gone to the brink of danger with Andrew and returned unharmed. Her breathing stabilized. She felt somewhat saucier. "You could get a pair of slingbacks," she said, "with an open toe."

Her suggestions threw Salty into a merry state. "Slingbacks!" he cried.

"An ankle strap would give you extra support. After that, you could wear regular pumps, or even mules."

Salty jerked his thumb at her. "She's nutty as a fruitcake," he said.

She was making straight for the car now. She could feel on her breasts and belly the spots where he had touched and caressed her.

"I used to put on my mother's shoes when I was a kid," said Salty. "They were the old-fashioned kind, the kind with laces. They had little holes in the toes."

Columbine made a face. She was feeling better.

"Of course, I didn't go outside with them," he said.

"I'm surprised your mother did."

"Kitten," he said, "I'm going to buy you a pair of alligator shoes."

Columbine looked at him evenly, as they came up to the car. "Alligator shoes cost fifty dollars."

"I like the way you walk," he said. "Hey, you deserve it!"

Columbine was waiting for him to open the door for her. She had recovered her aplomb. She was looking at him deadpan. Salty stood before her, with his hands in his pockets, the sides of his broad-shouldered primrose jacket thrown back sportily. He gazed at her in silence. His eyes changed color, growing dark, then bright. Then, leaning, he opened the door for her, but as Columbine stepped past him, he took hold of her from behind with both hands. He pulled her dress up over her waist, and then pushed himself into the car on top of her.

Columbine began to struggle, but Salty clamped his hand hurriedly over her mouth. He was already on top of her, undoing his belt. She was pinned to the front seat, but began to kick and thrash, her eyes widened in terror. With one hand she was clutching the steering wheel behind her, trying to draw herself away from him, while producing muffled cries and kicking her legs up and down as best she could. Salty was up between her legs, however, forcing her open, holding her in place with one hand, while tearing at his clothes. "Don't even know what's good for you," he said.

Columbine struggled to free her mouth of his hand, but she didn't scream. "Andrew, don't, please," she said frantically. "Don't."

"Don't even know what's fun."

"No," she was saying, shaking her head and wriggling backward on the seat. "Please."

"In ten minutes," he said, "old Saltyballs will have himself a real fine girl. Girl who doesn't even know what's good for her. Doesn't even know what it's all about. I'm going to look out for you," he said. "Nobody bums up my girl."

"Please," she was begging him to stop, squirming on the seat, her legs bicycling helplessly.

Columbine's underclothes vanished with a sudden deft tug, and she began to choke on her crying as she caught sight of him, of the reddish mass of coiled hair at the base of his penis as he fumbled with himself, clutching himself. It swung into view then in a sudden appalling manner, rigid and swollen. He was clutching it in his fist. Columbine's mouth opened in horror. Her eyes rolled backward.

"Nobody bums up my girl," he said, "don't worry about that." Salty paused to examine her. "You came to my door, Blackbird. I can't forget that. You see this?" He was showing her himself. Salty had pinned her chest with his left hand and was reared up above her. Columbine gazed in terror at the fat, slick, meat-colored head protruding from the opening in his fist. "You know what this is?" he was saying, his eyes gleaming. "This is Renfrew. See him? You looking at him? This is him," Salty said. "Renfrew of the Royal Mounted. The best friend you'll ever have. Oh," he said slyly, "I know what you want. With that fancy little snatch of yours. You don't even *know* what you want! You won't know it till you got it."

Salty reached and seized Columbine's head, grasping her by the hair at the base of her neck. His face was coming down to engage hers. She could see the green on his teeth. She couldn't move, but was still clutching the steering wheel with one hand, pulling futilely. "Somebody help me!"

"You can bite me if you want!"

"Don't do this! Don't do this to me! Oh, Papa!" she cried. "Please, somebody come! Please, somebody come!"

"Bite me!"

"I'll tell the police!" Columbine cried. "I'll tell the police! I will. No, I *won't*," she pleaded. "I won't tell anyone! Please, stop," she said. "Please. I won't tell. Please, Andrew, don't! I promise! Please! Oh, don't," she begged. Columbine's face twisted out of recognition. "Don't do it! Take me home! I want to go home! I want my mother! Please! Don't! Andrew! *Please! Please! Please!*"

XVI

Henry did not know the meaning of dramatic irony, but even if he had, he would not have seen himself exemplifying it when he settled into his room late that afternoon and opened a ponderous anthropology volume whose initial chapter was taken up with colorful descriptions of the important roles played by virgin maidens in a dozen ancient societies. Of course, to Henry, Columbine was the epitome of pubescent beauty. It was she, he was sure, who would have been chosen by the elders to sit as oracle on the holy tripod chair at Delphi, or who, at Rome, would have been elected to keep sacred vigil over the altar fire in the temple of Vesta. She was the choicest of her generation, and always would have been, he was certain. As Henry read on, however, sitting in the failing, milk-colored daylight by his window, he came upon some rather more lurid practices, such as the gruesome picture of innocent Aztec maidens, marked out for sacrifice to the gods, being flung alive down snake-infested wells, or being borne in melancholy processional up to the little stone summit houses atop the pyramids where grave-eyed priests armed with razor-sharp daggers set about the gory business of cutting the virgin's beating heart out of her breast while she was still conscious, and of displaying her smoking heart to the heavens and the gaping multitude below. The mere thought of Columbine, in all her innocence, in a dilemma like that left Henry woozy and upset. He was thankful that such sanguinary customs had been stamped out. For a space of several minutes

.

Henry was filled with feelings of a very loving and protective nature for Columbine. At dusk, when Henry went outdoors to roll up his car windows for the night, the sky was lighted with a pale-gray light from one end to the other, except for a spot on the western horizon where the withdrawing sun had left a little bloodstain of color.

He was standing beside his car, his white trousers and shirt blending curiously with the watery atmosphere, when his reverie was upset by the echo of a car door shutting in the street. A moment later, Henry was subjected to a colossal snub by the very girl whom he had been thinking about in such loving terms. Columbine went past him in the alleyway, and didn't even turn her head to look at him. The moment she appeared, her footsteps sounding on the gravel, Henry greeted her. But there was never an instant when it appeared Columbine might reply. She strode hurriedly past the back of the parked automobile with a cold expression that was very different from the look of hauteur that she usually affected. The fact that her hair was mussed was lost upon Henry, as was the rumpled disarrangement of her dress. Henry was too busy vibrating from her spectacular rudeness toward him to distinguish the telltale signs of her distress. He didn't question why she had entered the avenue from the roadway behind the house, nor could he have guessed at the tumult of emotions in her breast. He only noticed that in the twilight her purple dress looked black, and a moment after that, just as she vanished behind the tall hydrangea bush by her own back doorway, he recalled something discrepant in her appearance. He was struck by her tallness. He had not thought Columbine so tall. It was something about her gait. Then he remembered. It was her shoes. She was wearing a pair of very high-heeled alligator shoes.

Henry did not see Columbine for several days thereafter, and when he did—coming up the stone stairway one afternoon—she snubbed him again. In his perplexity Henry went so far as to telephone Columbine that evening, only to have Columbine bang down the receiver as soon as she heard his voice. He had not been mistaken about the alligator shoes, either; she was wearing them all the time now. Every time she came down from her porch and clattering along the flagstone walk, the noise and the great height of her heels were as conspicuous as the blue agate finish of her eyes.

Further confusing to Henry, his mother had begun, at about that same time, to speak of Columbine in a glowing way, which was, of course, the exact opposite of her earlier denunciations of the girl. Henry couldn't decide at first whether his mother's sudden reversal was a further proof of her instability, or whether the girl's defiance contained some positive quality that only his mother was capable of perceiving. It was only after a short passage of time that Henry realized his mother's illness was lifting. She was getting better. She was becoming her usual sunny self once more, just as Dolly McKenna had predicted she would. The secret paranoid smile vanished, along with the sudden crying fits and the many peculiar quirks that had surfaced in her behavior these past months. Henry's father, although saying nothing, seemed relieved, and Henry heard the two of them, his father and his mother, talking together in their bed far into the night on several occasions. It was only, therefore, in her attitude toward the girl next door that Mrs. Flynn's period of mental strain appeared to persist. Henry guessed that his mother was working to rid herself of some of the guilt she felt over having maligned the girl.

"If I could," she said, "I'd take her in to live with me for a while. I would! I always wanted a daughter. You know that, Jerome."

"She would change your thinking about that fast

enough," said his father. "You'd do as well with ten cats and a terrier."

"I really mean it, Jerome. I'd give the world to have that girl come and live with me for a while. How lovely it must be to come downstairs in the morning and find a fine young daughter like that waiting in the kitchen for you in her pajamas. I've always missed that." May Flynn smiled distantly. "And I wouldn't mind, either, if she *were* a difficult child"—she raised her voice to forestall the obvious objections—"or if she were headstrong or impulsive or even rude sometimes. That's a very trying age. I would understand . . . I think I could be very patient and helpful. Sometimes when I see her these days, I get the oddest sensation, Jerome, that I'm seeing myself at that age, even though, frankly, I was a regular little coward who wouldn't say boo. When I was her age, I was still saving my pennies for ribbons and corncakes. I was! I was still playing with paper dolls. We had cutouts then, Jerome, just as they have now. I was a regular baby. Now the youngsters grow up fast. It must be the baby foods," she said, "the Beech-Nut and the Clapp's."

Sergeant Flynn laughed pleasantly. "No," he droned, "I don't think it's the baby foods, May."

"If I had worn makeup like that, I'd've been skinned alive."

"Her mother and her sisters will quiet her down, you'll see. Just give them a chance."

"She's a very pretty young woman."

"She's not a young woman," he sang back.

"She puts her makeup on beautifully," said Mrs. Flynn, with sudden laughter. "I swear, she looks like Gene Tierney! She really does, Jerome. With those high cheekbones and that skinny neck of hers, she's become quite a picture. Oh, she's going to become a tremendous heartbreaker. Even I would admit to that. And I suppose if she's very uppity, well, maybe it's just as well, if it keeps people back. It seems like the day before yesterday when Mrs. K. brought her outdoors in her carriage and parked it under the chokecherry tree and I went over to peek. There was a net over the carriage to keep out the caterpillars and flies. She was an exquisite baby, Jerome. You could tell even then. She was different. I used to think that if I had conceived ten girls, I'd've miscarried them all. We were lucky to have had a child at all, after what I went through."

"There's luck and there's luck," said the father absently.

"Sometimes we should just count our blessings," Mrs. Flynn rhapsodized in earnest.

"That is a fact," he muttered.

Within a week, however, Columbine was showing signs of running wild. She could often be heard shouting at her mother or at Helen or Anna; it was well known that she was keeping late hours, and she made no effort to conceal the fact that she was dressing up in a precociously provocative way. The Trumbowskis, who lived in the house next door to Columbine, began to show their consternation by complaining to anyone who would listen that the little girl next door was behaving, they said, "like a tramp." Mrs. Trumbowski had seen Columbine sitting on the back seat of the Hadley Falls bus, wearing a black beret and smoking a cigarette. Anna asked Nicholas to talk to Columbine, but Nicholas, being a little tongue-tied, got nowhere. Columbine called him a "thug."

By the time Helen's wedding day arrived, Columbine had extended her freedom to the point where she had been missing school and, without any attempt at subterfuge or concealment, was allowing her "date" to call for her in his black and cream Packard sedan. Regularly, after supper, the redhead would stop his car in the street by the stone staircase and blow his horn, and Columbine would come clattering out to him.

Sophie came home from Boston on Thursday evening, two days before Helen's wedding, and was so incensed by what she heard that she restrained Columbine physically, locking her in her room that night. About eleven o'clock in the evening, however, the Kokoriss house erupted in fighting, as all four sisters began to shout and contend with one another. The squabbling rose to a pitch, followed after a moment by a sound of breaking glass as Columbine fired her mother's steam iron through the kitchen window. The neighbors converged warily on the house, collecting in the June moonlight on the flagstone walk, where, to Henry's surprise, it was decided by all (including Henry's own father and the irascible Mr. Griffin) that Henry himself should act as emissary and peacemaker on behalf of the others. There was a great deal of shrieking inside.

"You go ahead, Herk," said his father. "The girls always liked Herk," he explained to the others. "March right in," he said, "and put a stop to it. Be firm. If you need help, I'll be waiting."

Henry glanced about at his neighbors, his eyes pausing for a second on Mr. Griffin, who was wearing a dark, striped bathrobe over pink pajamas, and at the Trumbowskis standing side by side, their two snowy heads tilted like lovebirds. Mrs. Blye was nodding vigorously, while Nicholas stood stupefied behind her, biting his lip and wincing over each new outcry in the Kokoriss house. The house was lighted up from top to bottom, and the shrieking battle inside was moving from room to room. Henry was filled with a sudden sense of the poignancy of the fatherless house sliding into chaos. He entered at the front door and found Mrs. Kokoriss sitting in the parlor looking stricken. She was speechless. An ungodly yelling was coming from the kitchen, where, presently, Henry discovered Columbine standing against the wall, with her three sisters arrayed before her. Sophie had been striking Columbine, and she was showing Columbine her open hand, saying, "I'll beat the daylights out of you, morning, noon, and night. Is *that* what you want to know? You'll do what I tell you."

Columbine's cheeks were on fire with color, either from the blows or with indignation, and she was talking at the same time Sophie was. "I go where I please! I do what I please!"

Suddenly Sophie hauled off and dealt Columbine another ringing slap on the face. Helen was trying then to stop Sophie, and Anna grabbed hold of Columbine because the youngest of the sisters had seized a crystal candy dish and was trying to hurl it at Sophie. Henry didn't know where to begin, but he got hold of Columbine's wrist and was reaching out at the same time for Sophie, when Sophie, turning in anger, hit Henry hard in the face with her open hand. She didn't stop, either, but tried to hit him a second time. She was in a fury. Feeling a sudden wave of unaccustomed anger, probably mixed with a native repugnance for Sophie, Henry released Columbine and went for Sophie; he seized her by both forearms. Before anyone could realize what was happening, Columbine gave a cry and brought the candy dish smashing down on Henry's head. Henry let out a yowl and clutched his head with both hands.

Everyone was yelling. The sisters were all around him. Helen hit Columbine, probably for the first time in her life, and in retaliation, Columbine went for Helen's face with her nails, scratching her like a cat. Anna, seeing the blood on Helen's face, gave a heartbreaking scream and rushed at Columbine, forcing her backward over a chair onto the floor. Helen fled the room in terror the instant she realized what had happened to her face, and when Mrs.

Kokoriss saw her eldest's bleeding face, she began to scream in the parlor. By that time, the neighbors were crowding into the house.

"I told you to call me, you goddamned fool!" Sergeant Flynn came barging into the kitchen. "What have you done here?" He was shouting at Henry.

"Get him out of my house!" Sophie hollered wildly, her eyes blazing in hatred at Henry, who was standing back a step, massaging the crown of his head and gazing down at Columbine sitting on the floor by the table.

"Somebody do something," Anna pleaded over and over.

Henry's father, given his professional sense of the situation, got Mrs. Flynn to take Sophie out of the house altogether, a measure which restored calm immediately. Henry's mother took Sophie home with her, while Sergeant Flynn and the Trumbowskis went to the living room and conducted an examination of Helen's face. When Mr. Griffin came into the kitchen, he didn't try to hide his solicitous feelings toward the youngest of the four sisters, but immediately helped Columbine up from the floor. Columbine was not crying, but Anna's face was streaked with tears as she seated herself in a daze at the table. Columbine was brushing off her clothes. Suddenly, though, in a gesture remarkable for its childish sweetness, Columbine turned and allowed Mr. Griffin to take hold of her in his arms. She put her head down on his shoulder.

"There, there," said the old man gruffly, surprised by her sudden daughterly reflex, "that's all right now, girl. That's all right, that's all right." He patted her back stiffly with his hand, comforting her in a wooden and embarrassed manner, but evidently feeling very favored and flattered by it. "Nothing to worry your head about." Nor did Columbine show an unwillingness to let Mr. Griffin pamper and pet her a little, for she remained in place leaning against him for a considerable time, while he reiterated his assurances, and then Mr. Griffin led her out the back way onto the porch, and sat with Columbine on the divan. Henry was in the meanwhile left all by himself in the kitchen, although he could hear the rumble of Mr. Griffin's voice sounding through the hole in the broken window. The front room was buzzing with voices, as everybody tried to console Helen about her scratched face. Anna got a washcloth and sponged Helen's cheeks, while someone else gave Helen a mirror in which to examine herself. When Helen saw the red, symmetrical, brier-like scratches on both cheeks, she began to lament anew, but one of the women, either Mrs. Blye or Mrs. Trumbowski, said that face powder would conceal the marks. Henry could tell, though, by Helen's crying that she was very alarmed. There was a fear that Helen's wedding might be ruined by what had happened. For his part, Henry felt in some way responsible for the actual physical assaults that had taken place, and he had a throbbing skull to remind him of it. He had a sneaking suspicion, too, that if the other neighbors had not rushed into the house when they did, all four sisters might suddenly have descended on him at once, scratching and tearing at him, as in a kind of massive retaliation for his having courted all of them at one time or another.

When Henry left the Kokoriss house, he went out the back way. Columbine did not even look at him. She was sitting up straight, with the crusty, wiry-haired old man sitting beside her in his robe and pink pajamas, and she was making periodic sniffling noises while gazing into space. As Henry went down the steps, he heard Mr. Griffin trying to comfort his young friend. He said something to her about starting her flower garden again. All of the hard work had been done, said Mr. Griffin, in preparing the earth. "Just a bit of raking over," he crooned encouragingly. "You'll see."

Henry, who was not small-spirited, could not help feeling touched by the picture of the two of them sitting in front of the shattered window, with the old man's soft, broguish tones of endearment resounding in the shadows, as of a grandparent or even a surrogate father. It seemed to Henry that the Kokoriss family, in the aftermath of Mr. Kokoriss's death, was going to pieces, and he even wondered if he were not himself the proximate cause of its rather sudden downfall.

Before falling asleep, he recalled the Easter-morning splendor of the four girls spilling outdoors in their colorful finery. This recollection was more than nullified by the look of sheer hatred he had seen burning in Sophie's eyes and, even more than that, by the vicious crack on the head from the crystal candy dish.

Early the following morning, Helen's fiancé arrived with two or three friends and some immediate family. Henry saw the young man standing outdoors by the chokecherry tree about eight o'clock. Determined to resolve the ugly episode of the night before, Henry went hurriedly over to meet him. Helen had repaired her face remarkably well, he noticed, although at close range fine pink channels could be discerned through the makeup on her cheeks. In fact, the unpleasant business of the previous evening was already becoming a topic of humor among the wedding party. Helen introduced her future husband to Henry, and while she went indoors to look after some of the other members of the recently arrived party, Henry and the young man talked together outdoors. Henry had seen pictures of the bridegroom, but found him to be a more imposing type in person. His name was Johnny Rys. Johnny hailed from Ohio, but was stationed in Virginia toward the end of the war, he said, and had met Helen in Washington. Johnny had been an Army photographer. He was in the Pacific for years, he said.

"I understand you were out there," he said to Henry.

"I was at a British base in the Tonga Islands," said Henry.

"I believe I've heard of them," said Johnny thoughtfully. "Yes, I believe I have."

Henry enjoyed talking with the young man. He was very soft-spoken but solid-seeming. In fact, Henry sensed in Johnny a solidity that might even have been wanting in himself. They stood under the tree by the dining-room windows, talking about the Pacific. Johnny said that he, like Henry, was in the Pacific Theater at the time of the early campaigns, and that some of his photos of American war dead were among the first to be released to the newspapers at home. "I photographed the dead on the beach at Buna," he said.

"I've heard of Buna," said Henry.

"I had never seen dead men before," said Johnny. "I didn't see the fighting there, either. When I came ashore, everything was quiet." Johnny was speaking softly, as if the two of them were discussing not just another time and place but another dimension of reality. "A jeep was burning," he said. "There was smoke drifting out to the water. There were dead men all over the beach. Helmets, rifles. It made me sick."

Henry remembered the Australian cruiser pulling in at Tongatabu. That seemed now like another life altogether. "I know what you mean," he said.

Johnny smiled, as he and Helen's old friend had fallen into the natural, easygoing posture of two veterans used to dealing with other men on precisely this basis. They stood talking under the tree.

"I took a picture of a boy who looked like he was sleeping. I often think of that boy," said Johnny, looking away. "One of his leggings was undone. In the picture I took you could see the sand in his shoe.

I thought I would never get used to things like that. It was worse later on." Johnny smiled at Henry. "Still," he said, "when I think about it at all, I always think of Buna."

"Everyone remembers one thing best," said Henry sagely, in a quiet voice, knowing that in his case it was a reef and surf and a rim of palms with the topmost leaves blowing horizontally under an enormous sky. There were no people in that picture. He couldn't even recall when or where it was.

Henry was on his way to work at the time, but before going he wished Johnny a lifetime of happiness with Helen. Johnny was impressed with Henry, with his modesty and intelligence and apparent sensitivity, and later suggested to Helen and the others that he would bet Henry Flynn would someday make a fine journalist. Sophie interrupted at that point to say that Henry was a nitwit. Anna and Helen challenged that opinion, but Columbine chimed in to say that Sophie had a right to her own views. "Maybe he is a nitwit," she said. As Columbine was still wearing her skyscraper alligator shoes, it was generally felt that she had carried the day in her battle to forestall further interference from her sisters.

The wedding was a small but tasteful affair; following the marriage ceremony, the wedding party drove a few streets to Malek's Inn, where a half dozen Lithuanian toasts were followed by several in the Polish tongue. Johnny's people, who were Polish, favored their Lithuanian in-laws with a few choice compliments for the proud and ancient Lithuanian race. Sergeant Flynn, not wishing to be outdone, presently caused a merry eruption of applause when he stood up in his proudest sergeant-of-the-police manner and delivered a wild and really exhilarating cascade of Celtic cheers, which left him breathless and red-faced. The small party was so vociferous, in fact, that a collection of Polish musicians who were warming up in another dining room for an anniversary party scheduled for mid-afternoon soon invaded the room, seated themselves on chairs placed atop a vacant table, and began pounding out polkas with enviable enthusiasm. Two of them played trumpets, and a man and a girl played accordions. Now and again the girl sang, and there was a great deal of handclapping on all sides. Helen and Johnny started everyone dancing; and for more than an hour the waiters from the bar were kept unusually busy. One of Columbine's uncles—Alexis —began to polka with Columbine and then, quite suddenly, effortlessly, hoisted her onto his shoulder, and was dancing then all by himself, going in circles while waving and pumping his free fist in rhythmic triumph and singing in a deep, powerful voice. This demonstration of virility and hearty good cheer brought everyone present to his feet. Sitting on Alexis's shoulder, Columbine, in her peach dress and peach shoes, was eye-catching; her jet-black hair was cut prettily, and she carried herself, as always— even on the precarious perch of her uncle's shoulder —with singular aplomb. The little four-piece ensemble paused for breath; someone handed a glass of champagne up to Columbine, and an instant later the music exploded and Columbine's uncle launched into a second virtuoso performance that was so stunning, if only for the sheer blinding speed of the big man's footwork, that the waiters and barmen crowded the doorway in a curious throng. There was a great deal of clapping and interspersed rhythmic shouts going up from all sides. Columbine held her glass at arm's length, spilling about half of it during the course of the rollicking polka, but managing with great sportsmanship to smile prettily from beginning to end. The uncle, a big-chested, balding foundry worker, concluded his performance by removing one of Columbine's peach shoes and drinking the balance of her champagne from it.

Henry found the company very congenial. He couldn't speak Lithuanian or Polish, but he had always possessed the quick, toothy smile and easygoing nature that endeared him to strangers. Also, standing among the stocky Balts and Slavs, he cut rather a picturesque figure, with his blond crewcut and the flawlessness of his blue cord summer suit. Add to that the three or four gin boilermakers he had downed in the space of forty-five minutes or so, and Henry was prepared to hold his own. None of the Kokoriss relatives went past without thumping him on the back or squeezing his hand. At one point even Sophie came to him and apologized for having slapped his face. Henry danced with Sophie after that, and while doing so remembered the night six years back when Sophie made herself seductive to him in the shadows behind her house. That night seemed to Henry part of an ancient past, a time when Anna was a young schoolgirl and Columbine a stripling child whom no one noticed. Henry danced with his mother, and he danced with Mrs. Kokoriss. Sophie had given her mother a pretty hairdo, and Henry noticed that Mrs. Kokoriss's hair was turning white. Henry made small talk for a while with Nicholas Blye, but was cognizant all the while that Columbine was ignoring him beyond all reason. In fact, had his existence depended upon Columbine's recognition of his presence in the room, he would have vanished like a sunbeam. She never once looked at him.

She seemed to be everywhere at once. Whenever he looked up, she was whisking past, or else she was at the center of the floor dancing with one of her cousins or uncles. Henry recognized the dress she wore as the one Helen had worn for her parents' wedding anniversary in 1940. Just before luncheon was served, the little band played "The Pennsylvania Polka," and everyone stood in a circle and clapped and sang while Columbine danced with Johnny in the middle of the room. Her extraordinary dancing skills were here apparent to all, and when the music stopped, a roar of approval went up. This outburst was followed by a second, when Columbine's Uncle Alexis suddenly swooped through the crowd and made as though to kidnap her, sweeping her up in his arms, and running pell-mell across the room; he planted Columbine in her chair at one of the long tables, sat down beside her, put his big arm around her, and downed a full goblet of ice water.

"I haven't enjoyed myself so much," said Henry's father, as all the guests followed Uncle Alexis's lead in seating themselves, "since Johnnycake Cochran married his aunt!"

"That wasn't his aunt," said May Flynn, blushing swiftly at the mere mention of her notorious cousin.

"You say it wasn't," said Sergeant Flynn, opening his napkin, "and Johnnycake said it wasn't, but believe you me, Phil Teehan in the City Clerk's office has a better story!" He gave a hoot of laughter, then raised his water glass to the bride and groom. "A long and happy voyage to you both!" he said.

"Well said," put in Helen's Aunt Teeka, and turning, she showed Henry's father a playful, come-hither wink. "Aren't the police handsome."

"She's just jealous of Columbine and Alex," said Leon Botyrius, a skinny, black-haired man with a gold tooth and prominent Adam's apple whom Henry remembered from the anniversary party six years ago. Leon played the balalaika.

"I like all the men in the room," Teeka said. She was a big, colorful woman with a pretty moon-face and yellow-gold hair.

"That son of yours," said someone to Sergeant Flynn, "he's becoming a successful boy."

"Who?" cried the father, hiding his pride under a show of forced incredulity. "Herky? Oh, he's got a long way to go yet. One of these days he'll learn what we all learned: Life is a long, hard row to hoe."

"There's truth in that," replied Uncle Alexis.

"What do you say to that?" Someone turned to Henry with an encouraging wink.

"It's a long lane that has no turning," Henry retorted, recalling one of his Grandfather Flynn's favorite aphorisms. Henry, by then feeling no pain, was smiling broadly.

Uncle Alexis exploded in laughter. "There! You see?" he cried. "That fellow knows something. He knows words." Uncle Alexis closed one eye foxily and tapped his temple with his fingertip.

At this moment Columbine spoke up for the first time, looking across at Henry in her usual grave, deadpan manner. "Herky Flynn," she said, "is a regular dictionary of words."

"Now I am wounded!" cried Henry good-naturedly, unaware for the moment that Columbine had called him Herky. "Twice wounded," he amended swiftly. "Thursday night she hit me on the head with a dish!"

"Right on his bald spot!" said his father, laughing thickly.

"Henry's not bald," said Anna gaily, as everyone laughed heartily at Henry's expense.

"At the rate I'm going," said Henry, "I won't survive the summer."

"He thought the Pacific was dangerous!" said Johnny, and everyone laughed once more.

"I hope you survive long enough," said Helen, "to publish a nice account of the wedding. Don't forget to describe Mama's dress. She's wearing lavender tulle with blue and lavender trim." Helen turned a loving glance on her mother, who was beaming with pride. A rosy flush invaded her temples.

"He won't forget a thing," said Uncle Alexis, tapping his temple once again in that canny, all-knowing manner.

"If anyone insults me," said Henry playfully, "I'll

pillory them in the newspaper. And that," he added, turning to Columbine, "includes delegates from the peanut gallery."

Columbine had just addressed her fruit cup and was delicately raising to her lips a cherry balanced on her spoon when Henry's characterization set off a salvo of laughter. The points of Columbine's cheeks colored brightly, and she paused, holding the spoon in mid-air. "I didn't hear," she said, and looked about in puzzlement at the crescent of laughing faces for a clue to the nature of Henry's remark. She turned then to Henry, her lips narrowing in anger. "What did you say about me?" she said. She turned to her sisters. "What did Herky say?" she snapped.

"The peanut gallery!" Aunt Teeka was lost in merriment over the witticism, especially as Columbine's vanity was a source of special delight to all her relatives. Teeka's sudden piping laughter set the others off anew.

"Peanut gallery?" said Columbine. She returned the cherry on her spoon to her fruit cup, and appeared angry enough to throw something at Henry. Uncle Alexis saved the moment by suddenly clutching Columbine in his massive arms and pretending to squeeze the life out of her while roaring like a bear.

"You gorgeous little woman!" he bellowed, and commenced kissing her face all over.

The moment of awkwardness passed, but Henry had not missed the look of cold hatred Columbine had shown him. At the tail end of the wedding reception, when everyone was outdoors and Helen and Johnny drove off in an automobile trailing a hundred white streamers, Henry confronted Columbine. He took hold of her elbow. He wished to apologize for having been rude. But Columbine withdrew her arm, regarded him with repugnance, and walked away from him. Henry was left speechless. He noticed, too, that his mother had found him out;

she had been watching them suspiciously. Everyone else was cheering the departing newlyweds, but Mrs. Flynn was watching the silent drama between Henry and Columbine. At that point, Henry was too dismayed even to care.

Columbine had by then joined Anna. She spoke to Anna with a supercilious expression. "Can't you just imagine Helen trying to get out of bed tomorrow morning!" she said.

Anna regarded her little sister with shock. "What do you mean?" said Anna, in a suppressed voice.

Columbine studied Anna candidly. "Well, what do you *think* I mean?" she threw out pertly, but with the slightly aggrieved air of a young woman having to remind herself constantly that her sisters were all like little children whom she had to humor whenever an adult subject was raised.

She was out of control. Henry knew by then that she was involved in circumstances beyond her years; still, he was reluctant to admit that the infamous redhead, Salty Sullivan, was her regular escort these days. A story was being told that Columbine was with Salty in an Ireland Parish nightclub one evening when Salty had drawn an Army .45 and set the muzzle to someone's head in the way of winning an argument. Henry was tempted to disbelieve wild stories, but on three or four occasions when he spotted Columbine coming and going in the street, his doubts were revived. Her appearance was eye-catching. At first, she had taken to wearing a black beret and black turtleneck sweater, which Henry felt gave her native precocity a distinctly provocative air. Always, too, of course, she wore the high-heeled alligator shoes, and was making no effort at all now to conceal her lipstick or her facial or eye makeup. She was smoking, too. In fact, as she went clicking past Henry's front porch one drizzly afternoon, she reached up to her lips and, with an insolent gesture, tossed her burning cork-tipped cigarette butt onto the Flynn walk in front of the porch. Henry was sitting in his father's rocker behind the leafy curtain of Dutchman's-pipe that covered the front porch. She passed so close by he could actually see the sticky red lipstick smudge on the tip of the discarded cigarette. Henry was very put out by this piece of impertinence, particularly as he was quite sure she had *not* seen him sitting there, and was not, therefore, merely play-acting. The moment gained an added poignancy in the fact that Henry was holding in his hands a letter that he had received from Columbine.

The letter was apparently not a recent one, inasmuch as the envelope, which had no stamp on it, bore signs of having passed repeatedly through a canceling machine at the post office. There were also handwritten notations on it, doubtless penciled in by various letter carriers. The envelope, apple-green, was soiled as well. Henry found the letter awaiting him in his basket at work. When he first opened it, a powerful gust of perfume escaped the envelope. Henry was initially excited at receiving the letter, and read it over many times before realizing, with a stab of disappointment, that Columbine had written it some while ago—in fact, on the day following the night of their last encounter. It was the letter that had fallen from Columbine's lap the day she saw Henry in the park with Mrs. McKenna. Someone had found it and mailed it. For want of a stamp, it had shuttled about for days.

Henry read it many times, but it only deepened the mystery of Columbine's revolutionary behavior (which seemed to Henry a total renunciation of the beautiful vows she had made him, faint resonances of which sounded within the letter itself). He found the letter to be both childish and compelling, though, and he read it over and over, as if hoping to discover in it the secret behind her abrupt change of heart.

318

Dear Starbuck,

Sister is in the cloakroom with Marjorie & you should hear the whacks! M.P. is in a vile mood today. She called Marjorie a conniving devil. She said she has a cure for conniving devils & is giving it to her now. Everyone is giggling. You should hear it! Ouch! It started when Marjorie said dative instead of ablative. M.P. said *ablative?* and Marjorie said *yes.* Sister said to her *You said ablative?* And Marjorie said *yes. You are a conniving devil,* Sister said, *you said dative!* Marjorie said *I swear I said ablative.* So M.P. opened her drawer and took out her stick (it's a board really) & practically *ran,* Starbuck, to Marjorie's desk! *You said ablative?* she said. Marjorie broke down & changed her tune when she saw the big stick in Sister's hand & said *No!—You said dative?* And Marjorie said *Yes!* Sister said to her *Come with me you conniving devil. I have a cure for a conniving little devil like you!*

Oops! I have to go.

Here I am again. It's afternoon. M.P. is in the corridor talking to Marjorie's mother. She says she's going to take Marjorie out of school. Not that *I* would care! She's a *wretch!* I have to go now.—Nope, I don't. M.P. & Marjorie's mother are gone down the hall to see S. Superior. I could tell by M.P.'s face that she would like to give Marjorie's mother a good solid whacking, too.

Did you hear what I told you last night? Someday you are going to be very famous with people coming to see you from all over, because I am going to make it happen if you don't. I'm very ambitious. I'm also much smarter than you think! You will have a long flowing beard & will look very wise, Starbuck, & when people come to see you I will keep them waiting *ever so long,* until they can't bear it any more. I will be very beautiful, of course! So they won't mind waiting *too much!!*

(M.P. is shouting. She's saying *Corporal Punishment!* and *Mind—her—manners!* It's quite a ruckus!)

It's fun writing to you. Composition is *not* my strongest point but I *am* getting better. M.P. is helping me a great deal in that way. She says I have a hidden genius & it is coming out this year. Do you think she's right???

Got to go!

I'm back. I am sitting in the coffee shop near the P.O. I want to finish this letter, especially the part about your flowing beard—& me in a long silky emerald-green gown going out to you in the garden to tell you who has come to call!

You're very gentle. Even when I play tricks on you, I feel safe. I don't know what I would do if you were not there for me to play tricks on! (I am being asked to leave—by a man with a big red Irish nose!)

Before I mail this letter I will soak it in (Antelope) perfume & when you open it at your desk everyone will come running to where you sit & you'll never speak to me again!

Love & faith,
Columbine

This letter caused Henry considerable anguish. He carried it about with him, sometimes taking it out and gazing with loving attentiveness upon the flamboyant violet signature, with its great flowing capital letter *C,* which seemed a very pretty decoration in itself. He was completely mystified, as Columbine's antipathy toward him, her insolence, her virtual hatred of him, mounted from day to day. It affected him in his work. He was often daydreamish, preoccupied. He worried.

Columbine's arrogance toward Henry and his family took an even sharper turn on the afternoon of the Fourth of July, when two of Henry's cousins, Peggy and Davey Mahan, were visiting. Peggy, at sixteen, was a voluble, cheerful soul who seemed not to have experienced an unhappy moment in her life, and illustrated this temperament and good fortune by being able to talk a blue streak on any subject at the drop of a pin. Her brother was naturally more taciturn. Davey was Peggy's junior by only a year or eighteen months, but he was very guarded in his dealings with his sister. Davey Mahan had learned long ago never to interrupt or contradict Peggy when she was talking, because to do so was either to invite a nasty thrust or have the effect of steering Peggy around quickly onto subjects aimed at Davey's own moral edification. By then, too, Peggy had transformed her brother's reticence into a pattern of virtues upon which she was not disinclined to expand, as was evident that holiday afternoon.

Davey was shooting off Roman candles in the Flynn yard while Peggy was singing her brother's praises to Jerome and May Flynn. Peggy had a glass of strawberry soda in her hand, and was standing in the sun by the back steps. "Davey is deep," she was saying. "Still waters run deep. Davey is like Grandpa Lacy. He doesn't talk much, but when he opens his mouth, people listen. He doesn't waste words. I talk in pennies, but Davey," she said, "talks in dollars. He knows how to listen, too. I'm not a person to put too much stock in school grades, either, so I don't think Davey's marks mean all *that* much, although it wouldn't hurt him to open his mouth in class. The trouble with Davey is, he can't write, and if you can't write and you don't talk, it's hard to lift your grades. Of course, Davey hates reading. And *mathe-*

matics," she cried, and rolled her eyes, "that is Davey's *curse!* Davey couldn't solve a problem in algebra in the time it would take a horse to learn Hindu. He has an ear for music," she said, citing that categorically, "and he's deep. He's thoughtful. He's considerate, too. Quiet people are more considerate. I'm a chatterbox."

"You are a chatterbox," said Henry's father.

Peggy laughed gaily. "Good heavens," she cried, "who is that gorgeous creature?"

Across the way, Columbine had just emerged to view; she had opened the lid of the garbage can and was knocking in coffee grounds. Her appearance was flamboyant beyond description. Mrs. Flynn gave a little cry of wonder. Columbine was wearing a fire-colored dress and red high-heeled sandals. The dress was filmy and was flickering in the sunlight. The crowning touch, though, took the form of a bright-red, big-brimmed straw hat that she was holding in her left hand, extending it cautiously to one side, while beating the coffee receptacle noisily against the inside of the steel bucket. Whenever she moved, the dress shimmered like a swarming of orange-red butterflies.

"What a ravishingly good-looking girl." Peggy breathed the words with fervor.

Davey, too, had stopped what he was doing, and stood gaping at the vision next door, the spent cardboard cylinder of his latest Roman candle dangling at his side. When Peggy learned from Mrs. Flynn that the figure across the way was only thirteen or fourteen years old, she grew very animated; she begged and insisted that her aunt provide her with a reasonable excuse for calling on the Kokorisses at once. "Oh, please, Auntie," she said. "Let me ask for a cup of sugar. Give me a reason, quick, quick, quick!"

Henry, who had just appeared in the doorway

behind them, retreated at once when he saw that his mother was about to relent to Peggy Mahan's exhortations. He had heard a rumor that Columbine had accompanied Salty Sullivan to the horse races at Suffolk Downs, and then gone with him on a spending binge in Boston thereafter, but the actual sight of the diaphanous red dress blowing in the sunlight on that Independence Day afternoon upset him. Henry's mother had meanwhile instructed Davey to pull up several stalks of rhubarb from the luxuriant growth at the back of the house and wash them thoroughly under the garden hose. Peggy and Davey were then dispatched to the Kokoriss house. "Tell Mrs. K. that we heard from Helen and that we enjoyed the wedding immensely."

"Oh, I will, I will!" Peggy vowed excitedly, as she strode out across the grassless space of what was once Sergeant Flynn's victory garden, crossed the invisible property line where the pine tree had fallen in May, and, with Davey at her heels, scurried directly up to the rear porch, and rapped on the screen door. What happened in the minutes to follow would have remained a mystery to Henry had it not been for Davey's presence.

"Look," said Peggy, "I have some rhubarb for you!"

"Who are you?" said Columbine in a thin, puzzled voice from behind the screen. She opened the door then and stepped onto the porch. Columbine was taller than Peggy Mahan and stressed this advantage by keeping her head and face perfectly level and lowering only her eyes. She was still holding the bright-red straw hat in her hand.

"My aunt," Peggy breathed her explanation with a note of awe, "sent some rhubarb for your mother." She signified the Flynn house with a flick of her eyes. "I hope you don't mind my saying so," Peggy went on, "but that's a *precious* dress you're wearing.

323

Is that silk? Is that silk chiffon? Where *ever* did you get it? What a dreamy concoction! Did you buy it at McAuslin-Wakelin?"

Columbine was staring flat-eyed at Peggy. "I bought it at Worth's in Boston," she snapped icily. "Would you like to hand me the rhubarb—or am I supposed to summon my mother?"

"Your shoes are so pretty!" Peggy went on. "Why there's nothing *to* them! I tried wearing high-heeled shoes, but I got such shooting pains I had to take them off at once."

"You probably have fallen arches," said Columbine. Reaching impatiently, with the sudden impulse of an adult running out of forbearance with a child, she collected from Peggy the entire handful of dripping, dark-red rhubarb stems, dealt Davey a swift, polite wince of a smile, and pivoted smartly on her heel. She hadn't a hand free for the door, however.

"Would you open the door, please," she said to the girl.

"Oh, please don't go," Peggy pleaded at once. "I was hoping to speak to you."

Columbine struggled to open the door. "I'm *busy,*" she said, with an arctic flash of the eyes.

Peggy Mahan turned sardonic at once. She was not used to being mishandled in conversation by anyone, but certainly not by skinny, precocious girls with funny names who just *happened* to be attractive. The idea of this girl treating her like a nosy, importunate child was more than she could bear. "I was hoping," she said then, in a sugary voice that dripped with venom, "that you might give me some advice."

"I will," said Columbine, speaking back to her through the screen of the closed door. "Suck a tit," she said.

———

Davey Mahan recounted this story to Henry amid such gushes of laughter that he was all but prohibited from reaching the climactic riposte itself; but once he reached it, Davey repeated it a dozen times, while re-creating for Henry the expression of dead white horror that immobilized his sister's face. "She was *ossified!* Jumping Jesus!" Davey was beside himself, as though he had not believed before that just retribution came to the wicked. "You'd've given a thousand dollars, Herk, just to see her face!" Davey rolled his head from side to side, clutching his temples in a transport of amusement. Henry, of course, was not in a frame of mind to appreciate the effect of Columbine's good works, or to share his cousin's fit of merriment over it, because everything that pertained to Columbine these days fed his anxieties and left him feeling more pained by it and even, perhaps, a little lovesick, too. Of course, Peggy could never bring herself to reiterate Columbine's insult (which was the beauty of it, so far as Davey was concerned), but while she sat ashen-faced at the kitchen table, and railed in general terms against Columbine's "vicious insult," Columbine herself was going past the front of the house. Henry saw her. Abandoning Davey, he hurried outdoors and intercepted her on the walk.

As she came past, her face was half hidden from view. The brim of her red hat was turned down on one side, while the opposite brim curled upward at a smart angle. She didn't even see Henry. He stood on the grass, taking in the sight of her as she came skimming along the walk with her head turned. Her toenails, he noticed, were crimson, her arms and legs dark from sunbathing. But the dress itself (even Henry had to confess) was a creation from another existence; it moved everywhere at once and shimmered and appeared both alive and weightless, putting Henry in mind once again of a cloud of red butterflies.

"Oh, it's you," said Columbine, stopping abruptly and regarding her next-door neighbor with unexpected geniality. Her face under the hat brim was a cool realization of American beauty. "Who was that gooney bird who just came to my door?"

"Her?" Henry croaked. "That's just a cousin of mine. Don't pay any attention to her."

"Don't worry," said Columbine.

"That's just about the most beautiful dress I've ever seen," he suddenly brought out.

"This is?" Columbine stepped back half a pace onto her left foot, while keeping her right leg extended straight out before her, as she displayed the dress modestly. "It was a birthday gift," she said, and looked up swiftly, watching with her best poker face for the shock to register on his face.

"Your birthday?" Henry was appalled. "I forgot all about it. It was in June," he said. He gazed at her dumbly. "I wish I had bought you something."

"Why ever should you?" she cried blithely, and showed him a dazzling but perplexed smile under the shadow of her hat brim. She was peering at him as if he had just sprouted a second head, or had spoken to her in Arabic or Portuguese. It was the look of a film star trying to cope with an admirer whose enthusiasm in her presence was running away with him. "You," she said, "wanted to buy me a birthday gift? Isn't that sweet. Listen, Herk," she added at once, "I'd love to talk, but I'm in a rush." She consulted the tiny watch on her wrist, if only for the purpose of drawing his attention to its existence, not to say its prettiness or newness. "I have a date."

Henry was done for, of course. Had Columbine suddenly produced a formal instrument of surrender, he would have unscrewed his fountain pen and affixed his name to the document without so much as reading a line of it. On a night in May she had given him tender promises, about loving and cherishing him in the far-off times to come, of caring for him even when he was old and gray, vows as lofty as the noblest protestations of all time, sentiments, Henry thought, that would have done honor to Thisbe, that would have befitted the likes of Isolde, or even of the incomparable Juliet herself. But since that night he had not received one civil word from her tongue. Henry stood on the grass before her, in his shirtsleeves, his arms folded, rocking nervously to and fro on the balls of his feet. He could not think of a thing to say. He watched mutely as Columbine went digging industriously through the contents of her handbag, turning up matches, a fountain pen, a set of keys, a compact, a lipstick tube, an amber comb, a lace-edged handkerchief, even a Kotex napkin, before locating at last what she was looking for, a handsome diamond-shaped cigarette case with a polished mother-of-pearl lid. The cover of this elegant little cigarette box was, Henry noticed, beautifully inscribed all around the edges with a fine, black, scroll-like capital *C*. Deftly, she popped up the lid. Inside was a layer of cork-tipped cigarettes lying in a neat diagonal row. Columbine selected a cigarette, snapped shut the box, and handed Henry a packet of matches, while she continued talking in a rambling, gossipy tone.

"Of course," she was saying, as she leaned stiffly forward and held the cigarette between her lips, touching his hand with her fingertips as he raised the lighted match, "she doesn't have to be a dimwit just because she's your cousin." She straightened and blew a jet of smoke straight up.

"I didn't say that," Henry objected in a hurt tone.

"I didn't, either," Columbine replied. She was talking off the top of her head, saying anything that came to mind, especially as she had now accomplished her aim-in-passing of showing him everything important, the dress, the hat, the shoes, the watch, the Kotex, the cigarette box, all of it. She was ready to pop along. By stopping, she had impressed on him the fact that she *did* remember who he was, and had reminded him as well of the wonders of a time not so long ago when such an exchange of pleasantries between them might even have been commonplace. An instant later, she was gone.

She was descending the stone steps to the street, going sideways down the staircase, holding the pipe rail in one hand, and making an elaborate but lady-like show of the awkwardness imposed on her by her stiletto heels. Suddenly she shot up her arm in a gay salute to the driver of the black and cream Packard that came purring up to the curbstone. Henry was rocking back and forth on the balls of his feet; he was staring blankly across the stone path to the wooded spot at the base of the cliff where the pine tree once stood. He heard the report of the car door shutting and then the smooth sound of the Packard shifting gears. From behind him came the sound of Davey's gurgling laughter.

"How can you people stand her?" he said, with a pressing, incriminatory smile distorting his face.

Davey's crack was the last straw. Henry lost his temper. "Don't you have any more Roman candles to shoot off?" he cried, with a flash of exasperation rarely shown among the members of the family.

Not three hours later, however, it happened again. Henry couldn't believe it. He was sitting on the porch steps, listening to the second Red Sox game, when she returned up the stairs. She came hurrying into view, not fifteen feet distant, her orange-red dress glowing like a cloud of fire, just as before, and she went sashaying right past him, with her face in the air, and didn't even look at him.

The radio crackled from heat lightning in the atmosphere. The announcer's voice rose and fell. On the lawn before him the brass water sprinkler was going round and round, sending out a long parabolical rope of water; a sudden rainbow recurred inside it each time it caught the evening sun. The click-click-click of Columbine's heels was followed by the echo of a door shutting. Henry didn't hear his father as he appeared at the screen door behind him.

Sergeant Flynn stood in his trousers and under-shirt, yawning after having dozed off on the sofa. "What's the score?" he asked softly, glancing at the radio.

"Fifty-four to nothing," said Henry.

His father looked away with chagrin. "You ask him a question," he said.

XVII

Columbine was drinking pink ladies and pink daiquiris, but the pink lady was her favorite. She had tried a Jack Rose once, which was a pink lady with apple brandy in it, and had tried white ladies, which contained Cointreau instead of grenadine, but she never stooped to drinking simple mixed drinks like grasshoppers or Tom Collinses. She sometimes preferred frothy concoctions, such as sidecars in frosted glasses, but said they made her sleepy. She also said that the barmen she had met in Ireland Parish couldn't frost a glass if their lives depended on it. Columbine showed Chick Orcutt, the bartender at Pangur Ban's, how to frost a glass properly by cooling it and swabbing the rim with lemon and twirling it in granulated sugar. She also explained to Chick why Cuban rum was the best rum for rum cocktails, and suggested that Chick take out a subscription to *Town and Country* in order to acquaint himself better with the tastes of the *haute monde.* Columbine's age and her manners and glamorous precocious appearance were making her quite a favorite. She had also absorbed some of Salty Sullivan's vocabulary and had set off a brawl one evening in a Division Street bar when she called the owner a "royal crud" for refusing to serve her and then extinguished her Viceroy cigarette in someone else's drink. On another evening, in a dice game at the Ack Ack Club, she cast the dice for Salty by blowing them out of her mouth onto the green felt of the billiard table, and got a spontaneous cheer as she made Salty's six-point on her first try.

Henry's principal source of information in tracking Columbine's movements was none other than Mrs. McKenna. It was she, for example, who told Henry that Columbine was known on the local circuit as the Ziczac Girl. Columbine had herself given this sobriquet to Salty's sidekick, Petie Zidek, a scrawny, long-nosed youth who followed Salty wherever he went, flattering him obsequiously, running errands for him, and sometimes even serving as chauffeur for the redhead and his girl. Columbine said Petie was Salty's ziczac bird. The ziczac, she said, had a bill as long as Petie's nose, and lived much as Petie did—by picking the teeth of a crocodile! After that, though, Salty gave the name to Columbine.

It was impossible, of course, to give credence to so many rumors, but Henry saw Columbine coming out of her house one evening and was surprised by her striking, if bizarre, appearance. Mr. Griffin had made a present to Columbine of a genuine kepi, the traditional cap of French policemen. It was a souvenir of Mr. Griffin's World War I campaign days with the 104th Infantry Regiment. He acquired it in the course of a street brawl in broad daylight between American and British soldiers, and had run off with it in the street, he said, with half the city of Paris chasing him on foot. The cap had a round pillbox shape but with a sloping front and a shallow leather visor. Columbine wore the kepi very smartly with a black sweater and the charcoal pleated skirt and black shoes of her school uniform. It was only when Henry saw her come swinging down the walk on Cottage Avenue with the kepi sitting perfectly straight atop her head that he began, finally, to believe some of the outrageous stories.

In time, Henry's imagination began to produce its own supply of lurid fancies concerning Columbine and her unsavory sweetheart, so much so that he couldn't sleep at night. About that same time Mrs.

McKenna appeared also to wash her hands of Henry; an entire week elapsed without his once seeing or hearing from her. He felt piqued. One afternoon at work, Henry picked up his telephone, and in what struck him as a magnanimous act, he called Mrs. McKenna at home, only to have her deal him an unexpected reprimand. "If I had wanted to speak to you, I'd've called you, wouldn't I?" she said rudely. "I have company!"

The color rose to Henry's cheeks as he realized that Mrs. McKenna meant to treat him in the bossy, cavalier way that a man might treat a woman who was behaving like a pest. If Mrs. McKenna hadn't apologized three or four nights later, Henry vowed he would never speak to her again. She took him into Jockamy's late one night and bought him a straight gin. Henry sat on a bar stool and Mrs. McKenna stood behind him, pressing her bosom against his arm, and called him Sugar and Babylove until Henry felt placated. When Mr. McKenna wasn't looking, Dolly kissed Henry's ear and showed him a warm, colorful smile of the type that lent her nose and eyes the sharp, predatory look of a tropical bird. Her eyes dimmed sensually. "I could eat you alive," she said. Then, about midnight, Henry and she bade Dicky McKenna a pleasant good evening, and Henry drove her up the hill to her house. Twenty minutes later, he was in trouble.

"What in hell's going on?" she said.

"It beats me," said Henry.

"It beats him, he says. What do you mean, it beats you?"

Henry shrugged. "It beats me."

"Listen, Herk," said Mrs. McKenna, speaking out in the half dark of her bedroom, "I want my plumping."

"I know you do," said Henry.

"When I get all ready for it, when I look like this, a man gets a hard-on."

"I know that," said Henry.

"I'm not being unreasonable."

Henry was sitting in the pale window light on the edge of Mrs. McKenna's bed, his shirt front open, his trousers folded up on the cushion of the armchair by the bed. He felt miserable. Several times a vision of Columbine came between him and his thoughts. He had heard all the stories he could stand about the pink ladies and the Cuban rum, and had pictured in his mind a hundred times the pretty, bow-shaped, zephyrlike lips blowing Salty Sullivan's dice to a successful six-point on the green baize of a billiard table. He pictured her, in her fiery orange-red dress, sitting next to Salty in the plush back seat of the big Packard, with Petie Zidek chauffeuring the two of them up the river highway in the moonlight.

"Maybe it was the gin," Henry said.

"There was nothing wrong with the gin," said Mrs. McKenna. She sat up then behind him and tried massaging him again with her fingertips. She reached forward, underneath him, and kneaded the flesh there round and round. Henry gazed down disconsolately at his own flaccid condition. He felt excited by Mrs. McKenna, but he could not form an erection. In the shadow between his legs Mrs. McKenna's diamond ring twinkled like a distant star.

"I guess these things happen," he said.

"They don't happen to me."

"It isn't your fault," Henry absolved her.

"Maybe we should try it on the floor," she said. "I think you liked it on the floor."

"I don't see where that would help," said Henry, a little primly this time, wondering why his friend could not accept inevitableness now and then.

Sighing, Mrs. McKenna got out of bed, put her shoes on, and went out of the room to get an ashtray and cigarettes. She came back smoking; she looked at herself in the mirror above the dresser.

"Ever seen this one?" she said and, coming to where Henry sat, turned her back to him and made an exaggerated show of sucking in her stomach, until she seemed to have no waist at all, then leaned forward so as to confront Henry at eye level with the spectacle of two creamy hemispheres with a dark, vertical furrow between. "Would you like to do something with that?" she said in a suffocated voice, while backing up to him. "Peep right in," she encouraged. "That could wind your watch."

Henry gazed vapidly before him into the tiny, dark tangle of what he ascertained to be the nethermost extremity of his hostess's digestive system.

"I don't see where that will help me tonight," Henry confessed. Mrs. McKenna straightened up.

"I'm not trying to pull teeth!" she said.

"I know that."

"And after all these delays!" she cried.

"I wasn't delaying."

"Look at you," she fired at him. "Were you with somebody else tonight?"

"Of course not!" Henry was shocked at such an idea.

"I'm not asking for the moon, Herk. I want my plumping! I want to know what in hell's going on! Put your hand here," she said, and placed his hand palm upward beneath herself. She was moist. She regarded him with the air of a nurse waiting for a thermometer to yield a reading. Finally, in exasperation, she climbed on top of him. "Goddamn it," she said, "I want my humping." She was getting angry now. "If I can't get it from you, I'll get it from somebody else. Then you can watch." Mrs. McKenna rolled Henry over backward onto the bed.

"What are you talking about?" said Henry.

"You know what I'm talking about." Mrs. McKenna was getting cryptic. "All that talk about people watching. Do you take me for a dummy? I think you'd like to watch."

Mrs. McKenna was up on top of Henry, clutching his head in her arms, his face buried in her stomach. She was moving her pelvis against his chest. Henry had a mind to put his trousers on and leave, but he hated to think what a vicious reaction that would excite in her. Mrs. McKenna could be a regular hellcat. Henry knew all about her loose tongue, too; if he left now, she would pull him to pieces in every bar in town. She would make him the laughingstock of all time.

Unable to guess what Mrs. McKenna was up to, Henry decided to go along with her. She seemed to be enjoying herself. She was lying flush on top of him, and was moving back and forth with enthusiasm. He couldn't hear too well because her hands were blocking his ears, but he knew exactly where he was. He could see her navel. It was the shadowy depression that rose and fell right before his eyes. Since Henry's hands were free, he reached and touched Mrs. McKenna's rectum.

"That's good," she said, "do that." Like any creature of instinct, she had a flair for improvisation. She was making do. She even said so. There was more than one way to skin a cat, she said. She would be goddamned if she would wait six weeks—or even six minutes, she said—for some fathead to make a sap out of her in her own house. He could hear her clearly now because she had changed her grip. She was clasping the top of his head with one hand and his nape with the other, but continued pressing his face to her belly. Her pubic hair was scratching his chin. The next time something like this would happen to Dolly McKenna, she said, the dead would be building igloos in hell. Not that Henry could blame her for feeling angry. His failure to respond to her blandishments had struck a blow at her pride. Mrs. McKenna was by then sweating freely. His forehead was soaked with the perspiration coming from her abdomen. She was moving ceaselessly on top of him, and making soft, windy moans. Henry lost the use of his hands when she got her knees over his elbows and pinioned him. In all this time Henry made just one utterance; he suggested that he might be able to gratify Mrs. McKenna after all. He thought he felt something stirring, he said. Hearing that, Mrs. McKenna stopped what she was doing and looked back over her shoulder at him. A moment later, however, she resumed her undulations. "You missed the bus," she said.

What happened next would have been deeply mortifying to Henry had his mind not immediately relegated it to a subconscious sphere too deep for recall. All he remembered was the sudden motion with which the woman threw herself upright upon him. One moment she seemed to be hugging him, and in the next she was sitting straight up on top of him. Henry, during his early manhood, had become rather broadminded in the matter of tolerating exotic beliefs and practices, but something in his natural conservatism was nonetheless offended by the memory of Mrs. McKenna closing her thighs upon him that way, as though he were a riding animal. An odor of seaweed and lavender invaded his nostrils. He was being raped. It wasn't just the hot, prickly sensation of the act itself that dismayed him, either, any more than it was Mrs. McKenna's sudden gleeful outcries, or even the actual weight of her torso squirming about heavily upon his head or face, but rather Henry's own willingness to placate the woman at any price. It was no wonder he cracked up his car later that night.

Henry was tooling downtown at a good clip, about forty-five miles an hour, his head filled with the ugly events he had just endured, as in the way Mrs. McKenna had shown him the door, throwing his coat after him as though he were some kind of prostitute or cheap gigolo, and making that crack about his being "one of Jack Meehan's boys," when he ran a caution light at the corner of Race Street, swerved to avoid hitting a car that came out of no-where, skidded out of control on the car tracks, and was hit broadside by an eighteen-wheel Reo truck coming through the underpass carrying a load of produce for night delivery at the Growers' Outlet. The Ford was demolished on the spot. Henry could have been killed. Later he had a recollection of the bizarre sensation of the steering wheel spinning freely in his hands while the car was flying through the air with its front wheels off the ground. The Ford hit the brick wall of Bissell's Hardware Co., shatter-ing the plate-glass window, then ricocheted over the cobbles in the direction of the covered stairway that led up to the railroad station.

Amazingly enough, Henry opened his door and got out of the car in the middle of the street, and walked away in a daze. When the police and ambu-lance arrived, he was standing on the curb with sev-eral other people, most of whom didn't even know him to be the operator of the car. He just stood among them with a frozen look on his face, staring out at the wreck. The police were on the scene sev-eral minutes before someone finally identified him and he came forward to explain himself. He was that dazed.

Henry had spent time in hospitals before, but he never enjoyed himself as much as he did on the day following his automobile accident. For one thing, he was pleased by his popularity among the nurses and nuns of the hospital staff. He was known to them through his work on the newspaper. All morning long they came trooping into his room, fussing and flirting over him, bringing him extra orange juice and magazines and coffee, and all chattering about the "miracle" of his being alive. All that Henry had to show for his brush with death was a sprained ankle, but because his swollen leg was the one he had damaged in the Pacific, he was ordered confined for X-rays. Feeling in excellent fettle, Henry was happy to be laid up for a few hours. The relief that came from having survived such a violent crash filled him with a remarkable sense of well-being. His complexion was almost rosy. Henry looked so robust, in fact, that both his father and mother were a trifle perplexed at the sight of their son sitting up in bed, flushed with color, talking animatedly, his face erupting in constant smiles. Of course, the adulation helped. Head Nurse Halpin visited Henry so many times that he wondered himself if she hadn't developed something of a crush on him. He overheard extravagant compliments being paid him by nurses going past in the corridor, too, one of whom went so far as liken him in appearance to Robert Walker, the movie star. "It's like a hive of honey bees in there all morning," said the nurse, in passing.

"Well, I wouldn't mind," said a second nurse in a playful provocative voice.

"Oh, you," said the first, "you have enough men already in that jealous husband of yours."

"Hold on a minute," said the first. "I could do with another, if they're going to be like that."

During the noon hour, his friends from the newspaper came to call, beginning with Tillie Flood, the corpulent switchboard lady. Tillie brought Henry chocolates. After that, young Nolan came, and then Jack Meehan himself (poking his rubicund, bespectacled face in at the door and making a humorous crack about Henry having been either the luckiest man alive last night, or the drunkest). Henry responded to the outpouring of solicitude with boyish pleasure. By then, he had thrust Mrs. McKenna from his thoughts. Dolly McKenna, he decided, was just a small-town barfly with a wild itch in her pants that would be her undoing someday.

At four o'clock in the afternoon, Henry was discharged. He was disappointed, naturally, that

Columbine had not come to see him, but guessed that she had not heard about his misfortune or, if she had, that she was too proud to come. He had made up his mind that the stories about Columbine were nowhere near so scandalous as some people made them out to be. She was passing through a rebellious phase. He was beginning to see the light. He actually smiled now at the remembrance of Columbine showing off with her new dress and the big scarlet hat, and treating him that afternoon like someone she had recently jilted. It was all stagecraft. That was why she had called him Herky, and why she had induced Salty Sullivan to spend money on her. She was spinning a web. She was doing what she had always done, using feminine guile to keep him in rabid pursuit. He was supposed to worry about her; he was supposed to feel neglected. That was her way of obscuring the great difference in years between them. It was a remarkable instance of the female quarry's instinctive capacity to incite headlong pursuit in the endeared one. It was the oldest trick in the book. Her summer escapades, he concluded, were nothing more outlandish than the flamboyant climax to tricks she had used all year long.

At home, Henry's mother got his cane down from the attic, and Henry hobbled about on it, testing his bandaged ankle.

"I'm lucky to be alive," he said.

"We're all lucky," said his father, expressing relief over his wife's recent recovery from the bizarre symptoms she had been exhibiting for weeks.

"I wish the automobile had never been invented," said Mrs. Flynn. "If God had wanted automobiles to serve man, He would have created them Himself."

"He didn't even create shoes," said Henry. "What are you talking about?"

"Please don't blaspheme," she reprimanded softly.

The Flynns were eating supper. The evening sun

streamed into the kitchen. From outdoors came the occasional soft clatter of cooking utensils and chinaware, as other families of the neighborhood settled down quietly to enjoy the ritual of the evening meal. It was that hour of a summer evening when the withdrawing daylight creates a golden and resonant spell. Sitting in his place, Henry was not unaware of the thousands of similar occasions when the three of them had sat quietly to supper in this room. Henry's mind wandered. He fell to thinking about his job at the newspaper and of how Mr. Meehan, while maintaining an outward show of good fellowship toward him, was constantly conniving behind his back to discredit him in the eyes of the Chief. Henry was not a simpleton. Whenever one of his stories happened onto Mr. Meehan's desk, it was chopped to pieces. The sad truth was that young Nolan, with his college degree and that shrewd way he had of concealing his sycophancy toward Mr. Meehan behind an air of steady Jesuitical reserve, was now pulling down the choicer assignments. That riled Henry, for he knew himself to be Nolan's superior in every way. He knew, too, that Mr. Meehan was helping Nolan. Not a day passed when Nolan wasn't to be seen pussyfooting around Mr. Meehan's desk, peeping over his shoulder, nodding solemnly, and watching with despicable meekness while the older man expanded and polished his work. That was not the whole of it, either. Nolan had a secret resentment for Henry. He resented his natural flair for words. He resented his likableness, too, and even his way of dressing. Henry realized, with bitterness, that even his time spent in the Pacific caused envy in his colleague's heart. There was the occasion, about a month ago, when Henry had made a perfectly innocent reference to his days overseas—something about the typhoon season in Asia—when Nolan had colored swiftly and loosed a jest that caused everyone to laugh. "Oh, come along!" he had cried. "Next he'll be telling us yarns about Pearl Harbor, or about the Jap battleships he sent to the bottom at Midway!" Henry was so startled by Nolan's onslaught, and by the malice he divined within it, that he had not the presence of mind to make an appropriate response. "I wasn't at those places," he had murmured apologetically. He would like to have told Nolan that it was carriers, not battleships, that went down at Midway, but by then, of course, everyone had walked away.

After supper, Henry took to his room. The excitement of events was by then taking its toll on his spirits. Mrs. McKenna, after all, had humiliated him, so much so, in fact, that he had come within an ace of killing himself. Now he was back where he started, limping about on a game leg, swinging a cane, and dwelling morbidly on the motives of people with malicious tongues who could wish a man ill. Henry pulled a chair to the window and sat in the evening sun. The gardens below were overgrown with weeds, while along the back fences the ancient hydrangea bushes were blossoming in profusion. The setting sun drew a diagonal line of light and shadow across the roof of the Kokoriss house, with the yellow light seeming to spill from the roof onto the front walkway. Mrs. Kokoriss's salmon-yellow tea roses trembled with light by the front door. Henry was experiencing an involuntary premonition, a foretaste of a time to come when he would not live in this house any more. Strange people, he thought, would climb and descend the stairs. The house would fall into decay. The neighborhood would grow old, its tenants scattered and gone. The fences would go down, and the vegetation grow thick all about, until, one day, one of the houses of the avenue would be abandoned altogether. That day would come. He wondered if, in distant times, he would remember the house as it was tonight, sitting in this window, here and now, thinking forward to that distant day, or if the very texture of his thoughts was not itself as transient and evanescent as the yellow light in the weeds below. Naturally, he thought about Columbine, too, for he had a premonition also about him and her, and of how she, Columbine, would be no more real or substantial to him at that forward time than the memory of the chair upon which he was sitting.

In the minutes to come, it would have been as well had Henry gone elsewhere that evening. He heard his father go trudging out of the house, starting down the hill to the station, and then, later, his mother going off to one of her many novenas. Henry didn't stir. He was watching the sunlight go. He couldn't remember a time since early childhood when he had watched the room fill up with darkness. A final slab of pale light cutting through the treetops above the Kokoriss house disintegrated, while below, on the back-porch steps, a glittering milk bottle subsided into darkness. It was at that moment, precisely, just as the shrubs and back fences were blending to form a common pool of darkness, that he saw the two of them coming forward in the field beyond the back roadway. They were coming from the direction of Old Bridge Street, walking soundlessly in the shadows of the sumacs, a man and a woman, walking almost as one.

Henry had been thinking about her, about being fatherly toward her. Now, sitting forward, he stared at them. The man was holding her about the waist, steadying her, as she wavered a little on her heels. His hand, lying flush upon her belly, was unnaturally white in the dusk, as though illumined from within. The man wore a hat. Henry knew who he was. He knew him by the size and angle of his hat. He knew him by his slow, splay-footed gait. There was something apparitional about them. It was the hour, no doubt, that reduced them like that, for they seemed to be floating on air. They came on in the field as though spellbound, or as if he, guiding her, were not so much a man as a force. At a turning in the path, they changed direction toward Henry, coming toward his window, and appeared for several seconds not to be advancing at all, despite the steady churning of their legs. They emerged into the back roadway, turning to follow the line of the fence. Then only their heads showed above the dark mass of the shrubs. Henry watched breathlessly as they climbed the steps and Columbine opened the back door of her house and let in her companion. The door closed and a light came on.

Seizing his cane, Henry went downstairs as rapidly as he could go. He was in a tumult of emotion, muttering oaths at every step. He could not believe Columbine to be so rash or stupid as to put herself in so perilous a situation. Reaching the kitchen, Henry realized he had no plan in mind. He paused, peered nervously about in the dark, then started back the other way. All he could think about was the ghastly sight of that spectral white hand stenciled upon her stomach. Henry went back and forth through the darkened rooms, swinging his cane, clutching at chair backs and door posts, while working himself into a froth. For one thing, the Kokoriss house should not have been empty at this hour. The mother, he surmised, must have gone away somewhere with Nicholas and Anna. From the side windows Henry caught sight now and again of the silhouettes of Columbine and her illicit guest moving to and fro across the lighted window blocks. Henry wished he had his field glasses, but could not contemplate hobbling upstairs to get them. He was too agitated. At last, in response to a battery of urgings, he let himself outdoors. He went out the front way.

Once outside, Henry's natural reticence fell away, and within minutes he was on his neighbor's property, stumping along in the shadows of the snowball

343

bushes, the rubber tip of his cane pressing soundlessly into the sod at every step. The first window emitted a soft, residual glare through the massed leaves. Henry stopped and listened. Night was rising. Crickets lent a silvery hum to the stars. A tiny galaxy of lights danced along the gleaming shaft of Henry's cane, as, presently, he swung it forth and began to inch his way up to the window. It was the hall where the telephone was kept. The window was slightly ajar. The soft glare upon the window glass came from the dining room; it lit up the surface of the piano in the front room, and fell across the parlor floor. Steadying himself against the wall of the house, he gripped the projecting sill and set his sprained foot down carefully in the grass. No sooner had he done so, leaning his weight against the clapboard siding, than their voices came resounding from the next room. Columbine was speaking. Her voice was hollow, as though she were speaking into a drinking glass. Then the man spoke. Then Columbine again.

"That's all you think about," she said in her uppity tone.

"It's all you think about" came the baritone rejoinder. "I have other things to think about."

"And what makes you think *I* think about it?" she snapped.

At that instant Salty Sullivan came into view just beyond the parlor door. The sight of the garish redhead, with his hat tilted back on his head and a big flowery necktie cascading over his shirt front, threw Henry into gloom. Salty Sullivan, with his pegged pants and great swag of a key chain looping downward from his waist, seemed to Henry the creation of a cartoonist. It was apparent even in the manner of his putting out his cigarette, popping it from his mouth in a sudden paroxysm of indignation, glaring at it with hatred, as though it were a fiery ember cast up from his own stomach, then mashing it out in the ashtray on the piano with a series of ferocious blows. Henry couldn't imagine what Columbine was thinking to invite such a clown into her house, and then, more puzzling still, treat him as she might any other guest. Henry's wonderment was as profound as his jealousy; he couldn't take his eyes down, but studied the Sullivan youth intently from head to foot, the flame-colored mop of hair, the capacious yellow jacket with the big pockets and no lapels, the pleated lime-green trousers, the hat, the gold chain, the pointy brown and white shoes. The big-brimmed hat stood back on his head at such a precarious angle that it appeared perpetually to be blowing away.

Extinguishing his cigarette with characteristic brutality, Salty exhaled two horn-shaped jets of smoke, one from either side of his mouth, and strode importantly across the lighted space into the dining room. He possessed a bit of a belly, Henry noticed. So far, Henry had not caught a glimpse of Columbine, but her voice carried out to the darkness with bell-like clarity.

"If you ask me," she was saying, "it's old Renfrew who's thinking about that sort of thing."

"That's what I pay him to think about," said the baritone, and Columbine laughed lightly.

"Renfrew has a one-track mind," she said.

"Renfrew does what I tell him."

"There's a fib."

"Royal Mounties," said Salty, in a thick, sententious voice, "follow orders."

Columbine's sudden gay outburst of laughter caused Henry to grimace. He fidgeted about at the window. He could hear the two of them clearly enough, but he could not plumb the meaning of their words.

"If they didn't," Salty added, "they wouldn't be Mounties."

"Mounties come to attention," Columbine reminded him.

"Yes, but not every minute," Salty replied, and both he and the girl laughed sharply over that remark.

Suddenly Columbine changed her voice, adopting the tinny, sugary, playful, wheedling tone that mothers use with infants. *"Is little Renfrew tired?"* she said.

"Oh, get off that," said Salty impatiently. "Get me some root beer. Go on," he said, "get a move on. Get me a bottle of Hires. You got any marble cake?" he said. "You people eat stuff like that?"

"No," she said, "we make our cakes out of tree stumps."

"Don't laugh," said Salty. "I know an old Polack who makes wine out of dandelions."

"We," said Columbine, "are not Polacks."

"Did I say you were?"

Outdoors, Henry hopped about uncomfortably, straining as best he could to peer in beneath the sash. He had a horror of being detected at the window, particularly by Columbine herself, and he was not unmindful of the severe handicap imposed on him by his injured leg. Flight was out of the question. Still, Henry was resolved to stay put until he had convinced himself of Columbine's security. The impression he had got so far was one of harmless bantering between the two of them. In a surge of generous feelings, he even began to wonder if Salty's renown as a womanizer wasn't just a lot of hot air. Behind the brash, swaggering exterior, Salty Sullivan was probably frightened to death of women. That, at least, was an encouraging thought.

From time to time, Henry glanced around guiltily behind him, toward the walk and stairway, to assess his own security. The white trousers he was wearing would have betrayed him in a second to anyone entering the avenue. Anyone seeing him there would instantly set him down as a Peeping Tom. It would be an impossible predicament, certainly for a

346

policeman's son. Since nothing harmful was happening indoors, he was tempted to give it up and go home. (He could always go upstairs and keep an eye on things with his binoculars.) While debating whether to stay or go, Henry noticed that the voices inside had dropped off. Two or three minutes elapsed in silence. Henry listened carefully but could not hear them at all. Then, abruptly, the dining-room light flashed out.

There are times when nothing is more unsettling to the human spirit than silence, especially when maintained in total darkness by wakeful persons. The idea of Columbine ensconcing herself in a darkened room with the likes of Salty Sullivan, and probably necking and petting, was too outrageous for Henry to think about. Transferring his cane to his left hand and digging the rubber ferrule into the grass, he began stealthily to make his way along the side of the house to the next window. He was determined to find out what was going on. Henry should, of course, have interpreted the switched-off light as a sign of a possible leave-taking, that Columbine and her guest might suddenly appear outdoors. Somehow, Henry ignored or rejected that possibility, even though a surreptitious perusal of the dining room revealed nothing more than the glowing surface of the white tablecloth, the gleaming finials of walnut chair backs, and, behind it all, the twinkling glass doors of the old china closet. His suspicions were mounting by the minute.

Moving more hurriedly, Henry returned to where he had started and eavesdropped again at the hall window. He knew them to be somewhere on the ground floor. By now the worry he felt for Columbine was giving place to perplexity and frustration. Presently, however, Henry heard a telltale sound, a little isolated noise that came out into the night like something with wings. It came from the front of the house, from the parlor. It was a creaking sound, as of someone changing position on a chair. Henry stopped stock-still, listening, his cane frozen in mid-air. A moment later he put caution to the wind and started to make his way around to the front of the house.

Moving over the grass and the concrete sidewalk in absolute silence, Henry was impressed with his own stealth. Even the porch steps conspired to muffle the sound of his footfall, withholding any possible groan or squeak. Pausing at the top of the stairs, he leaned against the slender wooden pillar and listened intently. Through the open porch window came a second soft creaking, followed by a wet, sucking sound. Hearing that, Henry made his way to the window. A white curtain ballooned softly, and as it did so, Henry, peering into the darkened parlor, found himself staring at point-blank range at the spectacle of two shadowy white forms showing above the back of the sofa, a vision of Salty's naked buttocks.

"What's the matter?" Columbine was speaking softly.

"I don't know," Salty grumbled.

Henry was so close he could have reached in past the curtains and touched the looming soap-colored buttocks. A thick spear of glossy hair stuck up from Salty's fundament.

"Are you sick?" she said from somewhere out of view.

"I don't know," Salty said.

"Why, you reptile," she said, "are you going to be sick?"

The buttocks moved perceptibly. "I don't know," he said.

Their two voices resounded hollowly from behind the sofa back. Then, after a moment, Salty was on his feet. Henry saw him suddenly unfold and come upright. He was standing on the carpet before the

348

sofa. He still had his hat on, and was sporting a prodigious erection.

Salty was clutching and rubbing his sides with both hands, and gazing into the darkness with an appearance of pained concentration. "It's my belly," he said.

"Why, you scurf," said Columbine, affecting a low-class insensitivity to pain. "You crud," she said.

"Get me some more root beer."

"Get it yourself," she said.

"Goddamned pork," Salty added, and continued to massage the sides of his stomach. "Goddamned Beelzie and her pork." Salty's stomach must have rumbled then, because he tried to bring up air, puffing up his cheeks and then rolling his belly in the direction of a hoped-for belch. Salty stood in profile to the window, his hat on the back of his head, and his manhood standing forth like a fungo bat.

"You have to go soon," she commanded.

"When I go," Salty made her a mock threat, "Renfrew goes!"

"If it wasn't for Renfrew," she said, "you wouldn't be here."

Salty gave a sudden bark of laughter. "The look on your face!" he cried at her.

"Hurry up," she said.

"I knew you had it bad, but not that bad!" he crowed.

Salty climbed back onto the sofa. An instant later one of Columbine's feet appeared to view, rising straight up above the sofa back next to the curtains. Her heel came to rest on the sofa. The foot was pale and slender. *"Oh,"* she said suddenly.

"That'll learn ya," said Salty under his breath.

"Oh," she said again, "Andrew."

Salty gave a soft chuckle while laboring his way forward; only his soap-colored buttocks showed over the sofa. "Splitcha in two," he said.

"Oh!" she said.

His hat bobbed into view, then vanished again. His buttocks shook.

"Oh!"

Salty laughed thickly under his breath; the sofa squealed softly. "Bimbos," he said, and plunged violently.

Columbine's foot shot into the air. "Oh!"

"That'll learn ya." He chuckled.

"Oh," she said, "Andrew . . . Oh . . . *Oh!*" she shrieked.

XVIII

That Sunday Mrs. Flynn, after months of trying, succeeded at last in cajoling Henry into accompanying her and his father to Mass. Until then Henry's apostasy was an embarrassment and sore spot for both his mother and his father. Henry's defection from the weekly sacraments was the one delinquency which Mrs. Flynn had neither the strength nor the motherly inclination to excuse. In fact, she had raised the question so often in private to her husband that he, Sergeant Flynn, found himself taking Henry's side for once. "Give him air to breathe," he would say. "Herky has a head on his shoulders. Well, he *does,*" he would cry, as though Mrs. Flynn was about to dispute that point. "Do you have even the foggiest notion what's going on in his head? Do you? Because I," he would say, "don't. He's mysterious, you see."

"He's not that mysterious, Jerome."

"*I*"—his father would lay his fingertips gently upon his own chest—"find him mysterious."

"I don't like the way he sits and broods," Mrs. Flynn complained.

"Maybe he's lovesick. Who the devil knows?"

"He seems so unhappy."

"Or maybe he has a vocation!" cried Sergeant Flynn on one such occasion. "It's happened to stranger ducks. But no matter how you slice it, I for one can't see where his 'everlasting soul,' as you call it, is in such 'grievous peril.' You don't mean to sit there and tell me that the great God Almighty, in His infinite wisdom and goodness, is going to fling

Herky Flynn into Hell, do you?" His father laughed merrily, poking his thumb into his eye to expunge a tear.

"Jerome, please," she protested.

"Can you honestly picture that, May?"

But Mrs. Flynn remained unmollified. She was deeply perplexed. "You wouldn't suppose that it was something to do with the war, Jerome? That something terrible happened over there, something —that—well, you know, sort of *haunts him?* Jerome," she said, half whispering it, "you don't suppose Henry ever killed anyone, do you?"

This notion sent Sergeant Flynn into a fresh fit of amusement as he tried to imagine his son, Henry, caught up in a delirium of homicidal frenzy, chopping some poor unfortunate mortal to pieces with a machete or bayonet. *"Herky?"* he kept saying.

"Well, it was a war," Mrs. Flynn argued in the face of her husband's uproarious reaction. "Heaven knows, people were killed. Horrible things were done. The newspapers are still carrying stories of it to this day. The crimes and atrocities! The sheer butchery. I find it incomprehensible. The millions and millions of dead. People did that," she said. "People who are alive today. Even young men from respectable homes. Isn't that possible?"

"Ah"—his father waved aside her worries—"he's not deep enough to be no good. It takes character to be wicked! He's just a silly galoot like the rest of us."

"Or maybe he *is* lovesick," said Mrs. Flynn. "I've noticed things. Little things. I've even wondered if it hasn't to do with . . . with one of the girls next door. Helen," she said, "or Sophie, or Anna. Or," she added, pausing, "even Columbine."

Indeed, Henry did take his parents to church that Sunday, but he could not have been more distracted if he tried. His thoughts were a mile away. All morning long his brain was beset with the most frightful imaginings, phenomena made all the more lurid and ironic by the soaring notes of the organ and choir, and by the sea of reposeful faces surrounding him on all sides, so much so that when, following the Offertory, he put his head down on the cool wood of the seat in front of him, it was not because of the rising heat of the day but because he couldn't get Columbine and her loutish lover out of his mind.

For several days thereafter, Henry moped about the house in a torpid state of mind. He slept fitfully, ate without enthusiasm, and whiled away long hours on the front porch listening to the radio or pretending to be reading. He was depressed. He was assailed by feelings of worthlessness. He saw himself as an ineffectual hypocrite. He couldn't even look at himself in the mirror without experiencing repugnance. Stranger yet, Henry developed a peculiarly morbid attitude toward the material particulars of his life. He nurtured, for example, a peculiar distaste for his own clothing, the source of which revulsion was a mystery to him, but which caused him to look upon his trousers, shirt, and shoes with feelings as uncanny as those an archaeologist might suffer were he suddenly to recognize that the ancient garments he had just uncovered in a sealed tomb were actually his own.

Henry was not, however, morose by nature. Feelings of suicide, for example, did not find a willing conductor in Henry. In fact, the idea never occurred to him; he simply was not prone to violence of any kind, even of the self-inflicted type, such as putting one's head into an oven or jumping down from a high building. He could sit on the porch and stare out before him into the deep-green leaves of the Dutchman's-pipe until the very leaves themselves seemed as exotic and alien to him as his argyle socks or penny loafers and never feel so much as a twinge of an impulse to destroy himself. Instead, Henry succumbed to sudden deviations of impulse. For instance, one afternoon he betook himself up to the attic, unlocked his duffel, and extracted from it one of his carefully folded uniforms. He selected the dark woolen uniform, the blue winter one, took it downstairs to his room, set his cane aside, and carefully costumed himself in it from head to foot. He set the squared white cap just so upon his head, and then regarded himself in the mirror for a full quarter hour.

On another occasion Henry bought himself a handful of cigars, one of each of several different brands, and smoked them one after the other while sipping Bombay gin from a half-pint bottle that he kept stored in the bandage around his ankle. By then, he was feeling a little better. Human beings with no real disposition toward self-destruction are like corks, and come readily to the surface once again. He was still detached enough, though, that, while he sat gazing about him, he was able to note in wonderment how strange this little street of houses would have appeared if presented to an eye altogether untutored in things human. Seen in that aspect, the houses of Cottage Avenue were not so much remarkable for their differences—the little unique features that his own practiced eye was so sensitive to discern—as for the really astonishing similarities they shared. Henry guessed that a shrewd visitor examining the planet Earth would instantly lump all these dwellings into a single category along with all the various types of nests and burrows created by man's fellow beings on the planet—the birds, insects, animals, and fishes—and find them to be overwhelmingly similar. Observations of this kind brought an improvement to Henry's spirits, which the gin only served to reinforce, for he was making profitable use now, he fancied, of the very feelings of aloneness that had assailed him by studying himself and his surroundings in this novel, scientific fashion. Henry went so far in his meditations as to realize that contemplations of this order contained an enormous irony, a sort of "metaphysical ambush," as he styled it, for the more he destroyed his surroundings and himself by dehumanizing them, the longer grew the shadow of the contemplating mind itself. That is, discoveries of this sort could only be made insofar as the investigating mind was able to stifle its own nature and history; to think about them, the thinker had to aim at annihilating in himself the very source of thought itself. The shadow grew longer and longer. Psychic suicide was a logical enormity. Henry pulled at his gin and thought about that for a long while.

Sitting behind the Dutchman's-pipe, he smiled sottishly over the wonderfulness of his own ratiocinative powers. It was, after all, a valid conundrum, he decided, in which the ironies piled one upon the other. One could be as objective as one pleased about trees and houses and starlight, or even about one's own clothing, one's hat or shoes, or even the oxygen one inhaled, as long as one wasn't so dumb as to believe he had got anywhere with it. As for an objectivity that purports to dehumanize the objectifier, that was what Henry called a "wind egg." Henry sat humming a Kate Smith tune, and sucking his King Edward cigar, happy once more to be thinking the sort of high thoughts that had been such a mainstay in the past to his sense of well-being. He was put in mind of an occasion when the great Bishop Berkeley had responded to an opponent whose philosophical views he could not countenance by saying, "We Irish do not think so." Henry smiled over that one, and determined then and there that whenever he should find himself engaged in a highbrow discussion and wished to show a sublime disdain toward his interlocutor, he would give out the Bishop's words as his own. Softly he spoke the words to himself: "We Irish do not think so "

Henry's ruminations were not so absorbing, however, that he failed to notice Columbine's comings and goings. He was not unaware, for example, that she was driven home one evening by a man whom Henry was quite sure he had never seen before. Nor was he unaware that Columbine was often in a wicked mood lately, and could be heard in her house shouting at the top of her voice, berating her mother, or hollering at Anna. Sometimes, in fact, the tremulous pitch of her voice caused Henry to wonder if she was not becoming a little unsettled in her emotions. When Henry thought of Columbine in that light, she seemed to him like a small child whom he loved as a father would his daughter, and he was moved by feelings of pity and tenderness toward her. At other times, of course, he was reminded of her appalling entanglement that night with her satyric lover, a recollection that left him shaken and dejected. One way or the other, he went on thinking about her. He sometimes held imaginary conversations with her, in which he pictured her sitting beside him, with her head elevated on the slender stalk of her neck, her lips compressed, her eyes coolly absorbing his admiration for her, as though that was how it was meant to be. She would rattle away on a dozen or more bright, insignificant topics, her mind darting from one to the other with the colorful suddenness of a red-winged blackbird flitting from one tree to another. Or sometimes he imagined himself leading the discussion, but always curving it toward her, toward things that concerned her, as though she, Columbine, were their only proper and fitting topic. He imagined her sharing his seat, or walking beside him in the heat of the afternoon, her grave blue eyes mirroring an undeniable narcissism, a passion for the solicitude of others, a deep egoistic core that fascinated Henry but endeared her to him all the more. For that was their reciprocity. He was her surroundings and her looking-glass. It was some-

thing they had always known, even in distant past
times when she, as a little stripling too young for
school, would appear in the doorway of his father's
tool shed, standing primly in the door light, watching him with that level, dark-blue gaze, waiting to
be made something of.

One hot afternoon Henry went, finally, to call on
her. He had seen her mother and Mrs. Blye going
together down the front steps, chattering away in
Lithuanian, and on a sudden impulse he started outdoors. Columbine was upstairs. She saw him coming. When he knocked on the screen door, she called
down to him. Indoors, he waited for her to appear.
  "Come upstairs," she said, "I'm getting dressed."
  This invitation struck Henry as unorthodox, but
he did as he was bidden; putting his cane under his
arm and grasping the rail, he started up. His heart
was jumping but he strove to appear casual.
  "I had an accident," he called up the stairs to her.
  "Yes, I heard" came her reply.
  "I'm coming up now," he said.
  "I can *hear* you coming up," she called back playfully, in view of the heavy thuds he was making on
the stairs. He was hopping up two steps at a time,
pausing, changing his grip, then hopping again.
  "That's why I'm taking my summer vacation
now," he called up from the landing. "They were
glad to be rid of me for two weeks."
  "There's a fib," said Columbine breezily.
  He still could not see her, even as he attained the
top step and put down his cane, the rubber tip of
which, he noticed, was missing. The cane made a
clicking noise on the bare wood floor in the hall. His
pulse was still rapid but he was out of breath as well,
and for a while could hide one tumult behind the
other. "Shall I come in?" he said. "Is it all right?"
  "Mm-hm," she said.
  She was sitting at the white vanity with her back

357

to the door. She glanced up at him in the mirror. She didn't smile.

"I hope you didn't break anything." Her seeming ignorance of the details of Henry's accident and injury was not an encouragement to Henry, except as he thought she might be affecting a lack of curiosity in order to distress him.

He paused in the doorway and glanced about him. Columbine's room was surprisingly plain, with its old-fashioned furnishings painted white, an exposed bulb in the ceiling, and the floor covered with faded linoleum. It was the sort of room to which an unwanted aunt might be consigned to spend her last lonely days. It was not a girl's room at all.

"You'll have to sit on the bed," she said, without turning. She was busy doing something to her nails, cutting or filing them, or perhaps coloring them, Henry couldn't tell. He lowered himself onto the bed, extended his leg straight out, very carefully, then put up his cane.

"What are you doing here?" she asked him in a quiet voice.

"Well, I'm home all week," he said, but, knowing that to have been a foolish reply, coughed into his fist.

"Bored?" said Columbine.

"What?" said Henry.

She turned then and looked at him over her shoulder. She regarded him with a steady look while slowly compressing her lips. "I said, are you *bored?*" Columbine threw out, with an impatient inflection.

"Oh," Henry cried, "I didn't catch what you said. No. I haven't been bored. Well, maybe a little," he confessed.

She was looking fixedly at him all the while, and, again, not in a manner that encouraged Henry to believe that anything enlightening, or even cordial, was about to occur between them. "Because if it were me," she went on, "*I* would be enormously bored." Her eyes blazed.

Henry clammed up. He could not imagine Columbine looking at anyone in quite so penetrating a way without it portending something even more unpleasant to come. His own glance was riveted to hers. When Columbine saw no reply in the offing, she clarified her views.

"You sit on that porch of yours as though it were a guard post!" she said.

"Guard post?" he croaked, caught off balance, as always, by the quickness of her retorts.

"I'm surprised you don't ask people to show you their passes." She turned back to the mirror and resumed her grooming. Henry was staring at the side and back of her head, the shiny crow wing of her short-clipped hair drawing a vivid line across her cheekbone. He was troubled by her accusation. She was not looking at him in the mirror now but was rummaging noisily through a tin box containing brushes, tubes, hairpins, and the like, searching for something specific. "You ought to get yourself a gun," she said, "and march back and forth with it in the street." Having located what she was looking for, Columbine leaned close to the glass and began penciling her eyebrows. "It would be fun." She sat back from the glass to examine her handiwork, then leaned forward once more. "You could ask people where they had been, or where they were going, and with who, or *whom,* and what time they'd be back. Then," she concluded, as she straightened again and looked at herself in the glass, "you'd know everything about everybody." Columbine threw the eye pencil into the tin receptacle and started to conduct another noisy, impatient search in the tin box, spinning its contents with her fingers. "Are you still there?"

"Yes," said Henry.

Putting the box to one side, she examined her teeth in the mirror. She worked her tongue back and forth across her teeth, then examined them a second time. Then she put on a pair of sunglasses and studied their effect, averting her head one way, then the other, and turned and looked back at him from behind the opaque lenses. "Do I frighten you?" she said.

"Sometimes," he admitted, at length.

Flinging down the glasses, she popped up from the vanity bench, strode very briskly across the room, and threw open her closet door. She was playing the actress now, peering into the closet with an air of studied refinement, her hands on her hips, and making low inconsequential throaty noises to signify her indecisiveness. She was wearing her alligator shoes and, while trying to make up her mind what to wear, was shifting her weight first onto the heel of one shoe, while raising and revolving the toe of the other, and then over onto the heel of that shoe, while elevating and turning the other toe about. Something in her histrionic behavior struck Henry as being excessive, even for Columbine, as he gazed up at her from the bed with a worried look.

Outdoors, the air darkened as the shadow of a cloud enveloped the gardens, reducing the light in Columbine's bedroom by half. The curtains wavered in the open windows. Henry's feelings compelled him to speak. He was looking at her. "You don't dance any more," he said softly.

Columbine shot him a recriminatory look. "You don't sing, do you?" she fired back. Her quickness brought a smile to Henry's face. It was never possible to keep up with her.

"Everybody gives up something," he said.

"Turn your back. I'm going to change."

Henry faced the wall. He lay his cane like a lute across his lap. It was so quiet in the house he could hear from below the soft whir of the refrigerator in the kitchen. When Henry went away to the Navy, the Kokorisses still had an icebox. Four or five years before that, the Flynns had one, too. It stood in the shed now behind the kitchen. There was a big yellow basin underneath that collected the water and that had to be spilled out regularly. The iceman's name was Jerzyk. Henry remembered the canvas-topped truck parked in the back alleyway, the canvas rolled up and the blocks of ice gleaming inside amid the shadows and sawdust. The iceman wore a pick in a leather sheath on his belt and had a leather pad to protect his shoulder. With his tongs he skidded a block of ice over the tailgate onto his padded shoulder. He entered at the back fence, walking with a list, his left arm out for balance, and the big cube of ice shining like a diamond. On a hot day the boys thronged around Mr. Jerzyk's truck, begging for chips of ice. He remembered the man's infinite patience, chipping flakes of ice with practiced blows. Henry was staring at the wall. Behind him, Columbine was changing.

She threw her top onto the vanity and went in her brassiere to the closet. Then she came back and took off her brassiere, fished another from a drawer, and, reaching with her two arms behind her back like a contortionist, put that one on while walking back to her dresser. "Did you hear," she tossed out airily, "that I got thrown over?"

"What are you talking about?" said Henry.

"I was thrown over," she exclaimed, and banged a drawer shut with her knee.

Not daring to turn to look at her, Henry made a puzzled face. He didn't know what she was talking about.

"My boyfriend threw me over!"

Henry kept his eyes on the wall, while behind him Columbine was creating a world of noise, opening and closing drawers, clacking across the floor, rattling hangers in the closet.

'Who are you talking about?''

"Whom?" Columbine corrected him. "Whom do you think? I'm talking about Andrew."

"I didn't even know that he was your boyfriend," Henry lied. "I didn't know you had a boyfriend."

Columbine laughed ringingly. "Can you imagine someone throwing me over?" she cried, with her usual vanity.

"No," said Henry truthfully, "I can't."

"Well, I couldn't have, either." This remark was followed by the reports of other drawers opening and shutting. Columbine dropped a wooden hanger on the floor, and with the toe of her shoe sent it flying against the baseboard.

"What happened?" said Henry.

"Nothing *happened.* I've been dumped. You can look now," she said.

When Henry turned, Columbine was wearing the same skirt and jersey. She looked exactly as she had before, except her hair was mussed from pulling things over her head. She stood only a few feet from Henry, facing him but not looking at him, as she started in busily to brush her hair. She had that cool, detached, distant look, her face and eyes glowing with it. Her moving eyes paused once upon him, then moved on. She was brushing her hair with even, mechanical strokes, pausing now and again to withdraw hair from the bristles with her fingernails. Henry was sure she had no feelings for him but that she was not above tormenting him in return for some deep but mysterious grievance she bore him.

"If you ask me," Henry suggested, at last, quietly, "I don't think you need a boyfriend." He looked up at her with earnestness. He had in mind a great many things he had wished to say to Columbine, but could not recall them. Her eyes, moving sullenly, paused upon him, and moved away. Her manner was not encouraging. He sat, toying with the cane on his lap,

362

while Columbine continued to stand over him, motionless on her feet, the hairbrush working incessantly. Her eyes came to rest on the wall above her bed. "A lot of young girls," he suggested, "have girlfriends."

"I don't have girlfriends."

"You could," said Henry quietly, knowing that they were speaking of very important matters, but not understanding them himself.

"I insult them," said Columbine. As she turned away, Henry detected the sudden childish pout on Columbine's lips. "I don't like girls," she said. "I never did. I like them, but I don't like to be with them." Turning in place, she looked at herself in the distant mirror. "My sisters taught me that."

A moment went by before Henry responded. "You have lovely sisters," he said.

Suddenly Columbine turned on her heel and let fly the hairbrush. The brush flew through the open doorway into the hall, where it hit the wall and skittered down the stairs. "Did you come over here to tell me that?" she shrieked. Her eyes gleamed venomously. *"Did you?"*

Columbine's sudden rage would ordinarily have frightened Henry out of the room; but this time it transfixed him, for her wrath seemed aimed not so much at himself as at some abstraction whose nature he could not guess. It worried him. Abruptly, however, the moment passed. Columbine went to the closet and yanked out a white skirt clipped to a wooden hanger. Before Henry could look away, she had unfastened that skirt and with a quick motion at her waist had dropped the skirt she was wearing onto the floor about her feet and stepped out of it. She was wearing white underclothes and gave the fleeting impression of a long-legged white bird with a ruffle of white plumage under its belly and behind, as she stepped briskly into the white skirt and squeezed its elasticized top up over her thighs and buttocks onto her waist. Henry looked on like a perplexed husband.

"Not that it matters." Columbine resumed talking about Salty in an impersonal tone. "He was a filthy enough hog. Although," she added, as a shocking afterthought, "I suppose I could have stood that." She was holding up blouses one at a time, examining each one critically, then returning it to the closet with an angry flourish and selecting another to look at. "It wasn't his dirty habits."

"What was it?" said Henry, pained by the callousness of her words.

Columbine turned on him. "I just told you. He threw me over! Like you," she said, with a thin, unpleasant smile, "he likes girls with big boobs."

"*I* do?" said Henry, blushing over his sudden inclusion in Columbine's expostulation.

"He likes cows. Andrew would like a girl to have breasts she couldn't even walk with, but just lie there on her back, like a big mountain of pus, I suppose." Columbine's indignation was finding metaphors that further upset Henry. "Or wear big, greasy, size-forty dresses like his mother, or like that aunt of his," she said, "who hasn't seen her own feet in fifty years. Did you ever see Andrew's aunt? The one they call Beelzie? She walks with two canes and has boobs on her that could suffocate an elephant. Andrew is her favorite. He tells her dirty jokes. 'Beelzie,' " she mimicked Salty, " 'did you hear the one about the farmer's daughter who choked on a corncob?' " With disgust, Columbine slammed shut the closet door.

Henry couldn't respond but watched in silence as Columbine pulled her blouse up over her head, mussing her hair all over again, and tossed it aside. She had selected a blue cotton top from the closet, into which she thrust her arms, first one, then the other, and prepared to raise it over her head. Before doing so, she paused, however, and turned her eyes to Henry. He was gazing at her modest breasts and bare shoulders. Her attention lingered on him. He should have said something.

Waiting, unconscious of her own deepest impulses, Columbine gazed back at him expressionlessly. It was the face of the girl in the door light. A moment later, she pulled the blouse on over her head. She resumed talking, but as she did so Henry had a sense that something which was intended to be had formed itself into a picture and was starting backward now into the past. He should have said something. Her breasts looked very pretty. Outdoors, a long, silent wave of sunlight curled over the fence and ignited the gardens. The sun shimmered in the curtains. Henry sat staring at her, his fingers turning the cane on his lap.

"He calls his aunt Mother and his mother Auntie," Columbine piped up disparagingly. " 'Saddle up the stove, Mother, I'm riding the range tonight!' " she mimicked. "He's such a scurf, I wouldn't put anything past him. He talks about 'cornholing.' Says he cornholed Beelzie when he was eight!"

"Columbine," Henry said kindly, troubled by her overwrought temper. She was working herself up, he thought.

"I wouldn't put a thing past any of them," she said. "You should see the two of them in Beelzie's kitchen when she brings him berries and milk in a dish and stands over him with her two canes, *gloating*," said Columbine, and she widened her eyes lustfully, "and watching to see that he swallows every spoonful!" Without warning, Columbine turned and darted suddenly out of the room and went down the stairs clacking noisily, and then came clacking noisily back up, and reappeared, brushing her hair again in smooth, rapid strokes. "And you just *know*," she cried, "it's the same dish she uses to feed the cats, because I've seen them at the bowl, five or six of them, big filthy black things with whiskers on them like paintbrushes." Columbine's lower lip went back in an unconscious sneer. "She calls Andrew 'Lambabaun' and he comes and puts his head down on her tits. It's revolting! She made love to him when he was eight."

"I think he talks a lot," Henry muttered helplessly.

"She is a huge, huge tub." Columbine extended her arms to illustrate. "She's about three hundred pounds, with little glittery eyes and four or five yellow teeth showing." Columbine resumed brushing; her eyes glided restlessly about. She was breathing with her mouth open and nibbling on her lower lip, while passing from one side of her head to the other with alternate strokes of the brush.

"Salty starts a lot of talk," said Henry. "He always did."

"She's a perfect walrus! She has those two canes, and when she's sitting down on her sofa, with her fists up to her face, the sticks in her hands are like two big yellow tusks, one going one way, and one the other. *'Lambie Pie coming for supper tonight?'* " Columbine paused here to mimic the old woman's lascivious manner. *" 'Lambabaun want some a my chowder?'* His own mother treats her like a queen. 'Let me help, Beel. Let Andrew help. Andrew'll do it. Andrew, get Auntie her eyeglasses. Andrew, get Auntie her favorite cushion,' and Andrew and Beelzie snickering and winking at each other all the while, and her *big bosom*"—Columbine took several swaggering, gigantic steps about the room in an exaggerated impersonation of Salty's aunt—"up in the air like this, like two watermelons. And . . . and she's ugly! She's old and ugly. She sits there with an egg whisk, whisking flies. Her house smells of flypaper and cats. *She* smells like citronella. She puts it on like perfume! Oh, and she doesn't look at you, either, unless you're Andrew, of course. The only time she ever looked at me was when she caught me staring at her tits."

"Columbine!"

"She grinned at me." Columbine displayed the aunt's concupiscent grin and her syrupy tone of voice. " *'You want some berries and milk, sweetie?'* It turned my stomach! It's a wonder I ever went back. She called me *'Ahndrrew's gurrl,'* and told Andrew to give me one of the kittens that her cat was getting ready to have." Columbine shivered in revulsion. She turned sideways on her heel and began shaping her hair methodically with the edge of the brush. Her eyes went to her reflection in the vanity mirror. "Andrew says she's been excommunicated."

"He talks."

"Does he?" Columbine challenged. "What would you say if I told you I saw them kissing? Not the kind of kissing you think, either. What would you say to that? I was supposed to be outdoors, getting something from the car, but I hadn't gone yet. I could see her leaning all over him at the kitchen table, her huge fat bottom sticking up, and all you could see of him underneath her were his two hands coming around her back, like one of those trick riders in the movies that ride underneath the horse. When she saw me, she lit up like a pumpkin. *'Oh, Ahndrrew, yer gurrl'll never talk to ye again! Catch ye kissin' yer own mother!'* Of course," said Columbine, "she's rubbing his face with them—and *cackling!* Aunt Beelzie is ten years older than Andrew's mother, and his mother's fifty-six."

"They weren't kissing," said Henry.

"If they weren't," she assured him, "they were doing something worse. Would *you* like to tell me what they were doing? What would you call it," she said, "if you saw her covering him over with her body, and their two faces stuck together, and his arms all the way around her rump?"

"Of course," Henry put in, "you didn't have to see him."

Columbine's expression changed. For a moment he even thought she might reveal the secret reasons behind her contempt for him. He was wrong.

"He had his good points," said Columbine disdainfully. "But he's not the only fish in the ocean. Is it fish?" said Columbine. "Or fishes? You would know that."

"He was not proper for you," said Henry.

"He went back to Susannah. *I,*" she said, waving her hairbrush, "was thrown over for a cow like that. I even had to walk home. He put me out of his car Tuesday night. I told Harold about it," Columbine spoke of another suitor, "and Harold said he would beat Andrew to within an inch of his life, but I told him not to bother." Columbine came back from the vanity, opening a lipstick tube; pausing in the center of the room, she gauged the light from the windows, then raised her compact mirror. "I don't want anybody getting hurt," she said. "Harold is like you," she went on, paying Henry a dubious compliment, "he doesn't like trouble." She was peering at close range into the little compact mirror, scrutinizing her eyes and lips. "He was just talking," she added.

Henry didn't wish to inquire into the identity of the man named Harold, but supposed him to be the individual who had recently driven her home. When it was apparent that Henry was not going to query her about it, Columbine told him anyway. His name, she said, was Harold Quinn.

"That name!" said Henry.

"Yes, I know," said Columbine, "it sounds like yours. It sounds like—Herky Flynn," she said, and looked round challengingly to catch his reaction to being called Herky. Henry was not put in mind, though, of his own name, but of Harlequin, and marveled over that for several minutes. He was carrying in his jacket pocket the letter Columbine had written him in May and was tempted here to produce it. He could not reconcile Columbine's cold hatred of him with the sweetness of that letter, the words and phrases of which he could have recited by heart. He sat on the edge of the bed, twirling his cane, while watching Columbine make up her face with great showmanship.

"You probably know him," she said. "He's in one of the high schools."

"Harold Quinn is a *student?*" said Henry.

Columbine flicked her eyes at Henry to confirm the jocular nature of his remark, then began spreading the lipstick gloss. "He's vice principal," she said. "He was a pilot in the war." Columbine interrupted herself here to set the toe of her alligator pump underneath the skirt which she had taken off and dropped onto the floor, and sent it flying into the closet. By then, Henry recognized the erratic component in her behavior. She was becoming volatile and undisciplined. She was soon talking again about Andrew and Harold, and about Andrew and his aunt, and then about Harold again and his wife and daughters, and said she didn't care if he drove his Lincoln Zephyr a hundred and fifty miles an hour so long as they got where they were going. "You can be brainy and still be a lunatic," she said. Henry tried to warn Columbine about riding in cars with maniac drivers, but Columbine replied, with reference to Henry's leg, that Henry was not one to talk. "I wish you still *had* your car," she said, "you could have driven me to town today. I told Harold not to pick me up. He has troubles enough already. His wife is getting suspicious. Andrew, who knows both of them, says Mrs. Quinn thinks she's Vivien Leigh and threatens to poison herself and their children if Harold doesn't take her back to her family's plantation in Virginia. Andrew says she's insane. It was Andrew who introduced us. Harold asked him if I was for sale."

"I don't think that's amusing," said Henry.

"I think Harold offered him money." Taking up her canvas bag, Columbine stuffed in a green swimsuit. Henry pushed himself onto his feet, not because he wished to go, but because Columbine was giving signs of an imminent departure. She stood with her back to him, putting on her wristwatch while gazing out into the sunlight. Henry was staring down at the top of her head. "In fact," she said, "I think Harold gave him money. Tuesday night Harold had a lot of money and Andrew was broke, and Wednesday night Harold was broke and Susannah was all dressed up and carrying a new white lizard bag. It was the first time I've ever seen her dressed up. She looked like she had her hair done by a raccoon." Columbine continued to stare into the sunlight while fiddling with her wristwatch. By now, Henry knew she had passed him by. There seemed nothing preposterous at all in the knowledge that she was going away to an assignation. She was going to meet her lover. Her attitude was not conceived to repair or restore anything, he felt. If there had been a moment for turning back, it had come and gone this afternoon in this room. Gazing down on the crown of her head, at the fine white line of her parted hair, he could not imagine that she was thinking about him—a suspicion she immediately confirmed.

"I wonder if I should be wearing these shoes," she said.

A pale fragrance rose from Columbine's hair. When she turned to go, Henry reached into his inside jacket pocket and withdrew the apple-green envelope containing the letter Columbine had written him. He produced the letter slowly, with an unconscious delicacy of effect.

At first, Columbine didn't recognize it. She had stopped in the doorway, glancing round behind her. Then her eyes focused on it. Henry started to say something but never got the words out of his mouth. Columbine made a sudden wild lunge and seized the letter.

"Where did you get that?" she cried, and began to tear it to bits. She tore it violently into shreds. "You read that?" she said, and shook the fistful of paper at him. "You read that?" A blue turmoil burned in her eyes.

"It arrived in the mail," said Henry.

Columbine was speechless with wrath, her face pale and fixed. After an instant she strode out of the room and down the stairs. By the time Henry got outdoors, she was nowhere in sight.

"You know," said Mrs. Flynn, "it's not wise to visit single girls when they're home alone."

Henry was sitting on the sofa in the parlor. "Is that a fact?" he said.

"She's growing up," said his mother. "Don't you think she's too big for that?"

Henry went upstairs. He was not in an amiable mood. He was thinking about the letter. He wished he had not shown it to her. The letter meant a lot to Henry, although he could not himself understand why, unless, perhaps, its ruin had come to signify, or to portend, the death of Starbuck. That's what he was thinking. He wrote Columbine a letter that afternoon, if only for the want of anything else to do. He was experiencing evil premonitions about her, so much so that he didn't believe the letter would ever reach her hands. Henry could not later on remember having made protestations of love in it, but guessed that he probably had. He knew that he had written it under a shadow of foreboding. It was, as he recalled it, a paean on the mere fact of her existence, or on the fact of creation itself, on all the individual souls pressing along in the darkness in their millions like pinpoints of reflected light. He folded the two sheets, sealed them in an envelope, and wrote her name and address upon it.

Columbine didn't come home that evening, but by then Henry was already out looking for her. At suppertime, he borrowed his Uncle Stephen's car. Uncle Stephen looked very white in the gills when he saw his nephew standing in the doorway, and Henry didn't know if that was because Uncle Stephen was on the wagon or because he, Henry, was himself as pale as a ghost. Uncle Stephen was one of Henry's lifelong favorites. He knew, too, that his uncle by marriage loved him dearly, and it pained Henry to realize that Uncle Stephen was ashamed of himself in Henry's eyes. The uncle sensed Henry's misery at once. Henry didn't know that his uncle was one of those persons who had seen him riding with Columbine in his open convertible that spring night. Uncle Stephen gave Henry the car keys and followed him downstairs to the street, looking even more miserable and concerned than Henry himself. As Henry was climbing in behind the wheel of the Buick, Uncle Stephen broke the taboo.

"It's that little girl, isn't it?" he said.

"Yes," said Henry, "it is."

"I could drive for you."

"That's all right," said Henry, "I'll manage."

Henry drove the six miles out to the beaches, but the search there was futile, the ponds thronging with swimmers and sunbathers, the parking lots full, families picnicking in the groves, and dozens of small pleasure boats plying the waters in every direction. By nightfall, Henry was back in the city, going from one place to another, asking for them. Columbine was known. Oh, yes, said someone, two nights ago she had leaped onto the bar at the Spanish

Gardens and performed a suicidal dance to a deafening jukebox recording of "Slaughter on Tenth Avenue." She was the girl with the military hat. They called her the Ziczac Girl. Tonight she had not been seen. Henry picked up their trail about ten o'clock, however, in the old French Quarter of the city. They had had supper, the girl and a blond-haired man, at L'Escargot d'Or. The girl was wearing a green bathing suit and sunglasses and was talking a mile a minute. The man with her was speaking French, or pretended to be, but insisted on speaking German to the waiters. A difficulty arose. If the girl was going to wear her swimsuit, the rules of the house would compel them to sit at the waiters' table by the door to the kitchen. The girl would have to sit out of sight. Mr. Archambault, who was the headwaiter (and who grew effusive when Henry showed him his press card), explained that it was he who permitted them to dine at the waiters' table. Mr. Archambault said further that the man's French was not even French, but some kind of gobbledygook. Mr. Archambault said he was familiar with every kind of French there was. "But the girl," he said, with a gesture of his fingertips, "spoke beautiful English. *Perfect,"* he said.

"That's her," said Henry, looking about hopefully at the three waiters standing around him, each with a blue towel folded over his arm.

"You have never heard such English," said Mr. Archambault.

"Where did they go?" Henry asked.

"And manners," said the headwaiter. "She had manners like that. Perfect. Everything. Speech, manners, all of it." He clicked his fingers.

"What time did they leave?" said Henry. "And where did they go?"

"If she had been dressed—wearing anything—" Mr. Archambault pointed a long arm across the dining room, "I would have seated them at table number one. Some people," he explained *sotto voce,* "you must never refuse. Never. It's bad business. Some people are always correct. I," said Mr. Archambault, "can detect them. A headwaiter in a top establishment," he went so far as to say, "lives or dies on that ability. What time did they leave?" He suddenly parroted Henry's question. "Where did they go? I couldn't say. They are gone an hour. The girl," he continued, "talks to everyone. She treats you like an equal. She talked to Louis, she talked to Gene, she talked to Mrs. Ostreicher, she talked to the boys, to me, to Anita, to everyone."

Henry pushed along. In Sheehan's Avidoir he discovered Columbine's picture hanging in the gallery over the bar. It was set in a new black frame and hung at the end of a row of pictures, next to a photograph that showed Angelo Bertelli, the football player, with his helmet off, throwing a forward pass. In her picture Columbine wore white tights and ballet slippers, and lay full-length on an elegantly set dinner table, with wineglasses glittering like diamonds about her, and a spray of gauzy white flowers emerging from amid the glitter in the vicinity of her navel. She was as languid as could be, except for her eyes, which looked back at you with a distrustful glow. Henry made inquiries of the barman, an elderly gentleman in a black suit and squeaky shoes who was constantly ordering the second barman about with subdued gestures and a system of winces and winks aimed at maintaining a brisk flow of business. "Not tonight," said the elderly gentleman to Henry, with the air of a prime minister refusing a glass of warm milk before bed, as he deflected Henry's attempt to question him. "I'm busy."

"I'm not selling anything," Henry explained in exasperation. "I'm looking for someone. I'm looking for Harold Quinn." He had to raise his voice. "Harold Quinn!" he shouted, for the old barkeep was hard of hearing. Henry pointed to the picture of Columbine. "I'm looking for her!" he shouted.

"Are you?" cried the old gentleman, his bushy white eyebrows going up insolently. "What are you *drinking?"* he wished to know.

"Never mind," said Henry dejectedly, as he noticed heads turning toward him all along the bar.

"Never mind!" the old man cried back mockingly, as Henry went on his cane toward the door. The barman was glaring at him. "Never mind what he's drinking, will you!"

Next he tried the hotels, then three different taverns on Division Street. His search was becoming like a mortification, as he hopped from one watering hole to the next, a spectacle in the eyes of the hundreds of noisy carousers packed into the smoky, humid bars that lined the street above the railroad yards. Someone had seen her, a girl in a green bathing suit with longish legs and short black hair. She was dancing the samba at the Parazard Club. The patrons were cheering her on.

"She looked about fifteen," said a big, jowlish bleached blonde who insisted on introducing Henry to her two barfly boyfriends. The woman showed Henry a deep, baleful wink that portended something severe. "I would know what to do with a girl like that," she said.

"He already knows what to do," said one of the barflies, and the two men looked at Henry and laughed unpleasantly.

Henry went on. He tried the Brian Boru Club, the Rooftop, the Famous Door, and the Ack Ack, so many nightclubs, in fact, that by midnight he was being greeted and poked fun at by drinkers who had met him earlier in other bars. His quest was becoming known. Henry's open-faced innocence inspired in others a playful malice. At the Pangur Ban Lounge, however, a man named Talty was helpful.

Henry knew Mr. Talty by sight from a few years ago as a tax assessor. Mr. Talty had seen the two of them in a Polish night spot by the river at about eleven o'clock. "She came in talking," said Mr. Talty, "and she went out talking."

"What was she talking about?" said Henry.

"You name it," said Mr. Talty, with a sudden guffaw, his florid face lighting up with pleasure. "Everything under the sun. The weather, the people, the music, the character she was with."

"Who was she with?" said Henry.

"A regular crackpot," said Mr. Talty, as he adjusted the knot of his orange necktie and fanned himself with his newspaper.

"That's what I was afraid of," Henry said.

"He was a Navy pilot in the war. They grounded him for buzzing Nantasket Beach." Mr. Talty laughed thickly, with his tongue showing between his teeth, his eyes roving up to the ceiling.

"It sounds bad," said Henry worriedly.

"I don't think you'll overtake them," said Mr. Talty sagaciously. The older man seemed to Henry a decent sort, particularly as he evinced suddenly a more intimate air. "Is she your sister?" he whispered hoarsely.

"No, sir," said Henry.

"I didn't think so. Doesn't look a thing like you."

"No, she doesn't," said Henry, despairing now by the minute. He was reaching the end of his rope, his leg throbbing, his worries for her mounting.

"Let me stand you a drink," said the man. "After all, she's as apt to come in here as anywhere else."

"She was that bad," Henry surmised unhappily.

"She was," said the other. "She couldn't stop talking, you see." He beckoned to the barkeep.

"No, thank you," said Henry, "I'm going along."

"Try the Showboat," said Mr. Talty. "They swim out there at night, and the Quinn fellow likes the place. They don't like him, but you know how it is with fellows like that—there's just no discouraging them." Mr. Talty made a gesture with his fist to signify the inevitableness of an undisciplined will.

"I'll try it," said Henry.

"Do that," said Mr. Talty.

"Good night," said Henry.

"It's a late bar." Mr. Talty smiled hello at someone going past, and returned the same smile to Henry. "You try that."

"Yes," said Henry.

"Good luck to you."

"Good night," said Henry.

He saw the lights of the Showboat shining across the water as he approached by car. From a distance, the nightclub, which was situated on the southern shore of the ponds, appeared indeed to be a ship floating on the surface of the water, a big, lighted steamboat, with the shadows of trees showing behind it against the starlit sky. Uncle Stephen's car banged and whistled on the hills, and an oily vapor came up from the floorboards. Henry kept his stockinged foot pressed gingerly on the accelerator. Only as he approached the Showboat and nearby beaches could he make out, amid the orderly profusion of lights and lighted windows, a dull, red light throbbing upward into the darkness. The red glow rose and fell with the regularity of a heartbeat. Henry paid it no mind at first, but as he came round a final curve in the road, the meaning of the light became clear to him. Dozens of men and women were milling about on the bathing beach. With each flash of the ambulance light, the human silhouettes lit up red. The scene was infernal. They looked like the shades of human beings assembling in the dark for a final journey over the water. Henry abandoned the car at the side of the road and made his way as rapidly as possible through the sand. The voices coming back to him from the water blended into a single ominous murmur. To one side,

377

a short distance away from the others, a man lay on his back in the sand. A policeman stood over him. It was a dead man. The darkness of his form contrasted with the white sand on which he lay.

No one was looking at him, though. The throng faced expectantly toward the water. Even the policeman, Henry noticed, was gazing far out across the water at what appeared to be the silhouette of a boat. Henry's mind was going in circles. He could not believe this was happening. All the while, however, he was negotiating his way through the sand toward the dead man, his cane sinking uselessly into the sand. As he got closer, he caught sight of the dead man's hair. Just as each crimson flash of the ambulance light expired, the dead man's hair lighted up to a sudden whiteness. No one even turned to look at Henry as he paused over the figure of the drowned man. The man, sopping wet, lay perfectly composed, with his hands flat at his sides, looking like a high diver standing at attention in a world that had turned over. The face was reposeful. One eye was open a slit. In the slit shone a tiny starlike gleam. The man wore white trousers and a white dress shirt, and had on a sleeveless argyle sweater. He looked like Henry, so much so that Henry noted the resemblance. The incoming boat was chugging toward shore, its prow lifted out of the water by the weight of the two men standing in the stern. At the same time, two men from the ambulance waded out into the water. But one of the men in the boat waved them back. By now, the crowd of onlookers had grown considerably, but all fell silent as the prow of the boat brushed a buoy aside and came aground.

"It's no use," said the man in the boat.

They had been in the water thirty minutes. Henry looked back at the dead man, then at the boat. He couldn't see her in the boat. He wondered if the dead man had tried to save her. Henry looked about desperately at the people around him. They were all well dressed, and all appeared appalled by what they were seeing. They were in a speedboat, said someone. They were going about a hundred. Someone saw it happen. It blew up.

Henry backed away. He saw the man transferring the body from the boat into the arms of the waiting ambulance men. Henry's thinking was distracted; he was in a state of shock, but was touched nevertheless by the solicitude of the four men. The men in the boat were policemen. Both of them were bareback, their shoulders and arms glistening with wetness. The policeman in the stern had picked up their holsters and shirts. The ambulance driver took the girl in his arms as tenderly as though she were an infant. Henry put his hand over his mouth and groaned aloud. He could see the crown of her head, the black helmet of her hair showing in the crook of the sleeve of the man's white jacket. Then the two policemen came ashore. They jumped into the water, one after the other, and waded in. One of them paused and ran his fingers back through his wet hair. He laughed nervously. "All in a night's work," he said.

"Whose boat is this?" said the other cop.

"Over here," said a man solemnly; he was standing at the edge of the crowd.

"Thank you for the use of it," said the policeman.

Henry was meanwhile moving with dreamlike concentration toward the ambulance to intercept the driver, to see her face. The second ambulance man opened the back door, and a panel of light flooded out to where the driver was coming through the sand with the girl in his arms. Everyone looked down at her in silence as the man carried her past. Henry got to the open door just as he arrived with her. Her face was bluish and a long strand of knotted black hair lay across her mouth. Seeing that, Henry gave a soft cry and bit his hand. It wasn't her at all. It was someone else. He saw the girl's teeth showing, and

379

long weeds clinging obscenely to her dress. The dress was a wheyish white and was plastered to her body. It was not Columbine at all.

Minutes later, as the crowd dissipated and the ambulance backed slowly across the darkened beach with its light out, Henry found himself wandering in a daze to a nearby jetty. Underneath the pier a collection of tethered rowboats bumped one another in the dark. He could hear the water lapping against them, and the sound then of auto engines starting up. There Henry lost control of himself. It came up from inside like choking. He might have wondered if it was not caused somewhat by his almost wishing death upon a total stranger; but in his heart he knew better than that, and leaning both arms against the pier, he broke down and wept.

He could have spared his tears, though, for at 2 A.M., acting on an anonymous tip, the police from Ireland Parish broke into a tourist cabin in Smith's Ferry, ten miles away, and arrested Harold Quinn and the young girl with him. They were arrested "in the act." Harold Quinn tried to scramble out a window, but was caught around the legs by a policeman; the girl—not identified by name because of her age—while struggling with the other policeman, struck her mouth against a bedpost, and let out a screech that could be heard, they said, a mile away. Mr. Quinn protested his innocence every foot of the way. He was said to have been incensed by being put into handcuffs, insisting, as he did, that they had the wrong man. He insisted on this point over and over, to such an extent—especially in the face of the compromising circumstances attending his arrest—that the police were said to have been greatly charmed and amused by the episode. The girl, Columbine, wasn't speaking. In the cruiser she held a handkerchief to her mouth, which was swelling, and said nothing.

"Believe me," Mr. Quinn said, "I know what I'm talking about." He repeated this over and over. "You've got the wrong man."

After that, Harold Quinn grew increasingly calm, almost nonchalant, as, apparently, he came to reflect upon the power of truth and justice to vindicate innocence in the end.

"I'm not talking through my hat," he said.

XIX

The stories got going in the morning and by suppertime had mushroomed ludicrously. They said that
Mr. Quinn had the girl propped up on the dresser
and was servicing her thus at the instant the door
burst in. They said he had her up against the wall.
They said he had her upside down against the wall.
Harold Quinn was characterized in the news broad-
casts as an ex-Navy officer and mental patient whose
tenure in the local school system had been twice
jeopardized previously, one occasion involving a
fistfight with a student and another a flirtation with
a student. The girl was not named, but was said to
have been handed over to the juvenile authorities.
Mr. Quinn was charged with adultery, fornication,
impairing the morals of a minor, resisting arrest, and
a half dozen related charges, while being held without bail pending a psychiatric examination. Columbine was sent home. Henry read about it in the
newspaper. Mr. Meehan had covered the story personally, the front-page account of which bore his
name.

Some little suspicion attached also to Henry, of
course, as he had been missing most of the night; but
when queried by his father, Henry gave a truthful
account of his doings and whereabouts that appeared to satisfy the older Flynn. In fact, his description of the drowning of the man and girl riveted his
father's attention.

"Isn't that remarkable," said his father. "In matters like this"—he tapped the newspaper—"your
hands can't be too clean, you know. It's all well and

good to sympathize, but don't mix in. Nothing enrages people more than the violation of a young girl. You do understand what I'm talking about?"

"Of course," said Henry.

His father grew red and cleared his throat. "You understand what I mean by 'violation'?"

The son nodded. They were standing outside the back door. It was a soft July evening. Boys with air rifles were playing in the fields beyond the back roadway. Henry avoided looking at the Kokoriss house. Columbine was inside. A strange equanimity had come over Henry in the knowledge of her being safe, a peace of mind that even a grave scandal could not damage. It was not because she was safe from Harold Quinn, but because she was alive. This sense of well-being persisted in the face of the news.

"There are people in this world who know what to do with the likes of that Quinn fellow," said Sergeant Flynn. "If I had my way, he would not get a fresh opportunity."

"I can imagine," said Henry absently.

His father's face and neck turned shrimp-pink as his anger intensified. "Believe me, he would never be the same again. Oh, yes, I would know exactly what to do with him. I would do to him what is done to any crazy, high-spirited animal. Where do you think geldings come from?" he asked suddenly.

"From people like you," said Henry.

"People like me?" cried the sergeant. "Are you even listening to what I'm saying? I was talking about criminals, about filthy-minded lowlifes who will destroy the life and happiness of a beautiful child just to gratify the beast in them! That kind of man should be carved up."

"Harold Quinn is a certified nut."

"That's a license for filth?" said his father. "For the polluting of virgins, for every gross form of depravity—rape, sodomy, adultery? What about incest and murder, Mr. Smart Aleck? Oh, yes," he said,

"I've heard all the excuses and special pleadings, believe me. Innocent by reason of insanity. Temporarily insane. Not accountable for his actions. Mentally deficient. Why, there are people walking the streets of this town that are not fit to pitch their tents in a stockyard. I could name you ten men that should be swung from a lamp post at the crack of dawn. And your Ensign Quinn," he said, "would stand tall among them." Henry's father adjusted the tight little knot of his necktie. "I'd like to break his neck," he said.

Notwithstanding the sergeant's fulminations, an impressive quiet had settled over the avenue. No one stirred all evening. Radios played softly; lawn sprinklers whispered; fireflies came out. After midnight, a gentle summer rain began to fall. Henry heard the first drops pattering on the roof, then on the sill of his open window. Across the way, Columbine's room was in darkness all night except for a five-minute spell about three o'clock in the morning when the drawn windowshades were briefly illuminated. Henry guessed correctly that the scandal had greatly chastened her. She had had enough drama to last her a good long while, he supposed. He was not himself in the least bitter, but was, instead, relieved in knowing her to be safe, like a patient breaking a fever. The rain provided a fitting accompaniment to the general purgation. That was how he felt himself, purged of worry.

The following morning, just before noon, Henry had a visitor. Mrs. Flynn called Henry to the front door, and there, standing back a little way on the porch, his hat brim decorated with silver droplets of rain, was Mr. Meehan himself. The big man stood at his ease, with his hands clasped before him in the attitude of a public speaker who was being introduced to his audience and was awaiting his time to speak with modesty and confidence.

"There you are," he exclaimed in a kindly voice

the instant Henry appeared in the doorway.

Henry replied to Mr. Meehan in a subdued tone. "Come in," he said softly.

"No, no, no," Mr. Meehan returned blithely, raising a hand of gentle protest. "I have already thanked your mother for an equally kind invitation. I won't be but a moment. So"—he altered his voice while presuming to take in the house with the uncritical eye of a tourist or pilgrim—"this is the old Flynn homestead, is it?"

Henry did not respond to Mr. Meehan's remark, but joined him on the porch. The swelling in Henry's ankle and foot had begun to subside but was still painful. On that foot he wore an unlaced shoe. He was carrying his cane.

"And I suppose," Mr. Meehan continued more weightily, with a tilting of his head, "that the house next door is the—"

"Yes, it is," said Henry. He was trying hastily to plumb Mr. Meehan's motives for calling on him, but for the life of him couldn't make even a guess of it. He took at once an exploratory tack, however, saying, "It wouldn't be suitable for me, Jack, to furnish any information about—you know—the—ah—the girl next door. Not that there's anything to tell, anyhow," he added swiftly.

"Of course not." Mr. Meehan flapped his hand in dismissal of the preposterous, then reached and took off his hat. Holding the hat from him, he shook away the raindrops, then placed it on the arm of the wicker chair nearby. "This is a morning that can't make up its mind. Look at that," he said, "the rain is slowing up again. I'll be damned if it hasn't stopped."

It was true. The rain was letting up even as they watched, and was replaced by a watery light flooding over the stone path. Henry waited while Mr. Meehan brushed the morning wetness from the shoulders of his sharkskin suit. The man's flair for building suspense struck Henry as a kind of art form, one at which Henry had known certain Irish priests to be particularly adept; nor was Henry fooled into thinking that Mr. Meehan's delays, any more than the patently benign airs he was affecting, augured anything good. Henry was by nature a trifle gullible, but not so foolish as to think that Jack Meehan would not stab him in the back if he could.

"How's the vacation?" was Mr. Meehan's next abrupt inquiry, his eyebrows going up with interest.

"Well, because of my foot—" Henry made an inconclusive gesture.

"Naturally, naturally. Well, then," said the other at last, with a cheerful if forced sigh, "suppose I might ask you a few questions?" Here Mr. Meehan stared suddenly wide-eyed at the young man. "I've heard so many damn-fool stories these past thirty-six hours"—he laughed vacantly—"I'm about ready to chuck the whole business. Herk," he said in a familiar tone, "you wouldn't *believe* the crossfire of wild tales I've heard. Of course, most of it"—he made a face—"goes in one ear and out the other. People's names are being bandied about. Hell," he said, "that's what a scandal is. It's in the nature of the animal. Could we take a walk?" he asked suddenly, and reached an open palm over the porch rails to test the air.

Mr. Meehan put his arm companionably over Henry's shoulder as they went at a snail's pace up the flagstone path. Wearing a shoe on his game foot for the first time, Henry discovered he could put most of his weight on that leg now. Another week and he would be rid of the cane altogether.

"My, my, what a pleasant, secluded little byway," Mr. Meehan rhapsodized, admiring the row of houses and their lawns and the various horticultural groupings that presented themselves to view along the way. "Very picturesque, indeed. How much do you suppose one of these houses costs?" He rattled on in this way for several minutes, asking the names of the tenants and commenting favorably upon whatever he saw, whether it was the Trumbowskis' peonies or the twin red maples at Mrs. Blye's front door. Even the apparent jumble of lumber and tools scattered everywhere around Mr. Griffin's house won a commendatory remark. "Now, there's a house that's lived in," he crooned pleasantly. "Do you notice, Herk, that the old fellow—what was his name? Griffin?—that he keeps the homestead clean underneath it all? It's a busy little house, but"—he raised a stout forefinger—"it's not dirty. That's one thing that can be said for the Irish," said Mr. Meehan. "They are clean."

"You've never been onto Old Bridge Street."

"Those are shanty Irish," said Mr. Meehan, "that's different."

"I knew they were different," said Henry.

Henry was wearying of Mr. Meehan's maddening avoidance of the matter at hand, but was trying his best to stifle the grimace that arose repeatedly to his lips. Ever since that night in the Brookfields on the road to Boston when Mr. Meehan had behaved in an ugly, forthright manner, Henry had not been able to look him in the eye.

"I'd give the world to have a little house on a street like this. Why, it isn't even a street at all," chirped Mr. Meehan. "It's more an old-fashioned lane, isn't it?"

"That's what they tell me," Henry let out wryly. He and Mr. Meehan stood side by side in front of Mr. Griffin's place, gazing in absently at a mélange of carpenter's horses, tin heating ducts, wire fencing, oil drums, kerosene cans, lumber, tarpaper, cinder blocks, and, spotted amid it all, a scattering of ragged bushes that appeared to be struggling to live. At the back of the house, behind the crosshatching wire of a runway, three brown and black beagles stood shoulder to shoulder, watching the two of them in silence.

"I expect the old country had lanes not so different from this. Cottage Avenue"—he gave the name a melodious innuendo, and gazed about meditatively. Mr. Meehan's dark, meaty face assumed an almost celestial glow as he contemplated the humble beauties of day-to-day life on Cottage Avenue. "Herk," he spoke up thoughtfully, "did you ever *go* anyplace with the Kokoriss girl? I mean to say," he added hurriedly, turning to Henry with a look of astonishment in his dirty, globular eyes, "ever take her off riding in your car? Don't answer that," he followed up crisply, noting the shock that registered in Henry's face. "There! You see? That's what a scandal is. Of course, you took her riding. You have—*had,* I should say—a new automobile, that's *one;* a pretty young girl next door, that's *two;* so you take her for a spin, and it all adds up to nothing. Correct?" Mr. Meehan's speckled eyes gleamed with satisfaction behind his spectacles. He was looking down at Henry as from a height. The cold glow in his eyes persisted for an unpleasant interval. "Your name," he added, at last, in a gravid whisper, "is being bandied about. Care to tell me about it?"

For all his wariness, Henry was nonetheless taken off balance by Mr. Meehan's sudden reference to his own possible role in the scandalous affair. "What is there to tell?" said Henry lamely.

"Herk"—Mr. Meehan tried to frame an elusive concept with his two hands, while peering away into the distance—"we're talking about a really serious charge here. That girl is talking. I was there. *I* think," he said, and pursed his lips tentatively, "you ought to just out with it, give it the lie. By protecting yourself, you can protect everybody. That's the beauty of it." Mr. Meehan and Henry faced one another at an intimate range. "Listen, Herky, goddamnit," Mr. Meehan gave out suddenly, "say *something* to me! You were out with her or you weren't?" The big man was glaring at him now through eyes hardened with a mixture of triumph and loathing. Suddenly, however, quick as that, he shot up his hand, like a policeman stopping traffic. "Don't," he said. "Think about it first. It's time for me to go, anyhow."

Mr. Meehan led the way back and was even swaggering now, for he had taken Henry beautifully by surprise with his sudden sally, so successfully, in fact, that he chose once more to postpone the peroration of his vindictive but delectable accusation. "I," he said, over his shoulder, "was swimming at the Y this morning. What a tonic! What a marvelous way to kick off the day. I feel like a thousand dollars. Old man Houle said I never looked better. Now, *there's* quite a jimoke! Long-gone Houle. He played one game for the Boston Braves, and was *long gone,*" cried Mr. Meehan, and he doubled over and cracked his knee in a fit of laughter. "One game!" he shrieked. "A walk, a fly-out, a fly-out, a ground-out, and two errors at short." Mr. Meehan clutched his head with both hands. "Ninety minutes in the majors! An hour and a half!" He ticked off the at-bats once more on his fingers. "A walk, a fly ball, a fly ball, and a grounder. That and two errors in the field. A bobble," he said, "and a wild throw."

Henry was following in Mr. Meehan's wake, the bigger man gesticulating wildly, casting his arms to the sky, rolling his head from side to side, and popping forward in sudden kinks of laughter. The fat seat of his pants was worn to a greasy shine, his rubber heels beveled with wear. Henry felt like a mortal sinner going hellward in the footsteps of an obscene clown.

"Say," said Mr. Meehan, "that would be a good job for you, Herky. Old Houle is retiring in September. They could use a fellow of your caliber in the locker room—you know, checking in the fellows' trousers and underwear, checking the temp in the pool, scouring out the showers." He gave a bark of laughter and lurched sideways, leaving the younger man several paces behind. By the time Henry reached his front porch, Mr. Meehan was on the top step, fiddling with his hat, while snuffling and blinking back the tears of amusement that flooded his eyes. He brushed at his cheeks with the back of his fist. "I don't know why I'm laughing," he said as he endeavored to regulate his emotions and breathing.

"I don't, either," said Henry.

"Well, now, what's the verdict?" said Mr. Meehan, creasing his hat crown with the blade of his hand. "Guilty, or not guilty?"

"I think," said Henry, looking as pale as murder at the foot of the steps, "that I have nothing to say about any of it, Jack. It's my business."

"Wouldn't it be wonderful," Mr. Meehan expanded, "if the world were as simple as that." Suddenly the big man turned nasty. "Why," he spat out insolently, "I've known all about you from the first day! The day you walked in! Little Miss Bucktooth!" he cried, and leered at Henry, "with his pretty suit of clothes and his fancy-Dan airs—pitching woo at a child!" After that, Mr. Meehan did not try to conceal his disgust. "With what I know, I could drag your miserable carcass across the front page of every newspaper from here to Boston!"

Henry was ashen. "That's a lie," he murmured.

"Is it?" said the big fellow. "Well, I've been waiting here patiently for a quarter hour, and frankly I haven't heard one word of denial. Not so much as a syllable. Oh, don't worry," he simpered, "I'll keep you out of it. Would I want to sully the paper's good name? Would I?" he cried.

"I suppose not," said Henry, scarcely aware of the note of complicity in his voice.

"Of course, I wouldn't. If you ask me," said Mr.

Meehan, taking a new direction, "you'd better take account of yourself, my boy. Get in with some decent-minded people for a change. You might consider joining the Knights of Columbus," he said. "As a member in good standing, I could probably pave the way for you. Young Nolan is going in at my instancing. You might give that some thought in your spare time. Let's be candid, shall we?" Mr. Meehan tapped his temple with a blunt fingertip. "You've got something jiggling up here. I'm speaking to you man-to-man. Your little teenage crush on Miss Kokoriss"—he blushed intentionally—"tells me something. Do you know what it tells me?" he added in an apparently conciliatory tone.

Henry was standing motionless at the foot of the steps, with his eyes on a level with Mr. Meehan's belt. Henry's insides were squirming as the older man continued to glare at him relentlessly, his spectacled eyes offering a cold, inhuman refutation to the mellowness of his speech.

"You need to talk to someone," said Mr. Meehan. "Oh, I could straighten you out myself, if I had the time, because I know what makes you tick. But, believe me, I'm not going to waste a morning and an afternoon doing it, because *no one,*" he cried, "can waste a fellow's time the way Henry Herky Flynn can. That's a goddamned fact." He fixed Henry with a penetrating look. "I gave you every chance in the book. Well, with me, sailor boy, you'd have some atoning to do." When Henry interrupted to speak, Mr. Meehan flagged him into silence. "Just a minute," he said, "I'm not finished." He stared at Henry a moment longer. "Now, then"—Mr. Meehan here drew himself up to full height in the manner of a magistrate preparing to impose sentence on a condemned man—"let me tell you what brings me out here this morning. I have been authorized by the Chief to tell you, Herk, that you," he said, "have been fired."

With that, Mr. Meehan flashed Henry a mechanical smile. He put on his hat, tapped down the crown with his fingers, and marched importantly down the steps.

Henry gaped in disbelief. "I've been fired?"

"Fired." Mr. Meehan expelled the word at close range. "Fired," he said, and betook himself past Henry with his face in the air and an expression of stern dutifulness.

Henry watched as Mr. Meehan waddled his way down the sidewalk and stone steps to his car. The humiliation of having stood still for Mr. Meehan's battery of insults, only to have been discharged in the upshot—to have been twisted every which way by the man's words, led hither and thither from one lewdness to the other—left Henry shaken with anger. In a sudden fit of frustration, Henry committed probably the only act of violence in his life. Raising his cane with both hands, he shattered the globe of the overhead light.

Henry's troubles were not ending, either. For that same day, while he was fretting and stewing over the vulgar way in which Mr. Meehan had tormented and manipulated him, Sophie Kokoriss arrived home from Boston. Being one of those people who are never at a loss in a crisis, Sophie at least knew what to do. When Sophie first heard what had happened with Columbine, she was not entirely dismayed by it. Her only regret was at not having pinned Columbine's ears back for her the last time she was home. But then, Sophie was not the regretful type, either. More than any of her sisters, she had inherited her father's harsh, sensible, pragmatic nature. She was level-headed, reliable, stable. As soon as she had taken stock of matters, she called the police. She even called the newspaper and spoke to Mr. Meehan himself. After Sophie hung up the telephone, she went upstairs and brought Columbine down and planted her on the sofa in the parlor. Mrs. Kokoriss cautioned Sophie not to go hard on the girl, but the admonition was not necessary, as Columbine showed herself at once to be very forthcoming and compliant with her sister's wishes. In fact, Columbine's lassitude was very touching to Sophie. It was Sophie who conceived the idea of moving Columbine out of the house altogether, and later that afternoon telephoned Helen in Washington with that end in view. She spoke to Helen, then she spoke to Johnny, Helen's husband, and then resumed her interrogation of Columbine.

Sophie was not nearly so interested in the facts of the recent scandal involving Mr. Quinn as the police had been, but chose instead to delve into the past, for Sophie recognized the roots of Columbine's pathetic undoing as antedating the time of Helen's wedding, when Columbine already showed herself wild and unmanageable. By three o'clock that afternoon, Columbine broke down and confessed that she and Henry had seen one another in secret.

"I knew it," said Sophie.

Mrs. Kokoriss left the room immediately. Sophie sat down next to Columbine on the couch. Columbine was staring blankly before her. In the minutes to come, Columbine, by wishing to minimize everything that had happened, instinctively directed attention away from the more vicious aspect of things and toward the more innocent and, by doing so, invoked Henry's name more and more. She told Sophie about the perfume he had bought her last winter, months before the onset of her recent escapades, and confessed about taking rides with him at night and about visiting him alone in his own house. After that, Columbine was putty in her sister's hands.

"In other words," said Sophie, in a reasonable voice, "he dated you?"

Sophie was very white in the face. She was still wearing the small gray hat that she had on when she came in from the train station. Getting to her feet, she paced to and fro in the parlor. The fury was mounting inside her. She paused in front of Columbine and stared at her.

"He actually dated you?"

After a brief space, Columbine nodded.

"This is beyond belief."

Columbine looked up at her. "Nothing happened."

Sophie went to the windows and looked out moodily across the gardens, then at Columbine again. "He dated you," she said. She set her hand flat to her face.

"Yes," said Columbine.

"Did he *kiss* you?" Sophie's voice rose.

"Yes."

"He dated you? He kissed you?" she cried. "He *touched* you?"

Columbine was nodding.

Without warning, Sophie spun about, seized a vase of yellow roses from the piano, and dashed it to bits on the floor. "The insufferable son-of-a-bitch!" she said.

Had Henry known what was happening, he might have thought that Sophie was settling some secret score with him, since, for a long while now, she had evinced a mysterious bitterness toward him. In this case, he would have been wrong. In her love of her sister, Sophie was trying to vindicate Columbine in her innocence and had settled upon Henry as the prime cause. The crowning feature of Sophie's investigation, however, turned out to be—ironically— the letter that Henry had written to Columbine, for by one of those unaccountable coincidences that had marked their two lives several times before, Henry's letter to Columbine had arrived in the mail that morning, and fittingly enough, like hers to him weeks before, it bore no stamp on its envelope. It, too, was smudged. Someone had found it somewhere and posted it. Sophie found the letter in Columbine's room, the two pages lying open on the vanity. What Columbine herself made of this letter is not known, but Sophie read it through from beginning to end and then, characteristically, closed the affair with Columbine by deciding to present the letter to Henry's own father. By now, the weight of the blame was everywhere falling on Henry. In that very hour, two plainclothes policemen from Ireland Parish paid Henry a call.

Before they came, the detectives, as a matter of professional courtesy, telephoned Henry's father. Sergeant Flynn, coming home at once, met the two city detectives in the street outside his house.

"Nothing to get rousted about," said one of them.

"It's about your neighbor," said the other.

The first detective, whose name was Woodruff, was known to Sergeant Flynn from his own growing-up years in Ireland Parish. The other man was a stranger to him.

"Where is he?" said the second man, a mirthless, heavy-faced individual with shortsighted blue eyes. Sergeant Flynn, who was secretly a little awed by his two colleagues, men he looked upon as "big-city shields," sensed at once the air of suspicion that brought them here, and he was, in a word, frightened.

"Take it easy, Jerry," said the man called Woodruff, seeing the deep alarm in Jerome Flynn's eyes.

"Where is he?" said the first man. "Indoors?"

"You take care of it, Jumbo," said Detective Woodruff to the man called Garvey. "It's not that earthshaking, Jerry."

"My son?" said Sergeant Flynn.

"We're clearing up loose ends," said the policeman, as his companion went up the steps into the avenue.

To anyone passing in the street, Sergeant Flynn would have seemed a picture of perfection in his uniform, his cap set squarely on his head, not a button or a thread out of place. In reality, however, he was a shadow of his usual boisterous self.

"Jerry," said the plainclothesman at his side, "for God's sake, get a grip on yourself."

"But what happened?" said Sergeant Flynn. "What's going on?"

"It's nothing, Jerry. It's about that girl. We're just trying to piece it all together. You'd do the same thing yourself."

"Of course, I would" was the sergeant's hollow reply.

"So there you are," said the other, and he tried smiling.

"Then tell me he's not implicated," said Henry's father in sudden desperation.

"Jerry, for Christ's sake," said Detective Woodruff, "this is serious business. We've got a young kid here who's been running wild with some unscrupulous men."

This last remark was by no means a balm to Sergeant Flynn's worrying heart. On the contrary, he construed it as the very opposite of a reassurance.

Upstairs, Detective Garvey seated himself on the chair by Henry's window and hitched up his trousers at the knees. Henry sat on the bed. Henry knew the man. He was called Jumbo and had a reputation as a dogged, humorless man. The policeman's face, colorless and big-boned, reminded Henry of a cough drop.

"Anything you tell me can be checked." He frowned as he opened a pad on his knee and unscrewed his fountain pen.

"I have nothing to hide," said Henry, maintaining the same note of surprise that he had shown when he first admitted the detective. In the minutes to come, Henry conceded the fact of his friendship with the girl next door, but found himself discomfited by the questions being put to him. Had he, the policeman asked, ever gone walking with Columbine in the woods?

"What woods?" said Henry.

"I don't care what woods," said Jumbo. "Did you ever take her into the woods?"

"No," said Henry.

"Where did you take her?" The detective shot up his eyes. The suddenness of the question and the seemingly logical connection between it and the earlier question left Henry tongue-tied. Noticing that, the policeman grunted knowingly and made an entry in his notebook. He continued to speak while writing. "Take her out in your car, Henry?" he asked in a pleasant tone of voice.

"Yes, sir," he replied.

Detective Garvey was writing busily. "Quite a few times?"

"Three or four," he replied.

"Three or four?" The policeman looked up swiftly.

"Yes," Henry breathed out nervously, after an interval.

"Picked her up at school, did you?"

"I can't remember."

"How many times? Roughly," said Jumbo. "Five or six?"

"Once," said Henry faintly, "if ever."

"Now, what kind of an answer is that?" Detective Garvey shot back. He then repeated the question, but the sardonic twist of his lips told Henry that he was not going to be believed. "How many times did you pick her up at school?"

"Once," said Henry, giving the appearance here of thoughtfulness.

"Once?"

"Yes, sir."

"You picked her up at school once in your car. Where did you go?"

Henry explained himself. He described driving

Columbine to Laurence Pratt's. He told what he knew, too, about the origin of the photographs that had been circulating, several copies of which were now in the hands of the police. The questions came thick and fast. Yes, Henry admitted, he had visited Columbine in her house. Yes, he said, she had come into this house many times. The more Henry delivered himself of the honest facts, the more he began to appreciate his own innocence. Detective Garvey pressed on relentlessly, nevertheless. He had set his pad to one side and was leaning forward, with his elbows on his knees. It seemed to Henry that Jumbo was now taking more of a personal than a professional interest in the subject.

"When you were parked under the trees, what did you do?" Detective Garvey leaned closer and dropped his voice. "Did you put your hand under her dress?"

Henry sat back in consternation.

"Well, what did you do? You did something. You didn't drive all over Massachusetts and then park out of sight under the trees just because you were feeling sleepy. Were you in the front seat or the back?"

"The front seat!" For the first time Henry's perturbation began to show. He scratched his scalp nervously and sent a savage glance into empty space.

"I don't mean when you were driving," said the detective, "I mean when you were stopped."

"Well, of course." Henry flared up. "I wasn't driving from the back seat! How could I have?"

"What were you doing in the back seat?"

"I wasn't in the back seat!"

"Did you put your hands on her?"

Henry nodded wearily. He could think of nothing that had happened in the past several weeks that was as lewd as this interrogation. Jumbo was half whispering, half croaking out his questions.

"Where did you touch her? Try to remember," he said. "Did you squeeze her tits?"

Henry threw down a book he had been holding in his hands and offered a protest. "She isn't like that," he blurted out in sudden pathos, not even conscious himself of the strangely pristine quality of the response, of how it formed such a true reflection on the nature and depth of his feelings for her.

Detective Garvey continued to try to steer the conversation to the more salacious aspect of things, but Henry was finished answering questions. He sat on the edge of his bed, gazing moodily out of the window. On the walkway below he could see Sophie and his father talking. Sophie was holding the blue sheets of letter paper, and was pressing them on his father. Henry knew his defamation was complete now. The letter of love to Columbine that he had never mailed had arrived nonetheless.

Henry saw Detective Garvey out.

Outdoors, the detectives thanked Henry's father for the opportunity to question Henry, rather in the manner of someone showing his appreciation for having borrowed a lawnmower or a hammer. Henry walked in a daze through the downstairs rooms of the house, and on out through the kitchen to the tool shed. The walls of this unlighted enclosure were decorated still with a variety of gardening implements that hung from nails, rusted hoes and mattocks and rakes, and with long shelves above the ancient workbench that were still laden with tobacco and coffee tins full of nails, bolts, nuts, screws, and the like. The dirt floor underfoot was as smooth as cement. Henry opened the back door and stood in the door light looking out. He was standing there when his father came into the tool shed behind him.

At first, Henry was determined to offer his father no explanation, but when he saw the deathly pallor on the older Flynn's face, he thought better of it and prepared to set his father's worries to rest. Henry took just a step or two into the shed, when his father came at him, raising his fist. He gave a little squeal of pain and struck Henry a smashing downward blow on the face. Henry dropped straight onto his knees. Sergeant Flynn hovered over him, speechless in his fury, his face and neck quivering violently. Two dark jets of blood spurted from Henry's nose, and after a moment his mouth began to bleed. A crimson film blossomed on his lips and chin. Henry sponged his mouth with the flat of his hand, then stared at his bloody palm. He looked up in disbelief at his father, who said nothing but turned on his heel and fled. Henry remained on his knees in the dirt. His head was going round and round. He was making no sense whatever of the blow struck him by his father; it was worse than the blows of war.

Henry sat back on his heels in the pale parallelogram of light. He was not feeling fear or anger or indignation, but was merely trying to generate a thought. He was trying to think. A big blood-colored bubble formed on his lips. The door light faded, grew bright, then faded again. The sight of the blood falling in drops onto the black soil between his knees mesmerized him. His shirt and tie were soaked with it. He was a sight. No one who had ever known Henry could have imagined him, ever in his lifetime, appearing so stricken.

What happened after that mattered less. Henry was finished with all of them. He didn't even try to reconstruct the network of rumors and half truths that had brought him to this pass. He turned to silence. He even kept his father's secret, by erasing every sign of his assault upon him. So far as Henry knew, his own mother heard not one word of it, even to her dying day. His bloodied clothes went out with the refuse; his tongue kept the secret of his loosened teeth. By the following day, Henry knew which of his belongings he would take with him, and which would be stored in the attic with his Navy things. Mrs. Flynn, going about her business in a state of shock, was too appalled even to talk to Henry, let alone to broach the subject of Columbine, and was even more mortified in her soul by her son's apparent indifference to it all. Not that she believed her son to be culpable of having tempted or harmed Columbine in any way; rather, she wanted him to be indignant. She wanted him to term it all preposterous, even, strangely, if it meant his lying about his feelings for her. Mostly, that is, she was confused.

Whenever Henry passed his father, Sergeant Flynn looked away. On one occasion, as they passed each other by, Henry stopped and stared after his father, and he felt stir in himself a certain feeling of tender sympathy toward him. The creases in his father's neck and the gray points of his hair held a poignancy of their own, for Henry could not imagine Sergeant Flynn as having time enough left to save himself from the coward that Henry knew his father to be. Outdoors, Nicholas avoided Henry on the walk. Mr. Griffin, always less subtle, favored Henry with a choice epithet that he flung out at him in a thick brogue as he went past. Henry was indifferent to them, but lumped them all together, with the possible exception of someone like his Uncle Stephen, or, of course, more importantly, Columbine herself.

No one knew at that time whether Columbine was leaving home for a week, or a month, or forever, but it was known that Johnny Rys was driving up Thursday from Washington, D.C., to get her. She had not set foot outside the house in three days, and Sophie was there every minute to be sure she did not. Henry would like to have left home sooner—at once, that is—but thought it somehow more appropriate to wait for her to go, rather like holding a door open for her. So he lingered a day or two. He wanted to see Johnny's car back out of the alleyway and roll off down the hill with her. It was understandable enough. He was glad Helen wasn't coming. He was glad, too, that Johnny was involved. He liked Johnny.

That Thursday, fittingly enough, was the hottest day of the year. The temperature climbed all morning. The air was dry and hot. The WBZ weather forecaster called the day a "blisterer," and said that a temperature of 100 degrees was possible by three o'clock that afternoon. Henry's mother and father ate lunch with a fan going on the table. Henry was outdoors. His ankle was in good trim for the first time, and he was cutting the grass. As always, he was neatly dressed, and seemed scarcely to be perspiring. He went past the kitchen windows at regular intervals, working the hand mower in a narrowing rectangle of grass. He would not ever mow it again, and was doing a nice job.

"He knew such lovely girls," said Mrs. Flynn, with that gently remonstrating air that recently informed such sudden exclamations. "Do you remember them, Jerome? Girls like Constance Paradise," she said, smiling distantly. "Or the Lecznar girl. He took Constance to see *Gone With the Wind.*"

"They were well off without him," said his father, as he bit into a radish and looked at it intently.

"That's not true, Jerome," said his mother.

"Isn't it?" said his father.

Outdoors, Henry had stopped mowing. A moment later he came past the windows, and then entered the kitchen from the back door. He put on his suit jacket in the kitchen. He was wearing the blue cord suit and a white necktie. Mrs. Flynn was looking at her son; his father wasn't. Henry examined himself in a mirror on the door.

"I'm going to say goodbye to Columbine," he said.

No one spoke, and Henry went out. His father and mother watched as he strode across the mown and the unmown grass and crossed the garden space where the fence was before the pine tree hit it, and made his way around to the front door. Henry was not hurrying, or acting impulsively, but was struck by the absurdity of his not even having contemplated going into that house. He was sure no one was going to stop him. He knocked loudly on the screen door but didn't wait for a reply. He just opened the door and walked in. He stopped in the hall and looked up at the stairs, just as Sophie came through the living room and, seeing him there, gave an angry shout. Behind Sophie came Nicholas Blye. Mrs. Kokoriss called through from the kitchen, asking what was the matter. But Sophie was concentrating on Henry. Her hair was drawn back close to her skull, and her anger appeared to be drawing the flesh of her face backwards in the same direction. Henry looked at Sophie, then looked up the stairs again. Seeing that, Sophie threw herself in his path at the foot of the stairway, but Henry pushed past her. "You go away, Sophie," he said.

Henry climbed the stairs to Columbine's room. Nicholas went up two or three stairs behind him, making a little show of appearing offended by Henry's abrupt incursion into the house of his future in-laws, but he had no heart really to interfere with Henry. Upstairs, the door to Columbine's room stood partly ajar. Before entering, Henry looked back to the stairway. No one was coming up. When Henry entered the room, Columbine turned to him but did not look at him directly. The room was boiling hot, though the windows were open. It wasn't the heat, though, that made Columbine listless, Henry knew that. It was the weight of events. She was sitting with a crossword-puzzle book open on her lap. She was doodling.

"I thought it was you," she said. She was wearing the same pale-green terrycloth bathrobe that she wore the morning a year ago when Henry was holding the injured grackle and she came up behind him at the fence. On her bed stood a big blue suitcase, packed and locked; on top of the suitcase were laid out a skirt and blouse for the trip. The skirt was purple. The blouse, which was white crêpe with a big white bow, looked new. Columbine stopped doodling and looked out the window to where the air above the gardens shimmered with a radiant heat. Like Henry, Columbine seemed unaffected by the stifling atmosphere. Her face and limbs shone with a cool finish, like a porcelain produced under great extremes of temperature and which was now insusceptible to change. Henry could not ascertain whether she was embarrassed by his presence or merely indifferent; but she avoided looking at him. When he spoke, however, her attention to his words was something almost palpable.

"Everybody gets to go away once," he said pleasantly.

"You did," said Columbine. She had resumed doodling on the crossword page.

Henry stood just inside the doorway, looking at the blue leather bag on the bed. She had put everything into it. She would not be coming back. On the vanity behind her, amid a heap of discarded odds and ends, lay the two blue sheets of the letter he had written her. She still had it. He guessed she had not made much sense of it. Henry walked to the middle of the room. The heat was stifling; the window shades were burning with sunlight, bright flesh-colored rectangles, while the humming of insects at the open windows gave the heat an audible tone.

"You heard, I suppose," said Henry, "about my vigil the night I thought you had drowned." He couldn't suppress a smile. "I thought I was Leander," he said. "You don't know who Leander was, but I thought I was him."

"You thought you were *he*," Columbine corrected him.

Henry laughed softly over that, then told Columbine how he had hobbled his way out to the water, and about the dark silhouettes of the onlookers, and the two policemen coming in in the boat. "I knew I was losing my grip," he added, "when I thought the dead man on the beach was me."

He turned to Columbine. "I was sure it was you coming in."

"Maybe it was us," said Columbine.

"That," said Henry, with a smile, as he pushed back the sides of his cord jacket and put his hands in his pockets, "seems unlikely."

Columbine smiled to herself, but did not look up. She was making circles on the page. "No," she said at last, "I would never go out in a boat. I was never much of a sailor."

"Neither was I," said Henry.

"There's a fib," said Columbine.

Henry had turned and gone to the window. He was fiddling with the little woven ring on the end of the pull string of the window shade, moving it onto and off his finger. "I was relieved it wasn't you," he said quietly.

Here Columbine did not offer her typically mocking rejoinder, for the suppressed passion in Henry's voice forbade it.

"Thank you," she said.

"I was upset, too, of course, by the sight of the dead girl, as though I," he said, "had somehow caused her death."

"You?" said Columbine.

"By praying it wouldn't be you," he explained.

"Oh, I see."

"The man's sweater," Henry went on, "was just like one I used to wear, a sweater I remember from a school photo, a sweater that I wore with knickers and long stockings, when I was"—Henry hesitated —"about your age."

"I understand," said Columbine.

Henry's voice was uneven. He let up the window

405

shade, gazed outdoors into the radiant sunlight, and moved thoughtfully to the second window. There, he began toying with the pull string of the shade. "What time is Johnny coming?" he said.

"Soon," said Columbine.

Henry nodded. He was standing close to her now, gazing down at the circles Columbine was drawing on the page on her lap, circles about the size of the woven ring on the pull string he was holding between his fingers. "I just came to say goodbye," he said.

Columbine nodded. Turning, Henry let the second window shade all the way up. Mr. Griffin was coming into the roadway below, his beagles running before him. Henry was breathing more heavily. The high-pitched drone of the insects went on and on, a thin, ear-piercing whine like the report from some faraway corner of the universe of a violin string forever breaking. The room was aglare. The light bounced off the mirror panels and created tiny bright blind spots in space. After another moment or so, Henry began, finally, to perspire.

The sweat leaked down from his scalp and ran in rivulets down the length of his face and made his collar moist. Columbine daubed daintily at her own forehead with a small lace handkerchief. Her upper lip, he noticed, was swollen on one side; a single bead of sweat glistened there. She was not looking at the book on her lap, or at the mirror, or even up at him, but was staring in the direction of his shirt front or necktie, as though she were trying to raise her eyes to look at him. Henry had run out of words, but was regarding her with great calmness.

"Why do you never sing?" Columbine asked abruptly, and then glanced up at him. Her eyes came up in a dark-blue flash.

"I don't know," Henry said. "I never think about it."

She continued watching him. "Helen remembers when you sang in a choir. She said, too, that you sang in high school, and everyone came to listen. You sang 'Jeannie with the Light Brown Hair.'"

"That's true," said Henry, remembering.

Columbine was perspiring more freely. "You should have sung at Helen's wedding," she said.

"Nobody asked me." He affected the smile of a temperamental performer.

Columbine paused before replying. "I wanted to ask you," she said. "But I didn't." She continued to stare up at him with a bewildering expression in her eyes. "If somebody had asked you," she said, "would you have?"

"No."

"I didn't think so."

"Was that why you didn't ask?" Henry said.

"No."

This exchange of words led to a silence. Columbine sponged her face delicately with her handkerchief, passed the handkerchief to her left hand and daubed again, but without taking her eyes down. Henry's face was slick with perspiration. They were examining one another in silence. Something was left unsaid, and Columbine was getting ready to say it. Henry appeared to be waiting for her to say it. She licked her swollen lip with the tip of her tongue, all the while looking up at him intently. When, at last, Columbine spoke, the words came out in a whisper. "You betrayed me," she said.

Henry said nothing immediately. Out of the stillness of the day a June bug came whirring in at the window and lit on the floor with a click. Henry's voice, when he spoke, was as soft as her own. "I don't think so," he said.

Columbine's eyes moved away to the mirror, then to him, then to her reflection once more. Henry stood over her motionlessly. She looked up at him.

"You would have sung for me," she said.

Henry smiled. "I don't think so."

"Yes," she said firmly, "you would have."

Henry pondered that, but could only shrug inconclusively.

"Thank you for coming upstairs to me," said Columbine, as Henry turned and started for the door. "It was important."

Henry nodded. The sun was burning in the mirror. Columbine sat at the vanity with her bare feet crossed.

"It was kind of you," she said.

Whether from superstition or sentimentality, Henry wanted the last word he would speak to her to be her name. That was easy. He said, "Goodbye, Columbine."

Columbine nodded, with conclusiveness. "Starbuck."

Downstairs, Mrs. Kokoriss, Anna, and Nicholas were arrayed like a set of dummies on the sofa in the sweltering parlor. No one moved when he came down the steps. They didn't look at him. Sophie was out in the kitchen. There was an odd cooking smell in the air. Without pausing, Henry went out the front way, noticing in passing that the hinges of the screen door had been oiled. Nicholas was making his presence felt.

Henry took off his suit jacket, and in minutes had returned to cutting the grass. He didn't look up once at Columbine's window. Later, when Johnny Rys arrived and parked his car in the alley behind Columbine's house, Henry chose not to acknowledge him. He was raking up the mown grass and didn't trouble to look over. Johnny went indoors, and minutes later was back out again with Columbine's blue bag. He put the bag in the back seat, closed the door, and got in behind the wheel. Henry then put up his rake, standing it just so against the house, and went and stood there on the grass in his shirtsleeves, waiting for her to come out. There was a pause, an interval of what seemed (for Columbine) an appropriate length, just long enough, that is, to build a little suspense without losing any of it. Then she came out.

She was wearing the purple skirt and the white crepe blouse with the white bow, and walked straight out through the gate to the car without turning her head. Henry stood with his hands in his pockets and watched as Johnny started up and backed the car along the dirt roadway toward the street. Columbine's face went by in silhouette. She was sitting up, straight as a rule, and gazing directly before her through the windshield. Everybody remembers one thing best. That was what he had said once to Johnny. They were talking about Buna. That time Henry was thinking about a fringe of palm trees with the wind in them by a lagoon that was not even on a map. This time it was Columbine looking straight before her through the windshield while riding backward in a car. Her face went by, and she was gone.

XX

Standing in the garden space between the two houses, listening to the diminishing hum of Johnny's automobile going down the hill, Henry found the power of the moment softened by the casual drone of an airplane in the sky, by the whirring of insects, and the smell of the mown grass, all of which encouraged the illusion that tomorrow would be like yesterday. For Henry, it was the end of an epoch.

Henry left home on Sunday, three days after Columbine's departure. Where she had gone south, he went east. In New England, everyone faces the city of Boston, and since Henry, unlike Columbine, was free to travel where he pleased, he naturally gravitated there. The big city offered him both the anonymity and the career opportunities that he had to have. On his first day he found lodgings in a rooming house on Hancock Street, in an unfashionable quarter on Beacon Hill. The brownstone establishment sheltered a collection of middle-aged men and women who, despite their rather sleazy airs, appeared to covet their privacy to an extraordinary degree. To Henry, his fellow tenants seemed no less furtive or surreptitious in their movements than the silverfish and cockroaches with whom they shared the building. Henry likened his condition in the Boston rooming house to that of the young artist of all ages, dwelling in his youth, that is, if only for a short time, among the people whom life had thrown away. For his own part, he was out of the house and hunting for work at 7 A.M. each day. He had three hundred dollars, paid him by the automobile insurance company, and was living from day to day on a paltry sum. He kept his money taped to the underside of the sink in his room, dispensing it to himself at a rate of two or three dollars a day. Every morning, however, he found himself standing in long employment lines waiting for job interviews and listening to the desultory talk going on around him among his fellow applicants, talk mostly about the war and about the hard times that were certain to strike now. Not one of the young men, though, ever talked, he noticed, about going back into the service.

He rode the subway and the trolleys or buses when it was imperative, but mostly he walked. He walked from Milk Street to Back Bay. He walked across the Common again to Tremont Street, then round through Scollay Square, and on to the West End, and on and on. He had a map, and he walked and walked. He went from job interview to job interview, until, in time, he began to despair a little. By then, of course, he had given up hope of finding work as a reporter. Wherever he tried—the *Herald Traveler,* the *Record,* the *Globe*—the story was always the same. The editors would not even talk to him. The papers were all overstaffed; the homecoming veterans had claimed the jobs they left behind. Henry knew by then that he would have to attack the matter of his future life's work from a rather embattled position, one requiring great reserves of patience and resiliency. In late August he got work as a temporary proofreader for *The Christian Science Monitor,* replacing a man on summer vacation. Once ensconced there, Henry hoped against hope that his employers would keep him on at the end of the two weeks. He guessed that he was being secretly tested and that at the end of the period might be invited to stay on. When that day came, however, Henry was discharged. The following week he joined the Fifty-two-Twenty Club, and began collecting the twenty dollars a week to which he was entitled by his Navy service.

For a brief span, he considered submitting free-lance pieces to the various newspapers, articles that would seek to illuminate, freshly and with humor and wisdom, aspects of city life as witnessed through the eyes of a discerning out-of-town young man. Henry got himself a bottle of gin and spent the better part of four or five nights composing more than one such pompous essay. He sat at a card table on a metal-backed card-table chair, with a water glass of gin and a second glass of sharpened yellow pencils, and toiled away the hours. Sometimes, too, he fell into a brown study, sitting there in his shirt-sleeves, with the moonlight outside his window etching out the dark skeletal framework of the fire escape, listening to the soft padding sound of the woman upstairs as she went softly to and fro across the floor of her room, while he pondered dreamily his future existence. In the beginning he saw the steps he would have to take—locating a job, or moving to more suitable quarters—as being as concrete and easy to visualize as the actual stone steps that stood at the head of Cottage Avenue, or the broad flight of steps outside the State House at the top of the hill, for example. After several weeks, though, Henry found himself taking a somewhat more exalted, if vaguer, point of view with reference to all that.

During his first days in Boston, he naturally thought a good deal about Columbine. In fact, she seemed to be a sensible part of his quest to establish himself there, almost as though he were an immigrant from an alien country who would one day soon send home for his bride. That was, roughly speaking, his attitude in the beginning. But by fall, as he settled into a new pattern of life, collecting his benefits from the government and staying up much of the night, scribbling and drinking a little and reflecting, she slipped out of his thoughts. That is, he could not accommodate thinking about her, because she was connected in his mind with the small, hard successes he had known in the past, while, on the other hand, the memory of her was somehow inconsonant with his life in this room. It was a shoddy, unpleasant room, with sticky floors and tobacco-colored walls, and as long as he lived in it, the memory of Columbine would prohibit his ignoring it for what it was. Henry, in short, was falling into a decline.

He was a little careless, for instance, in his personal habits. His clothes were a trifle rumpled; small stains on his trousers and suit jacket went unnoticed. He bathed infrequently and shaved only at odd hours, sometimes skipping whole days entirely. He ceased writing, but resumed his voracious reading habits. He went, in fact, every day, the mile or more to the Boston Public Library at Copley Square to return the two books he borrowed yesterday in return for the two books he would read this evening and tonight. By this time, he had become a denizen of the city. Often, on pleasant autumn nights, he betook himself outdoors, usually in the hours after midnight, and set out on prodigious walks, his favorite route taking him down Commercial Street by the harbor, where he walked among the silent warehouses in the narrow, silent streets, with only the sight of an occasional policeman, either driving or on foot, to upset the impression of a completely moribund world. If in later times he had been called on to reveal the character of his thoughts during the course of these nocturnal rambles, he could not have done so. He might have said, though—and correctly —that he was not despondent. He was quite sure that he enjoyed his solitude.

Temporarily he stopped looking for work. There would be no work now, anyhow, he told himself, until after the holidays. Henry had been a tenant of the Hancock Street house for three months before he got onto a speaking acquaintance with any of his neighbors. There was a man named Enright, who worked somewhere as a watchman, and must have had an insatiable appetite for oranges, as he seemed constantly to be bringing them home. Henry could later remember Mr. Enright coming up Hancock Street juggling three oranges with the skill of a circus performer. There was, also, an elderly lady on the second floor who never left her room but was cared for by a relative who visited her daily. It was the woman overhead, though, who befriended Henry. Henry's first impression of her was rather a revolting one. She was a woman advanced in years, with a fat, round face hidden under a layer of face powder, a head of bright-orange hair which, when it was not piled atop her head in a big topknot, created a garish, frizzy halo about her face, and lips that shone with a wet, cherry-red luster. Her head struck Henry as being made out of baking soda and upholstery stuffing, the Kewpie-doll lips crayoned in. He found her to be creepy, so much so that he developed the habit of stealing quick backward glances at her whenever she went past him in the doorway or street. She walked with a rolling gait in a huffing, out-of-breath manner, but was not unaware of the furtive interest that the well-dressed young man downstairs was regularly taking in her. Whenever they passed, she showed her contempt for his indelicate curiosity by scowling to herself, but then, typically, made an exaggerated show in the movements of her backside, particularly when climbing the indoor stairs to her room.

Henry's world had become so compressed, so tiny and unvaried, by the late fall of that year, that the woman overhead became as familiar to him as anyone he had ever known. She had two pairs of shoes; she had three handbags; she wore seamed nylons;

she discarded a great number of Royal Crown soda bottles in the trash basket at the back of the stairway; she drank Four Roses; she bathed on Saturday night; she listened to the radio every evening from eight to ten; and two afternoons a week a tiny, well-dressed man visited her in her room. Her name, according to the tape on the mailbox, was Beatrice Tully.

The first time Henry ever talked to the woman was on the night of an electrical storm. In the middle of the evening, while Henry was reading, and just as his upstairs neighbor had settled heavily into her favorite chair, with her radio tuned up for the broadcast of a weekly drama called "Death Valley Days," the lights flashed out in the house. Henry went out to the hallway and heard her coming down the stairs to the fuse box. He was holding up a lighted match when she switched a flashlight on in his face. She supposed, she said, that Henry blew the fuse by plugging in a steam iron. He could not see her face in the dark, but her whining, exceptious voice fitted perfectly his daytime conception of her as a sullen old grouch who fancied herself to be better than others. She offered to give Henry a candle, however, and led him upstairs, trailing behind her a scent of carnations.

Upstairs, under questioning, Henry explained that he was a writer trying to make his way in an unappreciative world, a claim that didn't raise so much as a ripple of a response on Beatrice Tully's candlelit face. She had lighted two candles for herself, then one for Henry, grousing all the while about the "Death Valley" episode she was missing. In view of the woman's sulky egoism, not to mention her utter lack of regard for the reference he had made to his noble craft, Henry proceeded then to embellish a little on his assertions about himself by explaining how his dedication to his work had required him to turn down a high-paying job at *The Christian Science*

Monitor. After that, Henry and the woman got talking in earnest. Each of the three candles created its own separate glow, like three moons shining, but with their light merging in a common glow in the vicinity of their two faces. In the soft light the woman's round, dead-white face worked an almost hypnotic effect on Henry, particularly later, after he had gone downstairs, gotten his gin, and returned, and had drunk a tumblerful of gin colored with a dash of Royal Crown soda. From time to time, Beatrice Tully found occasion to get up from her chair, as when going to fetch the soda from a box on the fire escape, or in pretending to fiddle with one of the candles, and each time made a great show of herself for Henry's benefit.

Within an hour's time, swept up in a state of agitation compounded of feelings of desire and disgust, Henry was lying on top of the woman in her bed, clutching her, and groaning. She called Henry "Honey-bo" and talked about "us cuddling up together like this."

"I knew you was sweet on me," she said in a hoarse voice, "when I seed you lookin' at me in the street."

Henry knew his neighbor to be a washed-out prostitute who lived on the edge of destitution, saved, perhaps, only by the generosity of that tiny, dapper gentleman who came to her as regularly as clockwork, doubtless paying her a pittance each time for the gratification of some aberrant streak in his nature. Henry, in the clear light of day—that is, on the morrow of his sleeping with the woman upstairs —reviled himself to such an extent that he made up his mind to resuscitate at once his quest for a respectable position and a better place to live. He spent a lot of money just to rehabilitate his wardrobe, with several trips to the laundry and dry cleaner, and to the tailor at the foot of the hill on Cambridge Street. Within forty-eight hours, though, he was tramping the old familiar route back to the public library, and before even another day had passed, he went, at night, quietly and guiltily up the stairs to the woman's room and knocked softly on her door.

"You was downstairs thinkin' and thinkin'," she said in a thick, wily voice, while watching him shrewdly from her round, onyx eyes, "and then pretty soon you got to thinkin' about Beattie waitin' up here all by herself, waitin' to put you inside her like a little fish into her creel basket. *Is that it?*" she mocked him. "Oh, I knew you was happy, with those big eyes of yours shinin' and nothin' to say to me when you went out but just *lookin'* at me!" She scowled disdainfully, as from an incredible conceitedness. She scowled then, and she scowled at him later on when he left and crept quietly back downstairs, and she scowled and didn't even speak to him when they passed one another in the hallway the following afternoon. On his third visit, Beattie made him pay. He paid her two dollars. "And that ain't including extras," she added glumly, as a forewarning against possible infringements on her own rights and privileges.

Henry did not go home to Hadley Falls at Christmas time. He wrote letters to his mother that were filled with untruths and exaggerations about himself. He told her he was working still for *The Christian Science Monitor,* and went on to describe his room and the street on which he lived in terms that he pilfered word for word from a rhapsodic account by Henry James of a house on Mount Vernon Street. Henry did not ask for news of Columbine, but merely filled letter after letter with a recital of colorful references to life in a big metropolis. Henry's reading was meanwhile growing ever more learned and abstruse, as he pored through volumes of Hakluyt, Joinville, Caulaincourt, Suetonius, Fénelon, Cassiodorus, dozens upon dozens of rare masterworks, all grist to the midnight mills. When Henry finally found work, it was only because it fell on him.

One January afternoon he was talking amiably with a man in Filene's basement. The man liked Henry and, since he was department manager, saw to it that Henry was hired on the spot. Henry worked in the department store basement nearly a year, learning about invoices and inventories, threading his way like a sleepwalker through the great throngs of bargain seekers, moving stock, changing sale prices, opening cartons, and answering the thousand and one questions put to him day in and day out by the store's rabid patrons. At night, at home, he sequestered himself in his room, reading his books and newspapers, or stewing over a variety of nagging, inconsequential matters, but attuned, too, all the while to the creaking footsteps overhead. He went regularly upstairs to her. Henry thought of the old woman with the doll-like face and orange hair as his personal "trull," and suffered her ill temper and garish looks for months on end, just for the sake each time of wallowing for a moment or so in the wild, purgative release of a set of feelings he didn't even understand. Sometimes he went to the movies with her. Beattie liked cowboy movies with singing in them. Her favorites were the Riders of the Purple Sage and Wild Bill Elliott. When Henry walked with her in the street, people turned and looked at them. Girls tittered. In Chinatown one evening a sailor across the way whistled at Beattie with a bosun's pipe, and his chums gave out a cacophony of amorous catcalls that set a hundred people laughing. Still, on returning home, Henry followed her up the stairs, his eyes attached blankly to the seam in her stockings and the familiar swell of her calves. By the fall of that year, he was unemployed again.

During all this time, however, Henry managed to maintain a view of himself that could accommodate, to some degree, both past and present realities He was, for example, still given to philosophical flights. It was about this time that he evolved on paper his theory of "consciousness as a form of combustion." He wrote aphorisms in the margins of library books. "Even chaos has limits," he wrote in one place. "Only living things burn," he wrote elsewhere. He fancied himself still to be a "recorder" of life, and imagined the day when he would emerge from this lurid circumstance, from Beatrice's fleshy arms and deep hothouse kisses, and walk out of it in white flannel trousers and a double-breasted blazer, and sail off to Cap d'Antibes with pen and notebook, there to give his observations everlasting life. Walking by the waterfront one autumn night, however, he was accosted by a policeman. The policeman asked what Henry was doing by the harbor in the middle of the night, and Henry told him. Henry and the policeman walked together several blocks in the windy street. Henry spoke briefly about the Navy, but realized while he was doing so he was not talking about himself at all but about a total stranger inside himself. The cleavage he felt between himself and the person he was talking about left him shaken.

The patrolman asked Henry to join him for a cup of coffee at an all-night coffee bar in South Station and then, in a very kindly way, suggested to Henry that he help himself. Henry listened in confusion as the policeman explained how his wife's brother, a man he called Victor, also had trouble "acclimating himself" to civilian life, and what wonders the Veterans Administration had done for Victor at a clinic in Jamaica Plain. The man was talking about a psychiatric clinic, and Henry listened in unbreathing fascination: the man thought him to be slightly crazy, and what was stranger, Henry saw the truth in it. He could not later recall the policeman's name, but always in future years looked back upon that late-night encounter at the Boston waterfront as the nadir of his days on earth.

The last time Henry ever saw Beatrice Tully came shortly thereafter, late one afternoon when he happened to be entering his Hancock Street house at the same time as the dapper little gentleman who came regularly to call on her. The man was truly diminutive, Henry noticed, as he held the door open for him, for the top of his dove-gray hat reached up only to about the level of Henry's biceps. He was as tiny as that, in his flawless dove-gray overcoat and gray gloves, and a small pair of black shoes polished to a waxy brilliance. Henry watched him as he went up the hall staircase, remarking how the perfection of the little man's movements, his imperial bearing and crisp footstep, made the house seem huge and all wrong in its proportions. All Henry knew of the man was his name—Anicet Considine—and Beatrice's once bragging about the little man being a "force" in the state legislature. Over the months Henry had developed an abounding curiosity as to what precisely was happening upstairs between the spruce little gentleman with the beauteous airs and his orange-polled mistress.

On this day Henry determined to find out, and with that purpose in mind let himself out his window and climbed the fire escape. As it was broad daylight, and Henry wished to avoid special notice from his neighbors, he made a little pretense of clearing away the fallen maple leaves that littered the grillwork of the fire-escape steps, all the while progressing methodically up the iron stairs to her window. Beattie, he discovered, was not entertaining Anicet Considine in her bed; the bed was by the window, and no one was in it. She was sitting in her easy chair, which was raked diagonally from the window, and was evidently reading the Sunday comics. She appeared dressed for the street. Except for the little dove-gray overcoat hanging on the swung-out door of Beattie's wardrobe and the dove-gray hat perched importantly on the tabletop, her visitor was nowhere in sight. Beattie had a kitchen chair drawn up before her, however, and had her two feet propped on the wooden seat. It was only when she licked her thumb and turned a page of the funny papers that Henry caught a glimpse of her bare legs and of the little man crouching before her in the space between the two chairs. Henry could not see Mr. Anicet Considine's head or shoulders at all, but just the arc of his back forming a low gray shadow somewhere below the level of Beattie's cushion, directly in front of her. The tiny fellow was evidently comporting himself in some hidden, depraved manner, while she, Beattie, was perusing the cartoons with an air of aloof preoccupation While Henry should have found such a spectacle to be absurd even to the point of being comical, he was, in fact, revolted. It was the knowledge that his revulsion stemmed from his own dark emotional entanglement with the old prostitute that sent him look ing for help.

Henry was married three and a half years later. He was then working for a newspaper in Fall River, and met and fell in love with a young woman from New Bedford named Rose Ann Carmody. Rose Ann saw all of Henry's good points, and Henry, it was supposed, saw all of Rose Ann's. They were married in a Catholic chapel in New Bedford on a summer morning in 1951, in a double-ring ceremony that was praised by all who attended for its decorous character. Henry had by then regained much of his lost weight and cut a splendid figure as bridegroom. He was twenty-nine years old. Photographs taken of the newlyweds show Rose Ann to have been as frank and open-faced in appearance as her husband —a trifle camera-shy, perhaps, but pretty—as all brides are—with her father's dark eyes and her mother's nut-brown hair. They spent three weeks honeymooning in Nova Scotia before settling into a house in Swampscott which they occupied for several years. During that time, Henry changed newspaper jobs now and again, but always stayed within commuting range.

There was an occasion, however, back in the time after Henry's removal from the rooming house on Beacon Hill but before his marriage in New Bedford, when he saw Columbine. Henry's father and mother had come one Sunday by train to Boston to visit Henry, and during that visit Henry's mother let slip the fact that Columbine was spending the summer with her sister Sophie, who lived at that time in Back Bay. Henry found Sophie's name and Marlborough Street door number in the Boston telephone directory, and he wrote Columbine a note suggesting they meet. He suggested a time and a place, and then waited to see if she would reply. Henry's spirits were at that time mending. He was working at one of the series of inconsequential jobs he held during that difficult period, and was renting a room in the West End. Each day, on arriving home from work, he looked into his mailbox, but no answer came. He could have telephoned her, of course, but could not bring himself to do so. Consequently, when the day arrived that Henry had, in his note, proposed for a meeting, he set out on foot for the appointment. He did not expect to see her, but nevertheless took pains that morning to get ready for her. He shaved three times; he changed from one shirt to another; he even debated whether to carry a book or a newspaper under his arm. It was a Saturday afternoon in August.

Henry had suggested the front steps of the State House as a place to meet, but as the appointed hour drew near, his nerves began to unravel. Then, too, no matter how appropriate or symbolic it might have appeared, matters were made worse for Henry by the presence of something totally unexpected that afternoon; for there, on the State House steps, assembled in the summer sunshine, drawn up to attention in six rows arrayed neatly one behind the other up the stone steps, stood a fifty-piece United States Navy band. Cymbals clashed, flags whipped in the wind, and the drums and blare of brass echoed the strains of a brisk martial tune. It was a gay scene. The bandmaster, a tall, resplendent figure, wielded an enormous baton adorned with a gold head and white and blue tassels. The men before him were uniformed in white; the flags and banners were white and blue and gold and red; and, above it all, like a great armored breast turned heavenward, shone the golden dome of the State House. It was five minutes to two o'clock.

Henry approached the site by way of the Common. He was carrying the morning paper folded under his arm and, while advancing slowly under the trees, was searching everywhere for her with his eyes. He looked calm enough, but in truth his senses were in utter riot. For Henry, Columbine had lost reality these past months and years, as had an alarming amount of his earlier life. She had become like the brilliant heroine of a story that had never happened. That made the prospect of her suddenly appearing, of her coming into view in the flesh, very unsettling to him. Also, she would be a young woman now. She would be different. She would see straight inside him, too, as no one else could, and see the great failure of spirit there. He was sure of that. So perfect once was their reciprocity. He considered, too, that she might come to excoriate him; she had, after all, a sharp tongue, and knew how to use it.

Inconspicuously, Henry drifted along among the strollers in the park, picking his way past figures reclining in the grass, but with his eyes turned now toward the band on the stone steps across the street. The music and the crowd of people confused him, since in his imaginings of the past week he had anticipated an empty street and a silent flight of

423

steps. The minutes ticked past. By then, he was all but hoping she would not come; the crowds unnerved him; he could try her another time. He looked about. She was nowhere to be seen, although the sidewalk along Beacon Street was teeming with people, with throngs of well-dressed passers-by, lingering or sometimes pausing altogether to listen to the Navy band and to admire its beauty. It was two o'clock. Henry was standing behind a gathering of milling spectators, just back a few feet from a bronze monument, when, glancing at his watch, he looked up, and she shot into view.

She was coming rapidly on foot up Park Street, up the hill, darting in and around past others, then striding hurriedly out into the street and coming on in full view. There was not one instant when he doubted it was her. She fairly jumped into his consciousness. It was Columbine.

Henry turned faint at the sight of her. He was not faint in the sense of being touched or moved emotionally; he was physically weakened. She was in the street before him now, skimming along, turning her head quickly this way and that, while passing crosswise through the throng of pedestrians not twenty feet in front of him. Her mouth was open, her lip curled back, her face a picture of human astuteness. She was walking hurriedly, turning quick searching glances from side to side. She went around the bandmaster, and around to the left of the band itself, and up the stone steps. She could have been a ghost for the way Henry stared out at her through the spaces between the human heads in front of him, his fingers up to his mouth. She was wearing a green dress. The tail of the belt of her dress jounced and fluttered as she went up the steps to the top. Her hair looked blue in the sun. She was taller. She was the same.

Henry didn't move. He didn't even come close to budging. The hundred-year-old tree standing behind him might have been as apt to dislodge itself from the earth and make its way up the steps as Henry might have been able, on that day, to detach himself from the collection of faces around him and go up the stairs to her. He saw her raise her hand to shield her eyes from the sun, scanning the street for a glimpse of him. She walked across the top step, and walked back again. Repeatedly the sun gave her hair a bluish glint, her hair was that black. She looked the same, he thought. She was taller.

A woman standing close to Henry asked if he was feeling unwell, and Henry said no. But he didn't move. Twenty-five or thirty minutes later he was still standing in the shadow of the tree, standing behind the pedestrians who passed before him on the walkway, standing with the morning paper folded under his arm, when at last she started back down the stairs. She came down the stairway, angled out into Beacon Street, crossed diagonally through the intersection, and vanished in the crowd going down Park Street.

Heaven rewarded Henry with three daughters. In the days before his marriage to Rose Ann, Rose Ann sometimes made intimate references to the fine, strapping sons that she would bear him, even though both she and Henry understood that these remarks were really intended to take the place of any petting or lovemaking that Henry might have had in mind at the moment. It was a way, too, of assuring Henry that he should not worry himself about the future by confusing chastity for coldness, for while Rose Ann Carmody was virtuous to a fault in the matter of preserving her innocence, she was not, she knew, a cold woman. Henry was naturally very correct with her always, so much so that Rose Ann sometimes wondered if Henry was not as anxious as she over the matter of the honeymoon bed. She even wondered in secret if he was not a virgin himself.

The two of them led a reasonably happy life.

Henry's spirits held up well, and as time went by, he worried less and less about ever suffering another such decline or collapse as he had known in the West End. It was, after all, an "age of anxiety," and he was not the only person ever afflicted. The girls, of course, were a joy to him. Henry never showed favoritism to any of them, and in return, no one of them seemed to love him more or less than the others. Eileen, the oldest, was a more responsible type than her sisters, which explained why he confided in her more, just as Marilyn, the youngest, having been a trifle spoiled by everyone, was shown a little extra patience. Ruth, the middle girl, was the brain in the family, and had neither the time for her father's confidences nor the need for demonstrations in parental patience. Ruth was always buried in a book. "By reading," Rose Ann would say complainingly of Ruth, "she's learned to do everything else with her eyes shut."

"Such as eating dinner," Henry would say.

At holiday time, Henry and Rose Ann customarily took the girls one year to visit Rose Ann's family in New Bedford, and on the next drove a hundred miles west to Hadley Falls to visit Henry's mother and father. One Thanksgiving Day, at a time when all the girls were still small, Henry took his family and his father and mother to a high-school football game in Ireland Parish. Sergeant Flynn and Henry enjoyed themselves by cheering for the local boys. The game was a runaway, as the hometown quarterback put on a display of passing and running that dazzled and overwhelmed the other side. The boy at quarterback was Casimir Bober, who, that year, was breaking all the schoolboy football records. He ran wild on the field. His name was familiar to Henry, but it was not till Henry saw him come to the sidelines during time-out and take off his helmet that he remembered. The boy's hair was blond to the point of whiteness. He was Casimir, the little boy who had stood on the front seat of Henry's Ford convertible on the wintry night when he and Columbine drove across the river together to get him. That seemed a long while ago. At halftime, Henry went with Eileen to buy refreshments for everyone, and was watching at the foot of the grandstand as the two teams came out of the locker rooms, the boys rushing past, in brown uniforms, then purple, and leaping over the rope barricades onto the playing field. In the mass of faces Casimir went past, and Henry was moved by what he saw—the glassy cheekbones and penetrating blue eyes. Henry had by then lost track of the Kokoriss family. He had heard that Mrs. Kokoriss had died, and that Nicholas and Anna had sold the house on Cottage Avenue and moved away.

In later times Rose Ann liked to boast that in ten years of marriage, or twenty years of marriage, or in whatever number of years it was, she and Henry had never had a serious argument. That was the kind of marriage it was, she said. It didn't matter to Rose Ann, either, that Henry had never won a Pulitzer Prize, or, for that matter, any special accolades. It was hard enough just to hold down a job and raise a family without aiming for the stars was Rose Ann's philosophy. Journalism, Henry explained, in the way of agreeing with her, was a profession on the skids anyhow. You couldn't blink, he said, but another newspaper was folding somewhere. It was only by Rose Ann's skillful managing that Henry and his family were able to sustain a pleasant and modestly gracious life.

In middle age Henry took to wearing a cardigan sweater and to drinking a little lager beer now and then, and even developed a fondness for pipe smoking. Eileen disagreed with Ruth's contention that all smoking was vile. Eileen said that her father's pipe gave him a gentle, distinguished air, and said how much she liked to see him coming down the street in his cardigan sweater, puffing at his pipe, with

Rumpus, the family Airedale, running before him in the leaves. In time he grew bald on the back of his head, and he added weight, and complained, too, sometimes, as in wet weather, of pains in his feet. For all these developments, he was teased and made fun of by his girls. Henry could not remember a time when he hadn't been the recipient of other people's good-natured raillery. He guessed it was in his nature. Of all those who knew him, however, it was only Ruth, his second daughter, who ever showed any suspicions about the character of Henry's life.

On a summer afternoon, in these later years, at a time when the family was living in North Reading, Ruth and her father went upstairs to the attic to look for a window fan, and Ruth gave voice to some of her curiosity. She questioned Henry about all the books he had collected in his youth. The books were packed in cardboard cartons.

"Did you read them all?" she said. Ruth was squinting at him, as she had left her eyeglasses downstairs.

"Yes, and a million besides," said Henry.

"You must have had great plans in mind, Daddy."

"I don't know what I had in mind," he said absently, turning aside book cartons and other storage as he pressed his search amid the clutter on the attic floor. The air was dusty and stifling.

"People don't read like that any more," said Ruth, who that spring had completed her freshman year at Our Lady of Elms College and was developing a mild form of elitist snobbery.

"You do," said Henry.

"But I read for pleasure," said Ruth.

"What do you think I read for?" said Henry, straightening up and wincing a little from the exertions of his spine. "Punishment?"

"I think it was different for you," said Ruth.

"I hope," said Henry amusedly, "that you don't think I was searching for the meaning of life!"

He noticed, though, that Ruth had grown suddenly very affected by their conversation. She stood
stock-still, with her two hands resting flat atop a
closed-up carton of books, and her lips were moving
in and out in the way they used to when, as a small
girl, she was about to cry.

"What is it?" said Henry. He regarded her in puzzlement. Ruth was not the prettiest girl, and whenever she appeared troubled, Henry grew instinctively very loving and compassionate toward her; he
saw a great depth in her sometimes. Ruth continued
to gaze across at the figure of her bespectacled,
stoutish father, with his thinning gray-blond hair, in
his perennial white shirt and striped necktie, but she
couldn't speak. Henry couldn't imagine what had
come over her. He turned away in embarrassment.
He had found the fan and was trying to dislodge the
electric cord from beneath the pile of boxes. Ruth
was watching him, with her lips moving in and out,
her hands lying flat on the closed box before her.

"Do you think of yourself as a failure, Daddy?"
she asked, at last, in a small voice.

"Am I so ordinary?" Henry exclaimed, raising his
eyebrows and smiling at her.

"There's nothing wrong with ordinariness," said
Ruth.

"Thank heavens for that," said Henry. "If I
learned one thing in all my reading, it was that the
beauty and nobility of life lie in its ordinariness."

"I think that's hocus-pocus," said Ruth.

"Well, probably," said Henry, irresolute in the
face of his daughter's almost tearful earnestness.
"Saintliness is probably the most ordinary thing in
the world to a saint, or genius to a genius," he added,
"or madness to a madman."

"That's what I meant," said Ruth softly. "Just to
be ordinary, one has to be oneself." She looked at
him wonderingly.

Henry had got the window fan free, and came to

where Ruth was standing; he was holding the fan in one hand, the rubber cord and plug in the other. Ruth's eyes were glistening.

"What happened, Daddy?" she said in a whisper.

"Nothing happened, Ruth."

"Did you love somebody besides Mother?"

"Ruth!" Henry said. "I never knew you to talk about romance." Henry spoke in a teasing voice.

"I'm not talking about romance," she said. "I'm talking about you, Daddy."

"When *I* was nineteen," said Henry, "I was in the Tonga Islands in the Pacific, and doing what you're doing, thinking high thoughts."

"Did you love somebody besides Mother?" she said.

"We've all loved somebody else," Henry said. He put his hand on his daughter's shoulder and started her moving toward the stairway. He had the fan with him. "We love somebody every day of our lives. Other people move in and out of our loving."

"Was it a great love?" said Ruth, resisting her father's effort to move her.

"Like all great love stories, it never happened," said Henry.

Ruth said nothing to that, but continued to show an emotional distraction.

"It's a capacity for love," he said.

"Was she beautiful?"

"Oh, yes," said Henry. "I'm sure she was."

"Was she clever and bright?"

"Indeed, she was." Henry started down the stairs, touched now himself by the tenor of her words.

"Was that in the Pacific, Daddy?"

"No," said Henry, "it wasn't."

"Was it in Boston?"

"No."

Ruth started down the steps behind him, squinting fretfully at the top of his head.

"Where *did* she come from?" she said.

"Where they all come from," said Henry.

"And where is that?" said Ruth, shutting the attic door behind her.

"She was the girl next door," said Henry.